It's Showtim
The Weirdos R

Matt Youth was born somewhere on E he's not dead yet. He didn't win the Nobel Prize for Literature, nor the Pulitzer or the Costa Book Award. He didn't write Harry Potter and he most probably didn't contribute to writing The Da Vinci Code, although, rumour has it that Matt is Italian, coming from a village not too far from the famous Leonardo's birthplace.

He wrote his first novel at the age of 19 (he is now bored and old, somewhere around his mid 30s?) but you don't want to read that one, trust me. Neither you probably should have a look at his second and third novels. They're either too good for you (you will never get to his rockstar status) or totally unreadable, awful, nasty pieces of you know what.

This one, instead, is a Literary Masterpiece.
If you don't trust me, you should read:

Praise for It's Showtime, Mate!

'Some writers excite you. Others make you cry.
Bukowski showed me the harsh yet comically sad side of life.
Kerouac taught me that punctuation is overrated.
Niven's banging action and satire really got under my skin.'
'What about Matt Youth?'
'Who?'
KATE - librarian

'Focken Hell, I can't believe it!
Do you really want me to review the latest John Niven's novel?'
'Nope. This is a book by Matt Youth.'
'Who?'
PHIL - hooligan

'Who the fuck is Matt Youth?'
TONY - bodybuilder

'Matt Youth is the new Jesus.'
St.PAUL - full-time atheist

'I love reading.
I'm subscribed to the Sun, The Daily Mirror
and I always read Metro, my supa very fav.
Ima tell all my TikTokers fans that Matt Youth is wow!
You're gonna Luv him!
Can I go now?'
MELANIE - wannabe popstar

'Matt Youth is addictive.
Like sniffing glue.
Snif-snif
SNIIIIIIIIIIIIFF!!
Christ, I love Matt Glue!
Youth. It's Youth.
Who?'
JENNY - amateur junkie

'disUrgent
unNecessary
unSolicited
A real unGem!'
M.S. - journalist at the disAtlantic

'Wrong. Wrong. Wrong. His real name is Matteo Agresti,
he's a lazy good-for-nothing Italian immigrant who will steal your jobs,
seduce your women and eat your sweets when you turn the other way.'
LORIS - Matt's Father

'Pizza-Chewing
PopCorn-Crunching
Finger-Licking
Over-Stellar + Black-Mattering
At once
For fuck's sake,
Buy my goddamn novel, folks!'
MATT - Youth

'Biblical-er than the Bible.'
DONALD - atheist psycho

'Godlike
Riveting
Astounding
Be-*what?* Be-*who?* Be-*say it again?*
Be-*ah!:*
Bewildering
whatever it means
Also
Perplexing?
Mastodontic
Mammoth
Whatever, I don't fucking care.
Can I have my money now?'
TOM - professional junkie

'Matt Youth's ghostwriter is exceptional!
I wish I had such a Literature Master to write my novel too!'
PETE - janitor at the British Museum

'Buy it. Now.'
MARIO - mobster

ALSO NOT BY MATT YOUTH

Ulysses
TWO A.M.
Kill Your Friends
The Morvar Company
Trainspotting
Death Valley 101
Innit?
Breatharian Style
The Divine Comedy
56 Poems to tell you that I L*VE You
Ask the Dust
Or Don't
I'm A(w)-kay, May-t
Dark Shhh*t of the Spoiled Kid
Factotum
Fac You
Fac You Too
The Greateresterest Gatsby
The Catcher in the Rye
UOI?
Shandy
Junk
I Quit.

{Only a few of these titles are from Matt Youth and they're available.
Some of the others either don't exist or I suspect they're not from Mr Youth.
Spot the lucky ones and you'll win a special prize. [No, you won't. (Sorry.)]}

It's Showtime, Mate!

MATT YOUTH

Copyright © Matt Youth 2024

All rights reserved.

Matt Youth has asserted his right to be identified as the author of this Work in accordance with the Copyright Designs and Patents Act 1988

ISBN: 9798647751584

This book is a work of fiction. In some cases true life figures appear but their actions and conversations are entirely fictitious. All other characters, and all names of places and descriptions of events, are the product of the author's imagination and any resemblance to actual persons or places is entirely coincidental.

For Me, for once.

'Don't Wake Me with So Much'

Daysleeper
R.E.M.

ONE
THE MORVAR COMPANY

UNE

'Everything comes to an end.'
　'Right.'
'Everything except dreams, of course.'
'Of course.'
'The only way to be immortal is to become a legend.'
'Become a legend, checked.'
'You shall die like a hero.'
'Evident.'
'And these, son, are just a few memorable lines we use at:'
'LULLA-BALLOON!' Albert shouted, interrupting the job interview for *Coffins & Coffins, Your Unmissable Funeralcare*. Then he stretched his arms and legs as if enjoying a rollercoaster ride at Disneyland. 'We done here? I really need to go, Arth.' he announced.
'Excuse me?'
'I said, I have to go. Thanks for your priceless advice.'
'Is it a joke? You... you can't just leave!'
'Yeah, well, you know.'
'What?!'
'Look, my friend's downstairs waiting for me. We're running late.'
'Late for what?'
'Aw, you're gonna like this: we're hitting the landfill, it's Inspiration-Chasing Day, Arth.'
'My name is Arthur, and , please, don't touch me!'
'I'm sorry, Arth, I didn't mean to upset you. By the way, you should ditch these dusty coffins and join us.'
'This is insane.' cried the man, about to explode. He was really this close to... but he didn't. Instead, he stood up, fixed his unmistakably black suit and combed his mane while snorting large chunks of air like an addict.
'You ok?'
'Sure.'

'Come on, what's with the long face? You look like you're going to a funeral.'

'...'

'Besides, it's nothing personal, you know it.'

'I said DON'T TOUCH ME, for God's sake!'

'Oh, don't be that guy. There's no need to be angry, Arth.'

'I don't want to see your face ever again.' he basically snarled.

'Gosh...' Albert sighed, relieved. 'Finally, we're on the same page. I really hated this job.'

'You...'

'Fingers crossed, I'll never get it. You sure you don't want to come over?'

'GET OUT!'

''Aight but you're missing lots of great things, just saying...'

'You, son of a...'

'Whatever, nevermind, see you next time, Arth!' concluded Albert, and slammed the door on his way out.

Arthur was steaming. He was so angry he would throw a chair against the window, and... yeah, he actually did it, twenty-five seconds after Albert left the room. What a day.

Downstairs, parked straight in front of the building, Steve witnessed in shock the fall of a majestic, hand-stitched, brown leather swinging chair from the 5th floor. The expensive piece of furniture swirled in the air like in the movies, 360-degree Matrix effect, and it floated along with a thousand shards of glass which sparkled light all over, in the most glamorous way. Then the crash happened: *SBAM.*, a very disappointing deaf sound, too real to seduce. No Hollywood explosions, no blast when kissing the ground. A large crowd immediately gathered around the crime scene. Steve was observing that mess from the luxurious interior of his custom black BMW when Albert popped in and whined a long, loud:

'Bo – O – Riiing.'

'Uh?'

'I'm talking about Arthur, the interview guy. Such a waste. News?'

'Man, you won't believe it.'

'What's that mob doing?'

'Someone threw a chair from up there!'

'Classic. And, obviously: *ladies & gents, welcome the cream of society, popping on the scene like mushrooms.*'

'You don't have to talk like a '40s radio presenter, Albert.'

'Tut-tut. *Here comes the edgy conspiratorialist psycho fueled by gallons of coffee (whatever a gallon is), affected by nervous laughing and, there you go!, he's joined by the Catholic fools, convinced that Judgement Day finally came.*'

'Well...'

'*And, as they all reach for their phones to film the event, we end our transmissions. Sayonara, folks!*'

'I'm speechless.'

'Innit? They're wonderful.'

'Who?'

'People! A bloody bunch of talking plushies programmed to reply with pre-recorded answers: I'm too busy; I'm too nervous; I'm aw-kay, may(t).'

'You sound stupid.'

'Yeah Steve, cuz I hate them.'

'Man, calm down, you're gonna have a stroke.'

'Sure. Anybody hurt?'

'Nope, the road was desert on that side.'

'Glad to hear it. That's great news. Fucking great news! Mate, I'm feeling supersonic! Shall we go now?'

'Hell yeah!'

So, the engine started, lights went on and the car roared away, somewhere around Sherlintock. Steve loved his BMW more than anything else, girlfriends included, and that was the sole reason why he was so excited. Speed went up, the new Whatshisname top of the pops album pumped loud from the speakers and Steve began drumming on the steering wheel.

'Man, why don't you stop doing job interviews?' he asked 'It's pretty clear you don't give two shits about them.'

'As a matter of fact, I do not care, my friend, but it's therapy.'

'Wow, that's...'

'Free therapy!'

'Like going to a shrink?'

'Yepsy. Each time is a test. A squalor-level check-up.'

'You're insane, man.'

'What? No, I'm not. Are you even listening?'

'I...'

'It's all about finding the strength for being yourself, fuck the system and its cliches, no compromise. Do I want to wear a stiff suit for the rest of my life? Hell no. Where do I see myself in five years? Fuck knows, Malibu? We shall never give in to society's rules, Steve.'

'...'

'And remember, it takes courage to refuse moulding into certain schemes. You need to train yourself.'

'I bet.'

'Seriously, it ain't easy.'

'So, job interviews, uh?'

'Hell yeah, my friend. Guaranteed.'

'You're an asshole.'

'I'm just a survivor, mate. If I'd ever feel down because of the way they look at me or how they treat me, please blow my brains out. You'll find my suicide note stashed in the drawer.'

'Woah, woah, I'm not Courtney, man!'

'Don't be modest, you're pretty nice too.'

'She ain't pretty...'

'Good point. However, I'll be stone dead either way, so who fucking cares.'

'Amen.'

The shimmering-black engined panther was slipping through the narrow streets of Sherlintock at a good speed, dribbling bikes, vans and whatever got in the way. Albert was observing his boring village scrolling silently outside the car window. They were almost there.

'Any chance you're gonna tell me what we're supposed to do in a landfill?'.

'Steve, you kidding me? It's the most inspiring place on Earth!'

'Is it?'

'We climb over the fence and wander around. Your eyes won't believe how many treasures there are.'

'Mmm...'

'Listen, the potential doesn't lay in the object itself. Real magic lies in what you can see beyond it.'

'Fab.'

'Innit?'

'So, Mr next-in-the-queue for the Nobel Prize, please tell us: you're gonna change the world, aren't you?'

'Fuck off, Steve, think about it: why else should we live on this planet if not to make extraordinary things? This is the only way I can explain my existence to myself. I'll probably fail, alright, but I want to live it trying my best.'

'Man, you're so inspiring when you go bonkers.'

'You for real?'

'Nah. But I'm gonna write your speech down anyway. A bit of drama always works great with birds.'

'You're a monster.'

'Thanks, man.'

'Pleasure.'

'So, Albert, have you figured out what to do with your life?'

'What a cheeky question, Steve.'

'Well...'

'Unbelievable. Besides, what do you mean?'

'Come on, you live right next to the campus, you attend every class and you're not even enrolled.'

'So what? I like studying things, not getting a degree.'

'How do you think I managed to buy this car?'

'With all due respect, Steven John Damn I am the Big Sales Deal in Town: I have other plans.'

'Fancy short nicknames, uh?'

'Shut up. Now, stop the bloody car and follow me, I feel lucky. Today we're gonna catch the sparkle that will ignite our brains and give us the idea of the century! My friend, we're about to change the world for good!'

TWO

There must have been two-thirds of Sherlintock's entire population in Central Park that day, flying kites, barbecuing, drinking pints... everyone was there but her. The sun shone brightly between lazy clouds and the air was warm enough to make youngster's tees blossom all around.

Victoria didn't even notice the clear skies. She was so busy she couldn't tell whether it was night or day. Like every morning, she put random clothes on, pretended to wash her face and quickly headed to her favourite place in town: the busy, noisy Sherlintock train station. She always carried a book, pencils, crayons and whatevers, all squeezed into the narrow pockets of her vintage cardigan. Armed to the teeth she was ready for secret mission "Enjoy Aloneness". At least that was the plan...

'You forgot your mobile, you fool!' said Rose as they entered the station.

'Did anyone invite you, at all?'

'You're welcome, honey.'

'I'm late.'

'You're always late.'

'Would you stop it?'

'Careful!'

'Uh?'

'BASH!'

Victoria crashed into something enormous, dressed in marble, with a sign that read: *Platform Two*. Rose was laughing out loud, almost in tears, still pointing in the direction opposite the giant pillar.

'You, idiot!' Victoria screamed in anger, gesticulating wildly and shouting at Rose, who existed only in her mind, unreal and beautiful like a trip to Hawaii.

Obviously, all the stray passengers populating the surroundings turned, puzzled by that bizarre girl talking to herself.

'Shhh...'

'Don't shush me!' Victoria yelled again.

A very refined, impeccably dressed old man was observing the scene with special attention.

'Are you alright?' he gently asked her, rushing there to help.

'Thank you, sir, I'm fine.'

'Are you sure, dear? Where are you going?'

'Oh, well, nowhere. Everywhere. I mean, I've just arrived.' replied Victoria, sitting on a dusty-old wooden bench.

'That's a graceful spot... oh, you dropped your book, here it is.'

'Marvellous.'

'This bench... why is it so special?'

'To me?'

'No, not to you, I'm trying to remember...'

'For what it's worth, this brass plaque says *Anthony Morvar's Thinking Temple*. Is it of any help?'

'Good God, how did I possibly forget it? Christ. Fuck. Shit!'

'There's no need to swear, sir.'

'No need to... do you know who Anthony Morvar is?'

'Should I?'

'Sh... ... I?' he was shocked 'What are you doing here anyway? What DO – YOU – DO on the bench?'

'Mmm... things.'

'Now we're talking! What sorts of things?'

'Let's see... I read. A lot.'

'Show me.'

'No way.'

'Show me.'

'What the hell? Sir, don't you think you're overstepp...'

'Show me.'

'Alright (bloody old man). Do you want me to read? I'll fucking read so you'll leave me alone.' Victoria thought to herself. She took a deep breath, closed her eyes, and opened the book, a beautiful hardcover leather-bound piece stuffed with blank pages. Her fingers delicately danced over the thick wordless sheets as she started enjoying the story. A quiet smile rested on her face, eyes still closed, mouth shut.

The curious crowd was now staring at her, carefully approaching Platform Two, the one bringing people in and out from London, every day, like the graceful dance of the oceans. Victoria was performing her silent show when:

'Wake up, the copper's approaching.' cut in Rose. 'Put that book of yours away, we're going to have trouble.' she muffled in the most discreet, impossible whisper.

'Trouble? Why so?'

'Just chuck it in the bag. Now!'

'Good afternoon, madam. May I ask you to stand up and show me your ID?' politely asked the uniformed guy.

'Don't you see she's reading?'

'Please sir, let me do my job.'

'Your job? And what would that be? She's just...' insisted the old man, trying in vain to impose a certain authority.

'Hello to you, Charlie, how are you doing?' intervened Victoria.

'I'm ok, kid. Listen, I have to check on you, it's nothing personal but, you know the rules. We need to keep an eye on everything weird around here, at all times.'

'I understand. So, what do I look like today? Am I an unattended item to be removed?'

'Look...'

'Can't you let me be?'

'Yeah, about that: people are getting quite uncomfortable with it. They're worried.'

'With what? Me, existing?'

'Thing is, they don't understand how you can stare at a bunch of blank pages for hours, pretending to read. They're pressing me with all sorts of enquires. They're convinced you're up to something bad like, I don't know, black magic, obscure witchcrafts, you name it.'

'I'm just reading, that's all, Charlie.'

'Yes, I figure but... they...'

'Jesus Christ, spit it out!'

'You look like a weirdo.'

'Nice touch.'

'They're scared. You know, these days...'

'I'm not a freaking terrorist. I'm having a good read, what harm can I do to anyone? Take a look at it yourself, it's just a book, Charlie!'

She placed that singular copy in the hands of the officer who looked sincerely sorry about the whole situation.

'Listen, Victoria...' he mumbled, flicking through the volume 'these are blank pages, there's not a single word printed on it. No pictures, no nothing.'

'So what? Besides, you knew it already.'
'You understand that the people are...'
'Hey, hold on. Close your eyes and read page seven.'
'Seven?'
'Seven.'

The elegant senior appeared delighted with the whole situation. It was as if he truly understood it all. As if it wasn't the first time he witnessed something like that. Victoria was serious, staring at the copper.

'Please, give it a try.' she begged him with her sweet doe eyes. 'Trust me, this book is overflowing with stories.' she insisted.

'...'

'Brilliant, Charlie! Now take a deep breath, relax, free your mind.'
'Well, I...'
'Just for a moment. Have a seat.'
'Alright, like this?'

The mob was scanning the scene from a distance, waiting for something to happen. 'What's going on there? Why is the policeman acting like a nitwit? Did she cast a spell on him?' They asked each other, spontaneously. The officer, now comfortably sitting on the bench, was just about to get somewhere with the odd book in his hands and his eyes shut. He was on the threshold of his thoughts when a man shouted:

'Fancy a cuppa?'

And the crowd burst out laughing, nervously, freeing their tension. Charlie instantly woke up finding himself in the middle of a nightmare, feeling horrible, humiliated and defeated for lowering his guard down. He jumped to his feet, furious at himself.

'Fine, you tricked me once again, Victoria, but that's enough. Stand up! NOW. Go home!' he sharply ordered.

'I don't think I will, Charlie. I have the right to stay. Period.'

'I think I'll join her.' added the old man knocking his majestic brass cane against the floor.

'Oh, come on you people, why don't you go out like all the others? It's such a great day.'

Victoria adjusted her black ribbon choker as if she wasn't even listening. Then she got back to her reading.

'You know what? Stay. I can't waste all of my time with you.'

'...'

'Just try to keep a low profile, would you?'

'I can't believe you sold out like that, Charlie. You know me, and I think you owe me an apology. This isn't fair. Why don't you catch proper crooks instead of pestering me every day?'

'Holy Jesus...' thought the officer, who, as usual, didn't have a clue of how to escape that situation.

'Actually, you know what?'

'Uh?'

'It's your lucky day, Charlie. I'm sick of being treated like a loony, a misfit, a nutcase. I am leaving. Happy?'

'...'

'Rose, let's go.' Victoria told no one. 'We're out of here.'

She tied her white Reebok's shoelaces and fiercely stood up, grabbed her bag and finally headed to the exit followed by her imaginary friend Rose and the odd senior who genuinely seemed to enjoy all that weirdness, as if he had been searching for it all of his life.

Victoria set her walking pace to the Richard Ashcroft-mode in Bittersweet Symphony, and the three of them cut through the mob like superheroes, the old man brandishing his golden cane and Rose impossibly smiling with pride. Heads turned as Victoria passed by like a Queen on the royal carriage back in the day. She was about to exit the station when she stopped. She adjusted her striped socks and faced the staring crowd.

'You... Wankers.' she declared out loud with a slight squint of her deep blue eyes, without moving her lips, no sound whatsoever. Then, she disappeared.

The old man escorted Victoria towards a blossomed lonely tree sitting in the nearby garden. It looked like an inviting and harmless place for giving an end to the marvellous story she started reading on the Morvar bench.

'Do you like it here?'

'I love it.' she said, making room for him to sit next to her, on the grass.

'Thanks, darling.'

'Aren't you tired?'

'Are you implying I'm old?'

'Duh?'

'Hey, I might not be a teenager anymore but I still have some life to live.'

'Yes, you look good, even happy in fact. How do you do it?'
'It's a secret.'
'Mmm... Is it somehow related to that bench?'
'Ah,' he replied, pleased, swinging comfortably on an imaginary swing chair.
'Why are you smiling?'
'Because. I knew it, the Morvar bench is still magic. He's not gone.'
'That Anthony guy?'
'Precisely. Morvar is still around and he'll never leave us alone. I just needed confirmation.'
'I'm not sure I understand.'
'Don't worry, kid, you will. Now, would you be so kind as to finish reading your story to me?'
'Are you for real?'
'100%.'
'...' Victoria didn't say, a bit confused, but then thought: whatever. She opened the book to the exact dog-eared blank page, she closed her eyes and slowly let that enchanting tale sail her away.

The last pages turned out to be absolute pleasure. No word was coming out of Vic's mouth but the story was perfectly audible to her guest. He was this close to weeping as she strived to slow her heartbeat down, tasting every single sentence like vintage wine. All around, a weird silence was broken now and then only by the harmonious chirping of baby birds while the two of them were staring at the void with their eyes shut.

Finally, her long fingers caressed the inkless paper one last time and closed the book with respect.

When Victoria opened her eyes, the well-mannered senior mimed the most elegant bow to her.

'It was a masterpiece.'
'Thank you, sir.'
'How do you feel?' he asked, perfectly knowing the answer.

Victoria was ecstatic. She was enjoying that place in between an accomplished thing and the next project on the way; the instant when you feel scared by the future, and you just settle for remaining safe in that tiny fleeting haven.

'Can you smell it?'
'What do you mean?' she replied, surprised.
'It's like the perfume of a rainbow, pervading the air, forcing his way

through the nostrils.'

'Yes! Yes! That's precisely it, how did you do it?'

'Experience, my dear.' he concluded, standing up.

'Are you leaving already?'

'Oh, I've lived enough for today. It was a pleasure to meet you, Victoria.'

'Nah... Will I see you again?'

'Indeed. You will indeed.' he replied, curiously absent but with a grin painted on his face, brandishing his cane and whistling a classic Sinatra tune, on his way to wherever he came from.

Victoria followed his shape disappearing in the distance. Motionless she was: amused. What a weird man.

'Shall we?' no one asked her and, 'Just one more second.' she told herself. She couldn't resist splashing about in that moment for a little while longer. It was like surfing a lullaby. *Wow.* Besides, she would have done anything to avoid facing reality, diving into modern times' mayhem again. *Unsafe.* Victoria preferred sheltering herself within daydreams, one after another, jumping into places not far from the truth where our emotions created puffy paths for us to follow.

'What's next?' asked Rose, waking up from afar.

'I am starving, let's go get dinner.'

THREE

The landfill tour didn't go as Albert imagined.

No shocking revelations about the meaning of life nor even tiny pleasures such as feeling like an astronaut lost on an undiscovered planet. Yet the day wasn't done and he had to attend an important meeting, a good-enough reason to buy new clothes. He was wandering along the anonymous curbs of Sherlintock when he spotted a fancy boutique and decided to pop in.

ding

'Hi, mate, how are you doing?' asked the shop assistant, with a plastic smile.

'Living the dream. You?'

'Oh well, I'm...'

'By the way, my name is Albert.' he said, firmly shaking hands with the guy.

'Great... Great. How can I help you?'

'About that. I'd like a wool sweater.'

'Do you have a favourite colour?'

'Mmm... nope!' he said, smacking his lips while his eyes roamed around the shop, distracted.

'Alright, no worries. What's your size, man?'

'Never knew it, it's a curse, believe me, every time the same story. I get into a shop and they ask me that. I don't know, should I measure myself? How does it work?'

'I...'

'Seriously, is there a way to figure it out?'

'Indeed, we'll get to that, I assure you it's fine.' answered the guy, starting to feel uncomfortable.

'If you say so.'

The shop assistant took a deep breath, preparing himself to shoot the next question listed in the handbook *"Satisfied Customers Only"* the one he bought for 60 quid in a posh London Daunt Books store. No way to make a mistake ever, guaranteed, and he knew each word by heart.

'Did you notice anything in particular?' he asked, now with a certain, confident tone.

'Just a gold-plated sweater.'

'But... we don't have it in the shop. I'm not even sure it exists.'

'Oh, of course it does. I found it last night on the web!'

'I see, our online store always features new brands. Was it in stock?'

'Guess so, it was on Google Images. You know when you type random words and a cool picture catches your attention? I love strolling about the net without a purpose. You need to get lost to find your way.'

'Ok...' the guy hissed, almost in a panic. He wasn't trained to improvise and he was running out of topics. People usually approached him asking idiotic questions, looking for dumb answers in return, and he was great at sealing those kinds of deals. Basically, his everyday job consisted in giving people what they were meant to want. Thanks to bloggers, magazines and zillions of everyday ads, you were already told what to buy. People don't like surprises and Shop Guy was happy with that.

Albert was a totally different story.

Shop Guy was soaked in sweat.

'I'd like one made of wool on the chest part, you know, to keep me warm in winter. For the rest, cotton sleeves would do just fine, I'm sure my arms won't get ill.'

'I... let me... let me check if we have something in the stock room. Can you please wait here for a second?'

'Okey-Dokey.'

So, Shop Guy literally ran to the back, desperate. He shut the door and, iPhone in hand, he dialled his girlfriend.

'Honey? What am I supposed to do? There's this customer who wants... yes, I know, but... what do I... no, no, it would be the first time ever and I'm sure the manager... ok, alright, thanks, sweetie.'

When he made his entrance back into the room, he was armed with a new face, confident, he was prepared for any challenge like a US Marine on a mission. He placed himself behind the counter, cleared his throat and announced:

'I'm sorry, sir. We don't have what you're asking for.'

'I understand. Do you sell trousers?'

The whole world seemed to crash on Shop Guy's head. He felt a cold shiver running up his back; his body nervously started to tremble, revealing the terror he was holding tight behind his made-up face.

'Trousers... er... did you notice anything in particular? What size?'

'Mate, I told you already, I...'

'I'm terribly sorry, sure, you don't know that, so...'

'What can I say, I just need a pair of warm ones... like... no shit, this is sheer luck. I want those!'

'Those?'

'Yes, they look perfect!'

'It's a wetsuit!'

'Would it keep me warm?'

'Absolutely, it's designed for Arctic diving.'

'And you sold it, mate!' yelled Albert, scaring the other customers, possessed by a sudden, foolish joy.

'But... sir, it's not meant for everyday use.'

'How much is it?' Albert asked, completely immersed in his fantasies.

'It's 155 pounds 20p, sir.'

'Deal.'

'Contactless?'

'Contactless.'

'*Beep*' said the debit card.

Do you need a bag?'

'I'm cool, thank you.'

'Good.'

'Goodbye.'

And

ding

'TERRIFIC.' was the single word pounding in Albert's mind as he got out of there. He pictured himself wearing his new outfit during the cold winter and it just felt awesome. So freaking awesome that he stopped in the middle of the busy street, cleared his throat and:

'I don't mean to offend anybody, please don't bother me, folks!' he politely informed (shouted to) the unfortunate passersby right before pulling his old jeans off with a sharp move and slipping into his new wetsuit. Aw...

Warm. Tight as Jim Morrison's leather pants, fit like Jagger's Sticky Fingers. Marvellous. He was finally ready for his meeting. The Morvar's Gate was waiting for him.

FOUR

The off-licence around the corner was as cosy as a dump but Victoria always liked it as it was anyway. Also, the guy working there was totally nice to her and that was a big plus.

'Have you made up your mind, madam? Can I help?'

'No, thanks! I'm just having a look!' she shouted.

'Sure, sorry...'

'An apple or... maybe a peach... Rose, what do you suggest?' Victoria barked at her imaginary friend.

'Stop screaming, you fool. Geez, take off the bloody headphones!'

'Uh. I didn't realise...'

'Yeah, as always. Look, pick whatever you want but hurry up. I've had enough of this place! I know every corner of it by heart, and it's not something to be proud of.'

'I see, but...'

'The peach! Take the damn peach.'

'Hey girl, behave...'

'Behave my ass, it's been...'

'Ok, alright, we'll go for a sweet, deliciously ripe and tasty peach, happy?'

'...' replied Rose jutting her lower lip in a dramatic pout.

So, holding the precious fruit in her hands, Victoria approached the till and her eyes met the bewitched sight of the shop boy now standing behind the counter.

'How much is it?'

The young guy waved his hand in the air, shaking it as a perfect idiot in love, trying to say something with no positive result. Then he smiled, combed his hair and finally remained still, frozen like a statue.

'I'll take the peach' Victoria tried again.

'That? It's on me!'

'Fuckin' hell, the dummy can speak!' commented Rose.

Victoria couldn't help but laugh. 'Are you sure?' she asked him.

'Thank you.' his mouth, for some reason, stupidly said.

Victoria was nicely embarrassed and her cheeks reddened slightly, just that much to make her even more attractive. She fixed him for a second, undecided, then she ended up saying:

'Well, it's so kind of you.'

That delicate voice mixed with her hypnotic blue eyes gave an electric shock to the guy who, somehow, suddenly woke up. He gently took the peach from her hands, carefully placed it into a paper bag and handed it back to her adding a weird nod to the already awkward situation. And what did she do? She blinked at him, the fool, causing the fragile guy almost a stroke. Most definitely a stroke. And, as he silently fainted behind the counter, she simply left.

Victoria was feeling good. It was a good day.

Once on the street, she put her headphones back on. Music dictated the pace of her steps, bringing her by the hand through the noise of the city. This was one of Victoria's tricks to escape reality. She always felt like a rockstar when her favourite songs filled her ears. It was like... freedom. She was floating above the mass shielded by a gigantic rainbow bubble. From up there, people couldn't grasp how she was feeling, they couldn't know what she was experiencing or where she actually was. They couldn't touch her. In those moments, she felt gifted, endowed with a precious secret. Victoria was bobbing her head, shaking arms and chest, twisting her legs

'Hey! Been trying to meet you! Mmm mm mm m mmmmm...' she sang freely, in the street. *'Hey! Must be a devil between us. Or whores in my head, whores in my bed, but Hey!'*

Her long bare legs were gracefully flirting with the air while going with the flow. She was swirling and making faces, dragging Rose into that game. Rose was bonkers-like-good at this stuff as if she had literally been created for it. Within seconds, the impossible couple started singing back-to-back.

'Where have you been?'
'If you go, I will surely die!'
'We're chained hey hey hey, we're chained...'

It was so much fun, they were walking three steps above the pavement and yet no one was really paying attention to that ongoing play anyway. People were too busy with this or that, their faces lit up by the digital light of their brand-new smartphones. Nobody seemed to realise it but Albert, who happened to be right in front of the off-licence when Victoria got out. He couldn't help but recognise the famous Pixies line she was singing. He was so intrigued by that girl that he had to follow her. He was striving to find the right words to approach her when she literally bumped into him, without even noticing, so much so she was immersed into her fantasy world.

The peach fell from its paper bag.

'Yo! Stop! You dropped something!' shouted Albert, promptly gathering the fruit.

'I'm so sorry, she's totally absent-minded sometimes.' apologised Rose who witnessed the whole thing.

'No problema.'

'Thanks.'

'My pleasure. By the way, I'm Albert.' he said, shaking the ghost's hand.

'Rose. Look, sorry, I've got to go. My friend is leaving me behind, I'm sure she didn't even realise I stopped.'

'Your friend?' he wondered, a little distracted, turning towards that vanishing creature in the distance.

'Yeah, you know... she... however, take care, Albert.' Rose bye bye-ed, snapping out of there.

Albert's mind was as blurry as Kurt Cobain's face in the Come as You Are video. *'What just happened?'* He took a step towards all possible directions at once and he obviously stumbled. For some inexplicable glitch of the human mind, he was walking away from her. Why? God knows. Meanwhile, Rose was spying on him, fascinated by his figure: confident enough to wear a wetsuit in public but at the same time unstable and frail like a baby bird.

Albert was undecided whether to run after the girl or keep on his way. As in Meet Joe Black, he kept turning, hoping to find her face, her gaze. Was she still in sight? He would have loved having a chat with that girl, tasting the sound of her voice while staring into her eyes. How many undiscovered planets were hidden in there? He barely touched her and already he was drowning in her scent. The eighth time he turned, he glimpsed Victoria performing one last twirl before she would slide away in the distance. Again, Albert strived to catch a sparkle, the slightest hint from that one-of-a-kind girl he didn't even know the name.

But she didn't turn, not a single time. Till she got home.

FIVE

When he woke up the morning after, the strange girl was still haunting his thoughts. Albert had to free his mind, that's why he was returning to the one place that fixed him each time. Like a junkie, he was heading to his pusher for the 8th time in a week. One turn to the left and *zip!* he was almost there: the Morvar gate. The umpteenth cigarette tip had just been charred when Pete crossed his way.

'Yo!'

'Albert! Has anyone ever told you, you're not black?'

'Sometimes. But I can't help it, I've got rhythm inside. You put on any music and I get possessed, my legs twist and I get high, I start rapping like the brothers, rocking James-Brown-style! I could even breakdance right here, right now! Wanna see?'

'Are you done?'

'Mmm... yep.'

'Cool. Where are you going?'

'Morvar's'

'Aw, it explains why you're all dressed up.'

'This wetsuit's sick, innit?'

'Sure...'

'Come on, Pete, join me. I've got three plus one questions for you!'

'Guess it's my lucky day then. What about, Al?'

'Last time we went there, you said that beyond the gate are enchanted gardens. You told me not to get fooled by that crooked rusty entrance because, if I ever found its key, I would discover the unimaginable, on the other side.'

'Did I really say that?'

'Hell yeah, ma man. I was taking notes, look!'

'Impressive.'

'So, what's over there?'

'It's complicated, Albert. Some say that dreams and hopes had been forged in there for the very first time; others swear that over those bars there was something ethereal, so pure to be non-existent.'

'And what do you believe?'

'Me?'

'You.'

'Well... The building itself is only dust and concrete. It's soulless.'

'It looks like a bunch of old ruins, doesn't it? A giant kneeling elephant about to pass away.'

'Still, you're here. Every day.'

'Exactly my point. I don't know why but I always feel the need to come over, at least for a minute. It's like when someone you know is bedridden in a hospital. You have to be there, holding their hands.'

'Precisely! The people.'

'Uh?'

'This place was built on revolutionary ideas. See, once a man had a dream, a dream so naive and easy to comprehend that instantly spread like a disease, affecting everybody, everywhere. This warehouse means nothing if you haven't seen the faces if you haven't read the stories carved inside their eyes.'

'The Morvar people...'

'Yes, Albert, in that case, the old building is quite like a father.'

'Tell me about the day it all started.'

'Again?'

'Please, please, please!'

'... right.' Pete conceded with a smile. 'I was just a little kid standing among the crowd. Nobody had a clue of what was about to happen but there was a good vibe in the air and Anthony Morvar... darn, that man knew how to speak to the people. He got everyone moved.'

'...'

'His speech was like a tear of hope dropped in the human desert. At least that's what my father told me, I was a tad too young to remember anything but a sort of fuzzy sensation.'

'And how was it, Pete?'

'Pure magic. Morvar opened the minds and hearts of thousands, millions along the way and... but we're back at the starting point. The path is once again covered in dust.'

Albert always turned dead serious when it came to that matter. Somehow, he perceived that every single thing in his life was connected to that place. He was scared, but he knew he had to dive down that rabbit hole. His course depended on himself, on his actions. So, he kept walking towards the Morvar's gate. Perhaps that was the secret. Never give up on yourself? Trust your guts and jump into the void hoping you'll manage to fly like a bird? Who knows. Chances are, sometimes you just break your neck.

'Anthony Morvar was the painter of his own image.'
'Fuckin' hell, Pete, you're going metaphysical here!'
'I...'
'Are we getting emotional?'
'Fuck off!'
'Right, sorry.'
'Seriously, we need to wake up.'
'Who?'
'Me, you. Humanity!'
'Cuckoo...'
'We should search our empty pockets for the keys opening that rusty gate instead of wasting time with millions of broken locks.'
'And then what, Pete?'
'You'll find yourself, you asshole! There are no limits to imagination when your feet are properly stitched to your shadow.'
'Like Peter Pan!'
'Yes.'
'You high?'
'Oh, shut up, Albert.'
'Aye, I'm zipped.'
'Look, we've arrived.'

And there it was. The sometimes infamous yet more often simply decaying Morvar warehouse.

'What a marvel.' they thought at once, their eyes stuck on that gigantic structure. Rumour has it, it took tens of men and women with pulleys and ropes to raise the iconic six-letter sign:

M O R V A R

A name that quickly travelled the world ending up on expensive lips and educated thoughts. A name that almost changed everything. But "almost" doesn't count and history didn't go easy, gentle or fair with it. In fact, what Albert and Pete were staring at was just a broken sequence of four pathetic letters fighting against Gravity: M O V   R

Fucking pointless. Lacking any fascination, mystery or noir touch. That building was no more revved up by the kid's racket and their squeaks, squeals and shrieks, not during the weekend, nor ever. No more laughs and smiles polluting that industrial yard or the actual production line during workdays. Most of all, no more kites filling the sky with their colours, dropping nuclear bombs of joy all around Sherlintock.'

'Not today, Al.'

'Bummer.'

Albert was staring at those remaining massive letters. They cried revenge. They seemed to be holding on only for the next Anthony Morvar to resume the dream revolution from where it stopped. What could have Albert done to change the world? Was he destined for greatness? Only one thing was crystal-clear: *His Story* was lying beyond that battered metal threshold.

'What's on your mind?'

'Tell me, Pete: are we in or out of the gate?'

SIX

'You're out!'

'You silly human... you know you can't kick me off the door, don't you?' bellowed Rose.

'Yeah, you're only in my mind, I know you're gonna say it!'

'Exactly!'

'Perfect!'

'Whatever. Isn't that your car?'

Victoria mechanically turned and: a young boy was standing still in front of her derelict '60s Mini. He was fixing something, arms crossed behind his back, focused like an R.A.F. pilot.

'Tommy!' yelled Victoria.

Their eyes met and yet the boy didn't seem to care, he just got back to what he was up to. So, Victoria rushed to her car at the same time concerned and surprised by what she was seeing. Tommy, the next-door neighbour's son, was signing his first-ever piece of art with a sharp stone, right in the centre of the car bonnet. The screeching was getting nastier as his face gradually turned into a big grin. He was the living definition of carefree, innocent and sweet like a kiss in the morning.

'What are you doing?'

'A drawing.'

Victoria carefully studied the graffiti which spread all over her car. She looked at it in astonishment, then she burst out laughing.

'What?! You don't like it?'

'It's beautiful.'

'I knew it! Take.' he said, handing her a little rock. 'We can draw together.'

'Thanks, Tommy but I don't really want to ruin your masterpiece. Where are your parents?'

'Dunno. Mum went out early this morning and forgot to bring me to school. So, I thought it was the perfect time for creating something good, then I found your car and here I am. How come you know my name?'

'Easy-Peasy. Your mum is constantly yelling it. You must be a real brat.'

'And you must be a bad girl!'

'Hey!'

'By the way, is she a friend of yours?' asked Tommy, pointing at Rose.

'You... you can see her?'

'Sure I can. Why shouldn't I?'

'You're perfectly right. Hungry?'

'Geez, I'm starving.'

'Shoot, I might have some cake left. Do you want some?'

His eyes shone as bright as a beach in the Bahamas.

'Come on, kid, grab my hand.' said Rose escorting the rascal inside the decadent wooden building.

Victoria lived in an old pub. It was her father's whole life, business, and home. The pub was everything for the old man. He never travelled further than Sherlintock and he didn't even see the world during wartime, bedridden due to a problem with his right leg. His entire life could have been written on a tissue: waking up, preparing breakfast, serving lunch and dinner while carrying on a lifelong chat with his clients, till 9 pm. Then, after closing the kitchen, the man usually ended up stone drunk on the wrong side of the counter, barking and swearing obscenities at the telly. Till he died.

As you might guess, the pub had quite a strong sentimental value for Victoria and even Rose didn't dislike it, possibly because she was born within those dusty walls too, after all.

Tommy loved the place at first sight. He went straight to the counter and naturally settled in. From the top of his stool, he was holding a cuppa in one hand and a chunk of carrot cake in the other. Relaxed, like a natural.

'I always wanted to live in a pub!' he basically chomped out loud, spitting crumbs all over the place.

'You're only eight, what do you know?'

'Or... maybe in a toy store!'

'Don't tell me you have regrets already.'

'They're dreams, Vic. Dreams! And I can tell by the look on my mum's face that the more you grow up, the more you lose them.'

'...'

'But you seem different, I like you.'

'Thanks, mate.' she mocked him. 'So, where's your mother?'

'She's always busy somewhere but she'll be back tonight.'
'You must feel lonely, don't you?'
'Nah... I've got plenty of things on my plate.'
'Such as?'
'You won't get it.'
'Try me.'
'I want to create a Rainbow Room.'
'What? It sounds amazing!'
'It is!! Last month, mum bought me a tube of soap bubbles, I was so excited! I cracked the bottle open and started blowing them in my room, non-stop. I wanted to fill the whole space but, you know, they pop too quickly.'
'Soap bubbles?'
'Sure, they carry all the colours, they're magic! I want to blow so many that you won't even see through the room. Maybe, if we do it together...'
'Did you ask your friends to help you out?'
'I did, but they laughed at me. I've become the school joke. Bummer.'
'I'll tell you what, I'd be glad to help. We can also ask Rose, what do you think?'
'Wonderful!'
'Great! Get up, boy, let's give it a try!' yelled Victoria, possessed by a sudden enthusiasm, as if a spark just lit her mind on fire. She jumped to her feet, ready for some action when she realised Tommy wasn't following. He was still sitting at the counter with food stuffing his mouth, like a squirrel, looking smugly at her, shaking his head.
'It's not that easy, Vic.' he managed to say after swallowing some cake. 'We need sunlight. Otherwise the bubbles won't shine.'
'Sure, but I have an idea. Come on,' she gestured, 'There's tons of remarkable trash down in my basement waiting for us.'
'A basement?'
'Yeah. Let's find something useful for our project.'
'Yeeeee!'
'By the way, why don't you stay overnight?'
'I wish...'
'We can leave a note to your mum, so she'll know where you are and won't worry.'
'Seriously? That would be Super. Great! I love it, I love it!' said

Tommy, jumping all over the room as a perfect 8-year-old kid.

'Can I unplug him?'

'Oh, Rose, can't you enjoy life for once?'

'Let me think about it: no.'

'Vic, close your eyes! There's something I need to do before we start.'

Although she was curious as hell, Victoria obeyed the order without complaining. Her eyes shut reality out and she instantly got lost somewhere inside her mind. In the fleeting lapse of a second, she imagined waterfalls of light, thunderstorms and oceans crashing together creating new spaces. She dived into the sweaty warmth of Africa and she swam with Arctic penguins. She was just about to turn into a butterfly when a tiny hand pulled her sleeve, waking her up. Tommy was wearing a pair of aviator goggles, car driving gloves and a 32-teeth proud smile.

'I'm ready, Vic, let's do it!'

SEVEN

Steve's BMW growled loudly, adjusted its trajectory and, thanks to an expert manoeuvre, it spun with a burnout, perfectly lining up within the white parking stripes painted on the road. From the passenger seat, Albert was mumbling, flicking through the glossy pages of a fashion magazine. Something was wrong. Damn wrong. He took another puff from his ciggy and rested his eyes for a second. Then he snapped. He scattered fag and mag out of the car window and burst out:

'Nobody tells stories anymore!'

'What?'

'There's no magic around here. No poetry, no elegant terms unleashed on the streets like the Smiths did! No intriguing thoughts sticking to your mind, making you wonder.'

'And... you're telling me this now because?'

'I want to doubt, Steve. About everything. I want to stay up all night because of some existential question. I want to be moved by a stranger's story and cry like a fucking baby at the crack of dawn.'

'...'

'Can anyone shock my existence? Can a single word, even a flake of it, change a life? My miserable life? Please?!'

Steve, who knew his friend pretty well, let the healing silence do its job and, as by the book, Albert slowly calmed down after 3.56 minutes.

'Drink?'

Wrong-goddamn-question.

'Fuckin' hell, Steve, you know I hate those people!'

'Man, they ain't that bad.'

'Please, let's do something else.' moaned Albert glancing at the crowd outside the club on the other side of the road, the very people Steve regularly hung out with.

'Why do you always have to be like this?'

'Like what??'

'Jesus Christ, relax, let's have some fun.'

'Fun?! Fun?? This is ridiculous.'

'...'

'How can you not see it, Steve? There's no daydreaming here, not a hint. It's only harsh reality.'

'Look, Albert...'

'Close your eyes, try to imagine the scenario.'

'Oh, God, not again...' Steve thought.

'Just do it.'

'Cool, eyes closed. Go on...'

'Great. So, we get there, we walk in and, fuck me, what do we find?'

'I don't know, what do we find, man?'

'A bunch of dummies.'

'Right.'

'No smooth/smoky jazz music, no elegance, no hats on anyone's head. They all lie around the room as motherfucking fancy furniture, holding glasses, getting drunk on a thousand empty words, discussing money and success that no one ever achieves. Am I right?'

'Actually...'

'Brilliant. Pretending interest is the latest trending fashion. Everyone wants to impress so they're dripping fake praises over one another. Truth is, they're bored, incapable of imagining what's on the other side. Steve, what we just entered is a room filled with humans trained to refuse the truth, desperately holding on to a cyber, imaginary world tailored for them.'

'Don't be so damn tragic, man! We just came for a drink.'

'A drink. Unbelievable. A drink he says.'

From a distance, a distinctive guy raised a pint to the odd couple locked inside the shimmering car. He dribbled three, four, five drunken bodies on his way out of that clubbing mess and when he finally landed on the empty road his identity was revealed.

'Pete!' called Steve, waving at him.

Pete danced to the BMW and unhingedly shouted:

'WASSAAAAAP' right in Steve's face.

The DJ was spinning all sorts of classics from Marvin Gaye to Jamiroquai passing through Elton John. There was a good vibe in the air, a sort of *I'm o'aight, may(t)* mood that even Albert (who was still silently pissed off on his seat) would consider acceptable.

Steve and Pete high-fived, fist-bumped and did a couple of extra finger tricks like true locals.

'What's wrong with him?'

'He's sick with the whole world.'
'Oh, Steve, shut up.'
'Hey, he can speak!'
'Shut up you too, Pete!'
'Fuck off, Al!'
'What the fucking fuck, you fucks??'
'Did you swallow a dictionary by any chance?'
'...'
'Right. Get on your feet, we all know you're a dancer at heart.'
'So what?'
'Don't make me force you.' insisted Pete, now pulling the door and dragging Albert (his hand still gripping onto the handle) out of the car, over the tarmac.
''Aight, cool, I'm coming, it's just... you know.'
'Show me what you got, Al.'
'Woah, you sure?'
'Do it, Albert!'
'So be it. You asked for the Dance Master and here comes the Dance Master. Just give me a sec.'

He stood up, pulled the collar of his military jacket and raised his look to the clear sky. The night was dry-cold, so cold you were puffing smoke out of your lungs at every breath. It was one of those nights when you either get a move on and make something happen or you'd rather board yourself up at home for good, waiting in vain for life to knock at your door. He sniffed the air in search of a hint, a sign showing him the way, and there it was: a rock'n'roll thunder ripped through the people and smashed the airwave going from the speakers to Albert's ears. The Dj was scratching the vinyl so hard it sounded like a musical massacre, rough but precise, gradually killing the music, setting up the beat for something else. *Tick-tacking, scratch-scratching*. A chewy one-two, one-two countdown was leading the dancing mob towards a sudden change.

Albert couldn't help but twist his legs in a special move he only knew. His arms shook the cold away. His gaze landed on his shoes 'One two, FUCK YOU!' he shouted like a young Steve Albini. The tension was piling up when the rusty garage guitar of *Sabotage* made its entry, giving room to the Beastie Boys to rule that moment with a nuclear blast.

Albert was feeling awesome, the greatest damned L.A. rockstar on the planet. *'Time to rock'n'roll'* he didn't say while entering the club as irreverent as Liam and Noel Gallagher put together, and that was that.

Inside, the music was so loud that your thoughts got simply erased from your mind. Despite that, as soon as Albert bumped into the helpless faces of Steve's friends, a clear sentence emerged once again to the surface of his brain. It was pulsing like an infected vein.

'Nobody - tells - stories - anymore.'

That phrase was hurting him so badly that he struggled to breathe. It felt like when your girlfriend calls and tells you she's done looking at your ugly, stupid face. Albert was choking. Sweating. He carefully avoided every single glance as he stumbled his way to the bar.

'Hit me.' He ordered the bartender, and gulped down a random drink left on the counter. Attitude. That was his secret weapon, his only (if any) quality that attracted the opposite sex more than anything else. He had just knocked the tumbler against the solid marble surface when he spotted her: next to him, with crossed long legs and high heels, was sitting a girl he used to date years back. She was studying his face with a sensual yet very curious smirk smudged on her glossy lips. You never knew what to expect from Albert but, to her, he looked absolutely handsome, definitely worth risking something. Albert met her gaze and asked:

'Can you tell me a story?'

'What? Are you ok?' she yelled in order to be heard, breaking into a very embarrassed smile.

'Top of the world. Please, do you have a story for me?'

'Er... I don't know?'

'Hey, I ain't fussy, I can easily settle for a brief, spontaneous tale or... shoot, we could improvise and jam together, like a jazz duo!'

She scanned the room to make sure nobody was watching and, even though that was exactly the case, she felt all the spotlights of this world on her.

'Are you kidding me?'

He didn't appear to be joking.

'Look... what story?'

'A good one.'

She didn't know how to react so she just laughed again. Albert was dead serious and she wasn't prepared for that, but she knew pretty well how to escape any silence, any embarrassment. She gave him a look, one of those looks that only women know. Then she caressed his hair, whispered something in his ear and slowly licked his lips in a burning passionate kiss. *BLAST!* She immediately felt relieved, everything was going according to plan again although... as soon as their mouths separated, she realised Albert was still fixing her like before. With a surreal calm, he asked again:

'Can you tell me a story?'

'Shit. You fucking weirdo!' she didn't shriek on top of her lungs. Instead, she pretended to be cool.

'Listen, Albert... oh gosh, it's so late, I really need to go.' she lied as she grasped her stamp-size clutch bag and her lips mimed some nonsense like *'Call me'* while she slipped out of the club. Fast.

Albert was disappointed. Back to square one.

'Hit me.' he ordered the bartender again.

'You smutty scumbag, what did I just see?' asked Pete, getting hold of the vacant seat.

'You tell me.'

'I leave for three seconds and you're making out with strangers?'

'I just asked her for a story.'

'Damn, that was a kiss, Al!'

'I don't give a fuck about kissing. I just asked for...'

'Tut-tut, no need to get into dirty, filthy details.'

'But...'

'We need to celebrate. Bartender, give us...'

'Pete, stop.'

'... your best...'

'Enough.' Albert pounded his fist on the counter. 'I'm out of here.'

'Hey, hold on. What's the problem, Al? I mean, seriously.'

'What's the problem? You're always telling me about Morvar and the Morvar Company. Anthony Morvar was selling dreams and I can't find a soul to tell me a bloody story. What's the problem, you ask? What's wrong with the world, Pete?'

'Apparently, my dear impossible friend, grown-ups decided to put curtains against the night skies.'

'No more stars?'

'Nope. Unless...'

'Unless you leave the windows open, like Peter Pan, right?'

'It was Wendy Darling.'

'Thanks, Honey.'

'Idiot.'

'Dreams used to come from out there, am I right?'
'Well, these days only burglars get through open windows.'
'Fucking hell, Pete, you're a philosopher.'
'Yeah, man.'
'Yeah...'
'And where are you going now??' shouted Pete, but Albert was gone, lost among his thoughts, looking for a way out through the crowd.

Outside, the same embracing cold as before. Within minutes, Albert would have felt needles piercing his face but he couldn't care less. The sky was too beautiful to be avoided. He'd rather freeze his ass while staring at that marvellous show than idling in his warm room with a cold empty heart. He rolled a fag and admired the shiny holes cut out that velvety blue mantle. He was so abstracted that barely noticed the girl standing next to him. She was biting a peach, staring at the infinite sky with her eyes closed.

'Hard times for dreamers, uh?' she most certainly never asked.
'Don't tell me, stranger.' he surely never replied.
'Okay.'
'What are you thinking about?'
'The world needs a change. People shall see clear again and put everything back in its right place.'
'Hell yeah. Make a difference. Give dreams back to the people.' didn't say Albert, now excited and inspired by that imaginary telepathic conversation.
'Nothing will ever be the same.' she concluded.

Then nobody spoke. Silence. For a long while. But how long is too long? Nobody knows. What is clear is that in that moment a shooting star entered their eyes and scorched their lives forever. Or maybe it didn't.

'I'll become an inventor.' Albert finally said out loud, opening his eyes, hoping to find her.

But no one was there, next to him, anymore.

EIGHT

Tommy was absolutely tireless.

'Come here, Vic!'

'I'm Rose, you monster. How many times do I have to tell you?'

'Sorry... when is she coming back?'

'God knows. Apparently, Miss Perfection needed a breath of fresh air and decided to leave me, I mean, *ME*, to deal with you, the most annoying kid ever delivered.'

'Mmm...'

'Besides, she hates you.' Rose giggled.

'You're a liar.'

'Am I?'

'Hey, look at what I found!'

'Oh, Jesus. It's the 8th time in 10 minutes that you say it.'

'LOOK'

'STOP SHOUTING'

'Ok... but this time is for real! I swear.'

'Let me see.'

'It's a spotlight!'

'Nice piece of junk, indeed.' Rose commented, and then threw the metal piece away, without thinking.

'Wait, wait! It's important, look over there.' said Tommy, pointing his tiny finger at a marvellous pile of trashed spotlights.

'Anything else?'

'Anything else? This is it! If we connect all the lamps together, we can create our very own miniature Sun! This way the bubbles will always be shining, night and day. Colours will spread around, splashing and dancing over the walls like crazy!'

'Holy Moly, finally, a great idea. Nice work partner.'

'High five!'

'*CLAP!*' didn't sound Rose's ghost-hand meeting with Tommy's.

'Guess now we need to learn a bit about electric stuff, what do you think, guys?'

'VIC!! You're back!'
'About time...' grumbled Rose.
'Yep. I had to be somewhere.'
'Where?' asked Tommy.
'Aren't you tired, little brat?'
'I'm not!'
'It must be 1 am by now.'
'Where have you been? Can I come with you next time?'
'I think we can keep working on our project tomorrow. We're not in a rush, are we?' said Victoria, avoiding the question and putting an end to that gloriously dusty game.

Strangely enough, Tommy didn't argue nor moan. He pulled his goggles off and a couple of white circles appeared around his eyes. He was the exact negative image of a panda bear. Like a pioneer Harley / Davidson biker or an experienced steam train conductor, the kid was covered in dirt, but he didn't seem to care about it, he was bothered by something else altogether. He placed the coal-black filthy gloved hand under his baby chin and wondered:

'I don't want to go home...'
'You don't have to, didn't we leave a note to your mum?'
'Aw...'
'Besides, I just spoke with her.'
'Really?'
'Positive. There's enough space in here for an entire army.'
'Thank you, Vic! And...'
'Yes?'
'Well, I... can you tell me a story? It helps me fall asleep.'
'Sure I can, I know plenty of tales.'
'Seriously?? I can't believe it!'
'Follow me, tiny genius. Let's go to bed.'

Victoria brushed her hands against her denim shorts and led the way to the first floor of the pub. It was a vast open space once used as a dining room for functions, special events, weddings... Indeed, it was the most beautiful section of the building. It even had access to the balcony and to the priceless river sight.

'So, what do you think?' asked Victoria.

Tommy was enchanted. 'It's messier than my room.'

'Oh, thank you so much. You can sleep on the Chesterfield downstairs if you don't fancy it.'

'Nah, I'd trade all my toys to live here. My room is so small, it just fits a bed and a desk while you have... what is this, a ballroom?'

'...'

'How could you only use a mattress and a swinging chair?'

'Don't forget the handmade bookcase, mate.'

'Yeah, it's not fair and you know it.'

'I'm trying my best to decorate the place. For example...'

But he didn't listen, he just:

Run, jump, bed.

'Hey, what are you doing?

Jump, jump, bed again.

'Don't touch that!'

'This?'

Bed, jump, jump.

'Leave it there, please!'

Jump, climb, shelf.

'NOT THAT ONE!'

Grab, creeeeak,

'Gosh, you...'

crash, SBAM!

The bookcase collapsed, dragging all its contents to the ground. Tommy bounced on the bed and eventually hit the wooden floorboards like a faulty-autopilot-ed comet. No matter what, he was still gripping onto a leather-bound book he found on the crooked shelves. As it often happens to kids (and cats), he didn't feel a thing (are they made out of rubber??) and he didn't die either, the lucky bastard. Instead, he was already into something else altogether. He was flicking the pages of that weird volume when he naturally said,

'They're blank, Vic.'

She was staring at him, halfway between shocked and totally pissed off. *'Should I kill him?'* she secretly asked herself.

'Why there are no pictures, nor words?'

'Oh, Jesus...'

'What does it mean?' Tommy insisted.

Victoria took a deep breath, she fixed those innocent, glowy eyes and finally replied:

'It means that you can read all the stories you want, whenever you want. No limits. Each time, you can experience a different adventure around the world. How does it sound?'

'Cool.'

'Give me the goggles. And the gloves.'

Tommy surrendered immediately, without questions. He laid down and let Victoria gently caress the dirt off his cheeks. The mattress was super comfy and the duvet was soft, warm. When Tommy finally settled, she tucked him in. He felt like a baby bird, safe in his nest. So, Victoria sat on the swinging chair, cleared her throat and rested the opened book over her chest. She closed her eyes and...

'What's the title of the story?' asked Tommy, curious as a cat.

'Let's see... imagine an empty white room. No decorations, no characters for now. Try to levitate and escape your body. Then, slowly, plunge your feet inside that space and let the words fill it with the wisdom and the uniqueness of life.'

'Title?'

'Do you want to play this game or not?'

'...'

'Ok, now close your eyes. This is:'

"Jade Elephants' Graveyard"

IT'S SHOWTIME, MATE!

When she finally read the last sentence of that tale, Victoria couldn't help but lay her hands on the heart and breathe out a profound silent pearl of melancholy. Warm tears glided down the silk-smooth trails of her face. She let them caress her, like the soothing words of a mother, then... surprisingly, she found herself thinking about the strange guy she met out of the off-licence, the day before. The same fool she encountered out of the club. Or did she? A chill ran up her spine and she smiled. Was he important at all? She turned to Tommy, who was sleeping like an angel: his mouth open, fiercely snoring, lost in God knows what fantastic adventure. So, Victoria finally put the bookmark in place, wiped the tears away, and kissed Tommy goodnight.

One day she would read that story to the strange guy, looking straight into his eyes. And he would love it.

NINE

Cardboard's elephants twirling on the windowsill. Plastic tigers sliding up and down the tub saturated with hot air. Albert was utterly immersed in his new project called: *Creation*.

He sat on his shabby French chair, the one almost chewed away by Time (and moths). The bathroom was empty, overflowing with a thousand thoughts buzzing around like annoying flies. Impossible.

'I don't think so.'

'...' replied the empty room.

'Maybe it's just the location... let's try the kitchen again.'

ding-dong

'That's what I'm talkin' about! Can you hear it?' Albert asked no one, alone in his apartment. 'Astounding. Listen to the delicate flow of water petals licking the gutters, the elegant pounding of rain nailing on the roof... Creation...'

ding-dong!

'Like a Blue Hole in the ocean... or, no... yes, *The Sky is Fallin'*, that's the song I need right now.'

Puffing out smoke like a chimney, he hurried to the living room (one step). His hands rummaged through a box filled with vinyl records and grabbed the QOTSA album in a sec. Out of its sleeve. Slammed on the slipmat. Play.

Meanwhile, a solid cylinder of ash from Albert's cigarette finally surrendered to Gravity and landed right in the centre of the Sony turntable almost causing an international tune crisis, a sudden musical derailment. Luckily, none of the above happened. The LP kept spinning and the stoner rock hit the walls through the sound system, so loud that even Jackie, the blind-deaf 90 years old lady who lived downstairs, could hear it.

'Thump-thump, THUMP!!' violently knocked the broom handle against the ceiling below.

ding-dong, ding-dong

'Getting in the vibe, perfect. Let's light some candles, where did I stash them?'

'CUT IT OUT! I'm sick of your devil's music!' shouted Paul, the guy next door.

'Ciggies, I need ciggies... and Martini. A bottle will do.'

'Can you hear me, mate? *Woof woof*? You bloody bastard! I'll slit your fucken throat with a goddamn knife this time!!' insisted Paul. And his bulldog.

'Paint water on a blank canvas on torrid sunny days.' wrote Albert on the wall behind the couch, adding it to a long list of things to do.

diiiing-doooong, dooooooong!!!

'THUMP THUMP THUMP THUMP!'

Albert was about to faint. Being an inventor turned out to be too much stress. He had to keep things simple, lower his expectations. How? No clue. With a sharp stroke, he put an end to the heroic effort of the ashes piled up tight to his cigarette. He cleared his throat and, with a solemn "HemHMmm", stated that he was still far from a scientifically proven result. No applause for him. Yet.

'Fuck off, mate, this ain't funny, I'm breaking in!' yelled Paul, furious.

'There must be a way...' sadly thought Albert, on his knees.

Curses and swears were popping up around the room from all over the place, like pollen in Spring. The tension was reaching guard levels and the barking of the bulldog was getting nasty. Albert was somewhere else. Then the door slammed open and the music stopped.

'You fucker. They were about to call the police.'

'Steve! Why are you here?'

'You called me last night, remember?'

'Mmm...'

'Anyway, what's wrong?'

'Wrong? I'm feeling Supersonic!'

'It doesn't look like it, man: shutters down, fag stubs everywhere, you, laying on the floor, holding your head between your knees...'

'I need concentration.'

'Whatever. Can I help?'

'Well, you ruined the mood alright but... since you're here...'

'Blast my mind, I'm ready!'

'Cool. Sit down.'

'Shoot.'

'I want to invent something to make people feel better.'

'Aspirin. Done. Shall we go?'

'You got it all wrong, it has nothing to do with health... not directly anyway.'

'You figure.'

'I'm talking about objects, sounds, noises, images, perfumes or whatever else that, once perceived by the individual in question, would make him/her/LGBTQ+ happy. At least for a second, I don't aim to play God, of course.'

'Of course. And how's this project going?'

'Great.'

'...'

'Alright, mate. I'm lost, *perdido*, dead-end. I'm like a random John Doe dumped in a nameless alley.'

'Maybe you should start from scratch. What is that you want?'

'I... I was thinking of... like an epiphany, a mirage. It will be available in every grocery store, on Amazon, online shops... it must be something you can keep in your pockets and pull out when you feel down. Like a drug, but with no side effects.'

'Just it?'

'Yes... I think so.'

'So, everybody happy.'

'Obviously, there will be some discomfort. To be honest, happiness is rather dangerous. You can't take it just like that, without preparing yourself for later consequences. I was considering the idea of writing an instruction booklet, you know, to explain everything in detail.'

'Sure, and maybe you can use a headline like this one: *unless you find a way to jump over the atmosphere, landing will hurt. Train your legs.*'

'Holy shit, Steve. This is exactly what I'd love to write in it. How did you figure it out??'

'It was etched on the wall, look, here.'

'...'

'Listen, man, you need a break. I'm okay supporting you but don't you think you're aiming too high?'

'Too high? Too high. For chrissake, Steve, I can't waste my time chasing average ideas. Either I strive for the best or I can quit right now.'

'Beer?'

'Are you even listening?'

'Oh, shut that damn mouth for once. You can't push yourself like this, Albert. It's worthless. Sometimes you need to stop working to achieve your goal. Get distracted, mind-free. As soon as you give up chasing the idea, it will crash on your head like a 10 tons, black weight and *SBAM!* There it was. Creative jobs are complicated, you never know when or where the intuition would come from.'

'Nice.'

'New ideas act like clouds, they're fleeting, continuously changing shape. You only need to take the picture at the right time.'

'Wow, thanks Steve. It doesn't sound like you at all.'

'...'

'Pete?'

'Ok, fine, I had a long chat with Pete.'

'Uh, what do you know.'

'Thought this would help you, man. You looked shattered.'

'Yeah, working at home isn't so good anyway, you might be right. I need to wander around, meet strangers, fuel myself with life, experience the danger, the evil, the obscure.'

'Point taken, man.'

'I wanna listen to secret tales and get into dim situations, dangerous alleys. You know, Steve, those are the places where words flow slow but sincere.'

'I bet. Now, put on your coat and meet me downstairs. I'll be warming up my baby.' Steve replied, already one step out of there and: gone. He was gone.

Albert was pensive. He lit another cigarette while fixing the void inside the bathroom. *'Should I go searching for that girl or wait for destiny to do its course?'* he asked no one and no one replied. His hands reached the military coat and he was about to leave when he glimpsed something weird happening in the back of his retinas: by then, the cardboard elephants were soaked in hot air inside the steamy tub, and tigers were getting hungry after hours of plastic exercise. Albert didn't want to witness a massacre. Besides, he really needed a break.

'Don't put your life in the hands of a rock'n'roll band.' he reminded himself. 'I'm gonna find her tonight. Fuck procrastinating. Fuck destiny. I won't sit and wait for my car to fall right off a fucking cliff.'

TEN

Victoria almost smashed her Mini into the well-painted iron bollard installed in front of the pub. She jumped on the brakes just in time, making the tyres screech hysterically.

'I wonder who gave you the driving licence, darling. Maybe a dead body? Strapped to the passenger seat?' said Rose, shaking her head.

'Shut up.'

'And this is just because of a young, not-so-healthy yet good looking guy who *(I'm not finished)*'

'I said...'

'you happened to meet more than once without ever having the guts to tell him a single word.'

'Exactly. Can we move on?'

'Do you really want to?'

'Fine. I feel stupid and I regret I stood there mute as a fish. Happy?'

'I think so. What is the kid doing on the sycamore tree?'

Tommy was sitting astride a solid branch of it in the garden beside the pub. As soon as he spotted Victoria, he literally jumped down and, by sheer luck, he landed in her arms.

'You little crazy thing!! You trying to kill yourself??'

'What? No, I was searching for you. You know, the view from up there is phenomenal.'

'Is the kid high?' asked Rose.

'I wonder how it would be standing on the roof.' continued Tommy.

'Definitely high.'

'It would be trouble, believe me.' said Victoria, in anger.

'Bummer.'

'Look, we can go together if you want but, please, please promise me you won't do such a stupid thing again, not without me.'

'It wasn't stupid. You don't understand, I just wanted to...'

'Hey, hey, stop it right there. I perfectly get it, but you scared me. A lot. I don't think I can stand another stunt like that.'

'Oh... Alright then. But you will join me in the next adventure.'

'What did I just tell you?'
'Deal?'
'Sure, I was born for that.' Victoria conceded to Tommy, who looked more than pleased.

'So, what are we up to? Would you lend me one of your books? Can you tell me another story?'

Victoria didn't bother answering any of those questions. Instead, she threw the little brat over her shoulders like a potato sack and headed to her place. When they entered the pub, they found the lights on, a cappuccino was steaming on the counter and the turntable was playing a record. Weird.

'Do you like it?' promptly asked Tommy, fidgeting, waiting for an answer.

'What? You did this?'
'Yep.' replied his smug face.
'I can't believe it...'
'Me neither.' said Rose. 'You fucking broke in? What are you, a baby burglar? I mean, you fucking broke in??'
'Rose, language! Besides, what I meant was...'
'You a goddamn criminal?'
'I'm not, I'm sorry...' said Tommy.
'Baby gang? Teenage gang? Regular age for crime gang?'
'We got your point, Rose.'
'Un-fucking-believable.'
'So, Tommy,' Victoria tried again, 'you know Barry White?'
'Who?'
'The man singing the song.'
'Nah. I just loved the smiley face on the cover.'
'Oh, Tommy boy. You know who else is gonna smile?'
'Rose, please, leave him alone.'
'The police, cause we're calling them now, am I right, Vic?'
'No, we're not. Let's give this cappuccino a chance, instead.'
'Wait, wait. It's not a real one...' said Tommy. 'It's only hot milk mixed with the spare coffee I found in the pot.'
'*Slurrrrp*'
'...'
'DELISH! Thanks, mate!' joked Victoria. 'Next time I'll teach you how to make some froth too, alright?'
'YEEE!!'

'Don't yeee, you criminal.'

'Rose...'

'So... it was good, wasn't it?'

Victoria approached Tommy and gently whispered in his ear: 'I appreciated the thought, that's what truly matters. Never forget it.' and she kissed his puffy cheeks, which he immediately brushed with the back of his hand. Rose was visibly disgusted. Someone had to shatter that gushy moment, so she said:

'Why don't we go to the station?'

'What's over there?' asked Tommy.

'Trains, what else?! You kids...'

'Don't trust Rose, the place is filled with wonders.'

'Really? Such as?'

'You know... it's the same thing for airports, cafes... they are Stargates from the plain everyday world to somewhere you don't know yet. You get on your train wondering *What's on the other end?, Is she gonna be there?, Will I ever come back?.* There are plenty of these portals spread across the world, in different forms.'

'Are you serious?'

'Sure. I'm talking about books, movies, art, sounds, but you can also transcend reality by simply glimpsing at the sky, at the stars... all these things can ferry you through an amazing journey.'

'So, where are we going, Vic?'

Rose couldn't help but laugh.

'Nowhere. Everywhere. Oh my, you're confusing me!' almost cried Victoria. 'We can sit on the bench, reading a book while enjoying the scents of other places brought in by strangers. We could also read the stories written on the faces of the coming and going passengers.'

'Why don't we take a train?'

'We could, of course, but it would be limiting. What I'm talking about is an alternative way. I call it *Travelling Without Moving*.'

'Fuckin hell, Victoria, are you done with the bullshit? Let's bloody leave. Here's your leather jacket. And your mobile. You're welcome. Let's go folks!' cut short Rose. And that was that.

Tommy was ready. He was actually already gone, walking (should I say running?) along the green path. Victoria instead was rummaging through her pockets. Unsurprisingly, they were filled with a substantial amount of rubbish: pebbles, seashells, hairpins, *a teaspoon?*. She liked to think of them as splinters from her past. Every piece was a special treasure telling a unique story. She only had to touch them or play with their shapes, to see the faces, the places. It worked like an Apple memories' projector yet to be invented. For Victoria, life was all about simple little things. *Why didn't people get that?* There was more to feel inside a sunset than in any futuristic technological device. Sometimes even a single word can make you cry. It doesn't take much to shake your existence if you keep your eyes open. If you allow your heart to filter and absorb life, and...

'Tommy!' shouted Rose to the kid, who, in the meantime, had already walked half of the walk to the station.

'I can run faster than a cannonball!'

'Good Lord, you said that like I care.'

'You're mean.'

'And you stink.'

'What's that building?' asked Tommy suddenly stopping, putting his sugar-high overexcitement on pause for an instant.

'Morvar.'

'Who's Morvar?'

'A wise man.'

'Like Gandhi?'

'Better.'

'What did he do?'

'He sold dreams.'

Tommy sniggered at that. 'You can't sell dreams.'

'Says who?'

'Mmm...'

'Exactly. Now, why don't you shut up and walk?'

'And why don't you try to be nice, Rose?'

'You ask too many questions. You know, if we were in Italy you would have been whacked by now, just like this, SNAP!'

'Liar. Can we go in?'

'Sure.'

So, Tommy opened the rusty gate, hurried inside the abandoned park and landed in front of a gigantic crumbling warehouse. The courtyard of the decaying Morvar building was a creepy place sometimes. Ivy, thorny bushes and thick, prickly hedges everywhere. Rumour has it that ghosts and beasts of all kinds lived there. It was so creepy that even junkies avoided hiding around those places.

Rose hated it.

Tommy didn't have a clue.

Victoria absolutely loved it.

Each time she stepped over that threshold, she was overwhelmed by happy childhood memories. That was the place where her mother taught her how to fly a kite. Families and kids used to turn the huge playground alive every single weekend by filling the air with screams of joy and colouring the sky with restless smiles. It was a conscious mirage, one of the many things Morvar had been capable of. That man dedicated his existence to the purpose of making people happy, of creating a better world based on dreams. Then he just died, like any other ordinary human. One day you're up, the next you're not. Gone. His ideas, instead, seemed to be still floating in the air, like an eternal halo. They were resting in the background, waiting for someone to wake them up.

'Who's that guy?' asked Tommy, pointing his tiny finger to a weird figure dressed in wetsuit who was acting like a fool, inside the decaying warehouse.

Victoria couldn't believe her eyes.

It was Albert.

ELEVEN

The inspiration was around, Albert was strongly feeling it in his heart. Steve's advice didn't help at all and the night out had been a real pain, just as Albert expected. Yet, everything was about to change. He was on his way to meet the girl of his dreams, confused as never before, without having a clue of where she was. As if that wasn't enough, his brains were interfering with the crude reality, driving him to a quite adequate *(good)*, insane dimension *(not so good)*.

The more Albert walked the dirty pavement of Sherlintock, the more he got lost. His face was changing shape and colour as it reflected into every shop window, intermittent, like Christmas tree lights, but that wasn't the weird part, not really. Strangely enough, his confident walk was gradually downshifting as he got closer to the old pub by the river. Was she living there? Even though he couldn't possibly know the answer to that, his guts started rumbling and he panicked, so much so that he felt sick. Physically sick. Suddenly, his face emerged from the abyss of his thoughts and he recognized himself inside the window of a fancy Mercedes.

'You're a fucking coward.'

It was such a perfect definition that he couldn't help but give a firm handshake to his double self entrapped in the mirroring glass. *Idiot.* The car alarm screamed through its sirens as soon as Albert pulled the door handle. Stupid. So stupid he had to run. Fast.

He was panting when he reached the Morvar's gate, the only place capable of rewarding him with some sort of peace. Answers. Sometimes.

For the very first time, he decided to venture inside, and...

TWELVE

'Albert Hoover!'
 'That's me.'
 'Come in, it's your turn.'
 'You sure?'
 'Don't be funny. Professor Dali is waiting for you.'
 'So, Albert made his entrance. He finally completed his studies, he was thrilled, ticking like a bomb. He slammed the door open, ready to show everybody his value, determined to tempt fate. Albert was wearing his best sly face, eyes injected with a hint of perverse cruelty and fists clenched so tight that the knuckles looked spectral-white. He was about to kill that motherfucker in a clean, smooth bare-hand gipsy boxing match and... no, wait, that's another story.'

Albert was talking to himself, tip-toeing Gregory Hines-style around the desert ground floor of the Morvar warehouse.

'What is he doing?' Asked Tommy, hiding with Victoria behind some wild bushes.

'No clue, my friend. Let's see what happens...'

Albert was moving back and forth from a spot to another, pretending to be more than one person. There was no director, no cameras or spotlights, just a man rehearsing an absurd nonexistent script. Albert took a deep breath, shook his hands as if doing a yoga exercise and started again.

'It was a sultry afternoon, you couldn't breathe, and Mr Hoover was high as a kite because of the heat and the razor-blade cutting tension. He tried to knock the door down, realizing just a pitiful second too late that it was already open. Therefore, he missed it, miserably embraced the air and tumbled to the ground.'

'What a poor show, the commission muttered to each other.'

'He tried to regain some austere composure, a more appropriate seriousness for the situation. In vain. One by one, Albert shook all those highly-educated hands, then he exchanged an equivocal glance with professor Dali while approaching his chair.'

'Boy, sit down, enough with the jokes, said one of the board members.'

'Albert smiled, embarrassed, and obeyed the order. Professor Dali, the famous architect renowned in Sherlintock and all across the country for his incredible, futuristic works, began to comment on the boy's thesis. He spent time (a lot) focusing on the details, every single feature of the project, giving advice and whatnot till he got to the point, the final evaluation reached in agreement with his colleagues. He was glowing when he said:

Your expression is the fresh one of a young man thinking young. Your ideas, your inexplicable creativity that goes almost beyond the surreal, and your unique way of expressing it... allow me, Mr Hoover, you're brilliant.'

'Thanks.'

'I dare to say that, perhaps, you are one of the few members of an invisible movement of visionary creators. You, who have always shown a pure misfit's aptitude, you, the first in the University's history to introduce the grade D with shame. Tell me: how could you imagine such an innovation?'

'First of all, I want to thank you for mentioning the D with shame.'

'But this man here didn't achieve his goal just once. He collected four of those little bastards and this, let me tell you, it's not simple faith. It's genius work! Dedication. Passion. A real attitude towards science. This is what I call Fine Art!'

'Well... yes.'

'Your D with shame has become a classic by now. It's a trend, a cult, a dream that everybody pursues with ambition. As you all know, the shame rescinds the praise of your higher grades and this skinny boy got two, two miserable honours, but he managed to undo them all, and he certainly didn't stop there! His avant-garde spirit, typical of young people, could almost be defined as valorous, fearless, MAMMOTH!!, professor Dali screamed at one point, without making any sense, and continued: This man is sublime. Even after collecting six B minuses and four A's, he was still able to score the lowest average ever.'

'Actually...'

'Don't be modest, son. You're talented! You're the future! And I'm the one telling you. Me, father of four, married to a holy woman, the sixth out of five divorces; me, also cause of God knows how many other kids whose faces I don't certainly know, scattered around the world.

Allow me this: you are my greatest satisfaction.'

'Respect prof, Albert said, fist-bumping his chest.'

'Ok, let's cut the talking. I am proud to announce that, although in my opinion you deserved a noble A and magna cum laude, we reached the final decision of giving you a more than decent B minus!'

'Super!'

'You need to know that I ardently fought to get you this well-deserved grade. Son, I love you. Now, don't get me wrong. Some believe that I'm homosexual but, as I just told you, I have a wife and kids.'

'Crystal clear.'

'Unfortunately, all my previous five partners had complained about my... let's call it gay nuance, but this was and still is absolutely ludicrous. Anyway... screw all the students graduating with magna cum laude! To hell with these young elders who spend all their precious time studying, boarded up inside dark libraries without ever achieving shit! Fuck them!, prof Dali shouted, turning to the other members of the board. This is something completely different, new, better. Innit?'

'...'

'You are the fresh morning breeze, the sun after the storm, you...'

'I guess that nuance is becoming quite clear, prof.'

'Listen carefully: I, humble Salvatore Dali, propose that you rock the boat. I'm inviting you to not give a fuck about the degree board sitting in front of you, of which I happen to be honorary president, and consider my proposal.'

'A poignant silence descended upon the overcrowded hall.'

Albert was reciting these words out loud as an experienced Greek storyteller, marking each word with emphasis to galvanise his unreal audience packed inside the Morvar warehouse. His face changed. He turned serious, and dark, while inhaling a deep breath after another, getting ready for the last act of his play.

The three shadows behind the bushes were trying their best to hold back laughs and comments, focused and curious about what was going to happen.

'Mr Hoover.' Albert started again.

'That's still me.'

'Cool. I'm asking you to accept a C plus... CUM LAUDE MAXIMA!! I know, ladies and gentlemen, this has never happened before, but we are here today dealing with something I dare to define as supernatural.'

A deafening buzz switched on like electricity throughout the room. The Laude Maxima. It never happened. Never in this world. It was unpronounceable, just like Voldemort *(ups...)*. Albert almost collapsed, as if his legs couldn't bear the weight of that life-changing decision. Kneeling like a knight to his Queen, King, whatever, he placed his right hand on his chest, closed the eyes and pondered. He was about to accept the proposal when professor Dali incited the crowd again.'

'Everybody, let's change the world! Fuck yeah! C minus cum laude maxima, this is happening, folks! Make your choice, son, I trust your instinct, and remember: you're absolutely free to take the other offer too.'

'...'

'Holy Crap, boy! SAY SOMETHING! I'm shitting my pants here!'

'I choose C minus cum laude maxima, prof!'

'Goddammit, that's GREAT!! GREAT!!!! YAaaaaiiii!!!, yelled Professor Dali, insane, soaked in sweat, letting out a particularly pink high-note.'

And so did Albert, the real one, jumping around, screaming of joy and desperation at the same time. He was utterly, consciously delusional: *'LIFE IS WONDERFUUUULLL!!! TONiiiiiiiiGHT I'M A ROCK'N'ROOOOL STAR!!! I LOVE THIS FOCKEN SHITE!!'* he announced to the world, then he grabbed a heavy steel bar from the floor. He furiously swirled it in the air, fast, and threw it against a barely standing glass window which exploded in a thousand sharp shards.

'FUUUUCK'

Albert howled with all the air he had in his lungs. So, he picked up the bar again, and again he swirled it, approaching another victim around the empty factory. He was out of his mind: the bar hammered against anything, with rage, smashing, destroying, raping metal plates and glasses, leaving all sorts of splinters and slivers on its way. Albert was bleeding, covered in scratches, sweat and dust. Yet, he kept on smashing stuff for a while, shattering and kicking shit around till he finally collapsed, exhausted and overwhelmed by an unstoppable nervous crying. He let his wrecked trembling body fall to the concrete floor, he crawled a few inches and finally stopped, wrapped up in a foetal position.

At first, Tommy was surprised. Then he got scared. Then he found himself running towards the troubled guy.

'Tommy! Hold on!' Victoria shouted, losing grip on the kid's hand.
'How are you, sir?' Tommy asked the man on the floor.
'Who are you?'
'I'm Tommy. How do you feel?'
Albert tried to pull himself together. *What the fuck was going on?*
'Sir...'

He was still weeping when he glimpsed Victoria approaching. Blood suddenly froze inside his veins, but he patted his dusty coat and managed to paint a sort of crooked grin on his face.

'I feel terrific, kid! Why are you asking?'

Out of the blue, Tommy jumped over him and tightly embraced that shaking body. By then, Vic was standing right in front of Albert, holding some weird, embarrassed smile. She just met his eyes when her full lips managed to say:

'Hi, my name is Victoria.'

THIRTEEN

Jumpy.

Tommy was nothing but jumpy.

He was running up and down the stairs of the pub pestering Victoria and Rose with a million questions, overexcited by the unexpected visitor.

'Vic, are you cooking tonight? I think you should. You know, my mum always says that we need to be nice when we have guests.'

'Fair enough.'

'Yep, mum knows lots of things. So, what are we preparing for dinner?'

'Duck roast with potatoes.'

'Really?'

'I don't think so. Tommy, why don't you go upstairs and rest for a while?'

'Mmm... I'm not tired, I'm staying here with you. If you don't want to cook I can do it myself, you know, I'm pretty good at it.'

'...'

'Anyway, are we showing our project to Albert?'

'The rainbow room? Why should we? We just met him.'

'I sense he can help. He really seems like one of us, I'd say we can trust him. You know what? I'm asking him right now!'

'No way, hold your horses, cowboy.' she said abruptly, grabbing his arm. 'He's having a bath, do you really want to disturb a guest? What about manners?'

'Fine... but... you don't want me to do anything. You have changed since we met him.'

'Look who's talking, you've been running non-stop, for hours. Now, let's play a fantastic game. You go upstairs and plan tonight's activities or something like that. Can you make it all alone?'

'Wow, can I choose any sort of thing?'

'Let's say so...'

'Cool! You'll definitely love it!!'

'Sure, just wait for me to call you, ok?'

But Tommy was already gone, searching for the right pen and sheet of paper to sketch his idea.

Victoria was nervous.

Back at the warehouse, Albert was in such bad shape that she eventually offered him to stop by at her place, have a shower and, maybe, even stay for dinner.

'Please calm down, you're so tense you're making me anxious too.' said Rose, staring at her.

'I'm ok, alright?'

'Sure, and I'm not a creation of your sick mind. What's wrong with you? It seems like it's fucking Christmas or New damn Year's Eve! And what the hell is it that thing you're wearing? A pullover?'

'Expectations...'

'Brilliant, now you also mutter. You should pull yourself together honey, just saying...'

'I'm fine, period. Perhaps, just a little tired, that's all.'

'Bullshit. Marvellous bullshit. You're getting more and more human day by day. That's backwards progress, Vic. Congrats.'

'I think he can read my thoughts.'

'Finally, something serious.'

'On our way home, I was wondering about a great deal of stuff and guess what? Every time he spoke, it was like he was answering one of my unspoken questions. Can you believe it?'

'Of course I can, I'm not even real. Did you notice?'

'I'm going crazy, Rose...'

From the other side of the hall, Albert was not-so-secretly observing her foolish gesturing nonsense to no one. She was absolutely restless.

'Don't know about Rose but I don't believe you're nuts.' said Albert with a smile, popping out of the bathroom, his brown hair still damp. 'Any chance I can borrow a hairdryer?'

'How did you...'

'It's a secret.'

'What?!'

'Told you, it's a secret.'

'Fine... just give me a sec.' said Victoria, confused, rushing upstairs.

Once left alone, Albert, barefoot and wearing an oversized robe, carefully scanned the room looking for something absolutely fundamental:

Music.

His eyes found it right there on the floor: a splendid Pioneer turntable with a wooden base and transparent plastic lid. He couldn't resist it, so he raised the cover and switched it on. *Ella and Louis* started playing and Albert immediately got into the rhythm, snapping his fingers, tapping his feet, twisting around Josh Homme-style. He was in the midst of a quite intricate move when Victoria got back with the hairdryer and stopped to observe the twirling idiot, with curiosity.

'Here you are!' he said, shameless. 'Hope you don't mind, I put some music on, I love your taste.'

'Thanks.'

'No, thank you. The bath was superb and this robe is unbelievably cosy.'

'It's oriental... do you like dragons?'

'Only when they don't spit fire on me.'

'...'

'Pardon my insolence but, you know, you shouldn't be nervous.'

'In fact, I'm not.'

'Look, there's nothing to be ashamed of, I feel precisely like you.'

'But...'

'See? We should kiss right now, to avoid any later complications. Trust me, it works.'

'Yeah, for Woody Allen in Annie Hall. It's a movie.'

'I thought it was an excellent idea...'

'Forget about it.'

'...'

'... hungry?'

'Only if you are. Would you let me cook something special for you?'

Victoria blushed, and smiled, and tried to hide the warm, unusual feeling that was running through her body.

'It would be lovely.' she said.

'So let's do it. After you.'

Albert was happy. He hadn't been nearly close to this weird mood since so long he couldn't even remember. When Victoria brought him to the kitchen (a pro setting once used by the pub's chef) he barely believed his eyes.

'It's the first time we actually talk, but I feel like we've been telling each other stories forever.' said Albert, at one point.

'... are you a dreamer?'

'Are you an eagle? What questions are these?'
'Simple ones.' insisted Victoria.
'Right, let's see... I believe I got stuck in one dream today.'
'Tell me about it.'
'Sure?'
'If it's not a nightmare, of course.'
'Uhm... cool, but I need some space, yeah, like this.' Albert gestured while feeling the room where to set his play. 'Ready?'
'Go.'
'Super. I was acting on Broadway, New York, and the show was going so damn well that people re-booked their seats for the next eight weeks.'
'...' she told him with a puzzled face.
'Hey, it's a dream, isn't it? Anyway, I'm a famous actor *(definitely the best)* and everything related to theatre/movies/fame is basically chiselled into my DNA. Yet, somehow I can feel that something is ruining my performance. It's too perfect, if you know what I mean.'
'I do.'
'You do?'
'Sure.'
'Marvellous. So I need to improvise, shock the audience and... that's exactly when I see it: a big torch hanging to the wall. Its majestic flames are dancing as if nobody is watching. I grab it and, within seconds, that ancient flambeau is setting the wooden stage on fire, its flames getting higher and higher till they catch the stunning velvet curtains. Some guy in the audience freaks out, he starts screaming, as if that wasn't part of my plan. Amateur. So, I reach for the only thing available nearby and, gripping that dusty Louis XVI chair, I face the fire. I am beating the shit out of it, over and over, swinging the antique piece of furniture with violence till I finally *(heroically)* manage to defeat the flames. Silence. I bow to the void dark in front of me and *flash!* the spotlights switch on over the public like a SWAT attack, revealing thousands of people. Insane. They were giving me a standing ovation that still resonates in my ears.'
'...'
'...'
'Are you ever serious?'
'Seriously?'
'I give up.' concluded Victoria, turning her back at him, heading to the living room. She didn't quite make a step when Albert gently

grabbed her hand.

'To be honest... I don't usually tell my dreams while they're happening. I'm afraid I could wake up.'

'Ah, Is that why you made up another story for me?'

'Kind of...'

'I mean, there's no harm in telling dreams out loud, but if you don't feel like it, it's ok to me.'

'The thing is, I'm not so sure this is even happening. You know...'

'Well, I don't.'

'Oh, come on, you sneaky...'

'What?'

'Alright, alright. First, I've never been rescued, especially not by a beautiful girl and the oddest kid.'

'Hey, you forgot Rose.'

'And Rose.'

'You got it.'

'Second, I've never been given the chance to be part of something like... this.'

'Meaning?'

'Beautiful?'

'Shut up...'

'I don't know about you, but I'm pretty confident this ain't real.'

Victoria lowered her look as she approached him. She rested her head on his shoulder and caressed his hair. Now Albert was nervous.

'I bet I'm gonna wake up alone in my room, and I warn you, you might disappear anytime now like *POP-pop, blip, PUFFfff...* you will explode and vanish like a soapy bubble. It probably won't be funny by then.'

Even though Victoria was amused by his blathering, she pretended not to listen and when her lips reached his ears, they whispered something so sweet and honest to make Albert speechless. It was like one of those dreams when you strive to talk but your throat feels tightened up by an expert sailor's knot.

FOURTEEN

Day after. Forefinger pressing on a doorbell. Some imaginary ding-a-ling, the door opens and someone appears inside your retinas.

'Pete. Finally.'

'I made it as fast as I could. What's the hurry?'

'As I told you on the phone, I have a plan.'

'Yeah... about that...'

'Wait a sec, why are you sweating? And, how come you look like one who just walked here?'

'Because I...'

'Because you walked, you motherfucker!! We need your car, Pete, how can we possibly go to London without a car, Pete?'

'London?'

'Hello? Didn't I tell you this morning, Pete? Do you understand the magnitude of the disaster?'

'You never said anything about Lon...'

'Peeete??'

'We'll figure something out, don't worry.'

'Don't... DAMN IT!'

'Listen, Al, I already asked Steve for a favour.'

'Oh, yes. He's giving us his BMW, his baby, isn't he?'

'Not exactly.'

'I was sarcastic. He probably even sleeps inside that wheeled Space Shuttle.'

'He told me he might be free for the time we need him, stop by and give us a lift. Cool?'

'Cool.'

'Now, Albert, respect our deal and finish telling me your story. That's the only reason why I agreed to help you in the first place.'

'And you did right, my friend.'

'Great.'

'Super.'

'Albert, the story.'

'Hey, don't push it... what the fuck am I, a jester? These things require a certain mood, music, dim lights... don't you think?'

'No thanks, I'm alright. Just here for the story.'

'Fair enough, mate. Then I'll tell it in the most indifferent, cold, miserable way. You know what? Let's even switch on some fucking awful neon lights so we can properly feel like rats caged inside a damn lab fridge. Screw setting up the mood.'

'Perfect.'

'I'll spit out one word after another just to fill the air. I won't even look at you, and I'll yawn, a lot. Like a grizzly bear.'

'Sounds great to me.'

'Mate, I will be so indifferent that... hey, where are you going?'

'Home.'

'You leaving?'

'Are you telling the bloody story or not?'

'I... it's private.'

'You got to be kidding me.'

'Maybe. A little. But I'm not bargaining over the room setup. I refuse to speak in such average conditions.'

'Fine, Mr pain in the ass.' conceded Pete as he turned off all the lights except for the antique-style Victorian lampshade sitting next to the couch. He cracked a couple of beer cans open and pressed play on the turntable, letting Miles Davis spin.

The burgundy light filtering through the damask velvet shade immediately put Albert at ease. He gulped a mouthful of that amber fluid and finally laid down on the floor, just like Liam Gallagher on the cover of Definitely Maybe.

He was staring at the ceiling and:

'You should have seen her, Pete: the most graceful creature you could ever imagine. I was paralyzed by her beauty, stoned by her scent when, God knows how, I found myself embracing her, my arms around her waist, we were dancing. Her soft lips rested on my neck and breathed caresses from foreign worlds over my skin. I don't know, Pete, my heart was pounding so hard I most probably fainted.'

'Did you?'

'Did I? Good question. All I know is that when I opened the eyes, the room was transforming under my feet: the old pub walls crashed to the ground like ice panels, giving space to grand windows and gilded high ceilings. From the very middle of that ballroom, an invisible cable held an impossible chandelier made out of diamonds. It was suspended two fingers off the floor and that is why people had to dance around it.'

'Then what happened?'

'We were twirling like Caribbean birds with our eyes fixed on each other. I felt like she was telling me all her secrets, tales and adventures no writer could ever put down in words. It was absolute magic, the best delusional experience I've ever had. Mate, the chandelier was painting sparkles of pure light against the wallpaper and her eyes were glittering like a million crystals kissed by the sun.'

'Bollocks.'

'Right. Right? That's exactly what I told myself. Yet, some weird happiness I think I once knew possessed my entire body. I couldn't control it.'

'It sounds like a Jane Austen novel.'

'And it felt exactly that way. All the people in the room were staring at us, at our embroidered dresses. We were Queen and King of that night, Pete. Like silky rose petals, we were endlessly embraced. I was forever lost among the dreams jealousy kept inside her sparkling eyes and...'

'And??'

'We were about to kiss. Her full lips slightly touched mine when something blocked her, dragged her away for a glitch of time and then nothing. Again we were so close we could breathe each other, I shut my eyes and, but she was pulled by her dress, as if she got caught in thorns. As if someone was trying to get her attention. So, she turned. And there he was.'

'Who? Who was there?'

'The kid, mate.'

'No-Fucking-Way.'

'...'

'What the hell did he want?'

'Aw... he was hungry. He said *Vic, can we order something? I'm starving.*'

'Shit, Albert, are you abusing minors now?'

'Mate, I'm not! In fact, I immediately asked *Who's craving for pizza?* What a bloody suck-up! And, obviously, everyone loved you.'

'You got it.'

'So...'

'So, it has been a great night. The little genius picked a terrific movie and... Eventually, I fell asleep next to her.'

'On the couch?'

'Yeah, I was knackered. Then, the morning after... well, here I am.'

'She didn't say a word?'

'Nope. But I must see her again, tonight.'

'I can't believe she didn't write a single sentence on a damn piece of paper...'

'Nothing.'

'You don't want to read it to me, do you?'

'Pete...'

'But you have it. I bet it's there, upper pocket of your lurid flannel shirt. Correct?'

'I can't tell. Hungry?'

'What the fuck, you don't trust me?'

'It's not a matter of trust, Pete. It's... you should keep certain things private, otherwise, they lose all their preciousness.'

'You promised her you wouldn't share it.'

'Yep.'

'Alright, it sounds reasonable. Anyhow, I'm not hungry, just incredibly thirsty.'

'Here's another beer, Pete.'

'And here's Steve. I can tell the sound of his engine between a thousand. Now, my dear Albert, are you ready to meet her again? Are you going to tell her the whole truth this time?'

FIFTEEN

8:28 PM

'The truth is, I'm a serial killer. I'm sorry, I can't help it.'

'...'

'I killed today and I'm going to do it again, tonight, tomorrow... I'll keep on stealing lives until their souls will merge with mine, until they'll flow through my veins.'

'You... YOU ARE A MONSTER!'

'I don't care.'

'You fooled me. You, and your magic tricks, your charming manners...' she muttered in tears, crawling on the worn wooden floor.

'Enough! I'll get rid of you too if you don't stop it. You knew it from the start.'

'NO!' she screamed with all the strength she had left in her dying body. 'You kept it secret from me! You are a monster, a monster... Oh, Lord, save me, I didn't know...'

'You stupid woman, you've been my accomplice all of this time. No one can save you! Especially not your so-precious fancy God. Shut the damn mouth!'

'You...'

'SHUT IT!'

The Hackney Empire theatre was packed that night, and the play was so tense no one even dared breathing. The plot was a blast: an unusual serial killer piling up one victim after another, in his books. That weird intimate journey of a writer throughout his own fears and demons turned out to be an ongoing sold-out, and Victoria had been lucky enough to get an appearance. A very special one-off act.

* * *

8:31 PM

Vic was backstage, sweating fear. She was waiting for her turn.

'How are you? Ready?' asked Rose, a little concerned.

'Do you know the feeling when you're outside the doctor's room?'

'I guess…'
'No, you can't. You're not real.'
'Ladies and gents, give it up for Miss Grumpy!'
'It's frustrating. Time scatters every single second in your face. *Tic-Tac-Tic-Tac*. Every damn tick is a stab wound to your brain.'
'Right, now I get it. It's not just stage fright, is it?'
'…'
'He'll be here on time, you shouldn't be worried.'
'No, he won't.'
'Did you even invite him?'
'I didn't. At least, I certainly didn't use words for it. He reads my mind, so he knows, doesn't he?'
'Cookooo…'
'Maybe.'
'So, this would be your very first non-date.'
'What are you talking about?'
'It can't be a date if you didn't invite him. He probably doesn't have a clue of where the hell you are right now!'
'Whatever.'
'Yep. Nevermind.'
'Hey, can you spare a cigarette?' asked Victoria to one of the staff.
'You don't smoke.' said Rose.
'I do now.'
'*flick-flick, Frushhh*' said the flame escaping the lighter, burning the white tip of the fag.
'Thank you so much.'
'Congrats! You're making progress every day, Vic.'
'Cut it! Don't you see everybody's looking at us?'
'Perhaps, stopping talking to yourself would help. Also, you could avoid this back-and-forth dance on a single tile. You look stupid.'
'I hate you.'
'Shhh…'
The director's assistant approached Victoria wearing his usual grave face. 'Get ready.' he whispered. 'You're next.'

* * *

7:30 PM

The BMW was crazy roaring around random streets.
'Where to?' asked Steve to the guys.

'London Theatre.'

'There's no such place in Sherlintock, man.'

'In fact, it's in London.' said Pete from the backseat.

'What? You never mentioned no freaking Lon...'

'Calm down guys, it's just... a minor detail, innit?' intervened Albert.

'You motherfucker, I should have known better when you...'

'Steve, why don't you just drive?'

'Shut up, Pete!'

'No, you two shut up! We need to find this place.'

'I never heard about any London Theatre in London. Are you sure that's the name of the venue?' asked Steve.

'So, now you're a theatres expert, aren't you?'

'Are - You - Sure?' he insisted.

'I think there's a London Theatre in Sydney.'

'Fuck off, Pete.'

'Well, it's a theatre and it's in London. That's all I have.'

'Jesus, Albert. You're such an idiot. How d'you think we're going to find the place? There must be hundreds of venues in the city.' almost cried Steve.

'Is there anyone else who could know where we have to go?' asked Pete.

'Yeah, a fortune teller.'

'The kid!' shouted Albert, out of the blue.

'Who?' Pete and Steve asked together.

'Tommy! The kid. We need to get to the old pub by the river. Go, Steve!' commanded Albert, gripping on the handle as the BMW rushed, ripping the tarmac.

* * *

8:32 PM

'Do you remember when I used to wear glasses?'

'Back at school, sure. Hard times.'

'They were, Rose. I was crushed by the mocking, the looks those guys gave me. How can we be so frail at that age?'

'Who knows. I remember dad used to tell you that those idiots didn't actually give a damn about you and your glasses.'

'Right. *Once they get home, they forget about you. They're just killing time, but you are better than that. Don't let them touch you.*' Victoria said with a funny, old-man voice.

'And you did it. You bought the most-ridiculous glasses ever produced in the history of humanity, and you wore them with pride, every day.'

'Yeah... it actually worked after all.'

Out of the window, the soft drizzle was caressing the dark streets and their people. Victoria was lost out there, staring at the seductive reflections of the lights over the slick pavement.

'You should stop being afraid, darling. He will come.'

'Why am I feeling so stupid? I'm as insecure as a teenager. I thought I went past that phase but... guess we never evolve, do we?'

'Come on, don't fool yourself.'

'?'

'You're much worse now.'

'Oh, Rose, you're always so charming...'

Victoria fixed the black lace ribbon adorning her neck and carefully stubbed the cigarette into the sandbox against the wall. *Deep breath.* The play was going on great. People were still stuck in their seats, waiting for the next move.

* * *

7:36 PM

The BMW runs at full throttle through the streets of Sherlintock.

'SCREECH!!'

'MATE!!'

'What the fuck!'

'BEEP! BEEP! BEEEEP!!'

'Watch it, idiot!' Steve barked at the cab driver, miraculously dribbling him.

'Can you believe it?'

'...'

'People don't know how to bloody drive in this country.'

'Well...'

'Look at that. WANKER!!'

'Man, slow down...' finally managed to say a sweaty Pete from the backseat.

'WooHoo!'

'Steve!'

'Fuck, Pete, don't be a pussy. Look at Albert, how quiet he is.'

'I bet. He has completely spaced out. God knows what he's thinking.'

'Screeech.'

'I think we've arrived.'

The music went down as Steve lowered the window.

'TOMMY!! TOMMY!'

'TOMMY!' added Pete.

The little boy popped up as if summoned. He had his goggles on, ready for any adventure.

'Albert?' he asked.

'Yeah, no, it's Steve. We need your help, kid. Where's Victoria's play?'

'Straight to the point, uh?'

'Where in London?' asked Pete.

'Hackney Empire. It will take you about an hour.'

'An hour? How'd you know?'

'Victoria told me when she left. Is Albert dead?'

'Nah. Just a thousand miles from here.'

'Cool!'

'Great. Are we gonna make it in time?' asked Pete to Steve who was barely hiding the broadest of the grins, excited like a speed junkie for the challenge he was about to *race*.

'Oh, no...' they all thought at once.

SIXTEEN

8:42 PM
'The Secret. My Secret. You want to know it, don't you?'
'Look, mate, I don't even care anymore.' said the detective, annoyed to death. 'We've been here so long I'd rather confess myself.'
'Where are you going?'
'I'm out of here.'
'But... I did it! I am the killer!'
'Whatever.'
'I killed them all, just read my books!'
'Yeah, you told us a million times already.'
'It's all in there, don't you get it?'
'Sure.'
'Come on...' begged the writer, bursting in tears, sobbing like a little boy, his hands chained to the desk.
Drama.
So, two men from the psychiatric ward entered the scene, picked him up and dragged him away.
Lights slowly dimmed while Victoria was trembling by the side of the stage. It was her turn.

*   *   *

8:23 PM
'FUCK - FUCK - FUCK!' *(Pete)*
'We're gonna die, we're gonna die, we're...' *(Tommy)*
'...' *(Albert)*
The BMW got on two wheels approaching the last turn a tad too fast. They almost tip over, but they didn't. Like in a Matrix scene, time eternally froze, raindrops floated in space like crystal tears and the "spare" tyres of that mighty car spinned slow-motion in the air. Deep breath. *Woah.* Till that magic spell broke, reality resumed and they thumped heavily back against the pavement. Albert finally woke up.
'It's Showtime, Mate! Go get her!' said Steve, in a rush of adrenaline.

8:42 PM (again)

Victoria immersed herself into the crowd, one foot at a time, testing the waters. The silent stage was buzzing with dust, break-dancing within the conic void created by the spotlights. It looked as if a secret party was going on there, one Victoria wasn't invited to.

'Hem... check. Check.' she louded out from the speakers, across the auditorium, approaching the mic.

The puzzled audience was waiting for some action.

She was somewhere else.

'What is she doing?' a man seemed to whisper.

'Where is he?' she asked herself.

'Who?'

'Albert.'

'Is she going to say anything?'

'I can't see through the lights. Is anyone there?'

'It's crammed with annoyed people, Vic. Open that damn mouth of yours!' incited Rose.

'Show us what you got, honey!' the guy wearing a hat didn't shout.

'One more second...'

'We want our money back!'

'What a marvellous play. Silence. Isn't it brilliant?'

'It's not, mum. It's just boring.' replied the young girl to the *tailleur*-ed woman.

Victoria was waiting for a sign. She was imagining a door opening, tearing the dark deep sea in front of her with flashy lights. Then, Albert would appear from there, carefully holding a warm smile in his hands, a special gift reserved for her.

'That's it, I'm out.' thought the first row altogether.

'Ouch!' finally said the mic as Victoria rushed her hands to her leg, surprised.

'Did he really throw a Bible at her?'

'Who?'

'The director. Look at him!'

'No... it can't be.'

'Wow!'

'This is insane.'

'Absolutely staged. Brilliant.'

'Muuum??'

It was in that instant that the main door slammed open and flooded the auditorium with light. Albert spread his arms like a majestic eagle and screamed:

'I MADE IT!! I'm here!'

The Hackney Empire theatre turned at once to look at that no-one fool. Immediately, the security guys grabbed Albert by the arms, shut him up, and, just before they kicked his ass out of there for good, she finally spoke:

Nobody's coming down the hall
nobody echoes in my head
broken reflection out of luck
nobody ever needed Her

Beautiful senses are gone
Canary in a gilded cage
Singing
sweet soft and low
I will poison you all.

Silence.

Victoria bowed to the crowd. Albert couldn't believe his ears, nor his eyes. Speechless. There was an astonishing beauty in those words and the way she hissed them out into the mic. Even the security men loosened the grip for a second. And...

Gradually, two palms shyly touched together, then they clapped, alone, like a fearless raindrop diving into the Ocean. Instinctively, other hands joined that revolutionary act, one by one, domino effect, they were conquering the noiseless void. It was contagious. Like a sweet disease, the clapping grew louder, and louder, until it became hysterical, Beatlemania, and the Hackney Empire exploded in the most ridiculous, unexpected standing ovation. The elegant woman jumped on her seat, yelling some nonsense with joy, carried by the insane atmosphere.

'I told you, it was staged!'

'Shut up, mum.'

Cutting through the hall, an invisible wire connected Albert and Victoria's gaze, writing down such a gushy, boring story that anyone but them would hate.

SEVENTEEN

'A mobile, please.'
'Which brand?'
'Does it matter?'
'Well...'
'Whatever, just give me one. You choose.'
'Ok... do you like this?'
'I guess.'
'It's the latest model. It features the best camera ever made and it has lots, lots of storage.'
'I just need it to make a call. And send a message. Does it make calls?'
'Sure it does! It's a real deal. Do you want regular or wireless earphones with it?'
'I don't know what you're talking about.'
'Sorry, I...'
'No, I am sorry, I didn't even introduce myself.'
'...'
'Albert.' he said, shaking hands with the guy.
'I'm Josh, nice to meet you.'
'Manners. Never forget manners. It's a rule, innit?'
'So...'
'I need a mobile to call the most beautiful bird that ever sang songs from out of this world.'
'Ahem...'
'Last night she gave me her number but I don't have a phone and here I am, talking to you.'
'Right.'
'Can you believe she's a poet? And she asked me out for dinner?!'
'Sir, there's no need to tell me the whole story.'
'Sure, let's get back to business. What is so special about this... what is it called?'
'iPhone.'
'Exactly, that thing.'

'It's the Future. Once you start using it, sorry, *experiencing* it, nothing will ever be the same again. Let me tell you this...'

Albert was nodding like a car dashboard bobblehead, thinking about something else when his eyes stumbled across a chunky old device stashed in the back of the shelf.

'I want that one!' he interrupted the guy, overexcited.

'But... it's designed for the elderly, it has no camera, no internet connection...'

'Look at the keys, mate! They're huge!'

'That's the...'

'I love it! Love it! Love it!'

'You do?'

'Cha-ching! You sold it.'

'Wow, you really do.'

'Can you please wrap it nicely?'

'I see, it's a present.'

'Indeed, it is. I like rewarding myself every now and then. Isn't it great to unwrap gifts?'

'...'

'I'm absolutely thrilled! Nail-biting!! BOOM!!!'

'Yep. How would you like to pay, sir?'

'Cash.'

'Legend.'

'Thank you, young man.'

'Good.'

'Good Bye.'

Albert literally couldn't wait to get home to open his present. That's why he stopped at the first park on the way and, within seconds, he basically turned a perfectly regular bench into his office. He was tearing the package in pieces with such violence and rush that when a couple of slow-motion-strolling old ladies noticed him, they immediately became concerned: is he defusing a bomb? God knows. Albert managed to pull the black device out of the box and already he was about to smash it, trying in vain to force the (upside down) battery into its moulded slot.

'May we help?' the ladies asked at once, approaching him.

He suddenly woke up from his bubble world and said:

'Yhello, beauties! Thanks, but no thank you.'

They exchanged a pleased look, almost flattered. So, they insisted:

'You don't seem a mobiles' expert, my dear.'

'Oh, Jesus Christ. Look who's talking, the grand-bloody-mother of Eve, straight from the Eden Garden.' Albert silently thought.

'Can I see it? My son taught me how to fix it so many times.'

'Sure you can.'

'I must confess I'm pretty good with those toys.'

'Here it is.' said Albert, with a smirk on his face.

So the other woman spoke:

'You looked in a hurry, dear. May I ask why?'

'Well... *(you nosy)* Sure. I need to call my girlfriend, and...'

'I can't believe it! It's a love thing, did you hear it, Paula?' she told her friend, poking her ribs with the elbow.

Paula was so busy she didn't even notice. She already installed battery, SIM card, whatever, and she was about to enter the PIN and activation code.

'You didn't argue, did you? You seem like such a lovely boy.'

'What? ... nope... I just need to...'

'Let me guess. You're proposing.'

'Wow.'

'You have to. You can't fool around forever as a stray. You need to act like a man, my dear.'

'Hold on, she's not even... how can I say it...'

'She's foreign?'

'No, she's...'

'She's Muslim, isn't she?'

'For God's sake, she's not my girlfriend!' Albert burst out.

'Oh, gosh. This isn't right. Don't tell me she's also a married woman.'

'Precisely. Mother of three children.'

'Ahh! You want to see me faint, don't you?' she shrieked with a dramatic tone, holding one hand on her chest.

'I wouldn't dare, madam. I simply assumed that *such* young ladies like the two of you were looking for a good-old, intriguing affair story to tell.'

'I'm listening...'

'The truth is, we barely met once. I need to call her to arrange our very first date. Cool?'

'Now we're talking. Have you heard, Paula?'

But she hadn't. Paula was almost done with her unsolicited task, utterly proud of herself for fixing the phone in record time.

'I bet this girl is as beautiful as a wildflower.'

'She is.'

'I remember when I was young... we used to bite our lips to make them red. Oh my, does she have pretty lips?'

'Ahem...'

'Here it is.' Paula cut in handing the device to Albert.

'Thanks.'

'Good as new!'

'*(It is new, you dinosaur...)* I really can't express how grateful I am to you for helping me out. You've been incredible.'

Paula blushed like a schoolgirl. The other lady was clearly about to ask something else, but she managed to keep her mouth shut.

'Well, well, well, thank you and goodbye.'

'Goodbye.'

Albert got back to his things but the two women didn't appear to be willing to leave. Not at all.

'Ladies, did I forget to thank you, by any chance?' tried Albert.

'Oh, no. You did. And it was a pleasure, darling.'

'Very - much - indeed.'

'...'

He sniffed the air, took a look around, then started rummaging in his pockets, trying to look busy.

Nothing.

Granny's team didn't want to get the fuck out of there.

'...'

'...'

'So?' the ladies eventually asked, simultaneously.

'So, what? Do I owe you money?'

Whatshername exchanged a complicit glance with Paula and they burst out laughing.

'Fucking hilarious.' commented Albert with a smirk, 'Fucking hilarious indeed.' But his cheekiness lasted less than less since the couple didn't look so amused now. They crossed their arms and calmly said:

'Darling, we're just waiting for you to call her.'

EIGHTEEN

The cotton towel gracefully slipped to the floor, unveiling Victoria's peach-smooth long legs.

The bathtub was filled with soapy bubbles playing a funny game she couldn't wait to be part of. She closed her eyes and gently immersed her body into the steamy water abandoning herself to the heat, the peaceful solitude, and her face turned red, as usual, making Rose smile.

Victoria's breath was slowing down, every muscle seemed to relax, relieved from the constant battle against time, life and the infamous G-force. She plunged her head into the frothy lather and disappeared.

'One, two, three...'

Inside her ears, the heart was now beating heavier, louder.

'Four, five...'

She kept her head underwater, holding her breath. She was challenging her very personal world-record.

'... six.'

'Toc.'

'?'

'Knock-knock!'

'? - ?'

'Vic?'

It was Tommy, trying to get her attention from outside the bathroom door. Not a good time.

'Victoria?'

'You've got to be kidding me!' she thought out loud as she emerged from her secret refuge far from the world. 'Come in, it's open!'

She didn't even finish the sentence that Tommy appeared.

'You didn't use it!'

'What?!'

'I gave you mask and snorkel, don't you remember?'

'Oh, that.'

'How can you bath without them?'

'I know you're not the greatest underwater breath holder in the universe, but this doesn't mean we all have to...'

'You're weird.'

'Wow, that's new.'

'My mum says you are a weirdo.'

'Great, say thanks to your mother. And what the hell has it to do with the mask?'

'Nothing. I just remembered her saying so.'

'Fab.'

'Did my mum say something bad?'

'Let's see... I guess everybody needs to be classified in some way. What do you think you are?'

'Duh. A kid?!'

'Right. And that's how the world goes, then, at the end of the day, this is utter nonsense. You are much more than a kid and I'm not just a regular, average weirdo. I'm a professional.'

'I think weirdo means special. I like you, I want to be weird too, although...'

'What?'

'... what if people won't like me?'

'Oh, screw the people, Tommy! You need to be yourself, not me, not your mum, not one of your "cool" schoolmates. It may sound hard, but once you get used to it, you're free, and beautiful, or ugly, or...'

'I got your point.'

'Can I enjoy my bath now? And what was so urgent it couldn't wait?'

'Put on the mask first.'

'I don't think so.'

'And the snorkel.'

''Aight' she managed to say, chewing the plastic tube stuck in her mouth.

'You look funny.'

''Ommyyy!!'

'Ok, so, I think Albert called.'

Victoria spat the snorkel away, shocked.

'What? And you didn't mention it?'

'I'm telling you now.'

'What does it mean you "think" it was Albert?'

'Well, the connection was awful and people were chatting in the background. Then, an old lady got on the phone and said 8:30, somewhere. Can I come?'

'We already discussed this, Tommy. I'm sorry but you can't this time.' Victoria said with the warmest gentle tone but at the same time attempting to sound like an adult... despite the fact that she was still inside the tub wearing a diving mask and featuring a messy sort of punkish mohawk comb for her hair. If it wasn't for her sweet, innocent doe eyes, Tommy would have never agreed so easily.

'Bummer...'

'Yeah, guess my bath time is over, let's try to figure this out. Towel, please.'

'Here.'

'Now turn the other way, little fellow.'

Her left hand plunged underwater, reached for the chained plug and pulled it off with a sharp stroke. Like tourists on a rollercoaster ride, the soapy bubbles raised their hands and happily swirled down into the drain.

'If I ever happen to become a Buddhist, I wish I'll reincarnate into one of those glimmering spheres.'

'Did you really say that?' cut in Rose.

'I know, it's stupid...'

'And ignorant.' Tommy added with a real brat smirk.

'Cool. I'm a bad person. Now, can the two of you leave me alone for a second?'

'Rude...'

'Get out!'

'I think you should call him.' said Tommy on the threshold.

'I will. Thanks.' she cut short as she shut the door.

'You know it, don't you?'

'What?! What do I know, Rose?'

'You don't have his number.'

'I... I'm sure he will call again.'

'You really are a weirdo.'

'So what?'

'Have you ever considered trying to become someone?'

'Don't you see how busy I am at being a no-one already?'

'Very funny.'

'I know.'

'Seriously, you should make something out of your *thriving* creativity and *vivid* imagination.'

'Are you mocking me?'

'Maybe. But, no. I mean, think about Morvar.'

'...'

'He didn't have any particular skill. Let's be honest, the man didn't know nothing about making anything. But he had such a brilliant mind that he almost changed the world.'

'I'm listening...'

'He was selling dreams, for God's sake! Dreams! Don't you get it?'

'Well...'

'You read blank books, you record audio cassettes with sounds of: sunsets, empty spaces, orange cardboard papers, you name it. You even put on tape the *Vibes of the Darkness of my Room on a Soon-to-Be Sunny Morning of December*.'

'Crazy uh? My best take.'

'And now there's also Tommy. I hate kids but, let's face it, the boy is brilliant. Rainbow room? Oh, man, that's a game changer.'

'He's great.'

'Have you ever asked yourself how many people would love your work?'

'I don't know, Rose...'

'Morvar.'

'He actually convinced everyone...'

'Exactly. Selling dreams. Stick that into your bloody deaf ears, darling.'

NINETEEN

'So you've got yourself a date.'

'Yes, Pete. How many times do I have to repeat it to you?'

'Still, you're in front of the Morvar gate. Seriously, you have a problem.'

'It helps me think!'

'You don't have to think, you need a shower, you need to get dressed and show up at the bloody restaurant.'

'Easy peasy. And I already had a shower, FYI.'

'Great, now you also talk like an idiot. And what is this wet-dog smell?'

'What smell?'

'It's you, Al! Go shower.'

'Yes, mum.'

'Out of curiosity: did you call and inform her of this supposed-to-be-happening date, this time? Or... you simply wish that (somehow) she knows about it?'

'You really must think I am a fool. Of course I called her.'

'Did you speak with her?'

'Quite.'

'Meaning?'

'Meaning... I think I told the boy, Tommy, that we are meeting at 8:30 pm.'

'Great, you indeed are not a fool. And you didn't specify in which place, right?'

'Exactly. I like to be mysterious.'

'Call her again.'

'Oh, mate, you really are a pain in the ass. I knew I forgot something!'

'Call her again.'

'Er...'

'What?'

'I don't remember her number, Pete. She wrote it on my palm, but it faded away after I showered. See? Nothing good comes out of personal hygiene.'

'...'

'Come on, mate, I bet it happened to you too.'

'Don't you have a scribbled copy on paper or something?'

'I... might?'

'Gosh, Albert, you're a disaster. Get the hell out of here, and find the damn number!'

*   *   *

'Get out!' shouted Rose.

'You make it sound easy. Where should I go?'

'Out of here. Anywhere. You're too nervous.'

'I ain't. You are!' Vic shouted back with burning red cheeks.

'Tommy! Come here!!' Rose bellowed. 'Where's the damn kid when you need it?'

'He's coming, don't you see, you blind grumpy old bat?'

Rose snorted in the loudest possible way and when Tommy finally popped into the room, overexcited, she ordered him 'Bring the bloody princess out for a bleeding walk before I fucking kill her.'

But he wasn't listening. With a broad smile he announced:

'I've got great news!'

*   *   *

Albert dashed home. He heroically ran like a cheetah from Morvar to his place (less than 5 minutes walk), and got there absolutely exhausted, damped in sweat, short-breathing. 'I should stop smoking.' he told no one in the room, lighting another fag while rummaging through the drawers. 'It must be here, somewhere...'

It was 7:30 pm already, and he still had to do every damn thing including, obviously, find that magical sequence of digits and call Victoria. After cursing an indefinite amount of different Gods and divinities, he started ripping drawers off their slots, scattering stuff all over, swearing, puffing from his ciggy and swearing again. No luck. So, he gave up and sat his ass on the couch. And there it was! The damn mobile number had been with him the whole time, safely stashed inside the upper pocket of his jacket.

'Wow.'
'Innit?'
'Innit indeed.'
'Shower?'
'Shower.'

Albert was conversing with himself when, fully dressed, he jumped into the bathtub and unleashed a steamy-hot jet over himself. No time for cheap chats with anyone, he had to be quick, efficient, smart. He poured shampoo on his head, stubbed the old (soaked in water) fag and attempted to light a new one while dialling the number.

'Hi, it's me.' he said.
'Who?'
'I can't hear you.'
'Is it raining?'
'What?'
'Albert? Is it Albert?'
'Victoria, meet me at the Ship.'
'It's Tommy!'
'click.'

*   *   *

'Bollocks.'

'I swear, he called again!' insisted the kid. 'He said: meet me at The Ship, the Free House along the river.'

'Marvellous. Another fuckin' pub.'

'Don't be rude, Rose.' replied Vic, blushing.

TWENTY

The warm breeze ruffled her hair and those silky threads danced the void like gold flakes. Incandescent. She was surrounded by olive trees, vineyards and yellow-dry grass carefully painted by an expert dreamer on a wavy scape of hills. Steaming soil. Cicadas singing. Summer. She was immersed in the depths of those blue skies above, enjoying songs from the Mediterranean Sea carried there by salty winds, and sirens' breaths. Lying naked on an imaginary beach, she was letting the sun to embrace and kiss her pale skin.

Standing still, eyes shut, Victoria was waiting outside The Ship. She turned another blank page and sighed: 'darn, he's late. One whole minute late, and I'm already feeling as insecure as a man. Gosh…' She slowly lifted her eyelids and, for some divine coincidence, Albert gradually emerged from the future.

'Wow.' he thought.

'Thank you.' she replied.

He almost forgot she was capable of reading his mind, that's why he coughed an embarrassed cough. Rose was observing that little man with a giant ego with a hint of disapproval which, for her standards, was kind of an endorsement.

'Does she always have to stay with us?' Albert moaned.

'Nah, Rose was just about to leave.'

'Well, I didn't mean to…'

'Yes you were.'

'No, I… fuck, you got me.'

'Nice jacket, by the way.'

'Innit?'

'I love Korean collars. Especially those on military uniforms.'

'This?'

'That.'

'Thank you… it's… it's a long story.'

'I'd love to hear it sometimes.'

'Indeed. Indeed. Shall we go inside?'

'No.'

'What do you mean, no?' Albert said, cut off guard, one foot already over the threshold.

'The stars are beautiful tonight. Fancy a walk?'

'Isn't it something people do after dinner?'

'Last time, you wanted to kiss me straight away, and now...'

She didn't even finish the phrase that Albert embraced her and gently caressed her lips. They had a rose petals' flavour whereas he tasted like tobacco, in a strangely good way she didn't expect. In that splinter of a fragment of a half breath, he lost all his (few) certainties, their mouths met and together they faded into a peachy paradise.

Victoria was shining with inner light. Dazed like never before, she was striving not to think. The last thing she wanted was Albert listening to her thoughts. Not now. She had to be careful. And, *blew!*

A sudden gust of wind sneaked under her floral, blue smock dress trying to Marilyn Monroe her but, luckily enough, Albert was there, ready to stop it.

'Thank God I was here to rescue you.'

'My goodness, you're my superhero. I'm not even wearing panties!'

'Seriously?'

'No way. Who do you think I am?'

'I...'

'Come on, let's get inside.' she said, taking him by the hand.

'Now, wait a sec, what happened to the romantic walk, the silent night, and...'

'Shh! You're ruining it.'

'I don't understand.'

'You don't have to.'

'Okay' Albert didn't say and, like a real gentleman, he held the door, took her leather jacket off and let her sit first.

The pub was cosy, not really posh or fancy but, at the same time, it didn't smell of stale beer. So be it.

'I like it here.' said Victoria, combing her long hair into a very messy high chignon.

'You do?'

'Yes, it feels like home. You know, safe.'

'I heard they make delicious pancakes. We might have to come back sometime.'

'Are you inviting me to a second date already?'
'What?! Maybe.'
'Maybe's not an answer, fellow. Yes or no?'
'Definitely maybe.'
'Aha! Okay, let me check my Moleskine, I'm not sure I have any free slot for you anytime soon.'
'I should have known better and get in line months ago.'
'You mean years.' she giggled.
'Silly me... Talking about your Moleskine.'
'Don't tell me you also have one! Bought in Paris!! And you write too!!! Oh my goodness, you're an artist.'
'Are you done mocking me?'
'Sorry, I can't promise anything.'
'Fair enough.'
'What were you saying?'
'I bet you keep all your secrets in it, innit?'
'Not really...'
'Like the Queens of the Stone Age lyrics you read the other night, on stage.'
'What?' she blushed. 'Nah... you recognised it?'
'I did. The twist you gave to it was incredible. Absolutely enchanting. Fucking first-class poetry.'
'Aw... Checkmate.'

Victoria put her frenzy on pause for a moment to fix him. Despite the lame street-style talk, she could tell by his eyes that he was honest, even shy now. Perhaps he was regretting his complete transparency?, the compliment he just gave her? Whatever it was, she was delightfully surprised, so much so that her mouth only managed to say 'Thanks, mate!' in a cheeky way and her face turned to a shade of burgundy you can't easily hide. And,

Silence.

An impossible amount of awkward silence flooded the pub like sticky, paralysing mud. Only a proper Marvel character could have saved that situation. That, or Victoria:

'I love breakfast.'
'Breakfast.'
'Yeah, I...'
'You say the word and I smell croissants already. It must be a magical sequence of coded signs coming straight from Egypt, etched on a

pyramid or maybe, yes, it's a spell, no, wait: gosh... is it something Zen? Chinese, maybe?' he asked.

'I agree. Totally alien shit.'

'Like Mars bars, innit?'

'Now we're talking! How else would you explain the mouthwatering otherwise?'

'Jesus Christ, you're beautiful.' he didn't say, realising a second too late that she read his mind, lowered her gaze, and a smile curved her lips.

'Er... tea?'

'Now?'

'Well, yes, but no, I meant do you like tea?'

'Always. Like proper Bri'ish people.'

'I nu it!'

'Actually...'

'Shut up... so I didn't know shit, right?'

'Sorry, I'm more like a coffee person. I adore the scent of a fresh pot in the morning, it makes me feel... I can't really explain it.'

'An Italian Moka sitting on the hob. Blue, silent flames embrace it like blankets and finally, the warm gurgling of coffee comes out and wakes everyone up, spreading his aroma all around the cold house. Imagine: December. The fire is crackling in the corner and, outside, a white snow blanket covers the silence, keeping the world asleep.'

'Wow, you're good.'

'Thanks.'

'You had it ready, didn't you? Did you even rehearse it?'

'Obviously, I'm a pro.'

'I bet you stole it from one of those Disney-like movies.'

'Duh? Of course!'

'Well, it's nice, isn't it? I like to call it "Happy Family Effect".'

'Sounds just right.'

'Speaking about families, thanks for introducing me to your friends last night. They were really cool.'

'Who, Pete?'

'And Steve. Tommy told me he's mad for his car.'

'Mad? That's being generous. He lives in there. He eats in there.'

'Sleep?'

'I'm pretty sure he does that too although he denies like a politician.'

'...' she smiled.

'Give me your Moleskine.'

'No. Go buy one for yourself, you scrounger!'

'Sorry... I should have asked in a gentler way.'

'Hell yeah, cowboy! What about manners?'

'Dear Lady Victoria, would you please lend me your beloved extra super expensive paper bunch bounded in fake red leather?'

'You're the slyest bootlicker in town, aren't you?'

'Darling: I am.'

'Bravo.' she applauded. 'Take it, you earned it.'

She mimed a sort of regal bow and handed the precious book to him. Albert was absorbed entirely, taken away by her eyes. Her humour, the way she moved, the elegance in her tone, everything was sending him to the top floor of a daydream he couldn't afford.

'So? Whatcha gonna do with it?' she joked.

'I'm gonna draw a mega flower and a heart on each page.'

'You're not.'

'...'

'You're not, right?'

He was not, okay, but staying shtum was part of the fun. What Albert actually did was scribbling Pete and Steve's mobile numbers on the last sheet of her Moleskine. Then he opened it again, this time to a random page and secretly wrote: *you stole my heart and soul*, without ever telling her.

'Done.'

'Great, whatever you did.'

'I gave you my friend's numbers. Just in case.'

'In case of what?'

'In case I faint because of you.'

'Look, stop making me blush... okay?'

But Albert was blushing too. He was feeling lightweight, something close to lucidly drunk.

'How did I get here?' he thought.

'...' smiled Victoria.

'Shit, again?'

'Yep. I heard.'

'Brilliant... god only knows how stupid I look right now: silly and disarranged I bet, like those fools who fall in love and pollute the streets with their enthusiastic smiles.'

'Nah, you're way much worse than that.'

'In love?'

'I meant a fool, but you tell me. Or don't, yeah, don't.'
'...'
'So... you're not a lovers' fan.'
'I... well... hate when I get to a place and there's a couple exchanging glances, flirting and, you know, those things. Am I a horrible person?'
'Oh, you are indeed. Nothing to do with this, though.' she laughed.
'I probably shouldn't have said that. Sorry.'
'No, I get it. Sometimes I feel the same, not the hate part but, yeah, discomfort? Must be a sort of defence barrier we raise.'
'Exactly my point.'
'Sure... so, now we're a couple?' she implied with a smile.
'Er...'
'Please don't faint, dear.'
'... checkmate.'

Victoria was upbeat. She could feel the blood flowing through her veins in a way she never experienced before. Despite his best efforts to look and sound average, Albert was quite an impressive human to her eyes. The more they talked the more his passion about all sorts of insanities came out and, when asked about his vision on a matter (any matter) he completely spaced-out, deeply immersed in thoughts and ideas. At one point, he went so far from reality that he barely noticed Victoria's long fingers approaching his wrist and caressing it. They unconsciously ended up holding hands in plain sight, right over the tabletop, smiling like fools. Exactly. Like one of them silly couples Albert hated so much.

'... and music: don't get me started. Music is as vital as air. Music is everywhere...' *in*concluded Albert, leaving his last sentence on hold, as if asking a question.

'What's playing in your mind right now?'

She did it again. Another perfect question at the perfectly right time. Albert started *fearing* she was the playmate he had been looking for since forever.

'Where have you been all my life?' he silently thought out loud as a shiver thundered up his back and she silently pretended not to hear.

'I might have a few monkeys fooling around an acid jazz riff. We're sitting in a downtown smokey club and the groove is *shaba-daba-doo* whoop! I'm sure you'd love it too.'

'Monkeys, uh?'

'Do you prefer giraffes, darling?'

'Maybe a full set of ducks and gooses. With a rhino sitting in the back, hammering on the drum set.'

'Bonkers.'

'You don't like it?'

'I love it.'

'Ah. And what about...'

She was evanescent as ocean lather which explodes on North Sea cliffs and penetrates your dirty lungs; the same mist that turns into rainbows on one of those days. Victoria was telling him about imaginary islands, unreachable stars, planets and strange visitors from outer space.

Albert was ecstatic. All the pebbles piled in his pockets didn't seem so important anymore.

TWENTY-ONE

It had been like meeting with your best friend after years of being apart: you just have to start talking and everything flows on its own, forever, as if the world was written in a secret language that only the two of you could read.

Dinner was ok, God knows maybe even exquisite, although Vic and Albert barely noticed the food. They were still discussing thoughts on their way home. A wide range of impossible ideas and foolish dreams were exploding in the sky like fireworks, intertwining in shapes you'd never imagine. When they arrived, they were dancing to some music no one could hear.

'And here we are again. In front of your Royal Castle.' Albert said, miming an ancient bow.

'Beautiful, uh? Welcome to my stinky pub refuge.'

'Looks pretty cool to m...'

'WOAH! DON'T MOVE!'

'WHAT!?'

'Shh...'

'Is there something horrible on my face? Spider? Spider??'

'...'

'How big is it? Hey!'

'Oh, shut up please, your face is fine.'

'Is it?'

'...'

'What are you doing now? Why are you searching your purse?'

'You're terrible. Just trust me.'

A cassette recorder was pulled out and, since Albert was incredibly restless, Victoria stuck her hand over his mouth.

'click,'

-

-

Silence

-

'click.'

'Perfect, thank you.' she said, breaking the stillness.

'What was that?' Albert whispered. 'Should I worry?'

'Sorry, I had to do it. It's for my collection.'

'?'

'It's a sound portrait.'

'A what?'

'I like taking pictures of particular moments.'

'Without a camera.'

'Yes, this is different, I prefer to record the vibes.'

'Uh-huh. And...'

'What can I say... the stars are shining, it's a quiet night, besides, you know...'

'What? Us?'

'Maybe.'

'Fuck, you did it again. Where have you been all my life?' his mind was repeating on an endless loop.

'Listen to these songs...' she said, getting lost among the immense blue mantle, her neck stretched towards infinity, vulnerable to his kisses. It was the perfect movie-like romantic moment everyone dreams about and yet, Albert was busy with something else. He knelt on the wet grass and proceeded on his four, looking for a couple of big rocks he eventually found and tried to force right into his pockets.

'Geez... and I'm the weird one. Seriously?'

'My dear, I need extra weight to keep my feet on the ground. I'm afraid I could fly away.'

As the last of those words came out of his mouth, Albert thought 'Fuck me.', regretting his spontaneity, wishing he never said that. Why couldn't he control his mind and keep his damn mouth shut for once? Stupid. Silly. Girly, or even gay for the macho people. *'Night's over, mate!'* shouted someone from the back of his head. But then Victoria got on her tips, hands tied behind her back Liam Gallagher-style, and landed a delicate kiss on his cheek.

'Thanks for the lovely evening.' she whispered.

'That? Oh... I... Er...'

'Do you want to come in? It's still early, we could watch a movie, how about it?'

'I was born for that shit.'

She couldn't help but laugh, out loud yet with a certain elegance, keeping her hand over the mouth.

'I mean, I'm the master of...'
'Bullshit. Come on, let's get inside.'
'You shouldn't finish my sentences, you know, it's rude.'
'Just hand me the keys, Albert.'
'Flowerpot?'
'Flowerpot.'
'Classic.'
'May I ask where you keep yours?'
'Doormat. I got your point.'
'Exactly. Shame on you.'
They stepped inside and

Dim light filtering through the windows. Full Moon.

Victoria's fingers were about to switch the switch on when he stopped her. The door settled in its nest without making any noise and Albert embraced her from behind. His hands gently covered her ears.

'Now you listen.' he said.
'...'
'I bet this room absorbed a thousand more stories, and melodies, and... there must have been people dancing, lovers kissing...'
'How can you...'
'God knows, babe.'

She looked at him disappointed and amused at the same time. 'No one can call me no babe, baby boy.' she thought, and he heard. Though he was right about the room. 'Sometimes it resonates so loud I can't escape it. Those vibes are soaked in the walls, vibrating in each of those paintings' strokes. They're nested inside the wooden floor.'

'You have to be patient enough to listen to them. But they're right here, all the time.'

'Someone should invent a device to let people enjoy these stories.' said Victoria, without thinking.

'Oh, it definitely should exist!'
'You get into an empty room, wear your special headphones, and *BLAST!* You're listening to what's in there.'
'Shit, we should build a Sound Hotel!'
'*30 quid a day, no sleeping please, dreaming only.*' she joked, making a

funny voice as she disembraced herself from him and started dancing around the hall.

'You little crazy creature.' he silently thought.

'That's a real deal! And, you know, we won't necessarily need multiple spaces. No matter what stories are in the room, your mind will always pick the one closest to your heart, and you'll hear it in a way no one else can.'

'Fuck, I love you.' he wondered in his mind without any control over it. Unleashed.

'Everyone sees what they choose to see, all in a different way, filtered by their mood, their own lives.'

'...'
'...'

'We should make it real.' said Albert, his eyes glittering with admiration, love and god knows what else.

'You think?'

'Absy-lutely. It would be like selling dreams, it might really change people's perspective. Ideas like yours can make a difference.'

'You know,' she said, getting closer to him. 'Tommy and I have an ongoing project involving soapy bubbles and rainbows.' she whispered.

'Sounds terribly wow.'

'He wanted to tell you on the very day we met but, you know, I had to check you out first.'

'Ach, right. So now I'll never get the chance. Great.'

'Who knows, maybe someday? Are you curious?'

'As a cat.'

'Come here.'

'...'

'Look, Albert, you should be careful when you think out loud.' she said while unbuttoning his jacket.

'You heard my thoughts?'

'I did.'

'Shi..p'

'I can see you're a learner.'

Her scent was affecting Albert more than any synthetic drug cocktail you could ever get from your experienced pusher. He couldn't feel the ground anymore, floating like clouds over the oceans. The warmth of her mouth sped his heartbeat up to some unreal level. So, he grabbed her by the slender hips and pushed her body against his, against the wall, feeling her passion, her full breasts, as he lifted her off the floor and her smooth bare legs embraced him.

They climbed the stairs, and fell, and rolled over the carpet. Clothes were marking each step of their drunken dance through the house, all the way from the hall to the bedroom.

Victoria's hands ventured along the paths of his body, eager to know, feel, taste him. Albert was simply stoned, overwhelmed by her kisses when she stood up, leaving him naked on the floor and something like a Greek goddess with butterfly wings appeared into his retinas. She blinked at him and, using her barefoot, played with his generous erection. Up. Down. Up. Down, then, she elegantly laid on the bed like a cat and, with a slight swing of the shoulder, she invited him over.

Their slick skins joined, Albert irremediably lost under her spell. Her fingers touched the tip of his nose then drew a silent request over his lips, a request that brought Albert's head, and mouth, and sweat sliding down along her body, obeying the order, tasting every inch of her salty skin, playing with the white lace lingerie she was wearing. So, she grasped him by the hair and dragged his head deep in the middle of her legs, slowly, panting, feeling his tongue. She was about to come when she pulled his mouth away and licked her taste off his lips, she kissed him, she sucked his tongue. And she knelt down on his sex. Like water lilies petals' caressed by the wind, her head swung in the dark room. Back. And. Forth. Albert couldn't resist her anymore. He pulled her up by the hand and stared into her enchanting doe eyes. God, she was a miracle. And she kept massaging him, her hand wrapped nicely around his pleasure, sliding up and down, oily, as he put his fingers in her mouth asking for her spit; as he caressed her spot with it and finally entered, index first, and it was wet, so wet he pulled the thin lace of her panties to the side and she let him in. Victoria arched her back and their bodies suddenly became one, trembling under sharp strokes and gentle waves until she gasped, once, and once again, biting his skin and moaning as he kept going in, and out, and she turned, craving his thrust from behind, feeling it whole inside her as she pushed harder, and harder, her face blissful, breasts pressed against the wall when he finally pulsed the final pulse and beaded her skin.

Under pure-white sheets, their bodies laid innocently embraced, whispering something secret, breathing each other in. Albert was pretty sure all that beautiful mess happened only in his mind.

TWO
SELLING DREAMS SINCE 1986

TWENTY-TWO

Albert woke up like every other morning. Trashed. Hangover. Even though he didn't booze up in days.

'The usual, please.' he joked with himself, asking an imaginary bartender for a drink. His eyes slowly opened. Rusty. As the eyelids released, he started scanning what was around him and, *'Woah'*, it was a real mess: trousers scattered on the floor (normal); Nirvana Inferno t-shirt hooked to the floral corner of a gilded French frame (strange); striped socks: one dangling from the door handle and the other on… a swinging chair (?); his wonderful white lace bra on the…

'Wait a sec, that's not mine! This is not even my room.' he loudly thought.

'Cuckoo'

'Shit, this is real.'

'Of course, it is. What were you thinking?' asked Rose, staring at him.

'Fuck, what are you doing here?'

'Here I am not, honey. Your guilt summoned *me*.'

'Now, don't get weird.'

'Look who's talking.'

Meanwhile, Victoria was resting over his chest, peacefully embracing him. Graceful. Perfect.

'This is too much… I can't do it.' thought Albert.

'Here it is. Guilt. Told ya!' said Rose.

'Oh, shut up please, you don't understand.'

'What, your li'l secret? The fact that you're leaving exactly today?'

'How do you…'

'Hey, she's sleeping, isn't she? I'm not Rose. How many times do I have to r…'

'Cool, you're my conscience. So you know it. Great.'

'Is it?'

'Look, I need some help here.'

'Just tell her.'

'What? I can't...' he replied, with a smirk.
'Tell her.'
'Jesus... I said no. No way.'
'She'd understand.'
'Yeah, well, that remains to be seen. And, even if she does get it, what do you think she's gonna say? *Thanks for the fuck, you can go now. Please, disappear as if nothing happened, we're cool, babe.*'
'Maybe...'
'No, no. No. That's not an option.'
'Why?'
'I can't ask her to come with me. She can't pack her bags and leave like that, *SNAP!* out of here, out of the blue. *My dear, would you like to put your life in my hands? Fuck yes, I was just about to ask you.*'
'...'
'... and what for? Me?'
'That's a good point. Now that you got me thinking... you should really dash out. Quickly.'
'Exactly. It wouldn't be fair to her.'
'Coward.'
'She would refuse anyway, so I'll tell you what: I get lost, no harm no foul. All Happy, right?'
'Right. You fucking coward.'
'Great. Let's get out of here. And please, be quiet, the last thing we want is to wake her up.'
'...'

Albert stealthily gathered his stuff, he was already approaching the stairs when he couldn't help but throw a last glance at her. God, she was beautiful. The burning desire to kiss her one last time was tearing him apart.

The room looked like a glamorous movie set. Sunlight filtering through a shabby chic framed window. Tuxedoed shadows painted over the floor, climbing onto the bed and stretching towards her face, like a velvety gentle caress. Victoria was still hugging the messy mess of white blankets in such a harmonic way that the whole thing could have been the glossy-pop version of a Schiele painting, or a goddamn scene from a romantic movie. The next thing you know is a cute little cat appearing on the windowsill, and a bunch of baby birds chirping love songs.

'I want to throw up.'
'Yep, so why are you still here? Go, mate, GO!'

'I hate to do this, Rose.'

'I bet. God knows, she probably even liked you.'

'...'

'Strange, uh?'

'That's enough.' Albert concluded, snapping her out of his mind like a rainbow-y stained soapy bubble *'Puff...'*

One step followed another:

- Stairs - *X* - *checked*
- Stumbling into the rug, therefore making an awful noise. - *X* -
- Living Room. - // - *done.*
- One last gaze at the place before disappearing like a thief. - *X* -
- Coward. - *X* - *checked*

TWENTY-THREE

Brilliant. Absolutely, weirdly, brilliant.

Victoria woke up super late for the first time since teenage years. She stretched, yawned, and rolled within the bed sheets for a while when she finally noticed the white rose bud carefully placed next to her head, on the other pillow.

'It smells so good...' she sighed.

'*... it smells so gooood...*' promptly mocked Rose, with a funny voice, blinking fast and holding her hands crossed over her ghostly chest.

'...'

'*Its petals are like heaven's kisses, Ahhhhh... breathe it in, let it out, breathe it in...*'

'Good morning to you too. Idiot!'

'*Blabblab-blabblab-blah! Idiot.*'

'You know what? I'm sorry for you, but you can't ruin my day today. Take it, girl.'

'*He's such a fairytale's Prince... ahhhh...*'

'Yep, and he left this one for me.'

'It's all yours, babe.'

'Sure it is.'

'I wonder what he had to be forgiven for.'

'You're a horrible person.'

'Thanks.'

'He didn't do anything wrong. On the contrary... well... I won't get into details.'

'Thank God!'

'Give me my t-shirt.'

'Here it is, but I'm not touching your filthy, lusty, dirty...'

'Panties! There you are! Ready for breakfast?'

'It's more like lunchtime, babe.'

'Brunch it is, then! Doesn't it sound fantastic?'

'We're living the dream.'

'♩♭ ♪ ♪♫♭ #♫ ♪🎼♪.♩...'

Victoria was singing, dancing, jumping from one spot to another. Happiness. Wow. She rushed down the stairs and 'What the heck?' Tommy was sitting on the top of her cupboard as if it was the most normal thing to do in the world. Whatever, she was too excited to get bothered by such nonsense so she just sang to him:

'Hey hey, little baby get down, before you fall and hurt someooooooone!' knee-sliding like a rockstar, pretending to be her hero Kim Gordon, holding an imaginary microphone with both hands while curling on the floor.

'??'

Victoria jumped back on her feet and smiled.

'Come on, Tommy, get down!'

'Why?'

'Because. What's wrong with you anyway? What's this hype for climbing stuff?'

'It's better.'

'Better than what?'

'Than staying there, with my feet stuck on the floor.'

'Darn, it perfectly makes sense.'

'See?'

'Still... my furniture? Seriously?'

'You said no more missions on the tree, you forbid going up the roof...' he moaned.

'Exactly.'

'What am I supposed to do?'

'Be quiet? For once?'

'You're such a bore...'

'Fine. Fine. Let's get on the roof, damn it.'

'Really??'

'You won. Brunch first, though.'

'Yeeee'

'Now, get prepared for the landing.'

'Yes, captain!'

'Goggles on?'

'Done!'

'Fancy gloves?'

'All set.'

'I'll count to three, then you can jum/p/OUCH!!...' and they both crashed to the wooden floor. Classic. Rose was having a good time, busy sucking on her cocktail from a striped straw.

'TOMMY!'

'Oh, honey, you asked for it. It's your fault.' intervened Rose.

'You did.' confirmed the boy.

'Shut up, Rose. And you... you actually jumped?!'

'Yeah?!'

'As if my furniture was a freaking trampoline? What's wrong with you?'

'But...'

'You two should go play in the Olympics!' croaked Rose as she caressed the blurred crystal glass of her drink.

'Hey, sunshine, what time is it?' asked Victoria.

'11.30 am. 31, to be precise.'

'And what are you having?'

'Double Martini. On the rocks.'

'It looks like a full pint to me. No sign of rocks either.'

'Oh yeah. So what? Here in LullaCuckooLand, I can do whatever the fuck I like.'

Tommy was trying to mask a laugh. She was skunk like a... sorry.

'Stop looking at me, folks! Don't you have better things to do? Like... get on the damn roof? Kill yourself?'

'Sure. Tommy, grab your jacket.'

'What about brunch?'

'Shoot, yes. Let's make pancakes!'

'Yeeee'

'Bloody hell, kid, stop shouting!' shouted Rose.

'Yeeeeee!!' he replied with even more emphasis.

'Rose, why don't you put some music on?' asked Victoria, from the kitchen.

'Ah... the good-old slavery days are back. Yes, madam. Sonic Youth, you figure. *Play*. Happy?'

'Happy. Now, Tommy, here's the final question: jam or Nutella?'

'What's Nutella?'

'The fruit of the Devil.'

'ROSE, enough! Chuck that drink away and have some coffee, for Christ's sake.'

'Bummer...'

'Right. Nutella is chocolate spread, my friend.'

'CHOCOLATE!!!'

'Orange juice or milk?'

'Gasoline.'

'Yeeeee'

'Are you both out of your mind, today? Come on, people.' Victoria begged, crossing her arms. Pout on.

'Okay, then I'll go for... 100%... ORANGE!'

'Deal. Anything for you, Rose? Black americano? Cappuccino? Valium?'

But Rose was distracted. She was fixing something on the floor, next to the turntable. She picked it up and read the first line. Her face turned grave.

'You need to have a look at this, Vic.' she said.

'What now?'

'I think it's important.'

TWENTY-FOUR

Desert road of Sherlintock, practically close to nothing in particular. The flat, monochrome landscape made of asphalt, post-war warehouses and the typically bleak British lead-grey sky was disrupted by a compact black dot. It had the shape of a car, a BMW to be precise. The whole thing looked so dodgy that, if anyone had passed by, they would run away or call the Police (maybe both) yelling *'BOMB!!, we're under attack!'* Yet, nothing appeared to be happening. The only soul on the scene was a homeless guy sleeping inside the car, sprawled on the hand-stitched, luxury leather seat. Weird.

'Ring.' apparently, the derelict man had a mobile phone 'RRiiing.' or was it an explosive device? 'RRRIIIIING!'

Panic.

'Hello?'

'Who the fuck is it?'

As if waking up from a 12-year-long coma, Steve managed to put together a few charming words and slur them out.

'It's Victoria, listen...'

'Slow down... what time is it? Why are you calling in the middle of the night?'

'It's noon.'

'What?'

'NOON.'

He checked his smartphone. Correct.

'Aight, just give me a sec...'

'Steve?'

'*Blurrrr.... Brwlllll.... Plurrrrr...*' he said as he shook his head from left to right, slapping some life out of his cheeks, rubbing his eyes. He also punched himself in the chest. Why? You should ask him.

'Steve?'

'Ready. Whatsupgirl?' he yawned altogether.

'Have you seen Albert?'

'Was I supposed to?'

'Er...'
'And what about manners, uh?'
'Listen,'
'I mean, we barely met once and...'
'I'M JUST ASKING!'
'Woah, someone's pretty nervous here...'
'He was with me last night and now he's gone.' insisted Victoria.
'Who are we talking about again?'
'Albert.'
'Oh, yeah. The good old *Hit and Run*. A classic.'
'Fuck you.'
'Hey, I didn't do nothing, for Chrissake.'
'I know, but... you just don't get it... he was...'
'Nasty. Dirty. Filthy sex. Great. I don't wanna hear it. Especially not now.'
'Where are you?'
'BMW.'
'What?'
'Well...'
'So, you really do sleep in your car.'
'Nope. No, no... it's just... you know... long night.'
From the speaker, Steve could hear a baffled laugh, maybe two if you included Rose's.
'Do you have any idea of where he might be?'
'Ahem...'
'Brilliant, you don't want to tell me.'
'Me? Not at all. I... I think you should totally call Pete.'
'He knows?'
'Definitely maybe.'
'Great, thanks Steve.'
'My pleas...'
'click.'

'RING!'
Another call, another mobile phone buzzing somewhere else around Sherlintock. A poignant darkness, thick as butter, was filling the air of a pretty small compartment.
Short breathing and a body arranged in a very intricate shape.
'RING' for some reason Steve was able to hear it too from his driving

seat. 'RING!' It appeared to be coming from his car boot.

'RING.'

'Hello?' Finally, a sort of chilled voice slipped out of someone's lungs.

'Pete, it's Victoria.'

'Good morning, sunshine!'

'Yeah, well...'

'How are you?'

'About that.'

Clinking of keys and footsteps approaching.

'What was that noise?' asked Victoria, quite confused.

'Pete?' Steve, shouting from the outside.

'It's nothing, probably some interference.'

'Is it Steve?' Vic.

'Pete?' Steve.

'Are you ok?' Vic.

The car boot opened, revealing its content. A human body. Almost alive.

'Hhhhh...' deeply inhaled Pete, released at last, stretching his legs out of that luxurious metal coffin. He was at the same time shushing Steve up and miming something like "coffee" to him who was mouthing back an explicit "don't you fucking see where the fuck we are?".

Victoria was getting restless.

'Sorry, Vic... it's a long story.'

'What on earth are you two doing on a night out? Are you insane?'

'Sure. Nope, argh, listen... as I said...'

'Long night, I get it. Where is Albert?'

'Stanstead.'

'What the...' almost cried Victoria.

In that abandoned space in the middle of nowhere, Steve was now swearing in silence, shaking his head, gesturing obscenities.

'What did I say?' Pete tried to go back on his words.

'Albert is at the airport... where to?'

'God... he didn't tell you.'

Steve's lips were now not-so silently spelling something like Y-O-U A-S-S-H-O-L-E to his friend.

'Tell me what?' Victoria was pretty close to a nervous breakdown. 'What the fuck is happening here? Spit it out, Pete or I'll get there, wherever you are, and kick your ass so hard you're gonna bleed from

your ears.'
Silence.
'Wow... you really are something.' said Pete.
'TALK!'
'Please sit down and take a deep breath.'
'SAAAAAAY IIIIIIT!!'
'... Albert is gone to...'

TWENTY-FIVE

The 886 flight to Pisa has been delayed. We apologise to all...
The intercom voice was loudly echoing throughout the airport. An endless parade of useless cheap shops marked the path to new Worlds, new lives and memorable adventures.

'Sir?'

'May I help you?'

'Do you have a lighter by any chance?' politely asked Albert, his roll up pending from the corner of his mouth.

'I do, but you can't smoke in here, man.'

'Yeah, I guess.' he grumbled.

'Take care.'

'Toilet?' Albert insisted.

'Pardon?'

'Do you think I can have a smoke in the toilet?'

'Argh, don't think so... sorry, I really need to...'

'Oh, come on, there must be a damn smoking area around here!'

'I'm sure there is, man but, look:' the guy gestured, tapping on his watch.

'Please don't go...' begged Albert like a junkie in need of a fix.

'But I'm missing my flight...'

'HELP ME!' he eventually shrilled, grabbing the guy's arm, freaking out a few people. The man quickly scanned the place in search of a way out.

'HER!' he screamed back. 'Please, ask her.' he said, pointing his finger towards an old lady wearing the classic airport cleaner uniform. Albert got distracted for a second, just the exact lapse of time the man needed to vanish. Forever.

'Excuse me?'

'Ahhhh!'

'What?! What's going on?' asked Albert, instinctively turning his head, trying to understand what was happening.

'You no smoke here.'

'Yeah, that, exactly! Is there...'
'NO.'
'No, what?'
'NO SMOKE.' she firmly stated, her voice croaky enough to be the one of a passionate whiskey-drinker, cigar-smoker.
'Lady, calm down. Do you happen to know a...'
'AAAH!'
'Oh, gosh...' Albert thought as he approached her.
'AHHHH!!! don't touch me! Police!'
'Hey, it's all right, for Christ's sake, don't...'
'POLICE!!!'
'Shhhhhh!!!!'

* * *

'Italy? What for?' asked Victoria, exhausted.
'You know, he's got a job offer...'
'That can't be real.'
'Don't tell me about it.'
'How long?'
'...' Pete was shooting glances at Steve, hoping for some help.
'How long since he knew about it?'
'Uff, he had confirmation a few months ago, happy? Geez, I shouldn't be the one dealing with this shit.' he grunted, his eyes firing cannonballs straight into Steve's face. Steve was shrugging.
'... why didn't he mention it?'
''Cause he was afraid you'd stop seeing him. That's why.'
'Bullshit.'
'Precisely what I told him.'
'...'
'He was meant to tell you last night.'
'Oh, damn well he didn't.'
'...' smirks.
'Full address. Now.'
'Fuck, you don't really want to...'
'Get a plane. Find him. Slap his face as hard as I can.'
'Stubborn and violent. Do you have any more good qualities, dear?'
'You might discover them soon if you don't give me what I want.'
'You're seriously considering catching a flight, uh?'

'That's exactly what I'm going to do, Pete. Now, the address.'
'...' Steve was shaking his head. 'Don't.' he didn't say out loud.
'Please, Pete.'
'Fine, fine, goddammit and FUCK YOU!, fuck Albert and fuck you two together for getting me involved.'
'Thanks, Pete, you're a gentleman.'
'He's staying at his grandma's house, at least that's what he told us.'
'Great.'
'Do you need backup?'
'You must be kidding me. You two?'

They stared at each other: Pete was lying against the opened car boot while Steve was circling around an invisible something that wasn't occupying any space of that desert whack-like, mobster scenario. As if that wasn't enough, their clothes were torn apart and their faces covered in mud, for some obscure reason. Pete sighed.

'Fair enough. I'll text you the address as soon as we hang up.'
'click.'

* * *

'What's going on?' asked an annoyed Police Officer armed to the teeth.
'He!'
'Yes?'
'NO SMOKE.' the cleaning lady said, tapping insistently on the sign over the wall.
'?'
'CIGARETTE. He smoke!'
'He ain't smoking, what is this lady trying to say?' thought the experienced, nearly retiring officer.
'SMOKE!'
'Please, madam, oh my... do we have a translator at all??' he asked the other copper. 'Where are you from, by the way?'
'Me? I'm Poland.'
The two officers couldn't hold a laugh.
'Ok, please calm down and tell me what happened.'
'SMOKE! CIGARETTE!'
'Look...'
'HE TOUCHED ME!'
'He what?'

Albert was silent, quietly listening, dangling and rolling the fag within his teeth. He totally looked like the dumbest of nitwits although he was convinced to act like a real gangsta.

'MOLESTER!'

The old policeman instantly reached for his gun. The other had the red laser dot of his rifle already stuck right in the middle of Albert's eyebrows.

'Wow, that's a big word, isn't it guys?' he said.

'DON'T MOVE!'

'Molester... what does it even mean?'

'Trying to be funny, mate?'

'Not at all, officer. I just wanted to have a smoke.'

'SMOKE!!'

'Listen...' Albert told the woman as he approached her again, this time trying to get a friendly arm over her shoulder.

'AAAHHHH!'

'DON'T MOVE!'

'MOLESTER!!'

'I SAID DON'T MOVE! NOBODY FUCKING MOVE, OK?'

The airport staff hurried there and, withing seconds, had the scene conveniently confined. They were busy reassuring the other passengers that everything was under control. Meanwhile, an army of coppers ran to the spot, SWAT-style.

'That's enough, mate. Hands behind your back, you're under arrest.'

'Great, finally.' Albert said, 'She's the real molester, by the way.'

'MOLESTER!'

'You should check her out too, just saying.'

'SHUT UP! EVERYBODY SHUT UP!!'

'YOU PRISON. Good police.'

'Please, bring the lady as far from me as you can, Paul, would you? And, mate...' he told Albert 'No more idiotic stuff. Are we clear?'

'Fine. Super.'

'What's wrong with you? Shut the fucking mouth.' said Paul the copper, as he showed the way to the Polish woman. Albert was being escorted in the opposite direction.

'Are we going outside? Is there a smoking area?'

'...'

'Do you smoke?'

'It's none of your business.'

'I wondered...'

'What part of SHUT THE FUCKING GODDAMN MOUTH you don't get?' the old cop burst out, then he bellowed 'YOU!' to a rookie 'Remove the damn fag from his lips.'

'Yes, sir. What do you want me to do with it?'

'Stick it up your fuckin' ass.' he didn't say. 'Destroy it.'

'Sir, yes, sir.' and so he got to Albert.

He was just about to touch the cigarette when Albert spit it out, roughly, in the copper's face. 'Fuck off!' he cried. *Panic.* An incredibly heavy boot instantly tackled Albert down making him scream like a girl. Or a boy. Or a they. Whatever. *Pain.* A waterfall of laser beams instantly flooded the scene and a thousand rifles popped from all over the airport, from spots you couldn't even imagine. Albert was fully covered by red dots, he was actually solid red now, with his lips licking the filthy rubber flooring. That was it.

'Christ...' murmured the old cop. 'You really are stupid.'

TWENTY-SIX

Pisa airport. It was so small it felt like being at Sainsbury's Local or Tesco Express if it wasn't for the foreign accents or the fancy police uniforms. Also, a very relaxed vibe was spread all over the place like chocolate cream. Nutella, as locals say.

'So, this is Italy. Cool.' said Tommy.

'Is the policeman yawning? And what about this impossible queue for passport checking? We haven't moved in the last sixteen hours.'

'Rose, quiet down...' begged Victoria.

'Besides, this bloody, constant, pestering noise is ridiculous. I mean, why is everyone shouting all the time? Have we landed in Deafland or what?'

'Just enjoy the fact we're abroad, ok?'

'Enjoy? I don't feel my legs anymore, I want to die right here. Now.'

'I love vacations!'

'Listen to Tommy, he's loving it.'

'Yeah, he sounds like an immigrant coal miner with four kids and the ugly wife, who barely ever saw the sunshine.'

'It's our turn, Rose, please behave.' begged Victoria, handing the passports to the officer.

'Is everything ok?'

'Yes, sure.' she blushed.

'Who were you talking to?'

'Me? Er...' she was almost crimson now 'I'm just...'

'Where are you from?'

'London? you idiot?'

'ROSE!' Victoria shouted to what people would call "a ghost", only realising it a split second too late. Deep Purple. Her face, not the band.

The officer shifted from bored-to-death, to curious, to alarmed. He studied the fool for a few seconds: threat?; psychopath?; regular clumsy weirdo?; Whatever. He was almost enjoying that little diversion, so, he simply smiled and dismissed her with a polite,

'Welcome in Italia, madam.' right before getting back to his awful, monotonous day.

'Welcome my ass, we still have to get our luggage.' complained Rose as soon as they stepped forward.

'Hey, look outside, it's marvellous!'

'Thanks for pointing that out, Tommy. In fact, it is so hot I'm sweating blood from my eyeballs.'

'...'

'I'm leaving trails of sweat on the floor like an old damp mop.'

'You are an old grumpy mop!' said Tommy with a grin.

'Come here, you li'l bast...'

'Our suitcases!' cut in Victoria.

'... I need a drink.'

Tommy grabbed his colourful trolley and hurried to the exit while Victoria was still picking her overstuffed worn-leather holdall from the baggage carousel.

'Shame on you.' commented Rose.

'What's wrong with my bag?'

'Oh, Vic, you don't get it, do you?'

'Nope.'

'You make us look like freaking hippies. As simple as that.'

'Actually, all the rock stars travel with vintage luggage. It has more character.'

'AH.'

'What?!'

'I knew you were an aestheticist.'

'Meaning, I care about myself?'

'Well... I won't say that, look at you.'

'Fuck off, Rose.'

'Ripped jeans.'

'They're mum's.'

'Converse shoes.'

'I always had them.'

'Torn-apart leather jacket.'

'Dad's.'

'See? You basically are a tramp! Get yourself a torn greasy hat and we're top of the list to get a decent busking spot. I feel we're making some good-old filthy money today!'

'You're ridiculous. For your information, this French blouse...'

'Yes, that white puffy atrocity with embroideries...'

'... costed me more than the whole...'
'The finest garment at the latest gipsies fashion week.'
'... trip we're having!'
'Say it again?'
'It's expensive.'
'No shit. 5 quid? A tenner?'
'That was mum's too.'
'There you go. My point exactly.'
'Where's Tommy?'

Tommy was outside. He escaped the baggage claim room as an inmate running for freedom. Sharp turn on his right and sliding doors opening. *'YEEEE'* he cheered himself up as a true champion *'YEEEE'* his arms now reaching for the sky, Rocky Balboa-style. He cut through the thick fog of dumb smiles stamped on the faces of people waiting for a friend, the rascal son, or maybe for the love of their lives; people holding ready-to-go gifts nicely packed by robots for whatever moving/breathing thing that gets out of an airport.

Tommy didn't even see those faces. He was ecstatic. His mum let him go after a quite weird yet brief discussion. Despite Victoria's effort in building her case on stuff like "travelling the world is more educational than going to school" or explaining the benefits of warm weather over Tommy's skin, lungs, etc, the whole thing came to an instant conclusion when she offered to pay for the journey. The mum shook her hand and the deal was sealed.

'SLAP!'

A sharp pat on the back told Tommy he wasn't alone anymore.

'HEY!'

'Are you out of your mind?' raged Victoria, worried as beep.

He couldn't care less. He squealed: 'It's sunny, it's sunny!'

'Do you want me to handle the problem?'

'Rose?'

'I can make him disappear. Italian style.'

'Shut up, Rose.'

'TAXIIII' Tommy randomly screamed, and a cab actually stopped.

Victoria's mind was about to blow. She didn't know whether to strangle the boy, kill her inner voice for good or... but the driver was waiting. She took a deep breath and said

'Hello, sir. Can you bring us to...'

'Ciao. Dove vi porto?'

'CIAO!' yelled Tommy, completely nuts.

'We need to go... here.' Victoria said, handing a small piece of paper.

'Firenze, uh?'

'Yeah, Florence. Our place should be in the city centre.'

'Bene, bene, salite.' he gestured, telling them to get onboard, and they did.

The cab quickly slipped off the airport mess and dived into a more fluent artery. They were rolling on the highway.

'He's gonna rape us.' Rose started.

'...'

'Cut our bodies into pieces and chuck them into some deep, dark well in the middle of nowhere. We're fucked.'

'No, we're not.'

'Bella giornata, eh?' said the driver, trying to be kind.

'Yeah, yeah.' they all replied without understanding anything he said.

'Is he cretin or what? We don't speak his useless language. Why should we anyway?'

'What's with all this hateful rudeness of yours? Be kind for once.' Vic said, trying to shut Rose up.

'BELLA, BELLA, GRAZI' was saying Tommy, his head out of the window like a dog, his hand surfing the air.

'Do you speak English?' politely asked Victoria, from the backseat.

'Oh, little, very little. Bella is... Beautiful, in Italian. Beautiful girl, beautiful day, beautiful sun, pizza...' and he went on for a while, listing all the words he knew, mixing and shuffling them the same way people do in the London Underground: Utter. Random. Nonsense. But he was nice, relaxed and friendly, constantly cracking Italian jokes no one understood, shamelessly giggling at them.

'I like him. He's real.' said Tommy, and Vic cheered to that.

I bet, he's a fucking deranged maniac.' argued Rose, but no one was listening to her anymore.

It took about an hour to get from the airport to Florence, and the same time again to enter the city and reach the apartment. I mean, sixty bloody minutes to do what, two miles? One thing was clear: traffic was a worldwide pain in the ass. The taxi driver stopped the car in the middle of the street (two wheels over the curb, to be fair), in a narrow medieval part of Florence.

'HONK! HONK!'

'Signorina! Help?' he asked, already busy unloading the car boot.
'Thank you so much, sir.'
'BEEP BEEEEEP'
'Eh, sir... mi chiamo Davide. My name: David.' he said, always smiling, looking like he didn't have a care in the world.
'HOOOONK!'
'Thank you, David.' said Tommy, jumping up and down the two grey sandstone steps leading to the door.
'BEEEEEEP'
The line of cars waiting for David to move out of the way was getting nasty. People were shouting at him and yet he carried on at the same pace as if that was the most natural thing in the world. Un-bother-able. Until he gave the middle finger to one of the shouters and snarled something back, a very short and precise local sentence that even Victoria seemed to understand. He had such an authoritative tone, a deep voice, rough and elegant at the same time. The barking man stopped raging for a second, lowered his gaze and carried on ranting horrible things, probably swearing some Italian God, in secret. Two more minutes and the job was done.
'Call, if need. Ok?' he said eventually, handing his business card to Victoria. It was a plain-white rectangle of quality paper with a telephone number and *DAVIDE MORIANTI TAXI* printed on top.
'You've been a real gentleman. Thank you, David.' she said, and she smacked an innocent kiss on the old man's cheek. He didn't expect that at all, so he blushed, at the very least.
'BEEP BEEP.'
'Ho fatto, Dio Cristo! DONE! Vattene a Fanculo!' David shouted to the honking crowd. No matter what he said, he didn't look angry now, he was more like... extremely confident. Being called a gentleman made him feel like a king. He felt like kissed by an angel, knighted by the Queen herself during a never-ending ceremony arranged for him only. Davide Morianti, the taxi driver. He winked at Victoria, started the engine with a big roar and slowly disappeared, smiling as usual.
Finally, Vic's crew entered the medieval building ready to face the last part of their journey. The apartment was upstairs, top floor (the 5th). Horrible.
'There must be a reason why someone decided to make the stairway so steep.' panted Victoria.
'Clearly, the man was studying alternative ways of committing

suicide. Smart, I reckon.'

'...' she didn't reply to Rose.

'Are we there?'

'Not yet, Tommy.'

'Why don't you jump backwards and die?'

'Like this, Rose?'

'NO!'

'Just kidding!' he said, and started racing up the stairs 'I'm gonna be first! Try to catch me! Yeeee!'

'Uff...' Vic was exhausted because of the journey, the impossible heat and the stairs, of course.

'Fucking hell. Kids. Stupid kids...' Rose commented.

'First floor!' announced Tommy.

'...'

'Second!'

'Still alive?'

'Third!'

'Are you expecting a motherfucking *"good boy"* and a pat on the back?' Rose, again.

'TOP FLOOR! Got it!!'

'Good, now hang in there.'

'Hang yourself, boy.' Rose laughed out loud.

'It's not funny, you are not funny, do you realise it or not?' burst Vic.

'I can't help it.'

'Guys, hurry up!' said Tommy, impatient.

And so they reached the last step too. It must have been 40 degrees up there. Italian weather. Wow. They knocked at the door several times but no one appeared to be in. No sight of Albert, no granny either. However, Vic had an idea. Something was burbling in her head.

'Doormat...' she whispered.

'Cuckoo-level reaching 7 points! Gettin' there hon, gettin' there.' said Rose.

'The keys... they must be under the doormat.'

'Right, Vic. Just because you do it, it doesn't mean that everybody's stupid like...'

'FOUND THEM!' yelled Tommy, grabbing the bunch.

'Track-track. Creeeeak' said the ancient door, opening.

And they were in. Graceful. It was a very small studio apartment with a bathroom, open space kitchen/living and a decent size bedroom.

Tommy jumped on the couch and Rose poured herself an imaginary pint of G&T straight down her throat. 'Who needs glasses?' She thought to herself, looking pretty satisfied with her choice. Meanwhile, Vic started checking the place: pine tongue-and-groove wooden walls and ceilings, laminate floors, roof windows and plenty of light. Tiny but cute. She was so drained that, as soon as she spotted the bed, Victoria abandoned herself over it. Comfy. So much so that she seriously considered spending her whole vacation laying on it. She stretched her arms, and legs, and she yawned, and her eyes were wandering around the room when she got transfixed by something: a dusty book was left on the side of the bed, right on the floor. It was a blueish paperback with a strangely familiar title embossed on top.

- The Morvar Company -
dream's sellers since 1986

TWENTY-SEVEN

'What's up, boys?'

'Albert??' Pete and Steve couldn't believe their eyes.

'In flesh and blood.'

'Shouldn't you be in Italy by now?'

'Well, Pete, I experienced some troubles.'

'You figure.' said Steve.

After spending the night at the airport in the company of a few police officers, it turned out that Albert didn't molest anyone, nor smoke, nor, in fact, actually do a thing. Thank you, CCTV.

'Do you have any idea of Victoria's whereabouts?' asked Albert.

'...'

'I stopped at her place but no one was in.'

'Italy...' mumbled Steve, quite embarrassed.

'Mate, I didn't go, did I? Hello? I'm here.'

'What he meant is, she flew to Italy.'

'Ok, Pete, now I'm getting confused. Did she take a vacation?'

'She went after you.'

'What?'

'We had to tell her your Italian address.'

'You... No shit. Idiots...'

'Look, man, you put us in a bad spot, alright? She was fuckin' furious, we had to do it, trust me.'

'Oh, my... You, Steve, you're unreliable and we know it but Pete was with you, right, Pete? How could you let this happen?'

'Actually... I told her.'

'Fuck. Fuck...'

'What about the job?' asked Steve.

'Uh?'

'You scored a job down there, didn't you?'

'Sure. I guess.'

'...'

'You look pretty rough, man. Why don't you sit down and have a beer?'

'Thanks, Pete.'

'What exactly happened, if I may?'

'Let's see: I got arrested, detained overnight and the rest is history. What about you two? You don't look fresh either '

'Arrested?'

'Did you go to that place again?'

'mmm... yeah?'

'Ok, that explains everything.'

'How come you got detained?'

'How come you went to that place again?'

'Long story, man.' cut short Steve.

'Sure.'

'...'

'Now, let's get down to business, boys. I need a favour.' asked Albert, fully operational.

'Forget about it, I ain't calling Vic, I won't explain no shit to anyone, it's your damn fucking problem.' burst out Steve, pretty edgy.

'Man, calm down, it's alright, everything is alright...' Pete lullabied his friend.

'Tell her what? There's nothing to be said.'

'Come on, Albert. You can't be serious.'

'I am, Pete. I didn't ask her to follow me. She'll soon figure that out.'

'So, what do you want?'

'I need a fresh start. I need insights about Morvar and you seem to know a lot about it.'

'This is all fucked up. A minute ago you were crazy in love with her, you dragged us to London, we got friends, then you screwed it all and now you act like you never cared. If you want my help you'd better come clean, man.' bellowed Pete.

Albert didn't reply. He was staring at the luxury black marble and stainless steel counter of Steve's kitchen. Perfect. 'Has he ever used it?' he wondered, plunging deeper into the soft leather couch as if trying to vanish. Then he took a mouthful of beer hoping to wash down his thoughts.

'How can you not tell her you're still here?' insisted Pete.

'I just do it.'

'But you love her, you should...'

'Love? Love?? Aw, Pete, what is this, the girls' corner? Have we become a crew of frustrated housewives sipping wine on a Sunday morning, away from home and the children, talking cheap-chat-crap about sex, life and husband's behaviour? Be a fucking man.'

'That's exactly what I'm talking about. You need to grow a pair and call her, you fucking coward.'

'...'

Steve was witnessing the whole thing in silence, arms crossed over the chest, head randomly nodding every now and now while chewing his upper lip. He didn't look alright.

'She came after you, isn't that enough?' insisted Pete. 'She bloody flew to bleeding Italy, for God's sake! I mean, she got her ass on a damn plane for you, you stupid cunt.'

'Yeah...'

'Yeah? Man, I don't know what I'd do to have someone like her chasing me.'

'I ain't ready to meet her again, I ain't good enough, 'aight?'

'Woah, you're the bullshit master, Albert.'

'Thank you.'

'So be it. Go ahead, fuck this already fucked up situation, be my guest. But you're gonna cry at some point, and when it happens, don't even try reaching for me. Okay?'

Steve was bobbing his head intermittently, like a robin, on cocaine. He looked absolutely stupid, almost epileptic. Or was he?

'About Morvar.'

'Jesus Christ...'

'I'm moving to London first thing tomorrow morning, didn't I tell you?'

'You fucking - obviously - didn't.'

'Stupendous. I need all available info about the legend.'

'Who?'

'Morvar! Are you even listening to me? I'm looking for inspiration and that man seems to be my only chance to get what I want.'

'Woah, that's new. And what exactly is that you want?'

'I don't know. Yet.'

'... bollocks.'

'Please...'

Steve was shaking. His face was spectral white now. Drugs?

Pete gave up.

'So, what time are you leaving?' he finally asked.

'As soon as. Why?'

'We're coming with you, right, Steve?'

His forehead was dressed in beads of sweat. He (barely) nodded.

'Now we're talking. That's the spirit!' yelled Albert.

'It's not about you, man, we need a break, that's all.'

'Oh, I can see that. What exactly happens in that place?'

'You don't want to know.'

'No, I don't.'

'...'

'Ok, cool, let's pack our stuff and get ready to rock'n'roll.' Albert concluded, joining his hands in a sharp, single, crisp *CLAP!* as he jumped on his feet. 'I have so many questions for you, mate. Morvar. Morvar. Morvar.'

'Yeah, what about it?'

TWENTY-EIGHT

When Victoria sneaked a peek out of the window, she was overwhelmed by the sight of the Cathedral's dome. It looked so close it felt like you could touch it. From that tiny attic, Florence appeared like a carpet made of roof tiles. That signature red colour was everywhere, meshing with clear blue skies and olive-green hills which literally embraced the city creating a unique palette. And if you lowered your gaze, there was the river Arno, cutting through that ancient painting, reflecting life on its glossy-dark mass of toxic water. Astounding.

So, to fully enjoy all that, team Victoria climbed over the roof from a narrow dormer and laid in between the shingles pretending to be on a Caribbean beach. Immediately, they were thrilled by the view, excited to be live-watching the evening's movie on the bill: Italian Sunset, a masterpiece. The incandescent blinding sphere touched the black line of the horizon and burst like an egg yolk, pouring its viscous liquid all over the sky, gracefully tainting the soft clouds that couldn't help but bleed beauty.

'Boring.' commented Rose, her straw plunged into something tropical.

'...'

'What are you reading, Vic?' asked Tommy.

'This? It's... nothing, really.'

'*Oooh, it's nothing.* she said, flicking through the pages as if holding the Ultimate Holy Bible of Alien Life. You suck. SLUURP!' mocked, Rose.

'What is the Morvar Company?'

'Oh, Lord. The boy can read, it's a miracle!'

'It's the title of the book, Tommy, are you still playing with me?'

'Yes, madam. We ignore Rose.'

'Exactly.'

'*Aaaaaa...* look at us, we're so special, we can think the unthinkable and we will change the world. *Uuuhh...* what a marvellous sunset, *Aaahh* taste this delicious marinated olive, *Ooohh* beautiful this, beautiful that, I love nature, I love people, I...'

'Can't you turn her off? Like a lamp?'

'Sorry, Tommy, no can do.'

'You make me sick.' concluded Rose, getting back to her business. Booze. Smokes. And even more booze.

'What is the book about?' asked Tommy. 'Is this Morvar the same Sherlintock's Morvar?'

'Indeed. I totally guess so.'

'Weird. Maybe it's the story of his life.'

'Well, there's only one way to find out.'

'Another game?'

'I have an idea, take off your goggles, boy.'

'Yeeeee!'

'Fantastic. Now, you read the first part and I follow. Deal?'

It was a deal. Tommy set aside the chunks of chocolate cake he was holding and tried to look professional. That game seemed to be somewhat important, he could see it in Vic's eyes. So, he cleared his throat and started:

'Sherlintock, 2 pm, a sunny afternoon. The packed town square was breathing a respectful silence waiting for the Mayor's speech to begin. Microphone feedback piercing ears, sound engineer adjusting the volume and hundreds of heads turn to the huge stage set for that unmissable event.'

'We gathered here today to celebrate the anniversary of the end of one of the most important industries of the last century: The Morvar Company, loudly echoed the Mayor throughout the speakers. Morvar wasn't just a kite factory. It was the innocent, childish smile of all people; the wishing upon shooting stars we seem to forget at a certain age.'

'Who's this loser?!'

'Shhhh' said Victoria, turning to Rose. Tommy went on.

'Anthony Morvar, founder of this daydream, was striving to remind us of all the little things, the details that can change our lives on a daily basis. As he used to say: *Life is an exciting game I'll never get tired of playing.* That phrase, too simple to be true, sounded absolutely silly to my ears; a spoiled recipe for spoiled rich people. And yet the man believed in it so much that... but I was in a dark place at the time, I needed the job money, not a lecture. He thought differently: one day he called me up to his office and asked:'

'What's up, boy?'
'I'm alright, Mr Morvar.'
'Anthony, please call me Anthony.'
'Ok.'
'I can see you've been away for a while.'
'Actually...'
'I know, you didn't miss a shift but you weren't really here, right?'
'...'
'You're so easy to read , son.He said with a smile.'
'I'll be more productive, I won't let you down, Anthony.'
'Nah, you'd better go home.'
'I swear, I'll do my best, I need the job. I'm sorry...'
'You're a good boy, but you need to rest. You'll receive your cheque as usual, don't worry about money. I just want you to get better, find yourself again, that's all.'
'Are you serious?'
'Sure I am. The condition you have is very common, it affects all of us, at times. Please, go back to your family, take a vacation, go fishing, go fuck yourself if you wish! Anthony laughed.'
'But...'
'I'll tell you what: grab a kite from the production line and play it with your kids. That should do the trick but what do I know? I'm just an old spoiled man trying to sell dreams to the world.'
'I... thank you. Thank you, thank you!'
'Tut-tut, go do whatever you have to do and, when you feel ready, just pop back in and have some fun with your colleagues. Deal?'
'I don't know what to say...'
'So, get the fuck out of my office.'
'I'll be back soon, Anthony.'
'Yeah, don't rush things, son, that's all I'm asking. As I said, you'll get your paycheck anyway.'
'...'
'Marvellous. Can't wait to see you smiling again, excited about creating something great for the world to see.'
'You got it, boss.'
'Do we have an agreement? Anthony eventually said, standing up, extending his hand to me. His eyes were piercing mine with such an intensity I thought he was reading my soul. We shook hands and I left.'

Victoria turned the page completely absorbed by the book.

'I escaped from the factory feeling ashamed, not deserving of being treated so nicely and I got drunk, so drunk I could barely walk. Another mouthful of gin and I was stumbling through the dark alleys of Sherlintock; time suddenly disappeared and I slowly faded away with it. When I opened my eyes it was dawn. I found myself under the old rusty bridge. My clothes were covered in mud and so were my shoes, my hair, even my face. I was still gripping the bottle. One last sip.'

Tommy was gradually disappearing into Vic's embrace as the story unfolded, as if he was upset, and maybe he was, but no one said a thing and the story kept rolling.

'... I got home and went straight to the basement. My hands were shaking, my head was pounding. I scattered the bottle to the floor and threw up. I was broken. Enraged. Ashamed. And I fainted, my head hitting the floor only a few inches from the thousand shards of glass.'

'When I woke up I was lying on the couch. The fireplace was crackling in front of me and my trembling body was wrapped in a soft, clean blanket that smelled of fresh laundry. That scent: it was the exact scent I fell in love with when my wife and I finally moved into our new house, our very first home. Back then, I was dreaming Future, chasing imaginary butterflies and kissing the stars goodnight while staring at that same damn fireplace.'

'How are you doing? my wife asked, sitting next to me wearing a painful smile that slightly curved her lips.'

'...'

'Here's a present for you, she gently whispered, handing me a silly little toy I almost completely forgot about.'

'It's your magic train.'

'Wow... how did that happen? How can we end up so far from ourselves? I thought, but she didn't listen. Instead she said:'

'What if we build the old railway model? The one you had when I first met you.'

'What, today?'

'Yes.'

'But... we're not kids anymore.'

'Let me see: you threw up, pissed your pants and moaned like a baby when I tried to undress you, and wash you, and... she ended up hissing, halfway from crying and smiling a sad smile.'

'I'm so sorry...'

'She was silent. I gave a second look at the toy train and something magical happened. Somehow, I realised I was holding the answer to all of my problems and, *fuck*... I whispered without thinking, to which my wife giggled and for a weird domino effect, we burst out laughing for the very first time in months, maybe years. And so *we kissed, we hugged. We were close, very, very close (sha la la)* just like the Sonic Youth song. My wife had handed me the key to open my rusty gate. I toyed with it for a week then I knew. I was ready. I walked my way to the factory and entered its gilded portal like Richard Ashcroft singing "I can't change my mould, no, no, no, no, no, no, no.". I knocked and, come in, the door's open!, Anthony shouted from somewhere behind his huge Victorian desk. Then he emerged and recognised me: bloody hell, you already? Go home, boy, he said, trying to muffle a grin.'

'And there I was again, on that same threshold, looking for answers.'
'May I ask what you're holding? What is it, a toy train?'
'Yes, sir, it was my father's. I used to play it with him on Sundays.'
'Looks like a real treasure. Bring it over.'
'I'm ready, Anthony, I can get back to work.'
'Bullshit, he replied, totally distracted by the little toy which was now rolling back and forth on his desk. Can you do me a favour?'
'Anything, Mr Morvar.'
'Lend me your train. You'll have it back in... he was counting something on his fingers... come back in 3 days.'
'But...'
'Fantastic! Now, let's take a picture of this beauty. Here, hold it. Anthony said, and then started rummaging through scuffed boxes and dusty drawers, finally pulling an old camera out of one of them.'
'Like this?'
'Great, great, yes, and smile please, what the fuck, we ain't attending a funeral! Give me your finest look, like that, bravo, gimme the real deal!, he was screaming and jumping from one spot to another, striving to get the best light, the right angle.'
'Are you sure there's any film in the camera?'
'Nonsense, who cares! Smile boy, smile! *FLASH!* There you go, fab, just fab! Now, get outta my office! He blinked at me as he was kicking me out. And so I left, no question asked. My life was changed forever.'

'What a fucking pile of crap.' concluded Rose, bringing everyone back to earth.

TWENTY-NINE

'How much for insurance?'

'It's...'

'Whatever. Do we really need it, Pete?'

'Actually...'

'Let's skip the bloody insurance.' decided Albert after a two-hour 16 minutes bargaining with the car rental guy.

Pete was sweating, Steve was still blurry.

'Okay, sir. But I must remind you that, in case of an accident, you...'

'I'll be fine, don't worry, mate. Keys?'

'Here, it's all yours. And please be caref...' he continued, although the crew was already in the parking lot, approaching the car.

'Fuck. Me.'

'Nice, uh?' replied Albert, glowing. 'Steve, where the hell do you think you're going?'

'Uh?'

'You ain't driving this beauty, I am. You can drop your ass on the back. And, Pete:'

'Albert?'

'I formally appoint you co-pilot.'

'Did we just get a bloody Mustang?'

'Mate, if you want to do things properly, you need the juice.'

'Couldn't we go to London with the BMW?'

'Jesus, Pete, look at Steve. Do you seriously believe he can drive?'

'Well, no, but...'

'Besides, his car don't match my NY cap.' Albert said caressing the curved brim, acting like a real pro.

'Your what?'

'Just get in the car.' he cut short, chucking the bags in the boot and slamming it down. 'Let's fly to London!'

'How long has it been since you last drove anything?'

'Four years? Six? I don't remember, Pete. Does it make any difference?'

'It does.'

'Steve, you ok?' Albert asked, turning his head.

'Yeah...'

'Fab. So, look, you start the engine, lights on and...'

'*VRRRRROOOOOOOOMMMM!!!*' growled the car, revving up.

Pete was pale, gripping the door handle.

'How do I shift gears?' asked Albert.

'What did you just fucking ask?!'

'Oh, here it is!' and he floored the gas pedal.

!!!!!!!!!!ROOOOOAAAAAAARRRRRRRRRR!!!!!!!!

VROOOM VROOOOM SCREEEECHHH the car screamed, raging in an uncontrollable 360, the burnout signing the tarmac forever.

Pete started screaming too. Steve was splattered against the side window. From the office, the car rental guy witnessed that madness with his jaw-dropped. Then, the Mustang, elegant and mighty as a black panther, slipped into the street and quickly disappeared.

'Come on, Pete, ease up a little, we ain't gonna die. I still know how to drive.'

'Oh, yeah. I feel totally safe after the shit you just pulled.'

'Music.'

'?'

'Put this on. It's a mix I made for the trip.'

'*Is this it?*'

'Yep, with a twist of Jamiroquai, and some gems from Nirvana, The Smiths, Oasis, Jesus Lizard...'

'Frank Sinatra?'

'Indeed. Indeed.'

'I reckon, you're fully into themed playlists.'

'You got it, Pete. Now, can we please talk about Morvar?'

'Again?'

'Again? You haven't spit out a single word yet.'

'...'

'Tell me about that big celebration they had for the anniversary. The Mayor's story.'

'The toy train thing that Anthony wanted to do?'

'Precisely that one. What do you think Steve, you up for it?'

'Go, man.'

'Right...' sighed Pete. And, as the Mustang kept clawing the asphalt with style, he started unfolding one of the many Morvar stories he knew: 'So, young-version mayor was this close to losing his mind when Anthony offered to help.'

'With the toy train!' shouted Steve, suddenly resuscitated from hell.

'Yeah... no, that was after...'

'With the toy train!' he insisted, louder.

'Right... Morvar borrowed it and asked the guy to come back in three, not four, not two nor even two and a half, days. Clear?'

'Clear!' Albert and Steve replied at once. 'What happened next?'

'The man walked to the factory pretty excited. Deep down, he knew something was going to be different but what? How? You could never tell what Morvar was up to and yet he was thrilled. As he entered the warehouse, an unidentified flying object almost crashed into his face.'

'*CHOO CHOOOO*' Steve yelled from the backseat of the Mustang. (they all knew the story by heart)

'*clickety-clack, clickety-clack* the man raised his eyes and found himself in the middle of a very intricate network of rail tracks. *clickety-clack, clickety-clack* He was surrounded by miniature trees, toy trains, tiny houses, bushes and whatever else you can imagine for a fantasy shrunk world.'

'Good-old Morvar...' grinned Albert, delighted.

'Yeah, Anthony knew he had to figure out something quite special for his fellow worker or, chances are, he would fall back to his darkness.'

'Bollocks, he did it for himself!'

'That too. From the very instant Anthony saw the train, his mind started projecting images like mad; ideas were twirling in the air like fire sparkles; imaginary trains spinning; chimneys puffing soapy bubbles out. He only had a few days to arrange that delusion of his, he couldn't waste any minute. Not for such a brilliant vision. Mr Morvar immediately grabbed the phone and rang the head of staff.'

'*I want every single soul gathered in the Conference Hall. NOW!!!*' Steve recited. '*Yeah, even the security guards, the janitors, whatever. What? Indeed. Shut the production line down. I'll see you in a sec!*'

'It was too important.' mumbled Albert, fully immersed in the story.

'Of course it was. At the end of the day, they were selling dreams, so be it. That was an extraordinary chance to create and experience first-hand a daydream, on a daily basis. It was like an indoor test of the surreal and Anthony couldn't care less about costs or actual feasibility.'

'It had to be done.' nodded Albert.

'Mr Morvar explained his vision to the chock-full hall and everyone went hysterical. They were totally wired, anxious to start moulding that foolish project. Anthony was collecting ideas straight from the crowd: *What would you like to have?'*

'A coffee train!'
'Coffee and doughnuts delivered to all stations!'
'A mail train!'
'Soapy Bubbles Steam trains!'

'A million proposals flooded the room, soaking the air with enthusiasm. Anthony was cherry-picking and considering every single bonkers idea shouted out loud. *ORDER PLEASE!* He looked like a Wall Street broker, with three phones hanging from unknown parts of his body and a pencil, *ORDER!,* busy scribbling nonsense on crumpled paper. *Ok, guys, I want rail tracks running all over the place. Make sure no one is off the grid. Each one of you must build his/her/its own station, your own way. Make it as personal as you can, it will be your unique stop. Are you following me?'*

'YEAH!' Albert and Steve shouted together

'*I want each one of you to show up with a toy train. It will be your miniature self on wheels so make it reflect your style and passions. You like bright colours?, fucking hell, make it neon pink! Your train must be noticeable, recognised as it runs up and down the tracks. Then again we need to organise the service. The coffee idea was clever. Let's have a massive long-flatcar running non-stop, loaded with orange juice, steamy teas and cappuccinos. It must be followed by a bunch of croissants, cookies, cake and sweets carriages.*'

'YEEEEEEE' again, Albert and Steve, out of their minds, as if they were actually there, among the crowd.

'*I want trees, level crossings and houses, mountains, clouds, even rivers and lakes, if you can! Darn, let's transform this goddamn factory into the craziest fucked up playground in the Universe. Let's have some fun!* And so he dropped the mic, Obama style: *Anthony's out.* he concluded, finally unleashing the crowd who couldn't wait a second more to start working.'

Pete paused for a moment. Silence. Inside the Mustang, each one of them was fabricating a unique image of the Morvar factory; dreaming the same dream in different ways.

'There must have been a hundred different wagons, locomotives and colours.' Albert thought out loud.

'Yeah...'

'Every morning, the concierge drove his modified steam Rocket loaded with beverages and cakes along the tracks. The chief engineer used his black Stanier to send out drawings and instructions to the assembly branch downstairs and every worker was delivering replies, comments and ideas to any office with their Big Boy or Adler or whatever train they had. On top of that, the Soapy Bubbles wagon choo-chooed around on loop, spreading excitement throughout the different departments.'

'I read somewhere that, at some point, Anthony even introduced toy planes. Absolute madness.'

'Heaven.'

'Mr Morvar was enjoying it so much that he often climbed over the rails structure and, wearing his Train Manager hat, he rode the tracks for hours, shouting, whistling, grinning like a baby boy. Everyone was so over the roof-happy that they broke any previous productivity record. The Morvar Company must have patented and sold millions of toys that year alone. It was as if a nuclear bomb of excitement and creativity blasted inside that warehouse.'

'I heard that workers didn't want to go home and used to arrive at least half an hour before their shift started.'

'True. And they were all allowed to bring their families to the factory during the weekend. Kids were freaking out. Literally. Tits-up bonkers.'

'Amen.'

THIRTY

'This book is weird.' said Tommy.

'...'

'And why Anthony's train was completely built out of mirrors?'

'Because he wanted to remind his workers they were the actual rockstars at the Morvar Company. Every time his train arrived at their stations their faces reflected into his train and they knew it. It was his way to thank them.'

'Cool.'

'You are pathetic.' commented Rose.

'And why is that? It's a beautiful story.'

'Undoubtedly. Very inspiring too. Yet, you two are wasting yours and my time on this roof, doing nothing.'

'Your point?'

'Don't you think you could do the same, darling? You, and the pain in the ass thing sitting next to you.'

'Well...'

'Fuck, Vic! Let's move, let's improvise, I need action. Your ideas could work, I'm afraid they sound quite decent to me. Rainbow Room? Mind-blowing. The idiotic recordings? Perfect scam. Blank books? Jesus, we even save on ink, Extinction Rebellion approved!'

'I'm not sure, Rose... can you even picture it?'

'Of course I can! I bet even Tommy-boy can. Think about it: zillions of misfits reading their own mental delusions with their eyes closed, occupying every single bench the city has to offer. The first ones might feel "observed" but they'll enjoy it, I'm sure. It's relaxing, it's intimate, it's freaking nature/environment-friendly. What can be wrong with it?'

'If you put it this way...'

'Then again, people don't like to take initiative so, it's your duty to make it a trend.'

'Me?'

'Who else!? You created it, it's yours. Unleash the fools and you'll see what happens. We'll be rich as shit, my dear.'

'Rose, it's not about the money, we do it because we like it. Right?' she sort of asked Tommy who agreed with a big smile.

'Whatever *(losers)*, do it for yourself, what do I care! Oh, and if this works out, you won't be pestered by cops anymore, no more dangerous-terrorist style profiling and you know what else?'

'Please enlighten me, smartass.'

'Do it for all the weirdos. Do it for the creative people, the fragiles, the shy ones and, Vic?'

'Uh?'

'Do it for Albert too.'

'Bastard...' she thought, lowering her gaze.

'He truly believed in your shit.'

'He's gonna get what he deserves.'

'Hell yeah, kill the motherfucker, babe! But he's not here now, is he? We can't waste our time waiting for a no go. Let's make something great out of this mission.'

'HE'S COMING! I know he is. We need to wait for him...'

'I don't know whether you're simply delusional or, worse, like... like in love. *Yuck.*' said Rose, disgusted.

'...'

'Look, we're in Florence, decent place, and I'm starving. What about getting lost among these decrepit, ancient streets?'

'I...'

'Shall we?'

'Yeah, Vic! Let's go out!' yelled Tommy, ready for a new adventure.

Victoria was torn. On one hand, she perfectly knew Rose was right but... the truth was that those words were coming straight from her heart and her imaginary friend was only repeating them out loud. Victoria didn't need to be convinced but she needed a push, someone who believed in her and supported her. Someone like Albert, but he fled like a goddamn stray cat and now he was... yes, 'Where the fuck are you?' she repeatedly asked herself. 'Shouldn't you be here already?'

THIRTY-ONE

Wickes, parking lot. 5:15 am

Albert was sleeping inside the Mustang, along with his crew. He was covered by plastic bags of any colour and shape, *stitched* together to form the most ridiculous homeless blanket. The umpteenth lifeless fag was pending from his lips and a John Fante book nested on top of his NY cap, for some reason. Nearby, a mob of job seekers were gathered in the cold, waiting for someone to pick them up. Only a blind man wouldn't have noticed the mighty sportscar, in fact, that was their leading topic.

'Tic, tic. TOC!' some rough knuckles sounded heavy against the window.

'You dead?' the same rugged man asked.

Albert suddenly woke up and jumped at the sight of the bearded face watching him an inch far from his nose. The plastic bags went all over the car, the book landed in Pete's hands and the fag finally freed itself.

'Who are you? What do you want?' Albert slurred to the man. He was trembling like a fool.

'Nice car, boss.'

'Is there anything I can do for you?'

'You can't sleep in here.'

'What?'

'CAN'T SLEEP IN HERE!!'

'Says who?'

'Come on, Albert, let's just go away.' suggested Pete, now fully awake, sensing a certain catastrophe approaching fast.

'Joe, come here, help me sort out this bloke.' shouted the builder to one of his mates.

'Why don't you go back playing with your li'l friends and leave us alone? Uh?' said Albert, getting arrogant.

'You looking for trouble, mate?'

'He was joking...' intervened Pete.

'I thought so.'

'Fuck you.'
'What?'
'I said fuck you. You deaf?' repeated Albert.
'(shit)' thought Pete, sweating.
'JOE!!!'
The builder's mob was approaching the car like an unstoppable steam train with faulty brakes.
'Open the damn window if you dare!' the man barked.
'Sorry, it's stuck.'
'Innit now?!'
'Please, Albert, let's get out of here.'
'Oh, Pete, you're such a pussy sometimes.'
'Get off the fucking car and I'll show you some manners.' threatened the man outside, getting ready for a good morning fight.
Joe and the rest of the builders were now a step away from the car. Someone was shouting obscenities, others were more into dismantling the Mustang.
'START THE BLOODY ENGINE!!'
'VRRRRROOOOM!!!' screamed the Mustang once again and its wheels screeched hard on the asphalt.
'BAM/SBAM/PUFF/SLANG/SBRAMMM' the car crashed against a sort of box filled with smaller cardboard boxes which exploded in a thousand shreds, scattered all over the parking lot. Mayhem. Then, trying to get out of the way for good, the Mustang 360ed over that paper mess making it even worse, if possible. On top of that, the builders started throwing cups of steamy coffee at the black growling monster, a handful of middle fingers flipped in the air like rifles and purple raging faces cursed Albert and his ancestors back to twelve generations as he managed to roar away.

Eventually, they were safe.
'What a marvellous day starter' hissed Pete, shaking.
'It went well.'
'What's going on?' yawned Steve as if he just woke up (he did).
'Albert almost managed to get us killed.'
'Fucking hell, drama queen in action! Why don't you do your job, Pete?'
'My what?'
'Co-Pilot, you're the co-pilot.'
'You're a psychopath'

'Yeah, well... thank you.'

'My pleasure.'

'Right, guys, we need coffee. A solid bucket of the hottest and strongest black juice. Any ideas?'

'I know a place!' shouted Steve, from the backseat.

'Good heavens, aren't you back from hell, Steve?' said Albert.

'Why?'

'Whatever. Where is this kiosk?'

'Straight down the road.'

'Don't tell me it's...'

'The Steel Coffee Van!'

'No way...'

'Yeah, we were regulars, remember?' said Steve with a grin.

'What is this place?' asked Pete.

'Unbelievable. You don't know it.'

'No.'

'Let me tell you a story.'

'Thanks, Albert, but no thanks.'

'I guess it was...'

'1994!' yelled Steve.

'Not really, more probably...'

'2016!' still Steve, laughing.

'Exactly, thanks. We were so damn broke we started going to the builders' stall around the corner, every day. It was cheap. And drinkable. But mostly cheap.'

'Quality first, right?'

'Mate, I once asked for a cappuccino and the guy threw a bunch of empty cups at me.'

'A true gentleman.'

'You bet. He shouted in my face: *I serve coffee. Coffee only. Regular, black, hot, steel-strong, coffee.*'

'And how was it?'

'It tasted like poison, Pete. It was so strong I seriously considered scoring some cocaine to chill me down.'

'Fuck, it can't be real.'

'Trust me. If it wasn't for the thief-like prices of London cafes, I wouldn't go back to the Steel Coffee Van but, as I said...'

'Cheap.'

'Exactly. Besides, after a while, we started getting along. I was making new friends: the builders went from calling me boss, mate, to finally insulting my mother and sister. At last, I felt accepted.'

'Such a moving story, you really got me Albert.'

'I did?'

'Let's go try this place.'

*   *   *

Florence, L'Opera Cafe. 11:30 am

'This cappuccino is delish!'

'Yes Tommy, the best in town, as advertised on the board.'

'Christ, Vic, you're so naive. Don't you see they all have the exact same shit hung by the door? They're Italians, they cheat, they're liars, you should know it.'

'Don't be rude, Rose. It's pretty good, isn't it?'

'Quite expensive.'

'And the view...'

'Ah: an ancient pile of rocks blocking the sunlight.'

'It's the Cathedral, can you believe it?'

'What?'

'We're having coffee and croissants in front of such a majestic piece of history.'

'Fuck, aren't we now?' commented Rose.

'What's the next stop, Vic?' asked Tommy.

'I don't know, we could wander about the medieval alleys, have a real gelato and, maybe, enjoy a walk along the river?'

'Yeee!!'

'Sounds like granny's plan. Why don't we also stop at the first Funeralcare on the way and pick a good-old solid oakwood coffin?'

'Shut up.'

'Italian quality, handmade refined boxes to swoosh down to Hell Land like jolly-happy ducks!'

'I said shut up!!' burst out Vic, loudly, precisely when an old lady approached their table. She was totally mortified.

'I didn't want to disturb...' she excused herself.

'Wow, your face turned crimson. Shame on you, Vic.'

'Rose! Shh...'

'What?'

'I'm so sorry, I don't know what I'm doing today. I guess I'm just mumbling things out of place. Please, would you like to join us?' Vic said, making room for the stranger guest.

The lady sat down.

'What's your name, madam?' asked Tommy.

'My name is Sophie. Are you guys British?'

'Straight outta Sherlintock.'

'Oh.'

'I'm Tommy, by the way.' he said, shaking her hand like a proper gentlekid.

'You're such a nice boy. Do you like it here?'

'We're just arrived, madam. This place is incredible, isn't it?'

'I knoOow...'

'We're still adjusting to the heat but these clear skies are phenomenal!'

'I knoOow...'

'And people are so friendly, so easy going...' continued Tommy.

'I knoOow...'

'Besides, the food: oh, the food is...'

'Stupendous' Sophie kind of cut short. 'And you are?' she asked, looking at Vic.

'Why don't you mind your fucking business, you fucking witch?'

'Gosh, I didn't even introduce myself. I'm Victoria' she said, sticking a hand into Rose's ghost mouth.

'Victoria. Like the Queen. What a beautiful name.'

'Thanks... I guess.'

'Indeed. Indeed.'

'Are you local, Sophie?'

'Aw, darling, no, no. I just have a vintage shop around the corner. Listen, why don't you and your friends come over?'

'Now?'

'Yes, it's such a rare thing to find Britons willing to have a chat in this city. We can have tea together.'

'Woah, that would be great! What do you think, Tommy?'

'Marvellous!'

*   *   *

Notting Hill Hostel. 1:15 pm

Steel Coffee was as harsh as it was presented.

50p a cup. Heart attack guaranteed.

They had to spend the following hours strolling about Hyde Park, chain-smoking, speed-talking and snif-sniffing like junkies in the vain attempt to chill out a little. Then, Steve and Pete said goodbye, good luck, and sayonara, and went back to Sherlintock as planned. The Mustang roared away leaving Albert alone at last, ready to start his new London life.

First things first: accommodation. He picked the cheapest Hostel in town, possibly the shoddiest in the whole world: *Notting Hill Hostel.* Albert entered the place, pressed a completely useless call bell, muttered something and, since the guy sitting behind the Ikea-wannabe counter didn't appear to be interested in him at all, he decided to use a heavy hand: waiting in silence, Siddhartha style. I know, what a horrible plan. Anyways,

Albert crossed his arms and stood still, fixing the guy's face with laser eyes as if trying, hoping, imagining to shake the bastard out of his bubble. Nothing. Apparently, the bastard was busying himself with the latest issue of Time Out. He flickered through the pages for a while, took a sip of his lager and finally asked:

'What can I do for you, mate?'

'A room please.'

'Do you have a reservation?'

'No reservations, thanks. Anything would do fine.'

'I mean... did you book online?'

'Uh?'

'It don't matter. D'you want a room with or without a view?'

'I like to see things.'

'... okay... number 56 is free. Is it ok with you?'

'I hope so. Do you think it'll suit me?'

'Mate, are you kidding or what?'

'I'm serious.' insisted Albert.

'Aight.' chewed the "concierge". 'The room is extra fucking comfortable, no view, no breakfast,'

'Lunch?'

'No.'

'Dinner?'

'Fuck no. As I was saying, it's the perfect choice for a gentlelad like yourself. How am I doing so far?'

'Terrific!'

'Great. It's 40 quid a day, shared bathroom, shared kitchen, private TV and...'

'Wait, wait.'

'What?'

'I don't want no telly. It talks too much. Do you have a radio, by any chance?'

'Ah. Let me think...'

'Well?'

'Nope. No radio. Sorry, mate.'

'Gosh... this isn't going the way I expected. I'll have to find another place then.'

'Hold on!' the guy shouted, grabbing him by the sleeve.

Albert was unsure whether to show him a couple of deadly karate moves he actually didn't know or to quietly listen. Frozen in a sort of Bruce Lee classic move, he decided to go for the second option.

'Tell me.'

'Now that I think about it, there must be a war relic somewhere. Not sure it works, though.'

'Holy cow, that's fantastic news! I want that!'

'No need to cheer like a fucking baby, mate.'

'This is the best time of my life.'

'Innit? Anyhow, I'll see what I can do. Mr... ?'

'Hoover. Albert Hoover.'

'Sign here. How long are you planning to stay?'

'More than three hours.'

'Good, good. The room is on the third floor, end of the corridor.'

'I can't wait to lay down. Last night I slept in a car, a fancy car actually. To be precise...'

'Room 56, here are the keys, mate.' the guy cut short.

'Okey dokey. When will I get the radio?'

'Soon.' he kinda giggled, pulling out a gloriously fake polite smile. 'It'll be with you ASAP.'

'Man, thank you so much!'

THIRTY-TWO

Vintage Wanders Shop. 12:15 pm
They crossed the threshold and a little bell announced their entrance. Sophie was an old, elegant lady with long grey hair running loose over her shoulders. It looked like all the life in the world filtered through her. Yet, she was shining like a crystal, vital and inspiring like no one Vic had ever met.

'She's a witch.' Rose whispered to Tommy.

'...' he replied.

'Ladies and gents, this is my humble refuge from the world. Please, touch everything and have some fun.'

'Can we, Vic?'

'Sure, Tommy, you heard Sophie. Just be careful not to break anything.'

'Oh, he won't. These ancient treasures were so well-made they're going to last forever. Is this little fellow your son?'

'You old crow, what a fucking question.'

'ROSE!!' Victoria silently shrieked in her mind.

'It doesn't matter, darling. By the way, who's Rose?'

'Oh... well...'

'You keep mentioning her. Is she a friend of yours?'

'I... yes. A very close one.'

'Dear, you don't need to be ashamed. We all have an imaginary mate in our lives. Some people drop it when they grow up, others put it in a corner. My friend's name was Margaret.'

'You figure. Typical 18th-century stiff name. She's a witch, Vic, a witch!!'

Vic was stunned.

'I'm so sorry to disappoint you but, no, I'm not a witch, Rose. And... you know, I can hear you.'

'Umph.'

'That's fine, I know you don't mean it. You're just afraid.'

Vic was speechless. Even Sophie could read her mind.

'And what would I be afraid of, Mrs shaman of my socks?'

Sophie was amused by Rose grumpiness level. She barely masked a delicate laugh and replied:

'Honey, it's clear you're terrified by the fact that Victoria will forget you as soon as she finds a charming man.'

'Bollocks.'

'Maybe... the love of her life?'

'...'

'You shouldn't be preoccupied, though. People like your friend will always be loyal, they can't live without their inner conscience.'

'Fab, I'm totally relieved now. Thank you, old witch.'

'Rose is incredibly rude but she's fun sometimes.' said Tommy.

Sophie smiled again. 'Let me close the shop and offer you something to drink.'

'Finally, a bloody G&G for me, pronto.' said Rose, but no one could hear her this time.

A hand-painted secret wall picturing a romantic Victorian garden scene suddenly opened and Sophie disappeared behind it for a moment. Her shop was a collection of marvels from all over the world. You could have spent days rummaging through those gems without ever getting to the bottom of it. Like Merlin's handbag, that place was bottomless.

'And here we go,' Sophie said popping back into the room. 'tea, coffee, orange juice?'

'Cookies! Cookies! Cookies!!' squealed Tommy, ecstatic, staring at the loaded fine porcelain tray embroidered with blue ink.

'Asia...'

'...'

'It feels like time doesn't exist here...' continued Vic, completely spaced out.

'I knoOow...'

'Each piece brings me to a different era, a different culture... everything has a story to tell: that ancient map of China, those wooden toys, the rag dolls...'

Sophie was observing Vic moving along the dusty narrow aisles of the shop. She was studying her expressions, her reactions as if Victoria was one of those goldfishes spinning in their perfect glass bowls.

'... and that yellowish, huge rotating globe... what is that?'

'We'll get there in a minute. Take a seat, please.'

'Sure, I'm sorry.'

'What's his name?' asked Sophie out of the blue.
'Straight to the goddamn point. You ain't that bad, after all.'
'Thanks, Rose.'
'Who's name?'
'My dear Victoria, it's clear you're chasing someone. From the very instant I saw you in the cafe, I could tell your smile was stained with pain.'
'Definitely a witch. Told ya.'
'Oh, my... Rose might be right this time. Are you sure you're not...'
'It doesn't take black magic to see through your eyes, honey.'
'...'
'More tea?'
'Actually... do you have something stronger? I'm feeling a bit dizzy.'
'Ah. This topic is making you nervous. Please, open the Globe Bar.'
'Uh?'
'You fucking cretin or what? Crack the bloody world open and give us the booze!'
'Yes, Victoria, that's what it is.' Sophie chuckled.
'I'm astonished. This place is a marvel!'
'I'm glad you like it. Would you pour some scotch for me too?'
'On the rocks?'
'Straight, please.'

Victoria had the same. She sat down, crossed her long legs and gulped her drink as if it was water. She really wanted to make an impression on Sophie. She wanted to look like an experienced woman, a lifetime drinker, but she wasn't. The viscous fluid cascaded into her body all at once and almost choked her. So, she tried in vain to muffle a long series of coughs. Her peach-smooth cheeks turned crimson for the 10th time in a chapter and silent tears dripped from the ocean of her eyes.

'Amateur.' thought Rose; Tommy was laughing out loud. It took a while for Vic to put herself back together.

'What were we saying?' she asked, eventually.

'It feels like you got trapped in a borderless hide-and-seek with your lover. Am I right?'

*   *   *

Hostel Room. 3:20 pm
'Right. Where the hell is my radio??'

'...' answered the empty room.

'This place is rubbish. Bed: probably infested with bugs. Sheets: are those blood stains? Basin: holy crap, this is the original one used for Prodigy's *Breathe* video, I need to tell Pete! Should I call him now? Perhaps later. Nah. Or... Later indeed.'

Albert was talking to himself, as usual. He had been in his new room for just about 63 minutes 25 seconds and still no sign of any transistor transmitting device. He was getting frustrated. He was sensing a nervous breakdown coming, and that's why he rushed downstairs, ready to fight for his rights, positive about getting his radio. As a professional punk, he swooshed down the stairs, his ass grinding the handrail. He was approaching the last flight at warp speed when a very old lady got in the way and stopped his race.

'Hello.'

'Hi, I'm Albert.'

'Beautiful name.'

'Thank you.'

'Can you help me out?'

'Sure, at your service, madam.'

'Follow me in the living room.' she said, pointing her walking cane towards the nearby wallpapered space.

Albert observed her as she planned, attempted and eventually executed each one of her careful steps. It was like seeing a buffered slow-motion movie where nothing happens. Slowness. Starring Granny. A Colossal capable of stopping the Earth from spinning. Albert considered the idea of lying down and simply waiting to age dead. They were never going to get to the room, not in this lifetime.

But they did.

'Shall we take a seat?'

'We shall, madam. We shall.'

'I always loved these Chesterfield chairs.' the lady said when she sat down. 'My husband and I had one in our home.'

'Sure. May I ask what am I here for?'

'I'm so sorry, darling, I might have gone off on a tangent. Can you please open this bottle for me? The cork doesn't come out and I'm not as strong as I was during the war.'

'I bet... *squeak, squeeeak... POP!!* there you go. I can see you brought a full set of super cool tumblers with you.'

'Yes, two crystal glasses. One for me and the other for my guest.'

'Marvellous.' Albert said, jumping on his feet, his hands meeting in a single sharp-crisp *CLAP!* 'So I must be going.'
'Don't!'
'But you just said...'
'... please, would you be my guest?'
'Aha! Nice trick. Nice trick indeed.'
'I'm always alone, you know, everyone is rushing around in this city. No one ever wants to stop for a cuppa or to listen to a good-old story.'
'Well, it's your lucky day, madam, cuz I do.'
'Really?'
'Uh-huh.'
'You're such a nice boy, Albert. Please, try this liquor, it's from my old town. It's handmade.'
'Thank you, but no thanks. I really don't feel like drinking. Besides, what time is it?'
'3:25 pm'
'Exactly.'
'What?'
'Isn't it a tad too early for your drinky-drinky?'
'Not at all. Not when it's a special occasion.'
'Is it now?'
'May I ask why you were running?'
'Shoot, about that.' Albert cleared his throat, turned to the reception room and shouted, 'I DEMAND to have MY RADIO DELIVERED to my accomodation! ASAP!'
'Asap?'
'It means soon, madam. CAN YOU HEAR ME???' Albert insisted.
'I love radios! Do you really have one?'
'I will. I hope.'
'Can I see it?'
'Absolutely. As soon as they give it to me.'
'I'm so thrilled. You know, I was listening to the radio all the time when I was a young girl.'
'Did you?'
'Yes. Please, take a sip. As I said, this is a special liquor, we made it in-house.'
'Actually...'
Albert was studying her eyes. She reminded him of his grandmother: same good, honest vibes; same boring, yet genuine, halo. He

surrendered.

'Give it to me.' he said, and guzzled the amber liquid without thinking. *Fire.* His hands immediately reached to his throat as if someone just poured gasoline and lit a match down into his body.

'Oh, my...' giggled the old lady, almost in tears for the fun.

'AAAAAAHHHHHH' screamed Albert, exactly like *Home Alone* Kevin.

'You were supposed to sip it, you know...'

'AAAAAAAHHHHHHHH!!!'

'Wait here, I'll get you some bread.' she offered, heading towards the main room as slow as a crippled turtle, her cane marking each second of some slowed-down downtempo.

'Water...' he hissed. 'HELP!'

'What? You're too far, I can't hear you!'

'You're not even past the chair, you bast...'

'I'll be back in a second, don't worry.'

Albert was choking but, luckily that wasn't his first rodeo. Once, he had the brilliant idea of gargling with vinegar. *What can go wrong with it?* he told himself at the time, *It's natural, it's healthy and all that shit. One shot and bye-bye sore throat.* Obviously, as soon as he tilted his head backwards, the spirited fluid caught him off guard and he gulped the whole thing down. No gargle (sorry). It burned so badly that he found himself on the bathroom floor crying for help, his eyes flooded with tears. So, screw personal hygiene, he decided after that casual attempted suicide. However, thanks to that li'l adventure, this time he was prepared.

'What are you doing?' asked the old lady.

'*CRASH!!*' screamed the window glass, shattering, and letting Albert crawl outside, straight on top of a beautiful flower bed.

'Water, water...' he was babbling as he grabbed the hose and sprayed the fresh liquid into his mouth, and over his head, like a thirsty bear.

'Are you alright, dear?'

'I am, you bloody...' he panted.

'Thank God we are on the ground floor. Can you imagine if...'

'I do. I most certainly do.'

'Should I go get you a towel?'

'NO, please don't move, I'm alright. I'm ready for your story.' Albert said, brushing his topsoil-dirty hands over the damp suit. {Oh, yeah, he was wearing a suit [not his wetsuit (jut saying)]}

'It's my fault, I should have told you it was a bit strong.'

'Madam, I can stand worse things than that. I'm a man.'

'Please, take my handkerchief, you're dripping water from your beard.'

'Nonsense. You should have seen me during the great war.'

'What? You're so young, you can't be serious.'

'I am. 1995: My scout mates and I fought the harshest of battles to protect our food provisions. No one got to touch our all-butter scones. True story.'

'...' she smiled. 'Tell me. This radio of yours, is it old?'

'Probably as old as this country. May I ask what's so fascinating about it? I mean, why is it so important for you?'

'You see... my husband was an R.A.F. pilot in the '40s. I was terrified he wouldn't come back, so many of his friends didn't, it was an awful time.'

'Yeah, I heard.'

'The only thing that kept me going was the radio. It was a sort of relief. It gave me purpose, a sense of community. As if that box, catching waves from the air, was connecting all of us around the country.'

'I never thought about it in these terms.'

'The radio quickly became a new friend in our home. It was part of the day, part of our family.'

'Ah.'

For some reason, that story was striking a certain chord in Albert's heart. Now, I'm not saying he was about to weep or that he was irremediably touched by it but, hearing that piece of reality first-hand had some effect on him. Evidently, no matter how important our virtual lives had become, the human touch was still the most powerful weapon.

'So... you like vintage, rusty radios.'

'I must confess. I have a soft spot for antiques.'

THIRTY-THREE

Vintage Wanders (again) 4:30 pm

'Albert. Victoria and Albert. It must be destiny.' Sophie sighed.

'Yeah, a Royal destiny.'

'You sound pretty harsh, darling.'

'What, me? Why? Just because he left me it doesn't mean I hate that bastard with all my heart.'

'Poor disgraceful wreckage of a woman. She's madly in love.'

'I know, Rose.' giggled Sophie.

'Oh, no, no, no. No.'

'Sophie?' intervened Tommy.

'Yes, darling?'

'How did you ended up in Florence?'

'Well, it's a long story...'

'Was it because you didn't like the UK?'

'Not at all, quite the contrary.'

'So, was it because of a boy?'

'I...'

'Did you finish the money?'

'Fucking hell, kids: they're bloody shameful these days.'

'Rose...' said Vic, in disdain.

'Truth be told, I'm not exactly sure why we decided to stay.'

'Liar Alert, Liar Alert, Liar Alert!'

'Who's we?' asked Victoria.

'Right. It was me and John, my husband. We came here for our honeymoon.'

'Jesus Christ, not another gushy crap story.'

'Rooose!!'

But Sophie just laughed. 'Nothing like that' she commented. 'We were enjoying the rural areas outside Florence, visiting every tiny little village on the way when we stumbled upon a true marvel lost in the middle of nowhere. Now that you got me thinking, that was the reason why we stopped.

'It must have been spectacular.'

'Indeed it was, Tommy. John fell for it at first sight. We were walking a narrow road that twisted up and down through the hills when we saw it.'

'What?? You saw whaaat??'

'On top of a long steep, laid a monument, like a replica of the Dome you can see here in Florence, Rose.' she replied with a smile. 'We hurried there and, the more we got closer, the more its details and beauty conquered us. All around, an endless landscape grooved by vineyards, dotted with thousands of olive trees and cypress exclamation points marking the rounded shapes in the distance, guarding the country roads like soldiers.'

'Wow...'

'Yes, Tommy, that's exactly what we said when we reached the place. Our eyes got lost among that immensity. Suddenly, we were standing on the centre of the world.'

'So, this dome... how come it was so isolated?'

'Ah. That's a bloody story. Literally.'

'Tell us, tell us!!' insisted Tommy.

'Yeah, give us some juice.'

'Ok, Rose, I'll try my best: the legend says that in ancient times there was a city called Semifonte flourishing among those hills, getting more important by the day. Obviously, Florence couldn't allow any competitors to interfere with its business and these guys didn't want to submit. Therefore, the most powerful Florentine families decided to destroy Semifonte and burn it to the ground to impose their supremacy. They erased it from history and eventually, they built a small replica of their *Brunelleschi* Dome in the very centre of the old city, as a reminder that no one should ever mess up with Florence.'

'Mafia-style. Finally, something interesting.'

'Shhh!' Vic silently screamed to her imaginary friend.

Sophie was enjoying the situation.

'Did you ever come back to that place?' asked Tommy.

'We did, once a month like clockwork. Until...'

'Did something bad happened?' instinctively asked Victoria.

'Who's the witch now?'

'Only real witches can spot another witch.' intervened Rose.

'It's not true.'

'It is, Tommy. I swear on Victoria's life.'

'Sorry, Sophie...'

'No need for apologies, Victoria. It's been such a long time since I went up there but... on one of our last visits my John sketched five paintings of the landscape. Somehow, he fooled himself he could steal that beauty, bring it home and have it accessible at all times. He used to tell me "Just wait to see the five panels ready and assembled in circle!".'

'Woah, it sounds like a 360 degrees experience!'

'Something like that.' said Sophie lost in her thoughts. 'But he never got to finish them and... anyway, what he left, still kind of bring me back to those moments.'

'Vic, I think he got sick and died.' Tommy whispered without moving, keeping his eyes fixed on Sophie as if that way she wouldn't notice.

'I'm so sorry...'

'That's life, my dear. It was hard but I decided to stay next to him, in Florence. I kept the shop open.'

'So, you did it for him?'

'I did it for us, darling. He's my propeller, my engine, spinning me along the paths of life.'

'...' even Rose was silent now.

'Do you still have John's drawings?'

'Yes, they remained untouched. He planned to finish them on our glamorous comeback, you know, one of those sunny days perfect for a good-old picnic but, you know.'

'We should go there together!' proposed Tommy.

'Ah... I am too old for that. I don't drive, not on the wrong side anyway and... I don't feel like going on a journey alone.'

'Hey, you're not alone, there's us now!' said Vic.

'Yes!! Let's go see the dome!!' pushed Tommy.

'Mmm...'

Victoria's eyes were twinkling like diamonds. She had something in mind.

'Leave it to me, Sophie. I have an idea.' she said, without leaking the slightest clue of what she was talking about. Suddenly, she was ultra excited. Sophie was midway from confused and worried.

'Tommy, let's move.' ordered Vic getting on her feet.

'Where are you going?'

'Thank you, Sophie, thank you.'

'What for?'

'I'll get in touch. Soon. Very soon.'

'But...'

But Victoria's Dream Team was already one foot out of the shop, walking the streets of Florence, rushing somewhere, for some reason. Sophie was standing still on the threshold of Vintage Wanders: *'What the heck just happened?'*

They had just disappeared around the corner when Vic stopped and:

'You wanted adventure? Here comes the adventure.'

'That's my girl, rock'n'roll, babe!' cheered Rose.

'Tommy,' Vic continued, 'do you still have the business card of David, the taxi driver?'

THIRTY-FOUR

Mile End, London - 5:00 pm
'UBEEEER!!!!'
'?'
'UBEEEEERRRR!!!'
The grumpy, uneducated, gross man at the reception turned out to be a big fat liar, therefore, Albert didn't get the radio. Actually, there was no radio at all, it never existed, so he decided to pack his stuff and leave the hostel. The old lady was truly sad to see him go but Albert swore he would maintain his promise, whatever that was, if any. He was now out on the streets, in search of a proper place to stay.
'UBEEEEEEEEEEEEEEEEEEEEERR!!!'
'Fuck, man, what the hell are you screaming for?'
'Oh, hello. My name is Albert. Albert Hoover.'
'Cool. Stop shouting at cars.'
'I need a Uber, mate.'
'Jesus... it doesn't work that way.'
'What do you mean?'
'You need an app.'
'A what??'
'An app, for your phone.'
'Ah. I don't understand.'
'You go to your AppStore and download the...'
'Just tell me where this store is, I can walk there.'
The stranger took a matrix 360-degrees-look around in search of a camera. 'This must be a joke, a prank show. Have I been *Punk'd*?' he asked himself.
'Is it far from here?'
Nope, It wasn't a joke at all, and no Ashton Kutcher or any other TV guy was in sight.
'Alright, where do you need to go, Albert?'
'I'm looking for a room in a flatshare.'
'Great, so you might want to go online and check for spareroom dot

co dot... wait, wait.'

'Yeah, I lost you.'

'I could tell it from your face. Let me think... There's an estate agency just around the corner. JB Link, you can't miss it.'

'JB Link, around the corner.'

'Exactly, they have a massive blue neon sign hung over the door. Go there and talk to them.'

'Coolio! Thank you so much, mate!'

* * *

Florence, random street 5:00 pm

Team Victoria was waiting for Mr *DAVIDE MORIANTI* on a narrow curb.

'What the fuck is going on?'

'Rose, I have an idea.'

'Thank God.'

'What is it, Vic?'

'Are you guys ready for a secret mission?'

'Yes, madam, yes!' squealed Tommy.

'Great.'

'So, what is it?'

'Exactly, spit it out. Let's hear the ultimate delusion.'

Vic cleared her throat and straightened her back, trying to attain some sort of importance.

'Dear Rose, my little fellow Tommy: we are now officially stepping into the daydream business!'

'Right. We should totally call a doctor.'

'Rose, let her speak.'

'We will steal images, panoramas and details from little villages and towns. We will catch those precious fragments and bring them back to the people who lost them. As a present.'

'Sounds more like a charity crap enterprise than a business. Where's the money, Vic?' promptly asked Rose.

'We'll be paid back in smiles, hugs and...'

'Fuck me...'

'... hopefully, no one will get angry.'

'Angry? Angry at what? Angry for what? A bloody free service? ANGRY??'

'You know, not all memories are good, Rose. Bringing those details back could/should? awaken dusty dreams, emotions that got left behind because of the course of life. Our special clients will look at the photographs or listen to the provided sounds or, gosh, they could even smell vials filled with scents of their moments. They'll instantly know,'

'Know what? That you're a scam artist?'

'I'm ready, Vic! I like it!' yelled Tommy.

'Shit, it's getting weirder and weirder.'

'Okay, but it's perfectly clear in my mind! We just have to steal back those fragments of time, venture into B-side places where someone left a part of their heart. We will plunge into narrow dodgy alleys where life did its course for a while. Maybe, one of these pics will be the key evidence in solving a crime, no, a murder!'

'You're bananas, let's get out of here. Come on, Tommy boy.'

'What? This is brilliant, Rose. Think about Santa Claus: we can be a sort of Santa's helpers!! We give away gifts to the people and everybody turns into better humans!'

'Bullshit.'

'Haven't you seen *Klaus*?'

'What?'

'The Netflix movie! The whole village shift from being horrible to nice and friendly.'

'Fucking humans, they give up so easily.'

'They start to enjoy life and want to do good. Good deeds get viral!'

'Viral is good. Viral is business...' Rose suddenly thought.

'Absolutely. Our small gestures will be priceless presents to others. We'll be like Santa, all year round. No reindeer or red hats. We'll jump off cliffs, climb rocks and mountains just for the pleasure of giving.'

'They might be willing to pay after all...'

'Our company will be based on this principle: making people happy. Are you with me???'

'YEEEEEE' said Tommy.

'Hell YEAH!' added Rose. 'Let's fucking screw the bastards and pile a shitload of money!!'

* * *

JB Link. 6:00 pm

'How much are you willing to pay, Albert?' asked a tiny, short man from behind the fishiest desk in the world.

The place was as fake as Courtney Love's face. The area? Worse: '80s Bronx, but dodgier.

'What do you mean?'

'What's your budget?'

'I don't have much but... whatever, I want a decent place. I can spend some money after all.'

'Brilliant. Perfect. We're here to help, you don't have to worry about a thing.'

'That's what I call exceptional service!'

'We'll take care of you.'

'I knew you were going to be nice people. I can clearly feel it now.' said Albert, rolling up and down the flimsy IKEA chair that almost cried, this close from snapping into pieces.

'Let me show you this beautiful flat:'

'What is this smell?'

'?'

'Did you do renovations?'

'Excuse me?'

'I can smell fresh paint, did you move in recently?'

'Ahem... yes, but we have many other branches around London, this is only a small part of our expansion.'

'Wow, you must be real pros.'

'We are. Indeed.' the agent said, grinning, rubbing his hands.

'Seriously, it feels like you appeared in the hood overnight. Everything is brand-new, like this coffee table...'

'NO!!' the agent cried, watching the cheapest piece of furniture ever made crumbling into bits over the oakwood-printed vinyl floor.

'Sorry...'

'...'

'So, you guys new in the area?'

'We have connections, don't worry. You must understand, this is London. Everything moves fast but you can trust us, we ain't going nowhere.'

'Yes, I can see it in your eyes. Honesty. So hard to find in this crazy world. One day you feel safe and, the very next, you've been robbed.'

'...'

'Rumor has it there are agencies popping in the street like mushrooms and disappearing the day after. New name, new setup, same people.'

'Er...' he started sweating.

'Some say the smartest agents rob their clients for a while then they bail to exotic places. Bad people.'

'Absolutely, those bastards...' the agent said, thinking with envy about his lucky colleagues. 'You don't have to worry, you are in safe hands, my friend.'

'Absolutely. How do you deal with thieves and untrustworthy people?'

'We take care of them.'

'Oh...'

'Yes, well... We take care of them.'

'Of course, and you don't have to worry about me either, you can trust me, 100%. Here is my latest statement.' Albert said, handing over an A4 with all his bank details and the precise amount of money currently available in his account.

The agent's pupils widened as if he just snorted a chunky fat cocaine line.

'This is quite a sum.' he said, trying to hide his excitement.

'They're my life savings. As I said, I'm not rich but I can handle paying the rent.'

'Indeed. Indeed. So, you wanted a room only, am I right?'

'Precisely.'

'Let me see if I have any ready to go options for you... oh, look at this one, it's your lucky day, Mr Albert.'

'Really? I'm so thrilled, mate! What is it?'

'We just refurbished a whole apartment in Eric Street, very nice area, less than one minute from the Central line, District and...'

'Shi-p... I promised myself I'll go for a room only. I can't take the apartment, sorry.'

'We can offer you a very, very good price. Give me a sec.'

Tick-tlack-click-click,point-click,tarattattack. sounded the keyboard from behind the ridiculously oversized monitor.

'Yes, this is certainly your lucky day. You can get this apartment for a discounted price of 1850 pounds a month plus some nonsense fees.'

'Wow! Should I reconsider?'

'You must.'

'How's the place?'

'Spacious, full of light.'

'I mean, how many rooms? What about the fees? You know, I don't want to sound scrooge but I shouldn't throw money away.'

'Are you implying I'm not offering you the very best we have?'

'Never! I trust you blindly, but...'

'I was joking. The house is in perfect condition: new mattress, new laminate floors and, woah, we just installed a shimmering, brand-new touch control ceramic hob.'

'How about the rest?'

'It's the latest-design modern studio apartment so you will have a stunning kitchen sitting straight in front of your your bed, a built-in bathroom, and, wait for it... a breathtaking Juliet balcony.'

'Sounds a little small...'

'Tut-tut. It's a jewel, believe me. No better option in London, not for this exceptional price.'

'I think you're right. What about the fees?'

'Sure. It's nothing, really. We ask for threemonthsdepositinadvance, 100poundsfeeforthecontract and a silly, tiny, ridiculous agency renewal fee of eightyninepoundsfiftyfivepence every two months.'

'I'm not sure I got what you said but what can I do about it? Am I an expert like you? Do I work in finance or deal with estates? I can only trust your word.'

'Brilliant, perfect, indeed, indeed. I'm printing the contract now. Please grab a pen, you can sign...'

'Here!'

'What?'

'I'd like to live here. What's this place?' asked Albert, tapping on a gigantic map of the area taped straight to the wall.

'But...'

'Treby Street. Is it any good?'

'Oh, that's luxury, my friend.'

'Any spare bed over there?'

'You got it. A tenant just left a stunning room facing the street. You'll have plenty of light, plenty of space and many, many friends to meet!'

'Super! How many?'

'This house has five rooms, 8 people max. Guaranteed.'

'...'

'Did I mention the one toilet and the one bathroom? Oh, and it features an immense rear garden.'

'What?! Are you for real?'

'It needs some maintenance but... yes, it's a traditional British garden reserved for you only!'

'Deal!'

The agent's jaw dropped.

PRINT PRINT PRINT PRIIINT screamed the printer like a steam locomotive about to explode. The guy was dripping salty drops from his forehead and his eyes burned like hell. He was already picturing the new sports car he would buy off this majestic scam. 'No time to waste, seal the deal, seal the fucking deal, AHAHAHAHA fucking idiot!!!' he was repeating in his head, his eyes stuck into Albert's eyes, fidgeting with the cheapest plastic pen, half a breath away from a heart attack.

'About fees, rent and the odd extra charge...' the agent carefully tried to slip into the conversation in a sudden, unlikely rush of honesty.

'Man, I'm tired. Just give me a good price, ok?'

'GRRrrRrRRrRRRrREEeEEeEeeEeAAAAATTTTT!!' the agent didn't scream like a hooligan, trembling and twitching junkie-style.

'Biro?'

'HERE, take it!'

'Thanks.'

'What a fucking great day, what a fucking great day!!'

'*scribble-scribble, frusshhh*' the pen said, signing the contract.

'Perfect. Thank you, Mr Albert. May I offer you a ride to your new home?'

'Very kind of you but no, I'd like to walk there. You know, I love to wander around until I find the places. No maps, no nothing. It's a good way to explore the surroundings and make friends with the locals.'

'Yes, yes.'

'I'll ask around.'

'Marvellous. Here are the keys, then.' the agent said, handing the bunch, ending the transaction.

But Albert stood up, serious as hell, and started fixing the guy.

'Oh, my bloody fucking shit. He's a cop, a goddammit copper!! I'm done with this crap, I don't want to rot in prison, please, please God, don't do this to me, I'll get better, I swear, no more tricks, scams, overcharges, false indications, *kidnappings?* to newcomers.'

'...'

'I promise I'll get rid of all the firearms. And the illegal furs, the counterfeit Armani suits, the drugs... I...'

Then, Albert spoke:

'Mate?'

'Y...es?'

'It's been an honour to meet you. Thanks for your time, for being so kind to me, and, again, your honesty.'

The agent started crying, silently, from the inside of his numb face. The rush of adrenaline was so strong that his heart almost cracked.

'Too many compliments?' thought Albert, pretty embarrassed by the awkward situation. 'Look, I'll take the keys and leave, cool?'

'...' he didn't reply.

'See you around, mate!' Albert concluded, shutting the door on his way out.

The agent collapsed on his fake leather, fake everything swinging chair. He bounced and tumbled on the floor. 'Fucking Hell.' he thought. Then he reached to the inside pocket of his suit and smiled. He rolled the shutter down and double-locked the door, ready for his well-deserved white powder award.

'What a good man. It's so hard to find people like him these days.' thought Albert, heading to his new home.

THIRTY-FIVE

Countryside, 45 minutes away from Florence
Davide Morianti (the taxi driver) arrived on time, wearing his usual carefree smile. The proposed journey was pretty long but, although it was pushing him far from the city, he decided to do it anyway and only charge a special discounted fee he made up for the occasion.

'All-day, 150 euro. Only because you, ok?'

'Thanks, David.' Vic said, kissing his cheek. Then they hit the road.

As improvised detectives, the three (maybe four if you can count imaginary friends like Rose) improbable characters sitting in the car were about to get to the bottom of their very first, very unpaid and totally unsolicited case.

'Why we go here?' asked David, trying to make conversation, perfectly aware he wouldn't understand any kind of answer anyway.

'We're helping a nice lady!' Shouted Tommy from the backseat.

'Good lady?'

'Yes, we want to steal glimpses of a special day she spent up there. You know, we have to dig into the scene to find the key element that triggered the indelible emotion which marked her heart forever.'

'Jesus Christ, Vic. Couldn't you be a bit more technical with David? He doesn't understand shit, you know it. He's like a goat, he moans, and he laughs, and he...'

'Good, good.' replied David.

'Rose... that's extremely rude. He's a nice, humble man. Shame on you.'

'Shame on you!!!' added Tommy.

'Beautiful day, uh?'

'It's enchanting, David. Thank you so much for taking us around!'

'Thank you, thank you. Very hot here. Hot and beautiful. Sun, breez, wind, sky...' and he went on with one of his monologues made out of the few English words he knew.

'One thing must be said though.' commented Rose. 'He's magnificently shameless and confident. Damn, I love men like him.'

'Rose loves David, Rose loves David...' sang Tommy while happily playing with the wind, his hand caressing the air like a jet wing out of the car window.

Vic was smiling. Rose was wearing a pretty uncomfortable red face.

'So, what's the plan? Are we gonna take pictures? Record some shit?'

'I've no idea, Rose.'

'Good. Brilliant. Hyper professional.'

'...'

'Thank God you decided to borrow (or should I say steal, you thieves?) a bunch of idiotic things from Sophie. That will totally help us out.'

'What, the compass?'

'And the ridiculous Sherlock Holmes hat that Tommy added to his goggles and gloves cretin outfit, as if it wasn't enough already.'

'You don't understand, this helps set the mood. It's a great way to dip into our new job.'

'Sure. Ladies and gents, here comes the Freak Show!' laughed out loud, Rose.

'Come on, what's the point if we don't have fun? Besides, this is our first mission, the pilot of a super duper exciting new job, isn't it, Tommy?'

'Yes! I'm already picturing Sophie's face looking at what we'll bring back to her. I bet she'll be sceptical at first, but then...'

'She will burst out in a smile.'

'Yes, Vic! Or... well, let's hope she won't end up weeping.'

'That would be good too, Tommy. However, let's focus on our task. All we have to do is catch that unique butterfly capable of darting straight in the centre of her heart.'

'YEAH! Let's kill granny!' shouted Rose, enjoying herself.

'Ahem hem... then, after our memorable first success, we will be contacted by others, and more missions will come up. More work, more smiles.'

'Super!!' cheered Tommy.

'We should try filling the ever half-full tank of happiness.'

'We'll be rockstars!'

'Who knows, we might even end up getting jobs all around the world, visiting the Middle East, Asia...'

'...Scandinavian places, Alaska!'

'Sick.' concluded Rose, probably distracted by what was appearing in the distance.

'Almost arrived, ladies.' announced David, pointing to the stunning dome structure standing elegantly on top of the hill.

*   \   *

Treby Street, getting Dark.

Albert was lost, you figure. East London at night is cool, artsy, hipster and vibrating, according to TimeOut or bloody Foxtons. In reality, it's just fucking dodgy, and Albert was wandering as a stray around its wild streets.

'Boss, you smoke weed?'
'Uh?'
'Take my numba.'
'Finally, someone. Mate, can you help me?'
'Weedcokepillsacids?'
'I can't understand what you're saying, bruv.'
'Yo, you don't call me no brother, man! Fuck.'
'Yo, yo, yo... don't push me.'
'What's wrong with you? Stop Yo-ing.'
'I need some help. Listen:'
'Coke?'
'No.'
'Weed?'
'No...'
'Pills?'
'I just have to find this place.'
'Heroin?'
'Seriously?'
'Acids, then. Take my numba.'
'I don't do drugs, mate.'
'Sometimes?'
'Bloody hell, you're a pain in the ass.'
'Umph...'
'Where's Treby Street?'
'You're on it, man.'
'What?'
'Take my numba.' he insisted, handing over a glossy freshly-printed business card.

'Whatever, ok.'

'Call me.' he said, dashing away like a supersonic ghost.

Albert was playing with the keys of his brand-new, fucking amazing, luxurious apartment. Life was good. He already made a new friend too, Mr... WEEDALICIOUS as the capital letters bumping out of the crisp-white business card said. 'That guy's fly, what a fab start.' he actually said while standing in front of the door leading to his new life.

From out there, the place didn't exactly smell like luxury, to be honest. It looked more like a council estate, with the cracked plaster, the worn-out wooden door and

'What the hell??' Albert yelled, jumping on his feet at the sight of a filthy-dark monumental rat running by the brick wall. Even the scariest bully cat would think twice about challenging that thing. 'God bless rabid London foxes.' Albert thought. Then he hurried his hands to reach the keys. 'Get in, get in!' his busy mind repeated in a frenzy. For some inexplicable reason, he felt confident that beyond that crumbling door was a stunning, modern, beautiful space. Was he totally mad? Anyway, he waited a moment too long standing still on the threshold. You shouldn't do that in London, everyone knows it. People approach you, in the best-case scenario.

'Mate, smoke weed?'

'Yo, I'm local.'

'Uh?'

'I already have my contact.'

'Take my number.'

'I don't do drugs.'

'Sometimes?'

'You must be fucking kidding me.' Albert thought as he finally opened the door.

* * *

Semifonte City Centre. Sunset

Happiness. Anthony Morvar was often talking about Happiness. Where can people find it? Can you stumble across it by chance? Can we set an appointment with it? Eventually, those questions were the reason why he started the Morvar Company. Selling objects capable of triggering a smile, recall happy moments, that's what he was into. For example: kites. Flying your kite with your son, with your friends or even alone, seemed like something powerful. Selling kites was selling dreams, for Anthony. He believed it was a sort of sneaky trick to connect people, make them spend time together out in the fields interacting with nature and its secrets, its beauties. The force of nature. Is it where happiness comes from?

'I'm starving. Are we done here?' moaned Rose, staring at a paralysed version of Victoria. Since they arrived, her gaze got lost in the void of time and space, eyes shut, arms spread like Christ the Redeemer in Rio. Anyone sane of mind would have thought Victoria was on peyote, ayahuasca or some other psychedelic drug. But she wasn't, and no one appeared to be worried about her.

'Hold this, Rose.' asked Tommy, ultra busy.

'Kid, give me a fucking break.'

'It's important. I'm searching for clues, you know, details...'

'You haven't stopped pestering me since we landed on this forsaken dump.'

'This is the last time, I swear.'

'*He said for the eleventh time in an hour.* Forget about it.'

'Please... Rose...' he begged, using his big watery childish eyes as a weapon.

'Oh, just give it to me and fuck off doing whatever the fuck you do.' she spat out, grumpy as ever.

Tommy didn't even listen and immediately jumped back to his job. He was sniffing stuff, sensing the space, rubbing surfaces like a well-trained pedigreed detection dog. So much so that his face was utterly covered with dust, dirt and soil. Rose snorted. As loudly as she could.

'Why don't you lay down and rest like David?' said Tommy.

'He's not resting. He's dead.'

'He's not! Look: DAVID??' he called, without getting any feedback. David was somewhere far, deep into his R.E.M. sleep.

'See? He's dead. Now, get lost.'

'But...'

On arrival, David had the brilliant idea of kicking his shoes off and laying on the grass. He meticulously picked his spot and occupied it like a Roman Emperor. Then, he engaged in relaxing and sunbathing without shame: vest and gold chain off; shirt off; trousers rolled halfway up showing his manly, hairy legs and a pair of silly striped socks. He was now snoring like an old bear. If you were to walk by you would think a gipsy caravan just stopped there for good.

It was quite late when Victoria finally opened her eyes. The sky was blushing like a little girl, burning clouds and landscape simultaneously while falling into the horizon along with the sun. Vic was overwhelmed, she couldn't believe what she was looking at.

'There!'

'What?'

'Shhhhhhhh'

'...'

'...'

'Tommy,' she whispered, 'camera.'

'click.'

'shoot.'

'bzzzz'

'fab...' as a professional surgeon's assistant, Tommy proceeded with handing her the recorder.

'click.'

'rec...'

'...'

'click.'

'now, the vial...'

'POp.'

'blurb...'

'tap.'

Victoria broke the silence with a sonorous smile.

'Great work, team!'

'We done? I've had enough of all this nature.' said Rose.

'We got it!! We got it!!' Tommy, yelling, jumping around the place as a Native American dancing for a glorious rainfall.

'Ready?' asked Davide, back in his uniform, excited for being part of that unusual venture.

'Yes, thank you, David.'

'For what? I drive. You do things.'

'What a man.' said Rose, with respect.

'Let me tell you:'

'?'

'Brava. You very good.' he solemnly stated, smacking a rough kiss on Victoria's head.

'Er... thanks?!' she blushed. But he wasn't finished.

'Con-gra-tu-lay-tions.' he added, properly articulating each syllable, as if to give more pathos to it.

As the old wise man once said: Crazy people always get together., nobody said.

'Whatever.' puffed out Rose and,

'Shotgun!' yelled Tommy, running to the front seat of the TAXI.

Victoria was ecstatic.

Where the hell was Albert?

* * *

45 Treby Street. Night.

Albert was lying on top of the plastic-wrapped mattress of his new room. He still had his coat on and was focused on something. In his hands was a book, a weird one, printed with blank pages.

'How does it work?' he asked himself, puffing smoke out like a chimney. 'Is it upside down? Let me see... yeah. Nope.'

A worn-out fag dangled from the left side of his mouth. Albert sucked on it one last time before chucking the butt to the wooden floor.

'Ahem... hem!' he cleared his throat before starting to read:

'The Station Master grabbed the boy by the pussy, no, no this is all wrong. Damn, bloody president Trumpet! ... he grabbed him by the collar, right, better. The boy appeared to be an ok lad, clean and well-dressed, but he made one miserable single mistake in his life: he didn't buy a ticket for that particular journey.'

'What the hell were you thinking? said the Station Master.'

'SLAP! THUMP!'

'I swear to God, I will sue you, you bastard!'

'Shut up, scumbag! You thought you were smart, didn't you? Come here!'

'SBAM! CRACK!'

'Screamed the wooden baton of the uniformed man cranking up on the boy's eyebrow which immediately split open as if human flesh was made of butter and modelling clay. Bloody tears poured down the scarred face like brushstrokes: crimson, thick, oil paint matter.'

'Shit, you're insane. cried the boy, finding his hands covered in that burgundy warm fluid.'

'HEY!'

'I said, SHUT UP! shouted the officer. He had the boy cornered, a couple more blows and he would permanently knock him down. The poor bastard was silent, he had probably fainted by then, and the other passengers cringed, scared to death, trying their best to get the fuck off that fucking station. Fast. Some covered their eyes and ears. Others just looked the other way. All of them but one. A flimsy skinny boy, emaciated but fiery in his heart. He muscled into that massacre and, like the last of western movies' cowboys, he said: What the fuck you think you're doing?'

'The Station Master laughed at him. It took a split-second before he drew his firearm with a threatening frown in his eyes.'

'You wouldn't dare. said Skinny Boy, fearless, but'

'BANG!'

'roared the gun, sticking a bullet into that young right leg.'

'BANG!!! BANG!! BANG!!'

'shot after shot, the Station Mas...'

Suddenly, Albert realised that no one was shooting, neither in his story nor in reality. Instead, someone was knocking at his door. Whatever. He lit another fag and sat down properly, holding his face in his hands. He closed the magic blank book but forgot to dog-ear the page. Amateur. He should have known better, he would never find the path to enter that place again. No way to know how the story ended. Where was Victoria? She would have warned him. 'Too late.' he thought. That moment was already gone, vanished. Forever.

'KNOCK! KNOCK!'

Albert's head was airtight-sealed. He was on another planet.

'Tic-tic-tic-tic...' his pocket watch repeated without feeling any fatigue. That sound slowly emerged from the abyss, reaching Albert's mind. It had him think about the old lady at the Hostel. The radio...

'MAN!'

'She must have it, it belongs to her, to her generation... that's why she wanted it so badly.'

'THUMP-THUMP!'

'Those people... they knew the secret of doing everything with nothing. They were capable of loving life while appreciating the importance of the little things... yeah... the little things...'

'Mate?'

'I will find them all and return them to their owners, one by one, and... Victoria would understand. Indeed.'

'KnOcK-KNoCK!'

'Gosh... Mr Hoover, would you repeat one more time, why on Earth you left her?'

'Tic-tic-tic-tic...' said the pocket watch again.

'KNOCK-SBAM!'

At that very moment, Albert remembered that little game Vic had called Crying Lightning... nope... that was another thing...

'I'm Josh, your flatmate. OPEN THE DOOR!'

'The Sound Hotel! Yes, that's the one. That silly, annoying recording habit she had (who am I kidding?). I should entrap the ticking of my pocket watch on tape. That way she will know. She will read through that sound and see my face, my thoughts and the feelings I carry around with me all the time. Time...'

'SBAM! SBAM! SBAM!'

Subconsciously, he pulled his brand-new mobile phone (courtesy of Steve) out of his pocket and tapped rec.

'blip...'

'Tic-tic-tic-tic...'

'No matter how far we can be, the thousands of miles that separate us, one day we'll share this moment. Stop.' he didn't say.

'Blip.'

It was saved, safe within the depth of the electric circuits of his phone. 'For you.' he typed, naming the audio track. Albert was satisfied. He was feeling so good he lit another fag and cracked his sixth beer can open. *Living the dream.* Also, the obsessive knocking on his door had stopped and silence was now vibrating inside his empty room.

'Vic...'

THIRTY-SIX

Florence. Rooftop Apartment.
'Come on, Tommy, Sophie will be here any minute now.'
'So what?'
'The boy is right. Why do you always have to worry about things??'
'This place is a mess, Rose, we need to tidy up a little!'
'You sound like a fucking mummy.'
'Meaning?'
'You're annoying. And pathetic. Chill out, girl.'
'Mmm...'
'*ding-dong*'
'She's here, she's here!!!!'
'Unbelievable.' sighed Rose as Vic opened the door.
'Sophie! It's such a pleasure to have you here.'
'Thanks for the invitation, darling. Is this your home?'
'It's... er...'
'We're occupying some stranger's property. Like burglars, but with style.' explained Rose.
'Uh, should I be worried?'
'Not at all. Not - At - All (ish). We think the apartment belongs to Albert's grandmother.'
'And... I suppose she knows about you, am I right?' asked Sophie, a bit concerned.
'She... probably... has no clue. But, hey, we're good people and I'd really love to meet her, or Albert...'
'...'
'Look, if anyone pops in, we can always explain the situation. They'll understand, I'm sure we'll be a pleasant surprise.'
'Yeah, keep on dreaming, babe.' said Rose. 'If it was me finding you in my apartment, I'd shoot you in the fucking face.'
'... let's hope Albert's relatives are reasonable people.'
'May I ask why you wanted me here?'
'Sure, Sophie. Tommy, you ready?'

He was. They had a proper presentation set up for her but it wasn't anything hi-tech, no Steve Jobs slideshowing life-changing items onto the walls, no virtual special effects either. They just rehearsed some sort of ancestral, ridiculous theatre scene. Rose hated it but, at the end of the day, well, she couldn't care less.

'Please have a seat.' Vic said, pointing to a magnificent, upholstered vintage chair set in the middle of the otherwise empty room.

'Are you going to blindfold me and tight my wrists with rope?'

'Yeah, burn the witch, baby!'

'Rose... not at all, sorry, Sophie.'

'That would be funny. So, what do I need to do?'

'You'll see it in a moment. Tommy: dim the lights, please.'

'Done. Lampshade on, ready to spin.'

'Oh, Jesus...' snorted Rose, shaking her head.

The room went dark for a second, then, thanks to some cutout images pasted straight on the lampshade, the tongue and groove walls of that tiny flat started carouselling a weird oriental motif. It was unstable, trembling as if alive, and it was, since Tommy, Head of Special Effects, was actually spinning the shade by hand. If you're asking yourself where the boy got that rudimental projector's idea from, I can tell you that it came straight outta YouTube: *Shadow Puppetry | a Chinese folk Art.* Tommy was so inspired by it that he fabricated his own simplified version.

'This is marvellous, I should do it in my shop too.'

'Thank you, Sophie!' he replied from behind his goggles, fully focused on his task.

'Now, Sophie, can you please hold this vial?' asked Vic.

'Like this? What is it?'

'It will be revealed to you at the proper time.'

'Interesting. Can I open it?'

'Sure...'

'POP!'

'shushhhh...'

The precious content was released and an invisible plume of air stolen from that mystic spot on the hills got to Sophie's nostrils. Victoria was electric, so much were her expectations about that very first experiment. Rose was smoking a cigar by the window.

'Mmm... it smells like...'

'Bloody nothing, am I right?'

'Well, Rose, I... I'm not sure. Am I supposed to feel something?'

'Yeah, we thought you might find God in it.'

'Nonsense,' cut short Vic 'this was just... a joke, yeah, a silly prank to break the ice.' she continued, clearly disappointed. 'One out of three, whatever.' she thought to herself.

'Ok. What's next?'

'Here, please have a look at these photographs. It's a bunch of details, close-ups... you know...'

'Wow. Who's the photographer?' Sophie asked, flicking through the album.

One after another, the images scrolled inside Sophie's eyes like a monochrome silent film. The more she got into it, the more she was getting quieter. Victoria was hiding her fingers crossed behind her back. Something was happening.

'Is this... no, it can't be...' Sophie mumbled, stopping at a particular picture. Then she returned to it, she fixed it for a while and finally sprawled a thick mantle of silence over everyone's head.

'Yes...?' Victoria whispered after a moment, ready to gloat.

'Aw, it's probably nothing.' Sophie said as she unblocked herself and went on, till the last page was turned. When she closed the album she felt something odd running up her spine. What was that?

'Victoria... would you mind if I keep it?'

'Not at all. It's yours, really. May I ask why you want it?'

'I sense something powerful behind these pictures, like some sort of...'

'Memory?'

'Maybe. It might be the colours, or... I really don't know what it is.'

'It's Failure n.2 by Chanel, honey.'

'What did Rose just say? Is this a test?'

'What? No. No... no.' hurried to reply Vic. 'You know Rose, she was probably burbling some nonsense out. Shall we move on?'

'Yes. What's in that box?'

'Exactly, it's a tape recorder. We put it there because our Master of Sounds...'

'It's ME!' yelled Tommy.

'... concluded that, somehow, the cardboard case modify the acoustic to a more intense experience.'

'Ingenious. Let's listen. Is it a song?'

'Didn't you just say "let's listen", goddammit? So, listen, you old witch!' didn't shout Rose, sucking so hard on her cigar that she almost choked.

'Ready?'
'Shoot.'
'click:'

The room was injected with white noise. Peace. Then, slowly, a few birds chirped in the distance and a pair of crunching shoes on gravel gave a touch of colour to the unusual soundtrack. Every now and then, cicadas sang their love songs, bringing the warmth of summer nights into that rooftop.

Sophie spaced out. She sensed a series of shivers running up her back like electric shocks. It almost felt like an unexpected massage although she wasn't relaxing, quite the contrary. A sort of positive tension was building up inside her, so she got on her feet, then abandoned herself and fell. Like water down the cascade path, her knees hit the floor.

The box. That hypnotic lullaby was poured out from the scruffy cardboard box in front of her. As if possessed by something beyond human comprehension, her hands reached the flaps, opened them and more sound was released, flooding the room, piercing Sophie's brain.

She couldn't help but grab the audio recorder. She lifted it up as if she was holding the Holy Grail, then she pressed it against her heart and started crying. Even Rose was shocked by then.

'What the heck is going on?' everyone asked themselves, Sophie included.

Vic was radiant, and scared, and *woah!*, at the same time. Did they just summon an ancient divinity, a supernatural creature? Was it dangerous? All the buzzing questions sharply disappeared from the air when the music stopped and the recorder clicked off. Sophie was weeping profoundly, like a child, a silly little baby. It was one of those moments when you sob so hard that you think you're going to die, you're short of breath and you're exhausted yet free. As if that painful stream of tears managed to carve everything out from your body; as if it washed your soul with bleach, removing the stains, all the bad vibes you forced deep inside yourself, leaving you with a sense of peace.

Inner calm.
Quietness.
Shhhhhh...

THIRTY-SEVEN

Early Morning. Mile End.
Albert was jingling a bunch of keys inside his pocket. He just got off the local Pub (they kicked him out, to be accurate) where a middle-aged woman mopping the filthy floor shouted at him, 'WE'RE CLOSED!!' her voice rising above a cool tune that was pumping loud inside the empty room. It was some classic hit from the '80s, one you can't help but sing along, and dance; one that immediately stuck into Albert's mind like a dangerous disease. In fact, he was now whistling it on his way to his new home. Albert was feeling supersonic.

'Yo!' he nodded to a local who was minding his own business, smoking a fag in his miniature front garden.

'Nice day, uh?'

'Innit?' the neighbour replied, flipping a very explicit middle finger.

'Rude... but we'll get to be friends soon.' thought Albert, confident. Two more steps and he was in front of his apartment's door. He pulled the keys and reached for the lock.

'Weird.'

The door was open.

'Creeeak...' it said, swinging on its rusty hinges.

The floor was littered with all sorts of shit. A few drawers were piled up next to the plaster arch leading to the kitchen and cheap cutlery was scattered all over the corridor.

'Who's there?' Albert asked to the insistent noise muscling out from the other room. 'Anyone?' he tried again when, suddenly, a very dark, very upset black face popped out from the decaying arch.

'Got a problem, man?'

'Are you a burglar?' asked Albert, naturally.

'What? Who the fuck are you?'

'Albert. I'm Albert Hoover. Nice to meet you.'

'...'

'Listen, mate, I don't have credit on my phone and, honestly, I'm not in the mood for calling the police anyway. Those idiots at the call centre...'

'Wait a sec.'

'... never let you speak, it's ridiculous. Last time I phoned... however, do you mind shutting the door when you're done with whatever you're stealing?'

'I'm not a burglar, man. I live here.'

'Excellent! One less trouble. So, do you have an unrestrained passion for mayhem or it's just a hobby?'

'Uh?'

'I mean, trashing homes. Is it your thing?'

'You looking for trouble or what?'

'Me?'

'Yes, you, you piece of shit. First, you accuse me of...'

'Woah, woah, no need to clench our fists and get violent, mate, it's all good now. Tell me: what did they do to you?'

'Some motherfucker stole my keys!'

'Bummer. Where did you stash them?'

'I always chuck them into the flower pot hung outside, next to the door.'

'Oh, you mean these?'

'You son of a...'

'Hey!, hey!' Albert yelled as the black guy grabbed him by the collar, lifted him a few inches off the floor and adjusted his slim body against the wall.

'I'VE BEEN LOOKING FOR THEM FOR HOURS, YOU ASSHOLE!!'

'Ahem...' said Albert, his feet touching the linoleum again. 'It's just a bunch of keys...'

'Give 'em to me!'

'Sure, why not. They're yours.'

'You're totally nuts, man.'

'What's your name?'

'Fuck off.'

'Nice to meet you, Fuck Off. Listen:'

'Oh, goddammit. Josh, I'm Josh.'

'No way... you were knocking at my door last night!'

Josh's eyes went mad again, his muscles tightened up and a pretty large vein started pumping like crazy over his forehead.

'Mate, I was busy. What was so important it couldn't wait until tomorrow?'

'You... I thought there was a fire. I was walking the stairs up to my room when I saw thick smoke flushing out from under your door.'

'Right, sorry. I couldn't open the window, it's probably broken.'

'So?'

'So, I lay down Liam Gallagher Definitely Maybe cover style, and puffed the shit out from that tiny gap.'

'Why didn't you go to the garden, man?'

'You know... it's cold.'

'...'

'Hey, I'm not a fool, I'm not planning to burn down this shack and kill the eight people living in it.'

'Ten. We're ten now.'

'Whatever, you can trust me.'

'Next time just fucking go outside.'

'Yes, mum. Where are you going now?' Albert asked, tailing his new friend Josh.

'I need coffee.'

'Great idea! Let's have it.' he said as if he was invited.

'Don't you dare asking for any milk, cause I ain't got it.'

'Oatmilk?'

'I said any milk, didn't I?'

'Almond milk?'

'You deaf?'

'Ok, why?'

'Why what?'

'You don't have it.'

'I don't like it, okay?'

'Childhood traumas?'

'WTF, man. Why don't you shut up?'

And, strangely enough, Albert got silent for a moment. He was distracted by the overwhelming chaos possessing the room. He needed some space but cleaning wasn't exactly his thing, especially in such extreme situations. So, out of the blue, he pulled the plastic tablecloth with a sharp stroke imitating what experienced magicians and tricksters do in their shows. Epic - Fail. Everything was shattered to the floor in a big *CRASH!*

The next-door neighbour jumped from his chair and hurried to the communal wall to shout a bunch of obscenities. It wasn't anything new but this time he sounded nastier than usual so Josh frowned a respect-man frown at Albert. Without saying a thing, he placed a pot filled with water on the hob and shoved three spoonfuls of dried instant coffee into two filthy, stained mugs. Then, he sat in front of Albert.

'Cigarette?'
'Cigarette.'
'frrrusssshh' said the lighter, burning the tips of their fags.
'PuFF, PUFFFF, PUFFFFFFFF!!!'

Silence invaded the kitchen for a while. They were chain-smoking a shameful amount of tobacco like damned sailors or freaking damaged soldiers. Time disappeared. Everything vanished from their minds, including the pot on the hob which was melting, incandescent, obviously empty by now, dripping tears of liquid plastic from the already wrecked handle. An awful smell was filling the room and the insanely toxic fumes blood-shot the guys' eyes like crazy. So, Josh stood up, turned off the hob and sat back on his chair. He crossed his legs and arms again and got back to his staring-at-the-void game. The clock was ticking without rest as they went on staring at each other. Not a word. No awkward conversations. The only interludes of that silent TV show were due to the obvious, primary-need questions:

'Cigarette?'
'Cigarette.'
'frrrusssshh' said the lighter, burning the tips of their fags.
'PuFF, PUFFFF, PUFFFFFFFF!!!'

They were so abstracted that, at some point Josh even guzzled the dried coffee powder from his mug forgetting that no one ever poured water in it. He coughed and silently cried for a while but never laid his sight off Albert's face. Other moves that occurred every now and then were the occasional legs' swapping and the seat's shifting, performed in order to let the blood flow back inside the pale-white parts of their bodies.

Finally, Albert took courage and asked:
'You're not a man of words, are you?'
'Shut up.'

And so he did. Feeling on cloud nine for having found such a great new friend.

THIRTY-EIGHT

Vintage Wanders, Late Night

The whole crew was still moved by what happened that day, up on the sweating-hot rooftop.

'Magic.'

'Pure Magic.' confirmed Tommy.

'Bullshit. It was just a coincidence, Vic.'

'I don't think so, Rose.'

'Actually, you're right. It was the perfect scam. You set it up like an old experienced medium that claims to be able to speak to the dead.'

'...'

'Great job, by the way. For once, I think I owe you my dishonest congratulations.'

'Yeee!!' said Tommy, excited. 'So, if Vic is a witch, that makes me a wizard?'

'You got it, pal.'

'Except we're not, absolutely not. Right, Sophie?'

'Indeed. There are no such things in this world.'

'Great. So, it does work. You did have that moment back in your hands, didn't you?'

'Ah, it certainly awoke stuff, I'm still shaking. However...'

'Yes?'

'... Rose has a point.'

'You got to be kidding me.'

'Well... the room was set in advance, and you were trying to control all the reactions, like the invisible hand of a puppeteer.'

'But...'

'I'm not saying it wasn't good, mind me, it's just... you might want to try it again in order to get better at it and avoid mistakes.'

'True...'

'Don't give me that sad look, darling. I'll have your priceless gift with me for the rest of my life. Every time I feel down, I'll reach for the pictures, the sounds and smell of that moment. I'll be forever thankful to you for it.' Sophie said, miming a graceful bow imbued with gratitude.

'*And so they kissed, made love and lived a long, happy life.* Disgusting. Let's cut the crap. What now?' said Rose.

'?'

'I mean, since you're so convinced you found the key to crack humankind's secret doors open, what should we do with it?'

'We will help all the people in this world!!' Tommy intervened.

'Yeah, let's win the next Mother Teresa's Award. You-guys-suck. Period.'

'Rose, be patient, we'll figure it out.'

'Patien... WHAT??'

'Chill out, Rose.' added Tommy, grinning.

'I AM FUCKING CHILLED!!! THERE IS NO TIME TO WASTE, YOU IDIOTS!!'

Sophie was giggling. She felt like she was either attending the worst-ever robbery meeting, or... no, that was it. She had to intervene.

'I think, and I might be wrong, that first of all, you should try it again, on different people.'

'Scientific approach. I agree.' said Tommy.

'Bollocks. Let's capitalise on it.' Rose cut in. 'Why don't you write a fucking book, Vic? Even mules and politicians do it these days. We should use the spiritual angle. The "Energetic Spheres" of my ass or the damn hippie-naturalistic bullshit. Let's call it *The Meaning of Life REVEALED*, or, better, *Enlightenment 101.*'

'Nah...'

'Please, Vic, shut up. What do you know about marketing??'

'...'

'Follow me on this. First: we google *oldest man on Earth*, we steal his picture and photoshop a freaking turban on his head (or we shave his skull like Buddha). Then we stick a red dot in the middle of his eyebrows. SBAM! done.'

'...'

'Second. We print your shit in every format: hardcover, paperback, eBook, audio crap, we could even drop books from a skywriting plane. Everyone must have it, hoboes, toddlers, grannies! Then...'

'Seriously?'

'Here's the juice. Figurines. And dolls of you healing people. Picture this: Holy-Vic Barbie, like the Pope of Derelicts. We can have one with your arm extended, intent on resurrecting the dead; one with praying hands.'

'I don't think so.'

'Umph... so... a movie! A fucking movie will do the ultimate scam! The Disney guys will make us superstars: red carpet, us wearing million-dollar long dresses while waving hands like Queens to the cheering crowd of maniacs. We must throw buckets of holy water in their idiotic faces and have real diamonds falling on our heads from the sky, like confetti while we perform our triumphant catwalk. Don't even say it. I'm a genius, I know. And finally...'

'Incredible. You have more?'

'Merchandise. T-shirts, freaking cheap plastic vials printed with our logo, official recording devices, approved photographic paper and cameras to shoot your goddamn healing pictures at home, Jesus Christ I'm on a roll, how can you not see the potential??'

Rose was speeding her ghost brain at full throttle. She was so possessed she wasn't even drinking or smoking no more. She was gesturing, drawing imaginary graphs in the air, on invisible blackboards. And, truth be told, all that delusional outburst wasn't news for Vic or Tommy, so they didn't really pay attention to the plan. Sophie, instead, was focused, analysing details and pondering options as if the whole thing was feasible, somehow legit and worth trying.

'Rose is right.' she said.

'Sophie?! You can't be serious. She's the Devil.'

'Yes, she's pretty radical, sorry, Rose.'

'Apologies accepted.'

'But, if you read within her words you will see that her approach is the right one.'

'I don't want to trick anyone.'

'You must not. All I'm saying is that since you guys have so many brilliant ideas, genuine expedients that can help lots of people, it would be a shame not to share/sell them to the world.'

'See? Money. We should make some CA$H for once!' said Rose, her eyes sparkling coins in the air like Uncle Scrooge.

'Yes, make something out of your talent.' continued Sophie.

'Not again...' thought Victoria.

'You know what, why don't you open a shop?'

'Like the Vintage Wonders, yay!!!' shrieked Tommy.

'But...'

'We could sell your blank books, Vic.'

'Hell yeah, Tommy boy.' said Rose. 'We could call them something catchy, like...'

'WanderBooks!'

'Horrible. But, at least, you're following me now.'

'Yeeee!'

'Besides,' added Sophie 'why not think about workshops, live experiences, or, I don't know, you could write a blog, use Instagram,'

'Insta what?'

'TikTok? I'm confident you'll end up publishing a book too.' added Sophie.

'Are you for real?'

'I am, darling.'

'You're all out of your minds...'

THIRTY-NINE

'I'm not crazy!'

'If you say so...'

'Please, Josh, sell me your radio, it's important! You will make an adorable very old lady touching the sky.'

'Christ, Albert, I told you, it was my grandfather's, I can't give it to you.'

'You're not using it, for God's sake! I bet you don't even know how to switch it on.'

'Do you?'

'What? Sure. I guess... fuck, we're missing the point here. The radio is not for me.'

'...'

'Give it to meeee!!'

'NOOOO!!!'

In a desperate attempt, Albert tried to grab the radio by sort of climbing Josh (yes, he's that big). Silly. Or, was it? Somehow, Albert managed to pinch Josh's arm quite hurtfully and the ancient frequency transmitter swung and twirled in the air like a soapy bubble. It felt like time froze and the camera did a full 360 around them as in The Offspring's The Kids Aren't Alright's video.

'Cool.' thought Albert.

Josh was crying inside. His radio, his precious granddad's relic was going to hit the floor in a split-second. All his life, he dedicated a dusty corner of his room to that priceless thing. The world was about to end for him. Doomsday's approaching. *Where are the locusts?* Isn't God on his/her/its way to kick our asses out of this planet once and for all? He was already weeping, knees down on the floor when Albert (don't ask how), catched the radio with one hand. Just one. I swear.

'Voila`. You can stop crying now.'

'Man, you're dead.'

'Tut-tut. Everything's under control. You're simply a compulsive paranoid.' said Albert.

'I KILL YOU!!'

'Aw, what a big word. Mate, I'm not gonna abandon your radio in a pawn shop, I will not crack it open to see what's inside and yes, I'm not willing to get any money out of it.'

'I don't fucking care. It's mine. Give it back.'

'You're impossible. I'll tell you what. When this beautifully gentle and kind aged lady will die with a sad face because of you, because you decided to deprive her of the joy of her life, she will haunt your dreams, forever. Her unhappiness will follow you everywhere, anytime. It will curse each step you take, and all of this because you didn't want to...'

'Fuck off, you bastard.'

'Uh?'

'Albert?'

'That's me.'

'Keep it.'

'Thanks, Josh.'

'Bring it to granny but I don't want to hear no shit about no fucking radio ever again in my life.'

'Deal! Mate, you're the best, I mean, thanks for the radio. You did right, my friend.'

'I ain't your friend and please don't mention the...'

'Radio, yes, absolutely.'

'Precisely.'

'Coffee?'

'Why not.'

'A steam-hot cuppa before delivering the radio sounds like a great plan.'

'Oh, my...'

'Mate, we need to celebrate! Let's put on some music, let's turn the radio on!'

Josh was undecided whether to kill or try to sedate him with the good-old odd television programme. He knew that deep down Albert was a softie, a sucker for cartoons, so, definitely, a cartoon channel would have done the job, it always worked with kids. And

tap.

He switched on the telly but instead of some Disney whatever, MTV popped on the screen. Dammit. Eels' *Electro-Shock Blues* played loud from the cheap flat speakers, spraying more chaos in the already tense room. But Albert, like a perfect nitwit (or a typical 90s kid) fell in the trap anyway. Suddenly, he was rapt by the screen. Fully zombied up. He even started dancing on the spot, true story! So, brilliant, settled at last. No matter how. Josh resumed shovelling instant coffee and pouring lava-hot water into their mugs. Coffee and cigarettes. Typical day at 45 Treby Street.

Outside the door window, a shy substitute of the sun was spilling a sort of light, a dim enough invitation for Albert to keep popping in and out from kitchen to garden for a glorious sunbath. The garden. Aww, the garden: as every other claim or promise made by the JB Link agent, the backyard wasn't exactly the English Garden marvel Albert expected to be. It was more like a dumping site decorated with piles of scraps coming straight from the poor renovation works done on the house. But there was more: a rusty bike and a kid's three-wheels topping a graceful bramble; door frames eaten up by thorns, bushes, and all; the occasional dog-sized rat strolling quietly around his private kingdom.

The only *good* piece in there was an adorable, rustic bench and table set. Ok, it creaked and squeaked but, hey, somehow it resisted Gravity. That was the place where Albert and Josh shared their common passion. Chain-smoking. Guzzling litres of coffee. Re-chain smoking. Re-guzzling dark shit.

'When will you deliver the thing?'

'So, now it's unpronounceable.'

'Yes, like Voldemort.'

'Fair enough. I'll bring "the thing" to the lady very soon. At the proper time.'

'You figure. Do we have more coffee?'

'Sure. I just turned the hob on.'

'Why do we have to use a bloody Moka pot?'

'Oh, Josh... seriously?'

'...'

'It gives us a classy touch. We should act like real gentlemen. High society cats.'

'Yeah... do you want more instant coffee while we wait?'

'Definitely, the Italian marvel takes a lifetime. But, when it works, it simply pours out the best five tiny drops of black nectar in the world. Five delicious, genuine...'

'It's worthless.'

'May be. Hey, Josh, it that the sun?'

'What?'

'That silver medallion hiding behind the clouds. Can you see it?'
'Well, it's round and slightly blinding. It must be it.'
'Fab. Amazing. Great. Stunning.'
'Innit?'
'Shit, I'm thrilled. Is it gonna show up?'
'Nah, it's still June.'
'Right. Silly me.'
'Silly you.'
'...'
'...'
'Josh?'
'What now?'
'It's radio time, mate.'

FORTY

The sinuous back of an imaginary snake was calmly gliding in the distance. Vic was observing the hilly landscape outside Florence for the last time, chilling on the front seat of David's TAXI. They were heading back to Pisa airport, on their way to a new mission, a big one step that was freaking Victoria out.

'Still brooding about Sophie's shop?' asked Rose.

'What else?'

'Right.'

'You know, this morning, before leaving the rooftop apartment, I was washing my face and...'

'You mean plunging your head into a sink filled with ice cubes?'

'It wakes me up.'

'I bet.'

'Anyway, I was staring at my reflection and asked myself if I'll ever find the courage, the strength to do what Sophie did with her life.'

'We are going back to England, aren't we?'

'Yes... yes. It's just... there are only a few ones like Sophie on this planet.'

'Hey, she had an idea. She tried it. It worked.'

'It sounds so easy when you say it like that, Rose.'

'It is, darling. Remember that movie we watched a while ago?'

'Nope.'

'The McDonald's story.'

'The Founder?' said Tommy.

'Precisely. You're not as useless as you might seem after all.'

'...' replied Tommy's grimace.

'What's so important about this movie, Rose?'

'One word: persistence.'

'Easier said than done.'

'You're such a thickhead sometimes. Let me tell you a secret, Victoria: the people willing to risk anything at all are just a small bunch. No one dares to face a genuine, straightforward NO. So, nobody makes a move. Wouldn't it be cool to go out and try grabbing a bloody YES, for once?'

'What are you blathering about?'

'How the hell do you think you're gonna change the world if you don't try hard?'

'Who said anything about changing the world?'

'You did, goddammit. You and your bloody Morvar Company stories!'

'Yes, you did!' confirmed Tommy.

'Well... I might have given you the impression, but...'

'Great. Great. So let's get back to good-old Sherlintock (the smallest, miserable-est village in the Universe) and sleep it off. We shall return to visiting the two-platforms-only train station and read blank books, get pestered by local authorities and play the fool. Let's re-embrace the safe boring routine cuz what else could you do in your life? You're just a coward, a chicken, like your dear Albert.'

'What?' Victoria burst out.

'Yeah, I never thought about it but you two are a great match indeed.'

'Don't you dare.'

'*Ohhh*, look at us, we're so special, we can make the world spin backwards. *Uhhhh*, we're so good, we want to help people, we want to fucking save the Planet, we...'

'ENOUGH!!'

David was trying his best to mind his own business and stick to the driving task but the situation was getting out of hand. Victoria was bonkers, yelling and even punching/kicking God knows what like a maniac while strapped to her seatbelt. She was obviously talking to herself since only a few humans could see or hear Rose. Long story short, inside that TAXI you could have witnessed a proper nutcase possessed by the Devil, speaking to Satan. The next thing you would expect is her head to rotate 180 degrees, like the girl in The Exorcist movie.

'GOOD, EH?' David said out loud, trying to calm things down, mostly for his own sanity.

'GOOD WHAT???' screamed Vic.

'There you go, they're gonna lock you up in a classic nuthouse and throw the key away just like Frances Farmer.' grinned Rose.

'SHUT - THE FUCK - UP'

'CALMA, CALMA!! STO GUIDANDO DIO CRISTO!' shouted David too, now unleashing the Italian language.

The deep, rough tone of his manly voice instantly silenced them all. Tommy returned to his seat and even fastened his belt for the first time ever.

Vic blushed of shame as if she just awoke from some trans-human experience, a nightmare, a bad trip.

Rose frowned and, 'ladies and gents, our Italian friend just freed out a marvellously clear expression that included the swearing of God. Geez, I love this man.' she declared, triumphant.

'I think he wants us to calm down...' whispered Tommy.

'I'm so sorry, David... so sorry...' apologised Vic, trying her best to erase the previous image of her from his mind.

'Eh, no. No fighting people.'

'...' they all replied together.

'Why fighting? So beautiful day, please! Airport is five minutes now. Smile, enjoy the sun, the skies, the...'

'There we go again...' thought Rose.

'Ok, I have solution. Smoke?'

'No, thank you, David.' replied Vic.

'Come on, you smoke, I smoke. Take it.' he insisted, lighting two fags at once and literally sticking one through Vic's lips. She was astonished.

'*PuFF, PuFF* like this. No really healthy but... you know, sometimes.'

'*puff, pUffF...*' tried Vic.

'BRAVA! Cosi', like this. Relax.'

'*PUFF, PUFF*' continued Victoria, now more confident and '*PUFF PUFFFF, CAUGH*, ARGH - *COUGH* - DAMN - *COUGHH!!!*'

'Bloody amateur.' commented Rose, shaking her imaginary head.

'Hey, I can see the airport!' cut in Tommy.

'Aeroporto Galileo Galilei. Two minute.' said David, with pride.

'Finally, this charade is over.' grumbled Rose.

Vic's face was now close to a whiter shade of pale.

The car stopped right in front of the gates' entrance, David turned off the engine and helped with the luggage.

'Hey, no worry face. Please.' David told to his new weirdo friends.

Victoria was sad to leave that welcoming country and sad to say goodbye to David who had been such a great host. She threw her arms around him in an endless hug and almost shed a few tears.

'Thank you, David, you've been the BEST!'

'The Best...' that was a term he easily understood. Best pizza, best football team, best...

'See you next time, my friend.' Vic yelled as she rolled her trolley away, through the sliding doors, waving goodbye.

'My friend.' David was jolly. Touching the sky. Not only he was now the absolute BEST taxi driver in the whole bleedin' world. He was also a friend, family. He was already picturing himself having tea at Buckingham Palace. 5 o'clock, sharp. God knows, he might also have received an invitation letter to visit the United Kingdom, personally signed by none other than Her Majesty the Queen. He then imagined grabbing the phone and making an urgent call:

'Hey, it's me, David. I need you to redesign and print my business cards.' he thought, in Italian. 'You should add a crown on top of my name. Yes, like the Royals, and don't forget to place a huge stamp somewhere, certifying that I'm the BEST TAXI DRIVER. The wife will be so proud of me.' he said to himself, drumming on the steering wheel, ready for the next client.

'Good Day. Good day.' chanted Davide Morianti, and smiled one of his broad smiles, as usual. He was glowing as bright as the Italian sun.

THREE

CLOUD NINE

FORTY-ONE

Mile End, summer: sun shining up in the sky, drug dealers, gangs freely roaming the streets and trash, scattered everywhere on the pavement. The amount of garbage was so overwhelming that you had to be a professional zig-zager to avoid every single bit. Stuff like: cheap fast food boxes assaulted by crows; empty cans; the occasional used condom; spare doors/crumbling furniture sitting against the brickwalls; *a fridge?*; bike's skeletons and, of course, shiny bags of crisps flavoured whatever. Ah, did I mention the hundreds of empty hippy crack bottles sitting next to the curb? God bless the East End. Albert was about to hit the road.

'Josh, I'm leaving!'

'Yeah man, never come back.'

'Such a funny guy.' thought Albert, then shouted 'You know, I'm on a *Top Secret* mission named Eagle's Beak: deliver the radio.'

'Not so secret now, is it?'

'Well... you're the only one who knows.'

'Whatever.'

'Nevermind.'

He shut the door, pulled his military jacket collar up and announced 'Yo! I'm living the dream!', introducing himself to the street mob who instantly turned at him like a wolfpack, wearing the usual serious faces. With a certain nonchalance, Albert flipped his baseball cap sideways and (somehow) put on his brand-new headset.

'tap, tap.'

'tap tap, tap. Play.'

'*'Cause you can't, you won't. AND YOU DON'T STOP!*' he sang, playback-ing the Beastie Boys track saved on his phone, starting the journey into *Ill Communication*.

'Who's that fucker?' a guy from the other side of the street asked his crew.

Albert was on top of the world and the music was pumping as loud as Dave Grohl beating the shit out of a drum set. He grabbed the old radio and pulled it over his shoulder as if it was a classic boombox coming straight outta the '80s. Although it wasn't. The odd case was made of pinewood, pretty ugly, with a chunky valve and other shit you could see from the opened back.

'*giggy giggy ch-ch-ch jaw gaga gaga jaw check...*', Albert was scratch-scratching random words along with the beat, feeling the hypnotic rhythm shaking his bones.

'What the fuck is he up to?'

'DO IT!!' he shouted.

'??'

'That's the song I need.' he said, tapping track 14.

'TA-RA, bum bum, TA-RA, bum bum, TA-RA...' he sang as he bounced on his legs walking his way to the tube station.

'TUM-TUM, ta-ra, TUM-TUM, ta-ra...'

Now he was even spinning imaginary vinyl in the air with his spare hand. That, and his upbeat funky walk, made clear to everyone that a complete idiot had arrived in town.

'Rappin' my shit out, mate!' he yelled to an unfortunate random pedestrian and 'Yo yo yo yo yo!' he fired around, like a machine gun.

It was all perfect until he crossed paths with a very healthy, very protein-shake, pumped-up black man who didn't appear to be happy about his day.

'YO!' Albert shouted in his face without even stopping.

A gigantic hand grabbed him by the jacket, demanding attention. It pulled Albert's headphones off and

'Yo, what?' the big man asked, with a grave face.

'Yo... brother?' Albert tried.

'What the fuck? You ain't callin' me no bruv, man!'

'Yo, list...'

'SLAP!' loudly sounded the black hand over his face.

'Woah... you really do work out at the gym, don't you?'

Everyone was observing now.

'None of your business.'

'It's alright, I guess this is just an alternative way of becoming friends, innit?'

'We ain't no friends.' the guy replied, still angry, still gripping on Albert's arm.

"*Never ask anyone about their bad days when they're clearly having a bad day.*" thought Albert, remembering one of the many priceless pieces of advice from Pete.

'Bad day, brother?' he eventually asked.

'Brother? You son of a...' the man didn't even finish his sentence. His huge hands (freshly manicured, by the way), grabbed Albert by the belt and lifted him from the pavement. The mob was giggling, circling the scene, increasingly curious about the outcome of that fight. An army of smartphones was filming from every imaginable angle.

'Yo, gimme some love, where's all this rage coming from?'

'DON'T - YO - ME. AIGHT?' he basically spat in Albert's numb face, an inch far from it. 'O'AIGHT?' he repeated, and, since Albert looked like he was about to cry, the man put an end to that poor scene. He eased the grip and let the annoying fool back down.

A roar of claps and woos crashed the silent tension as the big black man straightened his expensive suit and slowly walked away. He had just disappeared around the corner when Albert shouted:

'Yo! You're lucky I wasn't set on war-mode!'

'Get the fuck out of here, man.' a guy from the crowd told him.

And so he did. But without shame, without feeling pathetic, a loser or, I don't know, defeated. He couldn't care less.

Albert put on a fearless smirk and fucked off. Matters of inimaginable importance needed his attention. A precious piece of analogic garbage had to be delivered to granny.

FORTY-TWO

Greenwich, London.

Victoria's fool team was strolling about the busy streets filled with Sunday Summer Tourists (yeah, it's a thing.). After a quick stop at Sherlintock and a thirteen hours sleep to recover from the Italian experience, they packed their bags again and headed to the big city, where the streets are paved with gold and luck is waiting for you around the corner. Innit?

However, the dreamers' bunch was now fully immersed in the London vibe, unconsciously rolling along with the flow like pebbles in a stream, running a race with no winners or prizes, holding Costa coffee paper cups. Classic.

'Where are we going, Vic?'

'We're looking for the perfect place to open our shop.' she gently replied to Tommy.

'Really? I thought we were having another vacation.'

'That too.'

'I'm confused.'

'The trick is to keep on walking until the place will reveal itself to us, naturally.'

'Naturally...' commented Rose

'That's how it works, we just have to be patient.'

'Of all places, why on earth are we in Greenwich?'

'Because, Rose. It's beautiful.' simply replied Vic, her gaze lost among the clouds.

'It's damn expensive, you fool. And, please, stop staring at the sky, you're gonna end up bumping into a...'

'LAMPPOST!' yelled Tommy, pulling Vic away from a sure crash. She didn't even notice.

'Maybe, if Your Majesty would even care to look at the surroundings, we might find a decent shack.'

'Oh, Rose, you're so ordinary...'

'I'm what?? I don't even exist, you son of a gun.'

'Rude as always...' said Tommy, shaking his head.

'Ok, let me guide you. I'll be your eyes.' said Rose. 'Here comes the live commentary.'

'?'

'Ladies and gents, here is Rose for BBC One, reporting from Greenwich. The sun is shining high in the sky therefore all the miserable, the poor and the bloody tourists are polluting the streets with their smiles and sweaty, colourful t-shirts. Oh, my, BREAKING NEWS! A damn kid is yelling nonsense as if it's his mother-*beep*-fucking birthday party.'

'...'

'Too bad a double decker just missed him. Anyhow, we are now passing by Greenwich Market where street fooders and thieves, bargain their filthy rubbish for shitloads of money with the easy foreign preys.'

'Yummy!! I want a burger!!' yelled Tommy, licking his lips.

'Fuhgeddaboudit.'

'What?'

'Vic, can you hear me? I am now interviewing a dumb miniature man who doesn't know about the iconic Brooklyn-Mobsters say.'

'Yes, I can hear you. We're not interested, Rose.'

'What's your name, little monster?'

'You know my name. I'm Tommy!'

'Cool, so, Tommy, do you think we will ever find the perfect spot for our shop?'

'Yes!'

'Brilliant, he just replied he doesn't think so.'

'LIAR!'

'The kid looks emaciated, and sad, and he's crying, possibly because of extreme starvation, malnutrition, and the forced labour he is subjected to. I am thinking about calling Children Services, can you confirm from the studio?'

'There's no studio whatsoever, Rose, and you're not a reporter.'

'Exactly, let's call the Police.'

'...'

'Hey, hey, hey, great news! We're approaching the path towards the Old Royal Naval College where we'll probably damp the minor, for good.'

'Are you done?'

'Nope. Time for a quick commercial:' Rose said, stopping that gipsy parade. She cleared her throat and, posing like a real pro, looked straight into an imaginary camera: 'Join the Army, folks. Give some meaning to your useless existence.' she announced, sticking her thumbs up.

'Why are you always so mean?'

'Sorry, I can't hear you, we're experiencing technical issues and, WOAH, didn't we just take a sharp turn and head into a busy street? Holy yeah we did. Cars are stuck in traffic: oiks and foreigners are crossing the road from every spot causing chaos. Where are the damn coppers when you need them? Order, ORDER!!!'

'Stay quiet, Rose.'

'Unleash the batons, kill the lawless motherfuckers!!'

'ENOUGH!'

'Still, no vacant shops in sight. What do you think, li'l Tommy?'

'I'm not "little".'

'Have you been in the dream-selling business for long?'

'Vic, have you seen that sign?'

'Sorry, the child appears to be utterly deaf too. I'll try to ask him again. Have you...'

Finally, Vic shifted her attention from clouds chasing clouds in the air to a more common, horizontal view. On the other end of the road, laid a big red adhesive strip saying "CLOSING DOWN". She smacked a kiss to Tommy and, grabbing his tiny hand, she hurried to the spot.

'Ladies and gents, we are now crossing the road without any respect for the law and...'

'BEEEEEP!!!!'

'We've almost been run over by a car, this is getting interesting, folks, I might be dead in a sec, please remember me!' continued Rose.

'HONK! BEEEEP!!!!'

'And *phewww*, we just landed on the other side in one piece. Ish. But don't cry for me, Argentina! Ups, I'm afraid I just shat my pants.'

'Gross...'

'Right. We're finally standing in front of a shop for sale. Will it be the one? Do we actually care? I don't think so.'

'Bye-bye, Rose!' said Tommy, entering the building. Vic didn't even bother byeing her.

'And that's all for now. This was Rose for BBC One reporting from Greenwich. Till the next one. Try not to die, you mortals.'

FORTY-THREE

'*Buzz, buzz. BUZZZZ!!*' the doorbell outside the Notting Hill Hostel demanded attention.

'Not him... not him again.'

'Hi, I'm Albert. Albert Hoover. Remember me?'

'How could I not?' the *receptionist* sadly thought. 'Yes, you are the gentleman... is that, a radio?'

'Precisely. I'm here for a delivery.'

'?'

'Is Mrs... the old lady still here?'

'Sure, sure. Hey, don't even think about pulling some crazy stuff like you did last time. We still need to fix the window.'

'You have my word, mate.'

'Yeah, whatever... she's sitting in the lounge, please be quick and don't you dare making any noise.'

'Absy-lutely.'

The entrance door swung open and Albert jumped inside. Mrs Something was reading a book while sitting on her favourite Chesterfield chair (where else?). When she noticed Albert coming into the room, she immediately glowed of some inner light she probably had dismissed a long time ago.

'What a pleasure to meet you again!' she said, trying to get on her feet.

'As you were.' said Albert acting like Frank Reagan, the Police Commissioner from *Blue Bloods*. 'No need to do extraordinary physical exercise.'

'What is that? A box of veggies? For me?'

'Christ, she's blind as a bat.' he thought to himself. 'Let me help you. Here, take your glasses.'

'Thank you, dear. Oh my gosh... is it?'

'Yep, no veggies for you, sorry.'

'A Utility Radio! I can't believe my eyes!!'

'You shouldn't, really.'

'What?'

'I said, such a beautiful day, innit?'

'Indeed. Indeed. How did you do it?'

'Well, I didn't do much. The sun is shining, birds are chirping... it's a beautiful day.'

'No, I mean the radio... how did you find it? How could you know this was exactly the right one?'

'Look at me. I'm a professional.'

'...' she sniggered.

'Oh, whatever, I didn't have a clue, okay? I thought this one was old enough for you to appreciate and... Hello? Are you listening to me?'

The lady was speechless, almost moved. She slightly caressed the old relic while lost in God-knows-what age or time. Then, her face got closer to the dusty thing, so close that her nose touched the pinewood of the radio. She kept adjusting her glasses to try and focus on the details. Indeed, blind as a bat.

'So?' asked Albert, waiting for the final approval.

Suddenly, (I'm joking, it took minutes) Mrs Something stood up on her feet and threw (again, she wasn't quick) her arms over Albert's shoulders.

'Thank you...' she whispered, shedding silent tears, trying to keep the composure and dignity so common among the elders. Albert didn't expect that reaction, he didn't know how to behave or what to do so, he just let her sob and weep over his shoulder, where no one would see her.

Finally, they sat back on their chairs without saying a word. Albert was puzzled. He didn't expect to feel or cause emotions of such magnitude, and he even felt guilty for taking that game so lightly when in fact, it wasn't frivolous at all.

'Thank you.' the old lady repeated for the 10th time, now looking thirty years younger. 'My husband and I bought a radio like this one not long after we got married. It was the first thing we brought when we moved into our very first home.'

'...'

'You know, my Paul was so proud of our radio. He handed it to me one night, as a special gift for the days to come. He was always playing with me, so he wrapped it in tons of newspaper sheets and stashed the lot inside a very big crate which was filled with crumpled paper and contained a smaller box also stuffed with shreds, and confetti, and...'

'No way, like a Russian doll?'

'Yes. It took me ten minutes to get rid of all that packaging. Ah, my good-old Paul...' she sighed. 'When I finally dug out the present, I was happy as a child. We both felt like we were rich, as if we were owners of the most precious thing in the world.'

'I see...'

'I was listening to the radio at all hours, every day. It was my escape from the bad things happening in London and around the world.'

'Sure.'

'Anyway, shall we turn it on?'

'Absolutely.' replied Albert like a good soldier, although he had no clue on how to make that bloody relic work. He was trying his best when Mrs Something intervened:

'What are you doing?' she asked, trying to conceal a warm smile. 'You don't need to shake it.'

'Right. Should I pull one of these levels?'

'Yes, dear, but not yet.'

'I'm not exactly sure I understood, madam.' he confessed.

'It's very simple. First, you have to plug it in.'

'Aw, clearly.' Albert said, finally getting there.

'*BzzzZZZzzZ FRrushshs*' the radio was finally alive and the old lady started DJing with the knobs. She pushed the volume to the max.

'I can see that you pefectly know your way around it.'

'I told you, it was part of my life.'

'WHAT'S GOING ON THERE?' shouted the reception guy from behind his desk in the other room.

'MATE! I DIDN'T DO NOTHING!' shouted back, Albert.

"...LOVE, LOVE ME DO..."

The device was screaming from a vintage radio station

'SO, YOU DID SOMETHING!!'

"YOU KNOW I LOVE YOU..."

'Is there a problem, darling?' cut in the old lady who wasn't completely deaf, after all.

'I guess the music is a tad too loud.'

'What?'

'THE MUSIC IS...'

'CUT THE FUCKING BEATLES!' again, the reception guy.

'MATE, I'M WORKING ON IT!!'

"I'LL ALWAYS BE TRUE..."

'My goodness, I feel like dancing right now...'

'Mrs Something, please, turn it down!'
'What?'
'TUUURN IT DOOOWN!!!!'
'WHAAT???'

So, Albert snapped the plug off the socket with a sharp, expert stroke. He manoeuvred the cable like a whip, a leather-made whip fastened to the Indiana Jones belt. Mrs Something was clearly surprised, even slightly blushing like a little girl, as if she had been caught in the middle of a bratty crime. Albert was relieved.

'Bloody hell, that guy...'
'Is he upset with you?' she asked.
'Always. God knows why.'
'Let me have a word with him.' she proposed, trying to get on her feet.
'No way. I mean, there's no need for that. I had to leave anyway.'
'Already?'
'Yes, madam. Honestly, I shall go now.'
'Please, wait...' begged the old lady, gripping tightly on her new friend, the dusty Utility Radio.
'I... is there anything else I can help you with?'
'How much do I owe you?'
'What? No... no. It was my pleasure. Actually, you already gave me back so much that I think I owe you the change.'
'Don't be silly.' she replied with an amused smile.
'I'm real.'
'You're such a good boy, Albert.'
'...'

He stared at her for a second, as still as a riveted statue, as if facing a deadly cobra. No movements, no words whispered. She was silent and relaxed, therefore Albert took his chance and exclaimed 'Great.' performing a classic one-clap stand like Basil in Fawlty Towers. 'See you around.' he concluded with the confidence typical of a youngster (or a bloody fool), and started putting his stuff back together, always keeping his eyes away from her, trying to avoid any more complications. He was about to leave the room when she elegantly insisted:

'Wait... wait a second.'
'Again? What now?' he didn't say.
'Take this.' she offered, pulling a crisp-white handkerchief from her purse. 'My husband gave it to me when we got married.'

'Lady, I can't accept it.'

'I insist.'

'Mrs Something, it's embroidered with your initials. Seriously, I...'

'Give it to the girl.'

'What girl?'

'Look, I might be old but I'm not a fool. You're constantly thinking about her. It's clear, she's the one.'

'How can you possibly... ?'

'Just give it to her.' she said, placing the folded silk hankie into Albert's hands.

He was confused, moved? by that out of fashion gentleness.

'It's the least I can do in return for your kind gesture.'

Now someone was in the middle of an emotional fistfigh.

'Take it.'

'Ok, I'll give it to her. I promise.'

'Brilliant. Now, go, please. You don't want to waste all your precious time with an old lady. I bet you have a great deal of things to do.' she said, smacking a big fat kiss on Albert's forehead

And he was this close to panicking. 'Get off here, fast!' someone inside his brain shouted. Another nice word and he would start melting away like a goddamn candle. He needed no more surprises for the day. Next time he would be efficient, icy-cold. *Delivery - thank you - byeeeee.* Just like the robot-idiotic machines at Sainsbury's: you're still packing your stuff, and the bloody thing tells you to hurry up and get the fuck out of the shop. Bastard.

Anyhow, Albert gave Mrs Something a blink so quick that his face disarranged into a Picasso abstract picture. To anyone in the room, he was totally having a heart attack. *Good Deeds are dangerous.* he wrote down in a mental note, then he was off. Twelve seconds. This was how long it took him from not saying goodbye, to hit the road again. He breathed in as much air as he could fit into his damaged lungs and finally relaxed. Gosh, for the first time in his life, he accomplished something decent for another human being and it felt quite alright. Albert threw his gaze among the blue skies trying to evade reality. He was well into one of his favourite games called *Guess the Cloud* (don't ask), when his mobile rang.

'Pete! Is it you?'

'Of course it's me. What are you up to?'

FORTY-FOUR

'What time is it?' asked Victoria to the estate agent.

'I don't know... a quarter to five?' he replied, reaching for his watch.

'I knew something was missing.'

'Excuse me?'

'The clock! There is no Time in this room.'

'I'm sorry... er... what?'

'It's ok, I'll bring it here myself.' Victoria said, serious but friendly, like a proper schizophrenic.

'Christ, I can't watch this. Where the hell is the boy?' thought Rose.

Tommy was literally scanning the place. 'Vic, have you seen this? Have you seen that?' he kept saying out loud while touching every corner, every surface, in a hectic search for the key element, that little detail that always makes the difference.

'You look like a silly dog wagging its tail.'

'Rose, please... I'm getting there.'

'You're getting mad, I can see that.' she laughed.

'The flooring is quite old. Good.' Tommy noted while crawling on it like a toddler, studying every single wooden board composing the classic, striped pattern.

'Why don't you look up, or straight, instead of wasting time with the filthy shit under our feet?'

'?'

'There's so much more around, like... yeah, the chandelier.'

'Mmm...'

'Oh, now I get it. You're hoping to find a secret trap door. One leading to an obscure cellar filled with ancient skeletons and...'

'You're horrible.'

'Obviously. Just so you know, if we happen to find it, that's gonna be your own private room. Aren't you excited?'

'No way.'

'Go on then, please help us discover the macabre cage where we will shut you down.'

'That's amazing!!'

'Are you even listening to me? And why are you staring at the useless fireplace?'

'This is it.'

'You, silly boy... It's not even working. Look. They bricked it up, for God's Sake.'

Tommy pulled a microscopic notebook from his pocket and scribbled some stuff:

Fireplace. Possible uses:
1. Install a blowing bubbles machine inside it.
It should produce a magical rainbowy smoke that goes "backwards".
2. Set chairs around it and have a storytelling session each day.
5 pm? Tea and biscuits? <u>BISCUITS</u>*. remember this.*

He concluded his note, underlining the capital letter word many, many times, with emphasis.

From a distance, Vic was still pestering the estate agent with a multitude of questions that didn't make sense to him. She was blathering stuff related to the position of the sun, the sight of the moon at night, bad vibes and 'What animal you'd wish to be in your next life?' Nonsense. He just wanted to discuss money. He was the Seal the Deal Master. The Ultimate Sales Wizard. In his mind, there was only one thought: buy a new car and go fuck yourself to some Caribbean island.

'I perfectly understand.' he casually replied after a bunch of random nods and yeses.

'Still... I'm not sure...'

'Exactly. The monthly rent, including fees and a couple of extra charges, would be...'

'Please, don't tell me. I don't want to hear it.'

'But...'

At that moment, Tommy finally saw it: a majestic, rusty Victorian cast spiral staircase. Damn, it was there the whole time and he didn't notice it. How was it even possible? 'Can I use it? What's upstairs?' he suddenly asked the guy, who looked surprised.

'Is he your son?'

'Great question.'

'Thanks.'

'No, I mean, what's upstairs?'

'Oh, that. Nothing, really. It was used as a storage room but we're not renting it, it's not safe. You know, it's a very old building and...' he was saying when Vic and Tommy approached the decrepit metal composition. 'Please, don't!' the guy tried as the two adventurers climbed the squeaking thing up.

'Cool, someone's gonna get hurt. Finally, some action.'

'Shut up!' yelled Vic to Rose, who wasn't there; who wasn't smoking a hand-rolled Cuban cigar right behind the unfortunate estate agent who couldn't possibly know it and, therefore, took it very personally.

'What did you just say to me?'

'Sorry, I was talking to Rose.'

'Who's Rose?'

'It's me, you asshole.'

'ROSE!!!'

'Please, get off the bloody staircase!'

The guy was bewildered, *what the hell was going on?* He didn't know whether to be pissed off or call an exorcist. Vic was shouting stuff to someone who wasn't in the room or at least, who clearly couldn't be seen by the agent. No one was passing by either. No soul was sliding through the huge flimsy-glass windows. So, who was she screaming at? She was unmistakably insane.

Meanwhile, Tommy sneaked upstairs, into the dark storage room. He lit up a match and ventured inside.

'Vic!!' he yelled 'You need to see this place, it's wonderful!'

'I'm coming, Tommy.'

'No, you're not!' ordered the agent, hurrying towards her just a moment too late. From the ceiling, a creepy *creak* demanded everyone's attention and bits of plaster started falling on the head of the incredulous guy.

'Fuck.' he said. 'I'm calling the police.'

He exited the shop and reached for his phone.

Tap - tap - taptap - tap.

'What did you find, Tommy?'

'Look at this, and that!'

'It's just a pile of old rubbish.'

'Oh, Vic... will you ever learn?'

scroll, tap, scroll...

'I can see some light filtering through there. Tommy, can you pull that thing off?'

'Sure! Do you mean this chunk of fabrics?' he asked, grabbing the nasty clog, trying to clear the way.

'Yep, be careful though. We don't want to die buried under a thousand tonnes of dust, do we?'

'It's not that easy, Vic! Give me a sec...'

'Great, like that, you're almost through it!'

'I got it! I got it!' he yelled, pulling the messy cluster off the wall. That was it.

'Let there be light!' announced Vic, amused by the sun rays finally entering that forgotten room. It was enchanting. For a moment, the two adventurers felt ecstatic.

9 (first)

'Yay!'

'Good boy.'

'We did it! We finally found it!' Tommy squealed, jumping around.

'I don't know why you have to bounce up and down like a broken spring.' said Rose, who just landed on the secret floor.

'Dangerous...' wondered Victoria, for a moment

'Indeed, my dear. He's gonna get hurt.'

'Nah... do you think?'

'Absolutely, this place is clustered with junk. I can't wait to watch him cry.'

'Oh, my...'

'Blood will be spilt all over the place, so much so that it will soak into the floorboards and drip downstairs, flooding the whole shop.'

'Vic, grab my hands!'

'Tommy, please, calm down.'

'... the nasty-viscous, burgundy permanent mark will stain this place forever, haunting the brave ones who will dare to enter the shop.'

'Aren't you a little too dramatic, Rose?'

'Vic!! Dance with me!!' Tommy insisted, ready to perform his most audacious, never tried before, jump from the top of an empty bucket.

'What the hell are you doing?' she asked, without really wanting an answer.

'I'm gonna land straight into your arms. Ready?'

'Tah Dah! The boy's gonna die!' added Rose.

...and,

'JUMP/SBAM!!'

9 (second)

Tommy's head knocked into something pretty hard and sharp (a shelf?) that finally decided to surrender to Gravity.

'*CrrrrraaaAAkKK!*'

It cried, dragging whatever was on top of it to the floor. The disarranged impact was so loud that even the agent could hear it from the street. He was increasingly upset. 'Bad day. Bad freaking day.' a broken record was repeating in a loop inside his mind. He couldn't wait to get rid of those idiots.

'Ouch...'

'Are you ok, Tommy?'

'Yep... my arm hurts.'

'Shit. You didn't die?!'

'ROSE!!'

'COUGH, cough, COUUUUGH!!'

They all said at once. A dust mayhem raised from the messy ruins and was now filling the room in the form of solid, thick fog.

'Insane...'

'Shoot, Vic, I didn't jump from the fifth floor, it was just a bucket...' Tommy tried to excuse himself.

'Shhh! Look at this.'

'What?'

'Wow...'

'Can you see the dust particles twirling in the air? They've been in this room for decades and yet, nobody saw them, no one ever gave them the chance to shine.'

'You're delusional. I bet we just blasted a bag of pure cocaine.' cut in Rose.

'You're right, Vic! And it's all because of the tiny window over there. They are dancing against the light. Like... they're possessed by a magic spell.'

'You did it again, you little brat.'

'Did I?'

'This is gonna be the heart of our shop.'

'Yeah, the client's heart-attack if we don't clean this shit. I am choking already.' Rose said.

'This room... it looks like a romantic movie scene where, in an ethereal, dreamy moment, the characters find their way to a secret land,

and a fantastic, stunning, enchanting...'

'Fuckin' hell, I can't stand another blathering session of yours.' Rose thought as she opened the window.

9 (last)

A column of smoke puffed out aiming for the skies, right above the agent's head. He was so into his calling-the-coppers task that he almost didn't notice it. From his spot on the curbside, he simply sensed that the upstairs' situation was escalating. 'Enough is enough.' He said and finally tapped:

999 - DIAL.

His fingertip touched the big green button connecting his phone to the police. He was about to speak when two blackened heads popped out of the tiny first-floor window.

'WE'RE TAKING IT!' they shouted.

'What?' he was shocked.

'WE'RE TAK...'

'Alright, alright, I get it (you bloody idiots).' the agent said out loud, brackets included, suddenly realising he just sealed another deal. So he grinned, 'Who's the best salesman in town, uh, mum?' He was almost in tears, both for the cumulative stress and some weird vibe echoing in the air. Was that shop really magic already? Was he the very first Victoria's client/*victim*? Whatever.

'Guys, come down, you need to sign the goddamn papers. Christ...'

'I love this man.' thought Rose.

'You figure.'

'Vic, this is it. We finally have it!'

'Indeed, Tommy. Indeed.'

'It's like the Holy Grail!'

'Yep, the perfect room in the perfect shop with the perfect mood.'

'Sick. Isn't it fucking perfect?' thought Rose, sucking on her fat cigar.

FORTY-FIVE

'Pete? You still on the phone?'
'Sure. So, yet, nobody killed you.'
'Quite the opposite. After meeting with ma nu black brother, I...'
'Yeah, he's not your friend, Albert.'
'Mate, he is. However, now everyone's treating me as a local.'
'Meaning?'
'Well, the drug dealers, gang members, kids and even the black mothers of the hood are now yo-ing me with respect. Aren't we all brothers after all?'
'Hell yeah.' replied Pete from the other end of the line 'May I ask when this happened? Wasn't it today?'
'Absolutely. And they YO-ed me right after the scene.'
'I get it...'
'Hey, this is real. I'm not making stuff up, you know me, Pete.'
'... just be careful, man. We want you back in one piece. No more crazy stunts, ok?'
'What can I do? I'm spontaneous.'
'...'
'I've got boiling blood in my veins, I'm alive, I'm black, I'm white, I'm ready to fight.'
'Idiot.'
'Alright, Pete. Let's cut the crap. Why did you call?'
'Ahem... it's a delicate matter. Are you in a quiet place?'
'Not at all, I'm walking to the tube station. Almost there.'
'Cool, so I'll be quick and straight to the point.'
'No, no, no. I can't waste such great news. I'll call you later.'
'It's about Victoria...'
'What? Can't hear you, Pete. Sorry, I'm getting down, down into the underground.'
'Hey!'
'Byeeee.'
'blip.' said the mobile, ending the conversation.

Albert got scared as hell at the sole mention of Victoria. He screwed up so badly that any news about her was like a stab to his heart. He wasn't ready yet. And, truth be told, he wasn't exactly getting into the station either, he was nowhere near it. After leaving Mrs Something, he decided to embark on a mission he had planned a long time before: drawing a wordy portrait of London.

He got off Pret a Manger holding a pricey, shoddy cup of coffee. His headphones wrapped the baseball cap and pumped music into his brain. Everything was going according to plan so, he left MARBLE ARCH behind, ready to face the exquisite, chaotic mess of the city. Albert was craving that moment since forever, he had a whole ritual prepared for it but, first of all he had to stop:

Breath in - breath out. Breath in - breath out
COUGH!!

'Amateur...' he told himself. 'A true local would never take a deep breath, or even breathe at all when in the centre of his metropolis. You hold it as a free diver. Apnea. Until you turn crimson and die. Silently, cause nobody wants to cause no fuss, innit? Another thing you want to keep in mind is, you don't stop, ever. Not even to rescue that silly lost kid standing still in the middle of a crossing. You don't have the time, you have to move, run, faster than a cannonball, don't look back in anger, don't look back at all! You jump over the homeless, you bump into people like an American football player, and you spit out standard, fake-polite sorry-s to them, without even looking at their ugly faces and you go on, you can't bother, you don't want to waste air by excusing yourself. No way. Especially when it comes to the damn tourists. They don't deserve your apologies, they don't even understand a fucking word you'd say anyway, and they are slow, they're distracted, they are laughing, what the fuck are you laughing about? This is a fucking - goddamn - war, you idiots, you have to run, FUCKING RUN FOR YOUR LIFE!!! AAAAAAAHHHHHHHH!!!!'

Despite the animated conversations living inside him, Albert's face was numb. Stupid. If you happened to be there at that time you'd probably be worried. I mean, what do you do when you spot the perfect psycho, the one staring at the void with a paralysed expression, in the middle of some megalotropolis? You either run or report "something unusual" to the police. See it - Say it - Fuck me. Luckily for Albert, no one bothered doing such a great service to society.

That endless stream of thoughts was rolling somewhere behind his eyeballs like closing movie credits. He was still standing in front of the imaginary gate leading towards Oxford Circus, and already his mind was blowing up like a nuclear bomb. No fear. He had it all planned. The mobile screen unlocked and, with a few *expert* taps, Albert found the song he needed.

'George Gershwin's Rhapsody in Blue. That's the one.'

As the score started playing, his eyes gradually lost their colour function and the city desaturated into a black and white movie. Manhattan, Woody Allen.

'Let's get on with this shit.' he said, approaching the first step into his new screenplay: LONDON. *by Albert Hoover.*

He took a look around and: City Souvenirs (fuck that), Top Shop, PizzaHut, freaking Holland and Barrett and then Primark, Boots, more bloody tourists' traps filled with thief-priced junk. Right.

'Chapter One.' Albert said out loud.

'He adored London City. He idolised and romanticised it all out of proportion. *Great.* He thrived on the hustle, bustle of the crowds and the traffic. To him, London meant beautiful women and street-smart guys who seemed to know all the angles... enough. This isn't me.' he said, stopping in the middle of the busy flow of people who, obviously, cursed him in any language. Fair enough, he would have done the same.

Albert smiled and started again.

'Chapter One. He adored New York City. Damn, I should have rehearsed it. Again!' he cleared his throat and

'He was enchanted by London City. To him, that was the filthy damned place described by John Niven in his books, where people would do anything to succeed, even kill their own mothers if that would do the trick. Bloodshot eyes, cocaine, classy whores and male vampires dressed in suits, working up the ladder, fornicating in their fancy offices. Shitloads of money and thousands of litres of coffee shot directly into your veins to be more efficient, fitter, happier, more productive. Radiohead, Oasis, Blur (no, not the Blur). And then The Beatles, the Queen, the goddamn Sex Pistols...'

Albert was talking with himself along the way, experiencing the street as if he was into a video game. He was doing his best to avoid the thousands of mobile-zombies that sucked on their stupid electric fags while they walked, texted, checked the news or wrote their own precious no-one-will-ever-read stories, all at once, multitasking. Inside Albert's eyes, a glamorous commercial was rolling: Zara, Selfridges, the sick-cute Disney Store shit, and Debenhams, Swarovski, House of Fraser, John freaking Lewis, ladies and gents! Money is pouring from the sky when you're around BOND STREET.

'ORDER!' Albert shouted out of the blue. But no one cared, no one seemed to care about anything but themselves.

So, he carried on with his story.

'Albert loved London City. He was well-trained for it, therefore he was looking at each face with disdain.

- Man with a dark suit and briefcase: lame.

- SpiceGirl-wannabe whore girl chewing like a cow, covered head to toe in tattoos and piercings: why do you even exist?

- Businesswoman on the left: interesting.

She's so stressed out that she'd stab the first one who dares to get on her way. *Get a fuck, darling!* She is so tense that a slight touch would make her jump off her skin like a cat at the sight of a cucumber. She was smiling at all the fuckers, the tourists, the colleagues, the beggars, trying to keep an elegant composure. She's a high-class woman, isn't she? In her head though, she expresses her real self: *'Fuck you, fuck you too, you asshole, why don't you hang yourself instead of walking like a retarded handicapped? Downer. Pervert. Faggot. Cunt. Stay in the goddamn line, you miserable piece of garbage.'* She shouted inside the privacy of her mind without feeling any shame, no fucking filter, since no one could hear her.

For all the cows in the street, she was a very elegant, quite attractive woman in a suit who knew her way around manners. Very polite, indeed, a true good-girl. *'Bastard, up yours, I hope you Dido! Aw, finally a human being that doesn't smell like shite. Fucken Hell, even grandma had to come out today? Why don't you fucking lock her down into a fucking nuthouse where she belongs? Jesus Christ, what did you have for breakfast, the whole McDonald's Department? You fat creep.'*

She was utterly enjoying herself when she spotted a black guy, all suited up and probably bathed in perfume. He was fully immersed in a business call *what else?* but couldn't stop staring at her legs, and she noticed, and she smiled, although this time, differently. So, he blinks at her as she's approaching at supersonic-train speed. He's so experienced that he doesn't even stop dealing with the client while handing her his business card, shooting a second blink and mimicking a clear, mute C-A-L-L M-E with his lips. She makes a face, acting disgusted cause, hey, she's not that kind of girl, she's an entrepreneur, she's refined, she's... but, as soon as she passes him, her long fingers slip the card safe in her panther-black push-up bra. And she grins, fantasizing about her well-deserved, majestic fuck she'll enjoy that very same night.'

Albert was at full throttle, he couldn't stop his brains. He was singing too, now into another classic tune

I want to wake up in a city that never sleeps
And find I'm a number one, top of the list
King of the hill, a number one.

Some guy called Godknows looked at him as if he was the coolest thing, or a weirdo. A cool weirdo? However, Albert had better things to do, such as getting on with his story.

'He loved London. London was like being thrown into the ocean from a helicopter: you either die or learn how to swim. Fuck, yeah. London was his city. The place where opportunities floated in the air and you just had to catch that damn flick of light before the others. London allowed even the oddity, the artsy, the hipster fuckers to succeed. As long as you were ready to eat shit; to fistfight with your tears at night 'cause you're alone and miserable; as long as you were cool about sleeping in a filthy one-square feet apartment shared by dynasties of rats for the modest price of a million pounds a minute. If you survived it all, you would be ready to rock'n'roll. Aw, London. Garbage, crime, drugs, gangs, acid attacks, terrorist attacks, knife crime... fucking hell, he loved that city.'

'LONDON. LONDON. LONDON!' he chanted at some point like a drunken hooligan, approaching the stairs leading down the very heart of the city. One last glimpse around before dipping into the obscure universe buried Underground. H&M, NikeTown, TopShop, Urban Outfitters, Tezenis. The freaking centre of the World. Welcome to OXFORD CIRCUS.

'London was his town and it always would be.' Albert said slowly, concluding his chapter. Then he pulled off his headphones and sang:

'*If I can make it there, I'm gonna make it anywhere.*
It's up to you LON - DON, LOOOON DOOOOOOOON!!'

'Shut up, mate.'

FORTY-SIX

Greenwich was enchanting. Like a rare jewel stolen from the Queen Collection by a French gentleman thief.

'*The Cat.*'

'Now what, Vic?' asked Rose.

'Uh? Nothing... we should get a cat.'

'Why not? Let's introduce a flea-ridden tramp to the crew. One who eats and pisses all day long in exchange for the occasional purr. Indeed, worth it.'

'I'd love a cat!' cut in Tommy.

'You'd love whatever. Even a crippled turtle and you know why? 'Cause you're stupid.'

'Hey!' shouted Vic.

'Actually, can we have a turtle?'

'We're not having anything. Happy? Let's think about how to get through this shop-deal first. Shall we?'

'Right. Shoot.'

'Thanks, Rose. One: *figure out how to pay the rent.*'

'...'

'Two:'

'You have to sell the pub, dear. Otherwise, there's no number two whatsoever.'

'Darn...'

'Hey, Vic, I have some spare money if it can help.'

Victoria's heart shrinked to the point it hurt. And she almost shed a lonely tear. How could such a small creature be so kind? She loved him so much.

'I...'

'Come on, fuck the pub, you'll get another one in the future!'

'I don't know, Rose, am I throwing all my savings in the wind?'

'You ain't trashing no money! Look, things change, life needs to go on. Do you want to live a little?'

'I guess...'

'So, do it! Who cares about cash? You're betting on the right horse, honey, you'll be back on track in a second.'

'It's a lot of money, Rose...'

'Ok, so let's simply enjoy the easy life.'

'There must be a better way.'

'Yeah. Prostitution.'

'Shut up.'

'I'm just saying.'

'You could rent the pub to my mum.' proposed Tommy. 'She's always loved it. If it's not too expensive, I bet she'd be ready to move in right away.'

'Are you serious?'

'Yepsy.'

'Let me do some maths: the rent, plus my savings, minus the contract fee, the entry costs, the renewals...'

'We'll do all the refurbishments by ourselves. We want to give this place a special touch, don't we?'

'Er... yes?'

'It's going to be wonderful! And cheap.'

'Tommy, Tommy, Tommy.' said Rose. 'You really are a badass, aren't you? I'd say you're almost smart.'

'Thanks! Besides, I propose to build the furniture using the stuff left in the attic, and, wait for it, we could live in the shop!'

'Wow, I'm impressed, Tommy.' said Rose.

'Is it even legal?'

'Who fucking cares, Vic. Let's move in the damn shack!'

'Mmm... we could try.'

'It's temporary, and if it doesn't work out, we can always get back to Sherlintock and use the pub! It's enormous, I'm sure my mum would love for us to live all together!'

'Are we signing the fucking papers or not, Vic?' insisted Rose.

'Okay, whatever. Let's do it, folks!'

FORTY-SEVEN

Mile End. The day after yesterday.

'Albert, can you talk now?'

'I guess...'

'You don't want to hear it, do you?'

'I'm a big boy, Pete. Shoot me heart with your silver bullet.'

'We saw Victoria, in Sherlintock.'

'Urgh... she's not in Italy anymore?'

'Nope. We were passing by the pub and saw her outside, packing stuff on the roof of her Mini.'

'...'

'We stopped to say hello and...'

'You what?'

'Anyway, she had news, big stuff.'

'Such as?'

'She's moving to London, man.'

'Bloody hell, I'm screwed. Did you...'

'No, we didn't mention you're there too, if that's what you're wandering.'

'So...'

'Yes, she doesn't have a clue on your whereabouts.'

'Great news. Great.'

'Are you stupid or what? She's right there, call her!'

'Anything else I should know?'

'Actually, yes. She wants to get a shop.'

'Seriously? Did she become rich or something?'

'Well, she's not buying, she's considering renting a space. To sell her books.'

'No shit. The ones with no words?'

'Sure.'

'Fuck, she's great.'

'Told ya. It's such a shame you let her go.'

'Whatever.'

'I bet she's gonna need a shop boy sooner or later.'

'Yeah, probably.'

'I'm talking about you, asshole! You should apply for the job before, you know, somebody else... Bloody hell, she might still have some feelings left for you!'

'She most probably hates my guts.'

'She should, indeed.'

'...'

'Look, why don't you give it a try? You live in the same city now, it would be stupid to waste this opportunity once again. The more time it passes, the less the chances you have to get to her heart, man.'

'Sure. Let me think about it.'

'Chicken.'

'What?'

'You're a fucking chicken.'

'Yeah?'

'Yes.'

'Alright, maybe. But I can live with it.'

'If you say so.'

'Do you... do you know where is she now?'

'London?'

'Mate, this city is freaking huge!'

'Sorry, that's all I have. She was still undecided.'

'Any-how, thanks for the tip, Pete.'

'Hey, do the smart thing for once.'

'I'll call you soon, ok?'

'Take care.'

click

'Holy fucking shit. I'm thoroughly, unconditionally fucked. I need coffee. JOSH?' Albert screamed from the garden as if shouting the name would summon him, like an Indian divinity.

Josh wasn't there, you know, he had a life too. Every now and then he'd go out to grab some food, do the occasional job (don't ask) or, well, to do whatever he had to do. Besides, the coffee and cigarettes ritual had been going on for a while and they both started feeling uncomfortable with it. In any case, Albert was still barking his friend's name when

'SLAMMMM!!! :;,,....,.,,.,:.,,.,..,,,,,..,,....,' crackled the wall.

The door shut close and a very pissed off version of Josh stepped into the kitchen. Albert went to check the wall.

'Anything broken?'

'Not this time, Josh.'

'Listen, I bought a bottle of Bourbon. I am tired of coffee, I sense that it's not suitable for my guts anymore.'

'You figure. I'm not feeling good either. So, whiskey?'

'Yeah, and coffee too, but I'd rather cut down on that black shit. Change is good, innit?'

'They say Bourbon is for highly refined people. I love it.'

'Have you ever tried it?'

'Nope, but...'

'Let's give it a go. Pass me the mugs.' Josh asked, and filled them with the amber liquid.

'Cigarette?'

'Cigarette.'

'flick, flick frusshhhh.' said the lighter once again, burning the tips.

'There you go.' said Albert, sticking one fag through his friend's lips and sucking on his.

'Puff, PUFF. Sluuurp.'

'This isn't too bad, is it?'

'Why do you always have to speak?'

'Mate, I feel a certain bond is sprouting among us.'

'You're not my type, sorry Albert.'

'I mean, we spend entire days together sitting on this bench, smoking and drinking coffee. We might not talk much but we're sharing beautiful moments. Last night, for example...'

'Oh, shut up.'

'... we sat here for so long that we ended up watching the sunset, and the dawn, without saying a word. Without turning the lights on to avoid ruining such a romantic moment.'

'Are you gay?'

'Everyone's gay.'

'Whatever. Please spare me another two-hour-long monologue about your hero.' complained Josh.

'Kurt...'

'Drink your goddamn whiskey and leave me alone.'

'...' A few teardrops appeared from Albert's eyes.

'What now? You crying?'

'Nonsense. It must be the alcohol. This shit is strong, mate.'

'You're a pussy.' Josh replied, weeping a few tears off his cheeks too.

'*Slurp. Pufff. PUFF*'

'Fuck, you're really enjoying yourself.'

'Mate, I just found out that Bourbon mixed with smoke create a special flavour in my mouth.'

'At least you're feeling something. My taste buds went on vacation a lifetime ago and never came back.'

'Yeah…'

'You look thoughtful. What's buzzing in your mind?' Josh asked, immediately regretting it.

'What did you like to do when you were a kid?'

'I've never been a kid.'

'This is fucking rock'n'roll, mate!'

'…'

'Seriously, what did you…'

'I don't remember.'

'You must have had some sort of passion.' insisted Albert.

''Aight, I loved painting, but I don't wanna talk about it.'

'Why did you stop?'

'You deaf? It's complicated.'

'Bullshit. If you want to do it, just do it.'

'Fuck you.'

'You got it.'

'Do you have any idea of how much that stuff costs? You need paint, brushes, canvases…'

'Sometimes you make me laugh.'

'Sometimes I want to punch you in the face.'

'Yeah…' Albert mumbled.

He wasn't listening anymore. He was wandering around the kitchen intent on doing things that any person with a pinch of sanity would categorise as foolish. He put out his ciggy into the half-full whiskey mug and gulped its content, acting like a rockstar. Then, realising what he just did, he almost threw up, cherry red face and lots of sweating, spitting, cursing all sorts of Gods, et cetera. Josh didn't make a move. No sign of amusement or anything. Then, Albert disappeared for a minute, got to his room, grabbed the white duvet cover and hurried back downstairs.

'What does this look like to you?'

'A duvet co…'

'It's a freaking canvas!!' Albert shouted, shredding the thing.

'What's the matter with you?'

'Look,' he continued 'you spread it on the table and there you go. Ready for you to paint.'

'...'

'Josh, it doesn't take a genius!'

'Man, it's no time to play Masterchef, ok?'

'Shut up and observe.'

'Why anyone should mix coffee, whiskey and eggs into a bowl?'

'...'

'Marvellous. You just emptied the ashtray in it.'

'That's the secret touch, Josh.'

'Disgusting.'

'Give me your hands.'

'No fucking way.'

'I said, give me your big fat black hands!'

'Fuck off.' Josh didn't say while (unconsciously) obeying the order. He plunged his fingertips into the smelly awful swirling broth. Filthy.

'Perfect. Now, tell me Josh, what else do you need?'

'You are a motherfucking fool.'

'And you got no more excuses, mate. You wanted to paint? It's up to you now! You need colours? We can mix paprika with a couple of yolks. Yellow? Orange? Be creative, for fuck's sake. Let me see...' he continued, slamming random cabinet doors open, scattering stuff to the floor and finally reaching the spices "section". 'Turmeric. Ginger. Fucking cumin, curry and black pepper.'

'Man...'

'Let me tell you a story.'

'Please, don't.'

'Have you ever heard of Anthony Morvar?'

'Who?'

'That man would have helped you. He was selling kites.'

'I don't care.'

'One day,'

'I don't give a shit.'

'Cool, I'll give you the short version then.'

'...'

'Morvar was a patron, an inventor and a pioneer for all the weirdos, the artsy, the creative and sensitive people.'

'You said he was selling kites. What the fuck?'

'Exactly. Kites. You might consider them as nothing special, obsolete silly toys for kids. Am I right?'

'Sure.'

'Wrong. Those flimsy two sticks and cheap fabric things can fly across the skies like dreams, drag enchanted eyes as they hover in the air. You fly your kite and you're lost in your thoughts, far from reality, you get back to the happiest moments of your life. You are making space for your desires, you are playing, you are living. Anthony Morvar wasn't just selling toys. He was selling dreams! He was smart enough to use simple, innocent objects to trick people into happiness.'

'Now that you mentioned it, I had a kite too. My grandfather taught me how to fly it.'

'Precisely my point. A simple kite was powerful enough to connect people. It was a shrewd way to induce humans to spend time together. Out in the open.'

Josh was smoking, and drinking, and sucking on his fag again. He wasn't relaxed any more. He felt something growing inside of him, like that hitch he had repressed for far too long and now seemed inevitable. He was staring at the duvet cover laid on the kitchen table.

'What are you gonna do with it?' asked Albert.

'It's none of your business.'

'I agree, mate.'

'Right. So, now it's your turn.'

'My what?'

'You act like you know everything, like a Guru, and yet it's clear you messed up your life pretty well. You ain't telling the whole story.'

'I...'

'What is that you want, man?'

'Josh, I want to be an inventor. I want to dedicate my life to creating, just like Morvar did in his time. I want... I'd love to meet Victoria again and tell her that I'm sorry, that I was out of my mind when I decided to dash away. Truth is, I want to live by her side and share my days with her, 'cause I... I think I'm in love.' Albert didn't say. And he probably never would, not in the real world anyway.

Instead, he declared:

'I want to be a writer.'

FORTY-EIGHT

Victoria rubbed her eyes finding herself out of a dream a bit too close to reality. Eventually, they signed the contract, paid the deposit and the first month's rent. Time to rock'n'roll. As Rose told her the night before: 'Now you have to grind away at this shit if you want to succeed. There ain't two trains stopping at the same track at the same time. Don't fucking waste it.' Charming as ever. Victoria felt her bones aching as she stood up from the bare floor where she slept.

'Coffee?' asked Tommy, already fully functional.

'Thanks, I feel a bit dazed...'

'Here we go, take.'

Ssssip

'No, wait, wait!'

'??'

'You can't drink it straight away. First, you should breathe in the aroma, enjoy the warmth of the cup and...'

'Guzzle it, babe! Swallow the black poison down your guts like petrol, that's what I call waking up.'

'...'

'We're in London, folks, we are stressed, we're machine guns ready to shoot. Let's cut the romantic crap.'

'Sorry, Rose. It doesn't work like that.' answered Vic.

'Exactly! Aren't we creating this shop for a reason?'

'Oh, Tommy boy...' commented Rose.

'This is supposed to be a relaxed, out-of-time space.'

'Boring.'

'By the way, do you like the colours, Vic?'

Suddenly, Victoria realised that the room had changed overnight. Someone painted the whole space in the most uncommon, weird way ever.

'Where did you find the paint, Tommy?'

'Attic, buried under some stuff.'

'You are incredible.'

'What do you think?'

'I love it!'

'Of course you do, you didn't have to move a finger, you lazy ass.'

'It's not that, Rose. I really...'

'Have you noticed that each wall has a different shade of ugliness? Sorry, I'm spoiling the surprise.' grinned Rose.

'How... well...'

'We didn't have enough paint for the whole room. So, I decided to mix what was left in the buckets and...'

'Tommy, it's beautiful! Thank you.' she simply said, and hugged him so strong she almost choked him. 'You're special, my little friend.'

'...' he blushed.

'Freaking awful. We should call it the Harlequin shop.'

'It's just different, Rose. I'm sure we can figure out something.'

'Yeah, let's burn the place down.'

'Maybe, we could treat each surface as a different space.'

'Yes, with different music, a different experience.' added Tommy.

'We can put furniture or bookshelves, to separate each area. Now that I think about it, it kind of resembles a fairytale garden filled with wonders. Harmonious, delicate but also intriguing.'

'Dodgy and scary. One minute you are listening to some nonsense record named *Silence in a Victorian Bathroom* and the very next, a serial killer wearing a hockey mask is stabbing you in the chest.'

'Sick.'

'Innit?'

'No, I mean, we absolutely need music in here, something like birds chirping, waterfalls, raindrops...' said Victoria.

'Ladies and gents, welcome to the New Age Major Scam shop for all the silly Vegans, the Green Party idiots and other rich hypocrites who pursue good ideas in fanatical ways.'

'Why do you always have to judge people?'

'It's funny. Don't we all do it in our minds? As a matter of fact, you're doing it right now. You know, I'm just a creation of your *mental* brain.' proudly declared Rose.

'...' Vic vamped, feeling ashamed of herself.

'Listen, honey, this place must be nothing close to ordinary, I'll give you this. So, forget about the commercial stuff you just mentioned. You need to be more creative.'

'I'm afraid Rose has a point.'

'Tommy!'

'Yes, Vic. We might want to consider using noises and sounds to stimulate the imagination. Something capable of taking your inner child by the hand and bringing it to the deepest caves hid inside your heart.'

'How old are you, again?' asked Rose. 'Did Tommy eat a vocabulary for breakfast? Are you on acids?'

'I like to read.' he replied, crossing his short arms, making a pout.

'Ok, you're both right.' conceded Victoria. 'Our shop must be unique. People should feel at home, without anyone observing or judging them. They should be comfortable enough to leave their fears and society-driven cliches out of the door; kick their stiff shoes away and slip into cotton-soft warm slippers.'

'Oh my God, not another dull speech.' snorted Rose.

'Maybe they'd fancy lying down somewhere, like... there! Yes, we should provide pouffes, cushions on the floor, as in an Arabic lounge.'

'Shisha!!'

'Yeah, no alcohol or smoke allowed. Sorry, Rose.'

'You figure.'

'What do you think, Tommy?'

'SUPER!! And what about a device to make them feel like they're somewhere else?'

'Brilliant. Let's fool them thinking they're in a completely different store, a better one. Scam of the century!'

'You're right, we should ferry them to another time, different age and space.' said Vic, ignoring Rose.

'I'll study a way to trigger their happy memories!!'

'That's absolutely what you should do, Tommy.' cut in Rose, again, and she continued 'You must use any sort of medium to achieve the goal. No matter the means, or the consequences, kick that shit out of our bloody customers, boy! And, if it doesn't work, I'll fucking shoot the villains' brain off. I have my 45-caliber loaded already. Don't you dare not to be happy in our shop. You bastards.'

'Can you shut her out of the room?'

'Sorry, Tommy, I have tried many times before...'

'You don't want me out, cause I have the smarts. Listen to this:'

'Nooo!' Tommy and Vic replied together.

'We need Hollywood Stars in our shop.'

'??'

'You said you want music. Weird, fucked-up tunes, am I right?'

'Not quite...'

'Precisely. What's that misfit called... the one that looks like Johnny Depp. Does it ring any bell?'

'The White Stripes!'

'I'm shocked, Tommy. You listen to the devil's music.'

'They rock! I want to be Meg, playing the drums.'

'Of course you do, you're a girl.'

'I just like the dr...'

'Yeah, yeah, yeah, let's not change subject. We must have Jack White playing our shop with his crazy one-string-attached-to-a-nail guitar. People will pay gold to come here. Picture this: skyscraper-size ads pasted all over London; the tube flooded with our shop name printed in capital letters right next to Mr White's face; Gallons of Rubbing Alcohol flowing Through the Strip...'

'So, Tommy, what about a couple of mattresses?' said Victoria.

'Why? Why don't you ever listen to my great ideas??' cried Rose.

'I love it! Mattresses and proper beds! I will hang speakers around them so people can be fully immersed in their experience.'

'Indeed. That will help them read inside their hearts and find back the precious stories written on the pages of their blank books.'

'Pathetic.'

'We shall awake lost feelings, bring back childhood moments, and smiles, and'

'Lost love.' said Rose, jumping into Vic's stream of thoughts.

'What?'

'I didn't say a word.'

'Yes you did.'

'Don't be a fool, Vic, it was you. Gosh... you really can't stop thinking about Albert, can you?'

'...'

'How can you help strangers connect with their freakin' voodoo child when you can't even admit that you're still in love with him?'

FORTY-NINE

'A writer?'

'Yes, I'll be a writer, Josh. You know, people who combine words and create stories.'

'Thanks for explaining it to me. I'm so dumb.'

'I titled my next piece *"Tube People by Albert Hoover".*'

'So, this is not your first article, is it?'

'Well...'

'Have you ever submitted stuff to an editor or a publication?'

'What? No way.'

'Jesus...'

'Those bastards are rabid exploiters. They seek and steal stories, poems or any material written by people whose names they don't even know. I'm sure tons of envelopes land on their desks every day, like cows sent to the slaughterhouse.'

'I bet they don't.'

'Editors don't give a damn about you. Do they find a decent-enough story? They slap their name on it and they publish the shit.'

'No one sends regular mail anymore, Albert.'

'Details. How can you even consider giving your masterpiece to such monsters? You spend hours trying to find the right words for the presentation letter, you write your details as carefully as a monk copying the Holy Bible. Your phone number is there, impressed on expensive paper, circled by neon-white blank space so that even a blind man could read it. Are they calling me back?'

'I don't know...'

'God forbid if they ever do.'

'Have you tried?'

'Sure. No. Whatever.'

'...'

'Fine, Josh, let's imagine how this would work.'

'Let's not.'

'Let's yes.'

'Please, God, take me now...'

'Eventually, they give me a call:

Hi, this is Mark from FuckYou Magazine. I received your piece and it didn't make me vomit. Are you the author?

Yes, why?

You know, I found your story through all the shit we get every day and it didn't completely suck.

Thank you!

We are sending it to print today if that's ok with you.

Great. Fab! Are you paying me anything for it?

What? Who the fuck do you think you are, uh? You should be thankful for us to even consider the idea of using your insult-to-writing piece of garbage for our publication.

Alright, sorry. And thank you for the opportunity. I'm Hoover, Albert Hoover. I can't wait to read my name in a real magazine.

It's not gonna happen, mate. This story will be written by Jonathan Bruce. He's the one delivering the cool shit.

But...

Please send us more stuff and, maybe, one day, we might discuss the chance to use your name, ok?

Gosh... I will, indeed. My next goal in life is to become Jonathan Bruce. Can you thank him for me?

Impossible. The guy don't exist. We use a fake name to spoil you miserable poor writers. Have a great day, Mike.

My name is Albert...

Whatever.

click.'

'Look, man, I don't have time for your delusions.'

'It's a true story, Josh.'

'Yeah, just get out of here. I'm tired and I want coffee.'

'Ciggy?'

'I need time alone.'

'Oh... you...'

'Yes, probably.'

'Holy moly, I'm so glad you want to paint again.'

'GET THE FUCK AWAY!'

Josh couldn't say thank you or even admit to himself that his friend was right. Josh was a complicated human being but who isn't? Anyway,

Albert didn't like emotional scenes either so he instantly disappeared. He stuffed his pockets with the essentials: tobacco, papers, filters, lighter and... no, that was it. Within minutes, he was hitting the road.

'Can you tell me a story?' Albert said out loud, rehearsing his opening, and what a powerful opening that was. Is there a better question to crack an interview? I mean, is there a better question, period? Maybe, but 'You know what?' he asked nobody, 'Fuck the system, this time I'm sending my piece straight to BBC News. Yes, they're gonna love it and I'll be famous. Why aim for small, useless journals, magazines or blogs? This is London, goddammit! This is my city. If you want something, you go get it. From the jugular.'

He was strolling about "his" hood, like a God or, better, like an idiot who felt like God, but no one was even looking at him, obviously. It took him three minutes to reach Mile End station. He climbed down the stairs and there he was, slowly dipping into the beating heart of the city.

'Tell me a story. Tell me a story. Tell me a...' his mind was stuck on a loop. 'Excuse me, can you...?' he asked a guy who clearly had something better to do and dashed away.

'...there are minor delays on the district line due to engineer works between...' the speakers announced.

Down the stairs, an old lady was blocking the way to the platforms one step at a time, moving an inch further every 30-50 seconds. Youngsters in the queue were clearly about to jump over her head and parachute themselves right into the approaching train. Others pretended to *Keep Calm*, probably because he/she/it read that sentence on a mug and he/she/they was used to obey, good-boy style.

'A good service is operating on the rest of the lines.'

One way or the other, they knew they couldn't say a word unless they'd want to be frowned upon or labelled as nazis deserving an atrocious death. So, they simply waited for the perfect opening to literally throw themselves into the microscopic gap through that solid human mass. The air was filled with tension. Hate. Rage. Stress. All mixed in a food processor pouring out a weird self-control slop. Just another ordinary day in the London Underground.

'This fake politeness is indeed working.' tried Albert, with another victim.

'Uh?'

'Can you tell me a story?'

'The next train to Ealing Broadway will arrive in one minute on platform two.' echoed the hall.

And he got distracted for a fraction of a second: 'Bloody hell, he's gone too.'

The station was flooded by people, all merging into that underground hole like twirling bubbles down the sink when you plump out the tap. When the train arrived, the platforms were saturated.

'One every minute! Crazy, uh?' Albert told someone else.

'Uh-huh.' the man sort of replied, emotionless.

'Mate, it's packed! I bet you couldn't manage to squeeze in even...'

Wrong

'... if you were an underfed...'

The guy just conquered his place in the car

'... skinny teenager.'

*'This train is now about to depart.
Mind the closing doors, mind the closing...'*

Albert was shocked. 'How the fuck did he... whatever, I'll get on the next one.' he thought, and then again... Trains were coming and going like time, in London. Albert didn't know the rules of that crazy game so he was playing cool, letting people out, respecting the queue and doing all the shit a decent human would do in a normal environment. Yet, London is far from normal, it's a freaking warzone. You don't fucking act like a gentleman. Not on peak-hours. However,

'Please stay behind the yellow line for your safety.'

'I'm on it, mate!' some nervous guy barked, making no sense. The train approached like a Space Shuttle returning from the Moon. That tube bullet was fast, it messed people's hair, it ruffled jackets. Even so, an army of mobile phone junkies kept their feet over the filthy yellow strip separating life from death, doing whatever with their devices. They didn't even blink at the arrival of the rounded missile which didn't touch them only because of some divine perfect geometry.

Albert was scared. The slightest bump from behind and they would all end up 6 feet under the underground.

'Let passengers off the train first.'

'Yo, finally my turn.' he announced. Yet it wasn't: a business guy forced his way in; the bulky builders imposed their presence with a simple nod and, finally, a young mother wearing the glamorous "Baby on Board" pin smiled a *'Don't you dare to stop me, you male bastard.'* smile at Albert while jumping the queue.

Despite the overwhelming frustration, he couldn't surrender. He had been there for 15-20 minutes now, standing on platform 2 like an idiot, minding the gap, minding the doors, letting people out first. 'Jesus Christ...' he muttered, watching another train fade into the dark tunnel. He was learning the game's rules the way any other rookie Londoner did: getting beaten and humiliated to the core.

'Come on, Albert, fight for the next train! Fight for your life! They won't trick you no more, oh, they won't! Screw grannies, pregnant women, handicapped creeps. I don't fucking care about anyone!'

'The next train to Ealing Broadway...'

'Here we are, I can do it, I'm the best, I'm the b...'

The train stops. Doors open and a fistful of people squeeze out of the carriage. The stopwatch starts its countdown: one, wait for the whole bunch to be out and... 'WHAT THE FUCK???' An experienced villain cut his way through, crashing into the exiting passengers.

'Rude, fucking rude and disrespectful.'

The guy managed to stick his right foot steadily on the train, causing silent rage throughout everyone.

'Enough is enough.' Albert burst out.

He couldn't tolerate such bad manners anymore, so he snapped. He grabbed the guy by the arm and pulled him out.

'Hey!'

'Get in the line, asshole.' fiercely said Albert, finally conquering his turn on the train. A few commuters applauded at that, others just didn't bother. The cool ones filmed the scene with their smartphones. Albert was feeling over the top as he waved his hand to the cameras and the cheering crowd like a Queen.

'This train is now ready to leave. Stand clear of the doors.'

'I made it, I made it!' he gloated. But the bloody train didn't appear to be able to depart. It kept accelerating and stopping, roughly, as if it was shuffling a deck of cards.

'Ladies and gentlemen, please stay away from the doors.' the frustrated driver repeated for the third time.

Nothing. Another violent stop-and-go with no positive outcome. Again. No luck. Albert's stomach was already upside-down.

'Alright, people, we are not going anywhere...' buzzed the intercom *'To the gentleman wearing a long grey coat on the second carriage: what part of stand clear of the doors don't you understand?'*

'Sick.'

FIFTY

Victoria was depressed. After a good week of hard work, the preparations for the Grand Opening of her shop were done but she was lost among her thoughts, sliding deep down memory lane, approaching regret road. Close by who-the-fuck-do-I-think-I-am square.

'It's not going to work...' she murmured, sitting on a torn French-fabric sofa, inside the tiny American cafe opposite her new shop.

'More coffee?' asked the girl working the floor.

'I'm a failure by design.'

'Madam?' insisted the waitress.

'What? Yes, coffee me up, please.'

The steaming dark liquid splashed and swirled inside the cup, then the girl hurried to the next request, next client, more work. Vic's gentle voice was playing around a melody from the past, she was whispering words, and everyone listened in secret, cuddled by her soothing tone.

'Vic?'

'Uh?'

'They're staring at you.' said Rose, annoyed.

'A song. But which one?'

'This isn't cool anymore.'

'Oh, yes, Kool Thing. I always loved it.'

'Please don't...'

'I don't wanna...'

'You can't do it everyday. We're officially a circus attraction!'

'I don't think so.'

'People are coming in here just to look at you. You're the ultimate freak-show character. Aren't you ashamed? A little?'

But Vic wasn't listening.

For once, she decided not to go by the book which, in her case, would be *The Fool's Manual* (a bestseller), therefore she didn't close her eyes while singing. Instead, she fixed the void ahead, pretending to be the real Kim Gordon. At that very moment, an undisputedly unlucky *not-regular* client entered the cafe.

'Hey, kool thing, come here, sit down beside me.' Vic sang.

Rose couldn't help but enjoy that moment as if it was her birthday's party present.

'Uh?'

'There's something I gotta ask you.' she went on.

'Ok...' replied the stranger, sitting in front of her.

'I just wanna know, what are you gonna do for me?'

'What?'

'I mean, are you gonna liberate us girls from male white corporate oppression?'

'TELL IT LIKE IT IS!' shouted Rose, laughing out loud.

'Er...'

'Don't be shy...'

'I don't know what you're talking about.' he said, embarrassed, looking inside Vic's hypnotic eyes which seemed to be staring at him, although they weren't. She was in a state of trance.

'Fear of a female planet?'

'I'm sorry, I think I should leave...'

'I just want you to know that we can still be friends.'

'Ok.'

'When you're a star, I know you'll fix everything.'

'A star?'

'Now you know you're sure lookin' pretty.'

'Nah... thanks... I'm so flattered.' he was blushing like a schoolboy.

'Rock the beat just a little faster.'

'Do you always talk like this? Your voice is so sweet...'

The cafe crowd was savouring that moment. A different show every single day so, guess what? It immediately became a trend. Locals simply loved to stop by and listen to Victoria's voice. They were delighted by watching her doing whatever she was doing. One guy even started a YouTube channel called "Greenwich Oddities" (you should subscribe) and walked in there every day staying from early morning till dark with his laptop, camera and phone switched on at all times. He used to sit on the scruffy couch on the left, next to the toilets, quietly waiting for his new favourite rockstar (Vic) to pop in and start her daily gig. Obviously, he was there at that precise moment too, gear in hand, shooting another chapter of his next-to-be-released Netflix Series.

'Now I know you are the Master.' Vic kept on singing.

The stranger's embarrassment got to sweating level. She was stunning beautiful, with a dazzling voice, and she was talking to him (no, she wasn't), she just told him he looked pretty!

'Best day ever.' he thought, already madly in love with her. 'May I ask what's your name?'

'I don't wanna...'

'I'm so sorry...'

'I don't think so.'

'I actually am, you can trust me.'

'I don't wanna...'

'I'm Billy, by the way.'

'I don't think so.' she repeated, totally abstracted, following the lines of the Sonic Youth's song.

'How do you know? I swear, my name is...'

'Kool thing, walking like a panther...'

'Mate, she doesn't even know you're there!' a girl from the audience whispered, trying to save the guy.

'What?' he was slowly realising all eyes were on him.

'Come on and give me an answer...'

'Is this a joke?'

'She's singing, man. She ain't talking to you.'

'What'd he say?' Vic sang when her fans finally cracked up in a loud, contagious laugh which woke her up. And,

As she emerged from her imaginary world, everyone jumped back on their seats, pretending to do stuff like nothing happened. They absolutely loved her. She was their personal idol and that's why they maintained a certain respect towards her. No one ever approached Vic to ask questions, selfies or anything. Sure, people made drawings, wrote poems and letters, but they were keeping it secret since they feared they could break that magnificent spell forever.

'Hi, I'm Victoria.'

'I'm Billy.' he replied, his voice shaking.

'Do I know you? Why are you sitting at my table?'

'I... I have to go.'

'I'm so sorry, I forget things sometimes. Do you...'

Stranger guy was so ashamed that he stood up and left the shop in a great hurry, shutting the door behind him, probably on his way to killing himself, so much he felt humiliated.

'Nice one, Vic.' said Rose, still laughing.

'What did I do?'

'Nothing, you can drink your coffee now.'

'ting, ting, ting.' the teaspoon said, playing high-five with the ceramic cup walls.

'You know,' continued Rose, 'forget about all that marketing shit I told you the other day.'

'Don't tell me you came down to reason.'

'Nothing of sorts, honey. I was right, obviously, but I guess I underestimated your level of madness.'

'I'm perfectly normal.' she replied, sulky.

'Normal? Jesus, you're so weird that you already made more fans than Alexa Chung just by sitting in a freaking coffee shop.'

'ting-ting-ting' the teaspoon was spinning faster now.

'Every soul in Greenwich knows about you.'

'Nonsense.'

'Let me see...' Rose said while scrolling on her imaginary iphone.

'ting, ting, ting.'

'There you are: five blogs talking about the charming weirdo; eight Instagram profiles showing pics of our shop; portraits of you; videos...'

'ting, ting, ting.'

'... and even idiotic TikTokers pretending to be Greenwich Vic, singing your songs.'

'You are making this up...'

'Shit, despite your few attempts to look decent, somehow you are inspiring a substantial amount of fools with your personality.'

'...'

'And you know what?'

'Clink.'

The teaspoon marked its last stroke of the day. Usually the three-thousand-six-hundred-one, depending on Vic's mood. She pushed the coffee cup forward and crossed her arms. She was fixing Rose.

'Please, enlighten me.'

'We haven't even opened the fucking shop yet.'

FIFTY-ONE

The train was speeding through dark tunnels. To the untrained eye, its passengers would appear squashed inside the cars with a 3G-force air compressor like canned meat. *SPAM*. Reality was much worse. Despite the situation, Albert couldn't help but pester everyone.

'Mate, how much oxygen do you think we have?'

'?'

'I mean, how many breaths am I allowed to take for us all to survive?' Albert asked, his head bent forward to fit inside the car; his back literally bashing against the door like a bleeding flail.

The guy laughed, 'That's a good one.'

'I'm serious. Can you tell me a story?'

'Sorry, I'm off at the next one.' he said, tapping the tube map over their heads.

Liar. That wasn't his stop but he'd clearly rather walk a mile or two than deal with a weirdo. So, the stranger disappeared at the first chance. Gone, forever. Albert checked his pocket watch and said:

'Two minutes.'

'What about it?' replied the lady pressed against him.

'Station to station: it takes two minutes.'

'Cool.'

'It's a fact, I checked it out.'

'Please move right down the cars.' asked the driver, trying to load as many passengers as possible into his metal trap.

'Do you think we'll ever sit down?'

'Where are you going?' asked the lady.

'Let me see... I'm twelve stations to go.'

'Holland Park? It's such a nice area. Do you live there?'

'Nah... I'm an East Ender. A local.'

'...' she smiled.

'If we're smart and aggressive enough, we should conquer half an inch through the carriage for each station.'

'Are you a mathematician?'

'I'm a writer.'
'Seriously? So you must have a great eye for details.'
'As a matter of fact, I do. For example, look at the privileged.'
'Who?'
'People enjoying their seats.'
'Ah...'
'Don't tell anyone but,' he whispered to her. 'they're all spies.'
'What?'
'THEY ARE SPI...'
'Shhh! I heard you. What do you mean?'
'Take a deeper look: the I'm-pretending-not-to-see-you game is on.'
'Is it a thing?'
'Absolutely. Now, act discreetly, observe: white male on the left.'
'...'
'He's been staring at the Asian girl since she sat down. He's holding the phone but, look!, he did it again!'

'Nice...' the lady started enjoying Albert. He was indeed a character, something to tell her friends later at lunch. She decided to play along. 'What about the black guy?'

'Aw, he's the best. He literally Xrayed the bird next to him from the reflection in the dark window. Smart.'

'So, you said you're a writer...'
'I am.'
'Do you Tweet?'
'Do I tweet? Hell yeah I do.'
'Great.'
'And I chirp too! Mostly under the shower.'
'...' she giggled.
'I'm sorry, I'm not sure I got what you were talking about.'
'You're so funny. Give me your card, you know I work for... well, I am with a bunch of cool people.'
'Fab.'
'We are always looking for good stories.'
'Babe, I'm your guy.'

'Ladies and gentlemen, we are being held at a red signal and we should be moving shortly.' announced the driver, after stopping the train in the middle of a tunnel.

The roaring of the train suddenly disappeared and some 80's tune emerged from the headphones of a very pumped, very bodybuilder-ed muscled guy who didn't realise shit and kept mouthing lyrics, convinced he was safe within the ridiculously loud wall of sound machine-gunned into his brain.

'I'VE HAD
THE TIME OF MY LIFE,
NO I NEVER FELT THIS WAY BEFORE...'

Everyone discreetly turned at the guy, trying not to be noticed but... they were sniggering like schoolmates. They were all accomplices of the same crime and it felt so good for everybody. Albert was amused.

'Seriously?' he whispered to his new lady friend. 'I expected some industrial banger from him. Some techno monochromatic CLANG CLANG CLANG tune slapped in your face.'

'Yeah, or some work-out playlist. He's so loud.' she laughed.

'To be fair, is there any other way to listen to music on the tube? Either you manage to stretch the volume bar beyond the digital boundaries of your mobile screen, or you'd rather turn the damn thing off.'

'Isn't people wonderful?'

'Now we're talking.'

'I apologise for the delay. We are now ready to depart.'

'What's your name again?'

'Hoover. Albert Hoover.'

'As I was telling you, I work for a news channel. I really think they're going to love you.'

'Super-b.'

'You don't have a business card with you, right?'

'Right.'

'No worries, I'll google you later.'

'You what?'

'The next station is Tottenham Court Road. Please keep your belongings with you at all times.'

'Nevermind. It's been a pleasure, Albert. I must go now, this is my stop.'

'No, please, don't leave me alone!'

'Sorry, I can't be late, you know...'

'Stay with me a few more stations, we might end up getting a seat.'

'Er...' for some inexplicable reason she was still listening to him and... she was even considering the idea of staying on the train. She couldn't believe herself. What did he do to her? Maybe she was changing, maybe she...

'Aren't you curious?'

'About what?'

'About... things.'

'I guess I am. Why?'

'I'm writing a new piece called:
"Tube People by Albert Hoover".'

'Sounds cool. I should write it myself.' she thought. 'Perhaps, I could pretend to leave and sneak back in, into the next carriage? I bet I can witness whatever happens (if anything) from the rear sliding window.' she continued, concerned about making up a good enough excuse to feed to the guys back at the office. 'No one really cares about me so, fuck it. I'm staying. This piece will change my career.' the young journalist concluded, in her mind.

'So? Are you staying?' he insisted.

'Doors are opening. Please take your belongings with you when leaving the train.'

'Sorry. I'll be in touch!' she replied, dashing off the carriage and jumping back into the next coach, 'Excuse me, I'm a reporter.' she yelled to the compressed mass of people while forcing her way towards the designated spying spot.

'This train is now ready to depart, mind the doors, mind the closing doors.'

FIFTY-TWO

'FLOSS!! CANDY FLOSS!!'

'Why does the damn boy have to shout? There's a sign the size of the Empire State Building over his head saying *Cotton Candy*. Isn't it enough, for God's sake??'

'Come on, Rose, he's just having fun.'

'I bet. Till someone calls the Police.'

'No one's calling anything. Leave him alone.'

'Tommy boy. How much do you ask for a goddamn stick of that blue/pink poison?'

'Aw, it's nothing dangerous. It's sugar.'

'Exactly.'

'Please, Rose. I have to work.'

'Can I have two of the blue ones?' gently asked a young mother.

'Absolutely, I'll bring them over in a sec.'

'Thank you.'

'*Thaaank you...* lame. What's wrong with these people? Don't tell me they're even giving us money.'

'Shhh! They can hear you.'

'Yeah, no way. I don't exist.'

'You do, especially when it comes to kids.'

'You mean the monsters? Like you?'

'Whatever.'

'Rose, why don't you help?' intervened Vic.

'Fuck. Should I help? I wanted to, I meant to, but then you told me not to choke Tommy in his sleep.'

'Oh, my...'

'And you stopped me from setting on fire that absurd, awful shop sign.'

'The cloud?'

'Yes, that horrid... what is it by the way?'

'Isn't it obvious? Puffy wool arranged in a beautiful, fluffy...'

'It's a damn cloud. I get it.'

'It took us two days to make it, show some respect.'
'It looks like a cat's hairball.'
'Yuck… disgusting.'
'CANDY FLOSS!!'
'Bloody Hell…'
'What's the name of your shop?' asked a guy from the massive crowd gathered there for the Grand Opening.
'I'm not sure.' replied Victoria.
'What do you mean?'
'Now that I think about it, I guess we don't have one, sorry.'
'I'm a blogger, how can I review your shop if it hasn't got a name?'
'Mmm… good question.'
'Give the fucker a goddamn business card!' shouted Rose.
'Great idea.'
'?'
'Please, take one.' Vic told the guy.
'Ah, impressive. A white piece of paper featuring a scrawled cloud. Seriously?'
'Seriously?! Vic, let me show this clown how we treat the snobby bastards. Give me a chance.' said Rose.
'It's our logo.'
'Yeah, still…'
'Vic, unleash me. I beg you.'
'Right. Use Cloud Nine if you like. That's how locals call my shop anyway.'
'Uh-huh. And what do you sell?'
'Dreams.'
'What?'
'Would you excuse me?' she said, rapt by something else.
'Yeah, Vic, tell him like it is. Fuck. Off.'
'You're the guy from the cafe, aren't you?' asked Victoria.
'I am.' he said, holding his massive camera, as usual. 'Gosh, you're the best thing ever happened to Greenwich.'
'I'm flattered… and, sorry, I don't think I…'
'Can we take a selfie?'
'I don't know, is it something dangerous?'
'Not at all, it's just a picture.' he giggled.
'Oh, like an autograph?'
'Yeah… nope.'

'Whatever, let's do it. How does it work?'
'You just have to smile, like this.'
'FLASH!'
'Thank you so much, Victoria! We all love you.'
'Who's we?'
'The community. Hey, take care, V, I'll see you around.'
'Ok...'
'VIC!!' shouted Tommy from the candy floss stall. 'Come here!'
'What's up little genius?'
'We're running out of books. The last person bought five copies!'
'Five?'
'Yeah, he said he wanted a couple for the kids, one for his wife, one for...'
'Ok, I get it, he loved them.'
'You've got no idea. Look over there.'
'Where?'
'Inside the cafe. They're all reading our books!'
'No way...'
'This is happening, Vic.'
'I don't know... they must be locals, or... people from the community.'
'So you know?!'
'I'm not even sure what it means. The YouTube guy just told me about it.'
'Well, I can assure you it's not only them. And... Vic?'
'Tommy?'
'I think he wants to talk to you.'

A very well-dressed old man brandishing a brass cane suddenly appeared inside Vic's eyes. Had he been there the whole time? What was he doing in such a weird place but, most of all, why did he look so familiar? The elegant gentleman was staring at her, holding a smile.

'Are you the owner?' he gently asked, doffing his precious top hat.
'You got it. At your service, sir.'
'May I ask what you do here?'
'Oh, plenty of things!'
'Such as?'
'Let me see...'
'Shall we go inside?' he proposed.
'Sure, the place is easier experienced than said.'

'Good luck with it!' said Rose.

'Shhh...'

'Did you say something, dear?'

'Er... well...'

'I heard a voice, but maybe it's just me.' he laughed. 'I'm not a youngster anymore. I'm a bit rusty when it comes to speaking with imaginary friends.'

'Imag... what? Did you...'

'Yes.'

'Ah.'

'Exactly.'

'Alright then. Take my hand, sir. Shall we?'

FIFTY-THREE

'Whatever. She would only slow me down. No writer wants to be disturbed while working on the best piece of his career. Am I right? Right?' Albert asked a stranger, who gave him one of those looks, you know what I'm talking about. 'And why do they even bother installing poles inside these cars?' he tried with another commuter. 'We're so tightly fit that falling it's a teeny tiny impossible.'

'Yeah...'

'I mean, we playing Human Tetris?'

'Welcome to London, man.'

'Not really living the dream, are we?'

'...'

'Can you hear this music?'

'Do you mind? I'm trying to read this article.'

'Mate, this beat is fab!' Albert told the guy, as if he could possibly listen to it too. 'It sounds like *BUM, tu-tu-pa, BUM, tu-tu-pa...*'

'?'

'You know when you have a song stuck in your mind and you can't help but follow its soundwave? Surf it to the moon and beyond?'

'Nope.'

Albert started moving his hips, awkwardly "dancing" within the ridiculous space he managed to conquer one station after another which equalled the volume of his body. Everyone was pressed inside the car as if vacuumed into one of those transparent plastic bags meant for food, or blankets. You suck out the air with your hoover and that's it, you ain't a problem no more. Ready to be shelved. Anyways, Albert kept humming his beat:

'BUM, tu-tu-pa, BUM, tu-tu-pa...'

Big Poppa by The Notorious B.I.G. was playing in his mind, and he was singing it out, tilting his head and doing the Michael Jackson move. He was so much into it that his knees started forcing their way up, feeling the rhythm.

'What is he doing?' asked the puzzled crowd spying on him.

'Oh, gosh. A fool on my train. Thank you God, for the umpteenth unwanted present.'

'Do I really deserve this? Am I not stressed / busy / frustrated / on the verge of a breakdown already?' silently cried someone next to Albert.

'BUM, tu-tu-pa, blabblab blabblab blab...' Albert was muttering nonsense, not knowing a single word of the verse.

'I need a drink.' sighed someone, out loud.

'Man, let's hit the pub.' replied a stranger.

'Pint?'

'Pint.'

'Guys, it's 9 am!' cut in an almost young woman.

'So what? Do you wanna join?'

'Watch it, boy.'

'Who the fuck are you by the way?'

'Waaait a sec. Who the goddamn fuck are you!' replied the black lioness, now pointing and swinging her finger at him.

'No need to argue, I don't have time to make friends anyway, I...'

'I bet you don't. You sure look like a 24/7 professional wanker.'

'What??'

Something was happening inside that train while Albert was splashing about a parallel world of his own, his delusion slowly escalating to a more invasive level.

'I LOVE IT WHEN YOU CALL ME BIG PO-PPA!'

He shouted at some point, his hands reaching for the car roof, club-style. Squished against the doors, A white young mother was about to explode.

'Why don't you tell him something?' she yelled at the smart guy standing next to her.

'Uh?'

'Yeah, you. Be a man!'

'I'm getting out at the next stop, sorry.'

'You coward!'

'You bitch!'

'HEY!' she roared, grabbing him by the hair.

'Throw your hands in the air as if you's a true player' sang Albert as he actually did it.

A smart black guy dressed in a suit dropped the briefcase and raised his hands too, getting in the mood. Instantly, his pale-white-faced colleague did the same.

'Wow, this is it...' thought the BBC reporter, spying from the other carriage.

'I LOVE IT WHEN YOU CALL ME BIG PO-PPA!' they screamed all together like proper hooligans.

A typical London youngster, possibly a model, smiled at a cute girl not too far from him.

'U on T-I-N-D-E-R?' he mimed with his lips.

'...' she blushed.

'...' he blinked back.

'M-A-Y-B-E...' she replied.

'For fuck's sake, get a room!' the explicit frown of an old man shouted at them.

'To the honies gettin' money, playin' niggas like dummies...'

Albert was singing as more and more people joined the party. Some were hammering the beat on the metal poles. Others were beatboxing like drum machines, with their fist pressed against their mouths.

'What's going on?' asked granny to herself, shaking her head, enjoying that rare moment of humanity. 'Has the war ended?'

'Go granny, go granny!' a bunch of teenagers cheered as she brandished her cane in the air.

'I LOVE IT WHEN YOU CALL ME BIG PO-PPA!' the whole car sang in unison.

Albert was directing the crowd, fueling the air with energy and pumping out the beat, loud, like the resident Dj of an underground Soho club. His moves were shaping the human mass as water, as a giant jelly pudding made out of people from all over the world. That human wave was now rocking the carriage. It was so contagious it quickly spread further down the coach, and to the next car, and so on, conquering the whole Central Line train to Epping.

'MAKE SOME NOISEEEEEE!' shouted one.

'FUUUUCK!' cried the stressed out business woman, finally letting off some steam.

They were dancing like a 3D Keith Haring graffiti, hands up as if holding the metallic ceiling.

'If you got a gun up in your waist please don't shoot up the place!'

'The coolest underground club ever.' the BBC reporter quickly scribbled in her mind. 'Better than any New York City basement party.'

A guy lit a fag, another cracked a beer open and there you go. The first ever rolling club was born.

'Cause I see some ladies tonight that should be having my baby, baby.'

'SCREW MY OFFICE JOB!!' shrieked out a senior partner of some downtown firm.

Even the teenage riot grrrrl wearing the classic Nirvana t-shirt was now partying. She couldn't resist it.

'Fuck sadness.' her black rimmed eyes seemed to say.

The Tinder match was now finally close enough to catch fire. Their tongues were performing a pretty extreme twist.

'SHAG HER, MATE!!' barked someone from somewhere.

'YO! You ain't talking like this in front of my kids, 'aight?' barked back a pretty statuesque mama, protecting her children's ears with her hands from the devil's words. Then she picked the man by the ear as if he was a little brat, although he wasn't young, more likely in his forties. She was about to kick the shit out of him when the whole car cheered at that and a smashing standing ovation and applause crashed the party. Her kids were laughing, and dancing like pros, clearly they had rhythm in their blood. They were so cool that everyone was copying their moves.

'BEST TIME IN MY LIFE!'
'TOP MORNING EVER!!'

The BBC reporter was sweating excitement, filming, taking mental notes, trying to scribble stuff on the palm of her hand, on the wrist, gosh, she didn't have enough skin for that. 'Suddenly, everyone, no matter their colour, religion, gender or sex orientation let down their guard and enjoyed being together for a while. A miracle. A spark of light for the Modern Western Civilisation.' she scrawled on the spare space left on her forearm.

The train did its first stop since the party started. You could clearly see the serious faces of the people waiting outside, on the platform. They were nervous and sad, and when they witnessed the unimaginable happening inside the train, their jaws dropped. The doors opened like velvet curtains at the Royal Albert and revealed an odd bunch of people singing, dancing, having a good time.

'What the fuck?'
Nobody gets out.
No one can possibly get in.
So the train goes on.

'TO THE NEXT STATION!!'

FIFTY-FOUR

'ding' said the doorbell welcoming Vic and her new friend.

They stepped inside and

'Are we dipping into an abstract painting?' asked the old man.

'?'

'Wow.'

'Thank you.'

'What a marvellous waterfall.'

'I'm glad you noticed it. It's our Stargate.' proudly said Victoria.

'Your what?'

'A STARGATE!'

'Ok, ok, I'm not deaf. Not yet anyway.'

'I'm so sorry...' Vic apologised, her face instantly turning crimson.

'This place is Delilah!'

'Ah. Indeed.' she replied, totally confused.

'Can I see what's over there, in the middle of the cascade? Is that a passage?'

'It is.'

'I wonder how you managed to pull that off.'

'Oh, it's one of Tommy's inventions.'

'What, the cotton candy kid?'

'Precisely. He explained to me that, basically... a small pump pushes the water up and then the water falls down, sliding against the wall. Then again, it goes up and...'

'Fuck me. Can't you be more bloody incompetent?'

'ROSE!!'

'It's alright.' said the elegant man, smiling. 'You're not an expert, but at the end of the day, nobody is.'

'Yep... I just like it.'

'And that's the only thing that matters. We should spend all of our time chasing beauty, lazing around the unknown, living adventures.'

'I love your approach, sir.'

'Thank you.'

'Sir?'

'Yes?'

'Pardon my insolence but, somehow, I feel like we met already. Do I know you?'

'Do you?'

'I... I'm not sure.'

'Fucking hell, Vic! How can you be so useless??' Rose burst out and then, turning to the old man, 'Don't you see? She's a nutcase just like you!' she yelled at him, but he didn't look upset or annoyed in any way. He was simply fascinated by that impossible character. He didn't say a word.

'I'm so sorry...' Vic apologised in shame. 'I'm afraid she's right, I get so easily distracted sometimes and I forget things.'

'It's ok, dear.'

'Still, you seem familiar. Are you sure that... ?' she insisted.

'Let's get serious. What's over that tiny passage?' the man asked, avoiding the main question.

'Ahem...'

'Don't tell me you guys created such an enchanting entrance and it leads to nothing.'

'Not at all, quite the contrary.'

'So, what's the problem?'

'Well...'

Vic was embarrassed. She was staring at the crystal water-wall looking for the right words to say. To be more accurate, she was observing the point where the flow was interrupted by the invisible plexiglass arch, the one framing a kid-size door which allowed any curious creature to overcome the waterfall without getting drenched.

'So?'

'Sir, I'm not sure you can get through it. It's very small.'

'Nonsense.'

'Ok...'

'What are you looking at? Help me out, lady. We need to get there!'

'Right. Give me your hat, and the jacket, and...' but he already chucked the shiny cane and his expensive garments to the floor. 'I guess we need to...'

'On your knees, let's go!' he insisted, kicking off his shoes.

'What the f...'

The old man was already on all fours, radiating an enthusiasm and such an energy he almost forgot to have. Vic was pretty incredulous, yet she knelt down too and followed the elegant senior explorer through the narrow passage. One more crawl and *BOOM!* A room full of mirrors, cushions, Christmas tree lights and stacks of books welcomed the odd pair.

'What is this?' he sort of asked, shocked.

'I don't know, you tell me.'

'I feel ecstatic. As if I'm fourteen once again.'

'Great, and, what are you doing?'

'Checking my pocket watch.' he said, pulling the analog device from his waistcoat. 'There's no time in here, marvellous!' he exclaimed with joy.

'...'

'Can I grab a book?' he asked. He was on a roll.

'Indeed. But I must tell you...'

'I knew it! They're blank!'

'This is the way we love reading, sir.' Vic sort of apologised.

'Terrific. It should be a common practice.'

'Reading?'

'Reading blank books.'

'Ah.'

'Argh... we used to play this game with my brothers when we were kids.'

'Are you serious?'

'Sure. You close your eyes and...'

'... and you catch the stories floating in your mind.'

'Everytime a different one. A never imagined tale that no one knows and never will, because...'

'... it fades away in the wind when you stop the flow, like a dream.' Victoria said, concluding his sentence.

'Genius. This is brilliant.'

'smack!' said his cracked old lips over Vic's forehead.

Victoria was getting emotional. Did they really create a magic place? The old man was playing with the mirrors, flicking through the books, making faces, sticking his tongue out. He was laughing the hell out of himself.

'I'm so glad you like our place.' she said 'You know, we just started and... sir? Are you crying?'

'Am I?'

'And now you're smiling.'

'It's your fault, darling.'

'Thank you.'

'This is the most amazing place I've ever been in my life. Can I stay here for a while?'

'Absolutely, sir.'

'Please, call me Frank.'

'Like Sinatra?'

'You got it, kid.'

'Great. I'll see you later, Frank.' she smiled, sneaking out of there.

'Grandpa's gone for good, Vic.' promptly commented Rose 'We'll have to call the police to get rid of that relic.'

'Isn't he adorable?'

'Like a fucking puppy?'

'Yes.'

'What's wrong with you people?'

'Aw, Rose, I know you're enjoying it. Take a look around. Did you expect so many visitors?'

'You're right. I couldn't imagine London had to offer such an array of creeps. That man, for example.'

'What about him?'

'What about? He's been playing with the toy trains since we opened, mixed among a bunch of kids!'

'So?'

'He's dressed like a CEO, I saw him toying with his phone for an hour before coming in.'

'It's a good thing, isn't it?'

'Yeah... I'm not so sure. He looks like a pervert. Should we call the Old Bill?'

'Idiot. He's simply enjoying it, check his eyes.'

'Paedo.'

'Hey, there's Steve!'

'Oh - My - Goodness. Is it Christmas already? Who fucking cares.'

'Steve!, Pete!'

'Hey, Vic...'

'What's with the long faces? Anything wrong?'

'Well... you should turn the radio on.'

'What?'

'You know... Albert.'

'Yeah? Where is he?'

'He's on air right now.'

At that very moment, Tommy ran inside the shop like a fool. He was holding a mobile phone tuned in to BBC Radio London. The tiny speakers buzzed:

BREAKING NEWS

A young man has been attacked at Notting Hill Station. Police officers were escorting him outside when an angry mob assaulted him. The guy, Albert Hoover, is accused of chaos-starting, perpetrated in the form of a party, inside a packed Central Line train. This is a massive operation for the MET which, after stopping the vehicle, has arrested hundreds of people involved in the incident. We have the man of the hour on the phone:

'Albert, can you tell us what happened?'

'Mate, we were having so much fun!'

'How are you doing?'

'Where am I?'

'You've been attacked. They're bringing you to the hospital.'

'Oh, yeah. Where's the motherfucker?'

'Please, language. You're on air for BBC News.'

'What? Fucking hell.'

'Ahem... Can you give us a few details?'

'Absolutely. I was saving this city from technological oblivion, in the name of Anthony Morvar.'

'Who?'

'We need happiness, people interacting with each other. We need to start and spread a Dream Revolution!'

'Christ...'

'Can I say hello to Victoria?'

'You just did.'

'You know, she's great, she has a shop in Greenwich and she sells dreams. VIC, I'M SO...' he didn't finish shouting, since the reporter pulled the mic off.

'Thanks, Albert. That was all from Notting Hill. More news about the incident in the next update.'

FIFTY-FIVE

In every movie worthy of its name, bad news comes in the midst of the night waking the main character like a bucket of ice cubes thrown on the head. So, he/she/it runs to the streets still wearing a pajamas, still half-sleeping. At this point, the hero usually steals a car and starts a race against the clock breaking all sorts of law, ignoring traffic lights, shouting obscenities to pedestrians and cursing at the storm that (obviously) is sweeping the jammed big city away like one of those leaf blower cannons over a handful of confetti.

When Victoria got news that Albert was in a hospital, she burst out laughing. Was it a nervous breakdown? Was she glad that karma punished that silly boy for leaving her like that? Perhaps, it was a weird-happy reaction to the fact that Albert was still thinking about her, that, maybe, he never stopped being in love with her.

'God only knows what's wrong with you.' commented Rose.

'...' said Steve and Tommy together.

Victoria couldn't stop her nervous laugh. She was in tears, so much so that only Pete, the one half-sane person in the room, managed to calm her down after a while. He convinced her that, no matter what happened in the past, visiting Albert was a decent-enough thing to do. For some obscure reason, Victoria agreed. Without saying a word, she grabbed her coat and, with the sharpest of the gazes her eyes could slash, she never said:

'Whatever, let's give the motherfucker a chance.'

And so they went.

As they entered the sterile hospital room, they found a zombie-like human lying still inside a tucked bed like an Egyptian pharaoh.

'Mum...' slurred Albert, his eyes blood-encrusted, stoned by legal morphine.

'Is he dumber than usual?' asked Rose, amused by the hopeless derelict, but Victoria wasn't listening. She was't smiling anymore.

'Can we have a minute alone?'

'Yeah! Kick the shit out of him!' cheered Rose, leaving with the

others and.
Clack.

The door shut close as Victoria approached the bed. With the most awkward face, she managed to say 'Hey, how's tricks?' to Albert, attempting to look cool.

'... who are you?'

'It's Victoria, the one you dumped a few months ago, you bastard.' she didn't say although, he heard. Naturally.

'Bloody - hell.'

'Yep. Me.'

'Jesus... where am I?'

'London Royal Hospital.'

'I must have blue blood, then.'

'It's nice to see that you're ok, you didn't lose your sense of humour and, above all, you're so freaking happy to see me again. Well, I shall leave now.'

'Wait... wait a second.'

'I don't think so.'

'Where's my mobile?'

'What?' Victoria was staggered. 'Are you fucking kidding me? I'm not in the mood for any of your jokes.' she continued, pissed off.

'I swear, it's important.'

'Isn't it?'

'I mean it.'

'Right, here's your goddamn mobile *(stick it up your motherfucking beep, you son of a beep beep beeeeep),* what should I do with it?'

'Can you go to Voice Memos and play the first one?'

'Unbelievable...' she sighed.

'Please, trust me.'

'Whatever.' she finally said.

And she did what he asked, mostly to satisfy her sadistic curiosity, but also because of the feelings she didn't seem so good at repressing. She tapped play: the ticking of a pocket watch sounded from the phone speakers; weird noises like the flick of a lighter and the fuzzy sizzling of a burning cigarette tip joined the beat; someone was shouting in the background, knocking furiously on some door; finally, a long, deep breath expressed an unintelligible, precise thought and the track ended.
Blip.

'What do you think? Did you like it?' asked Albert after a

profound, silent wait.

'...'

'I was thinking of you... I'm sorry.'

'Bastard.' she thought, trying to avoid his gaze.

'I never stopped thinking about you.'

'How much morphine do you have in your veins?'

'Well...'

'Look, I didn't even want to come over.'

'But you're here now. Thank you.'

'Yeah, anyway. Did anyone tell you that you managed to get on the front page of every national newspaper?'

'What?'

'I brought the BBC article, I can read it if you want.'

'I want!'

'Okay, it goes like this: Tube People *by Hellen Moore.*'

'Fucking hell, that's my title!' burst out Albert.

'Can you stop lying for once?'

'Vic, it's true!'

'Choke him with a pillow, babe!' almost said Rose, spying along with the other from a tiny fissure left by the ajar door.

'Anyhow,'

'What did she write?'

'Do you want to hear it or not?' Victoria shouted, freezing Albert with a murdering look.

'...'

'Great, listen:

Tube People *by Hellen Moore.*

Builders and sales guys sharing beer cans and chanting football anthems. Strangers dancing, hugging, cheering along no matter their status, race, gender or sexual orientation. Muslim mums, Indian, Catholic, black, white, asian mums, all helping each other to protect their little cubs from the overexcited crowd. This is what Albert Hoover managed to pull out of his top hat today, on a regular Central Line train. The world has never been so little, equal and fair. London is back to Magic. What happened should serve as an example for everyone to observe and follow, if we want to build a better future.'

Victoria's eyes shifted from the paper to Albert who was embarrassed, as only guilty people can be.

'Comments?' she asked.

'Hey, I didn't do nothing. I just wanted to sing. So, I sang. Then... I guess people got along with me, and the rest is history.' he kind of apologised, incapable to hide the brattiest of grins.

'You are such a...'

'Idiot?'

'... freaking fool.' she finished her sentence.

'Thanks but, let's stop talking about me, I'm not the celebrity in the room. I heard the big news, congrats about your shop!'

'...' Victoria blushed.

'Pete told me there were like a thousand queuing people.'

'It really went well.'

'Can I come down, one day? I'm dying to see your new place. You're the most inspiring person I've ever met, Lord knows what you created this time.'

'Er...' tables turned, it was her time to be embarrassed. How could he be so shameless? One minute he was apologising and now...

'Did you come up with a sound room too? Do you remember the Sound Hotel?'

'I do. And I still love the idea, but...'

'Vic, I drafted new inventions, you know, I've been thinking about you a lot...'

'Gosh, the morphine is really working on you.' she thought out loud, then she said 'Listen... Albert...'

'Would you ever forgive me?'

At that very moment, Albert's phone rang. Some unidentified person was calling and Vic happened to have the device in her hands. What to do? She gave him a puzzled look and, since he replied *yes* to her non question, she answered.

'Hello?'

'Am I speaking to Albert? Albert Hoover?'

'Yes. Nope. I mean, this is Victoria, who are you?'

'I'm so sorry, my name's Hellen Moore. Are you the Victoria everyone's talking about?'

'I don't know, am I?'

'My goodness, yes, this is my lucky day! I really wanted to speak with you too, you're a hero!'

'Uh?'

'I'd love to interview you, if you have time for it. Your shop is a London's landmark already. Cloud Nine, isn't it?'

'That's the name locals gave to it, you can call it the way you want.'
'You're lovely. Lovely. I can't wait to meet you in person.'
'...'
'You, and Albert, of course. We want you live, on BBC Breakfast.'
'What? In Manchester??'
'Nonsense, that's just another fake news. The studios are in London, don't worry about it.'
'It makes sense.'
'Anyhow, it's going to be amazing, we're receiving so many letters from all over the country! People want to see you guys!'
'I'm not sure this is a cool id...'
'Tut-tut. I'll pick you up tomorrow, 7:30 am, in front of Cloud Nine.'
'Wait a sec!'
'Thank you so muuUuuch! See you later.'
'But...'
'click.'

Victoria stood up, stared at Albert's numb face for a second and then punched him in the arm.

'I'm so fucking happy you're back, you fucker.' she told him with a straightforward, silent frown. And she left the room.

FOUR

UNLEASH THE WEIRDOS

FIFTY-FIVE

Despite doctors' concerns, Albert managed to escape the hospital the very next morning. He slept like a baby for fifteen hours straight and his face regained a human-ish colour. Obviously, the morphine, the forced rest, and the many antibiotics IVs stuck in his veins did most of the job, but... seeing Victoria had been the real trigger. Her smile and her soothing voice did more than any synthetic drug. Like Asterix's magic potion she gave him an impossible strength. Albert was happily dizzy, what else could anyone ask from life? So he left. He slammed the exit door open like a rockstar and was out of the hospital, curbside of the road.

'TAXIII!'

'Man, I'm here, no need to shout.' said the driver, who was parked in front of Albert's nose. 'Get in.'

'I'm sorry, didn't see you. I'm quite confused, it must be the drugs.'

'? Are you ok?'

'Top of the world.'

'Cool, I don't want no problems.'

'You got it.'

'Where to?'

'I don't know.'

'You don't? Is it a joke?'

'I wouldn't dare. Do you know Victoria Sparkle?'

'Who?'

'Mate, she's the creator of Cloud Nine!'

'I don't give a damn if she's the President of the United States of my Ass. I need an address.'

'You a rapper?'

'Man...'

'But... that's exactly where I need to go.'

'Where?'

'Victoria's.'

The driver closed his eyes for a moment, took a deep breath and finally turned his head towards Albert.

'Alright. Does she live in this city, at least?'

'Of course. I think so.'

'I'll tell you what: I drive, you pay. Sound good enough for you?'

'Marvellous.'

'Just tell me where and when to stop.'

'That's great, thanks!'

'Fasten your seatbelt, I don't want any accidental death happening in my cab.'

'Excellent, me neither.'

The car started and immediately Albert spaced out into his personal imaginary closet where he stashed the most intricate thoughts. He was trying to put the top shelf in order, the one labelled *Morvar* with a permanent marker when, among tons of rubbish, he found a few good missions which seemed to have the potential for inspiring future projects. For example: delivering the radio wasn't easy but made Mrs Something happy; the audio recording of his room appeared to make an effect on Victoria no matter how angry at him she was. What else? Oh yeah, Josh. God knows, he might be painting his masterpiece right now.

'Greenwich!' Albert shouted out of the blue.

'What?'

'I just recalled that her shop is in Greenwich.'

'Ok, boss, heading there.'

'Where was I? Inventions, yes, and suitable ideas to be put on the shelves of Cloud Nine with a decent price tag. So, audio tracks: ok, they're certainly not conventional, but they're music, after all. I mean, what's wrong with *Sound of Empty Room 56 at Night*? or, *Inaudible Perception of Life Vs Death*? It's so easy. You rent a random space, sit in the corner and press rec. Some might say it's only a silent track but I beg to disagree. Whatever stream of thoughts you have in that very moment must end up on tape, even if you don't speak. Right? Great, we should start a Record Company. We could sell our LPs throughout the world, changing the listening concept forever, shifting it from conventional ears-brain path to a more complex system of communication between all the other senses. Track 1, *The Void*. You press play and there it is: a soundless noise that makes you think about a certain colour, then a taste, then you actually see the Void, the vacuum, and suddenly you want to skip to Track 2, *Absence*.

Mate, my girl and I are gonna be pioneers!' Albert told the driver.

'Fab.'

'We'll be on the cover of The Times, freshly Nobel awarded.'

'Do you want me to fake interest?'

'That would be superb, thanks, mate!'

'So, this Victoria is your girl, isn't she?'

'Well... we're not really together...'

'Cool.'

'You know, I...'

'Look, I don't actually give a fuck, I just asked the first thing that came to mind.'

'Indeed, sorry, mate.'

'Brill. Go on.'

The driver was a true, proper friend, Albert was so happy he found such a great person. Male's bonding is easy: no one asks tricky questions, no one gives disappointing answers, and the world keeps spinning smoothly, like wind licking the ocean's skin. Aw, perfection. 'Anyway, back to Morvar-inspired world-changing inventions: scents of daytime moments sealed in tiny glass ampoules, available for anyone, in every store. It's the future, I can see a huge market for it. Here's what I already tested: *September 12th's Dew*; *Lunar Eclipse n.2* (n.1 didn't work); *Buried Seed of a Centenarian soon-to-be-born Oak Tree;* and many others which I definitely (maybe) catalogued (cata-what?) in my (somewhere) Moleskine. Enough.

One-shot Essences, Unique like You.' chanted Albert. 'Do you like the jingle?'

'Absolutely.'

'People will go nuts for our vials!' he continued.

'I bet.'

'Really?'

'Man...'

'Fuck, my fault, I almost forgot our deal.'

'It's alright, brother. Now, do you recognise anything around here?'

'Uh? Are we in Greenwich already?'

'Man, you've been blathering nonsense for an hour.'

'Mental time-lapse. Wow.'

'So?'

'So what?'

'Please, tell me we're almost there.' begged the taxi driver, rather worn by the endless driving in circles around London, impossibly attempting to guess the right direction.

'I don't know... try the next road on the right, I feel lucky.'
'If you say so.'
'Sure, in fact...'
'Here?'
'Yeah, it could be... be careful, WATCH OUT!'
'*HOORN!!*'
'Yes, definitely, there, the next one.' said Albert, sweating.
'Don't worry, lad. I've been on this job all of my life. Relax.'
'Yeah, but...'
'Now? Should I turn or continue straight ahead?'
'No.'
'On the right?'
'No...'
'Left?'
'No. No! Mate, can you please stop the car for a moment? I need to stretch my legs, I can't think in such poor conditions.'

The driver loved the idea. He let the car skate on the tarmac for another ten/twenty metres then pulled over. To him, Albert was another weirdo in weirdo's town. At least this one didn't seem to be a professional sicko nor a serial killer/rapist. 'Aw, London.' he mumbled getting off the cab, doing a 1-2, 1-2 done stretching and finally puffing on his electronic fag.

Albert scanned the sky as if chasing the trail of an aeroplane that never took off and never would. He was so much focused on a specific imaginary spot among the clouds that even his new friend turned to look at that. Nothing.

'There's nothing.' commented the driver.

Albert wasn't so sure about that, but we're losing the point. All of a sudden, he happened to see the exact route leading to Victoria's place *(no, he didn't)*. He smiled and hugged the driver. 'I know the way.' he said.

'Fucking hell, about time. Get in the car.'
'Thank you, but I feel like taking a walk.'
'Whatever. How do you wanna pay?'
'Cash?'
'You're a legend.'
'Nah... I'm just a...'

But the cab driver couldn't care less, busy counting the notes like an expert bookie. He stashed the roll in his back pocket and, with the agility of a 99 y.o. man, he slipped back on his seat. The engine started and the car window rolled open. 'Try not to die, ok?' he gently said nodding to Albert.

' ;) ' he blinked back to his new mate.

FIFTY-SIX

Hellen Moore arrived on time-ish, finding Victoria and a little boy yawning on the curbside. She was shocked by their outfits: the kid was wearing a sort of so-called poncho that mostly looked like a tablecloth, or some cheap curtain pulled over his shoulders. As if that wasn't enough, he also had a pair of vintage aviator goggles shading his eyes. Victoria wasn't less outrageous, her style was possibly even a step forward: jungle print headband, loose hair cascading over a torn brown leather jacket, Sonic Youth tee and a pair of worn-out denim shorts, all enriched by a few kilos of medallions, necklaces, bracelets and whatevers. Uh, did I mention the silver hand-sprayed 60's boots? Those two looked like Jimi Hendrix and Brian Jones in the iconic '67 picture, only a tad (a lot) cheaper. How on Earth could Hellen bring them live on BBC Breakfast was a mystery.

'Daaarling, it's so nice to finally meet you in person.' she said.
'What a fucking fake. She hates you, Vic.'
'Nah, Rose, she's just polite.'
'Yeah, I told you not to wear the damn hippie gear in full.'
'Hellen, let me introduce you to Tommy.' said Vic, ignoring Rose.
'You are the Special Effects Master, aren't you?'
'Precisely. I curated the technological parts of the shop.' he proudly replied. Hellen was stunned. How old was that boy?
'Impressive.'
'Can we have coffee before leaving?' asked Victoria.
'Actually, we're behind schedule. Where's Albert?'
'God knows. He was in the hospital yesterday.'
'Ok... I guess I should call him.'
'Good luck with it.' said Vic, not sure whether she was annoyed or amused by the whole thing.
'What do you mean?'
'Albert loves to make surprises. Therefore, he switches his mobile off every time he's got an appointment.'
'Ah.'

'Come on, let's grab a coffee.'
'Right. I bet he'll be here any minute now.'
'Yeah, you wish, you corporate bastard.' commented Rose.
'Where the hell are you?' thought Vic.

* * *

Albert was literally around the corner, wandering inside Greenwich Vintage Market when he found what he was looking for.

'A rose, please. Red.' he asked the guy at the stall.
'Flame or passion red?'
'Red.'
'Do you fancy a semi-closed bud or a fully opened one like this?'
'I'd like it to be special, with a hint of eternity.'
'The taste or the smell?'
'Both. No, pardon me. It must have the flavour of the horizon, and the solidity of the skies.'
'Aw, you're an expert. It's such a pleasure to meet people like you.'
'I know, mate.'
'Just give me a second, I'll go get it for you. Are you in a hurry?'
'A bit. Why?'
'Don't. Please, relax. Haste is an utterly negative thing, isn't it?'
'You got it, boss.'
'Can you imagine if flowers would blossom instantly? If they'd come out of the soil in a matter of seconds? Where would the magic be?'
'I can't agree more with you. The thing is…'
'You don't have to justify yourself, it's perfectly normal to be in a rush. Perhaps, no one ever had the patience to tell you.'
'Tell me what?'
'Try to picture a world where everything happens in a matter of a snap. Close your eyes, follow me.'
'…'
'Let's say you want to admire planet Earth from the top of the Himalayas. You think it, and *PUFF!*, you're there. Beautiful, uh?'
'Fuckin hell, it is beautiful!'
'Now, remain there for ten minutes.'
'Do I really have to?'
'Just do it. Meanwhile, I'll get your rose.'

From that breathtaking height, Albert felt like a God. He was eagleing the skies, swooping through the clouds, diving and splashing into those frothy puffs like a kid, again and again. Then he began staring at the horizon. He tried to grasp it, grab it with his sweaty hands, well-aware that it was impossible but he was leaning forward, so much that he almost fell down. 'What a sight.' he thought but... he didn't know what else to do. Weird. 'Where the hell is he gone?'

The florist came back exactly ten minutes later, perfectly synced with Albert's awakening from the oblivion. He wasn't surprised at the sight of his client's numb face, it was always like that with the new ones, the first time.

'So?' he asked.

'I'm sorry, I fell asl*yawnnn*... can I open my eyes?' begged Albert.

'Of course. Now, before I give you the rose, please answer a simple question: was the top of the Himalayas as good as you imagined?'

'I don't know... it was at first, but then I got bored, even though...'

'... even though it was an absolute wonder. Classic.' the florist said, finishing the sentence. 'You weren't able to enjoy it, right?'

'Yeah... what did I do wrong?'

'Isn't it clear?'

'No.'

'You missed the journey; the fatigue, the pain, and the swearing, and the *why did I come to this miserable freezing hell at all?*, from the slopes to the peak.'

'Ah.'

'You missed trampling and stumbling on every single rock; the soreness of your feet.'

'...'

'If only you opted to reach the top by making an effort, by being patient and slowly enjoying the walk, tasting the air, breathing in the nuances, the colours, the shimmering of the mountain sky...'

'Are we getting anywhere with this?'

'... you'd definitely remember all those experiences, your memory would be rich with details and the final sight of the top would be unforgettable. Unique.'

'Mate, you're fucking number one!'

'Well... thank you.' the florist blushed.

'Is that my rose?'

'Yes, sir.'

'Fuck, it's astonishing.'

'It is, isn't it? Bring it to your lover.' he said with a smile.

'Sure do. One last question: what will I tell her?'

The guy grinned, pleased with himself.

'The words you are searching for are jealously guarded inside your lady's eyes. You simply have to enter her gaze and read.'

'Perfect, I'm screwed.'

'You can't be wrong.'

'I hope so. Thanks again, mate.' Albert concluded, and he dashed away, conscious of being unbelievably late to his appointment.

Luckily, he reached the cafe sitting in front of Cloud Nine in no time. It was precisely around the corner. From outside the window, he saw Victoria, her lips curved in a smile as she caressed the air and gestured impossible gestures. 'Gosh, she's ravishing.' he thought, pressing his hands and nose against the thick glass, fixing her like the n.1 psycho in the universe. When Hellen Moore noticed the curious peeping Tom, coffee cups flipped in the air and everyone was dragged outside in a hurry.

'Chop-chop, we're late! Everyone's waiting for you at the Studios!' she yelled in a frenzied state, grabbing Albert and Victoria's hands the way one would do with babies.

FIFTY-SEVEN

The back seats of the glossy-black Mercedes provided by the Studios seemed like a gilded cage to Victoria and Albert. They felt incredibly uncomfortable at sharing that space on their way to the location. Victoria was torn. She couldn't realise whether she was touching the sky or freaking mad at Albert. Besides, she had to leave Tommy behind, at the shop, and Rose was impossibly quiet as if that situation was too much even for her, so much so that she puffed away, leaving the two alone for the first time in months.

Albert was weird too. Weirder than usual.

'Guys, we're almost there,' started Hellen, 'get ready for make-up, hairdressing and...'

'No way.' interrupted Albert.

'What?'

'I'm not a monkey, I don't want to be touched.'

'Me neither. I don't paint my face, that's the rule.' added Victoria.

'But...'

'NO!' they replied at once.

'Right... what about new outfits? We have plenty of cool dresses and...'

'Thanks, but no thanks.'

'I agree with Albert. Why do you want to change us?'

'It's...'

'You should have known better. This is what you get when you ask for the Cloud Nine gang.'

'Ahem... you're not in the team, Albert.' whispered Victoria.

'Exactly.' he said.

'I'm sure we can provide the clothes of your dreams, guys.'

'NO!!'

'Fucking bastards. I'm gonna get fired.' thought Hellen, but then said 'Absolutely, whatever makes you feel good.'

'Can I go home?' asked Albert, causing almost a nervous breakdown to the reporter who suddenly turned pale. 'Yo, I'm kidding.

All good in the hood, Hel.'

Hellen was seriously considering the idea of murdering them. *Hel? Why don't you fucking call your slut mother like that?* She secretly swore. Then again, the almost five-figure check she had been promised for arranging that appearance put her back in her place. *You can call me anything you want*, she hummed, counting imaginary stacks of notes and finally sinking into a parallel world of her own.

She was almost jolly when the car stopped, waking her up. Instantly, like the most efficient cocaine-fueled robot, she switched back to hysteria mode and expertly manoeuvred the two out of the vehicle and around the corridors, like puppets.

The BBC Studios were huge. Not as much could have been said of the actual set, smaller than what a regular person could think. Shrinked, if compared to a London studio apartment (aka rat-infested closet).

'Bloody telly is fish eyeing everything like a magnifying glass.' commented Albert, blinking to Victoria who just didn't reply. 'Don't you feel like... plunged into an aquarium?' he insisted. Nothing. Not a single thought was escaping Vic's mind.

Since they refused any makeup (or other magic tricks) and, since they were *we'renotgonnamakeit* late, Hellen basically shoved them on the TV set. At that moment, Paul, the famous BBC presenter approached his golden guests with a neon-white smile .

'Hi, I'm Hoover. Albert Hoover.' he cut in.

'Pleasure to meet you. And you must be Victoria.' said the TV man, offering his hand to her.

'Yep. You can call me Vic.'

'Marvellous. Shall we start? Please, have a seat.'

'...' they both replied.

'Let me introduce the rest of the crew to you: here is John Blake, a critic from Oxford University.'

'Critic of what?' asked Albert, without getting a reply.

'and... the Mayor of London will be connected with us from City Hall.'

'What??' they shrieked unison-ly.

'*Ready in 3 - 2 - (1)...*' whispered a technician, and that was it. The theme song played loud in the studio, a million watts army of spotlights switched on, and the show started.

'Good morning, welcome back to BBC Breakfast. Today, we're honoured to host the couple of the hour. Everyone is talking about them, so please welcome Victoria and Albert.'

Thunderous roar of applause flooding the studio.

'First of all, we're not a couple.' said Vic, to break the ice.

A blizzard immediately overwhelmed the audience.

Albert lowered his eyes.

'Nice fucking start.' thought Paul, pulling a smile and expertly changing the subject. 'Let's begin with you, Victoria. There's quite a buzz about your shop, Cloud Nine, isn't it?'

'I guess...'

'Can you tell us what's so special about it? What do you sell?'

'Dreams.'

'Isn't she adorable?' the host commented looking straight into the camera, applying fake smile n.7 to his face, the one provided by the BBC for any occasion. 'Rumor has it that you also sell blank books, is it correct?'

'Indeed, Paul. I always loved to read that way. You know, what's better than flicking through the stories trapped inside your heart?'

'That's a great point. What do you think, John?' he said, passing the hot potato to the art critic.

'I don't believe their work is special in any way. To be honest, I consider her statement quite arrogant.'

'What? Selling dreams?'

'Precisely. I attended your opening and I must say that what I found was pretty close to ridiculous: a broken TV set?'

'It's the find-yourself, Reflection Screen.'

'Soapy bubbles...'

'The sparkling-light Rainbow.'

'... inaudible music...'

'That's the concept for a Sound Hotel.' Victoria said, giving a fleeting glance to Albert who was enchanted by her confidence.

'... empty vials...'

'You mean Scents of Lost Memories, I suppose.'

'Right. Your shop seems like a cheap amusement park, nothing more than that.'

'Cool.'

'I'm not saying it is garbage, although...'

'Can I kick him in the nuts?' Albert suddenly didn't tell Victoria, who almost smiled.

'Shhh...' she didn't reply 'They're gonna hear you.'

'How does this clown dare to judge your hard work like that?'

'Come on, be quiet.' Victoria insisted blushing at those words, instinctively reaching for his hand. Albert couldn't believe what just happened and neither could Victoria. That simple gesture calmed him down, he wasn't furious no more. His face shifted from angry to confident. Attitude. Albert's best feature. So, he had to speak up his mind:

'Mate, you might be an art critic but, clearly, you don't know shit about amusement. A bit rusty in that field, innit?' he provoked.

The cameraman couldn't muffle a laugh, barely capable of holding the gear steady. Finally, someone was giving Mr Blake what he deserved. The art critic was shocked, no one ever dared to challenge him, but he managed to keep it together. He replied:

'I must admit that I haven't been to the Circus in a long time.'

'You should.'

'Thanks for the advice, Mr Albert. But I must insist, what else do you have?'

'What do you mean?'

'I'll get straight to the point. There are the books, the quirky space, and... then?'

'Then what? What does this piece of *you know what* wants from us?' asked Albert, turning to Victoria, gripping her hand.

The production was on the edge, undecided whether to shut the show down and send commercials or capitalise on that fight. That kind of language couldn't be tolerated and they feared an escalation. Luckily, Victoria intervened.

'I'm sorry, Albert's not feeling well today.'

'Oh, I perfectly understand. It's always like that when it comes to artists.' commented the critic with a smirk.

'Yeah, us freaks... To answer your question:'

'Please, Miss Victoria.'

'I spotted you at the opening, it wasn't hard, you were the only one not having a good time.'

All the people in the studio giggled.

'... and you know why?' she continued.

'Enlighten me.'

'You didn't try any of our creations. You stood still, scribbling stuff. You didn't give it a chance.'

'I beg to disagree. I...'

'If only you would let down your guard for a second... have you noticed how many businessmen, senior bankers, old women and grandpas ended up playing with the toy trains, the mirrors, the Wonderwall Waterfall?'

'In spite of that...'

'Cloud Nine is all about giving everyone the chance to get back to their inner child, let go of the stress and find happiness again. If only we could focus more on the details, the little silly things, the noble humble gestures... I'm sure we would see beauty in this world again.'

'Well...'

'But one must find the courage to try. I'm afraid you didn't.'

'Yeah, you coward.' said Albert, displaying a full bratty smile to the cameras.

Paul, being an experienced TV man, instantly recognised the perfect break in the conversation and intervened, calling for the commercials.

'We'll be back to Victoria and Albert in a moment. Don't switch channels!'

FIFTY-EIGHT

Hellen Moore was checking the share, ratings, demographics of the show and couldn't believe her eyes. The BBC phone line was on fire, the email box exploding and comments flicked all over, on social media.

The host, Paul, appeared to have facial paralysis so much he was smiling. He loved that rodeo, he was born for that. He was adjusting his suit when the camera guy gestured something to him and again, theme song, *3-2-(1)...* and the lights flooded the room, making that tiny plaster box shine like the Chelsea Stadium.

'Welcome back to BBC Breakfast. Albert, can you tell us what happened on the tube?'

'Thanks for asking. It was a miracle.'

'Can you expand on that?'

'Have you ever been on the Underground?'

'Sure. Why?'

'We are facing a great change, Paul.' started Albert, acting like a real politician. 'People are increasingly alone, they avoid any interaction by scrolling on their smartphones all the time, especially on the tube. Everyone's locked inside their own virtual cage without knowing where they stashed the key.' Albert stated. Victoria smiled.

'Are you saying that we need more humanity?'

'Indeed. Let me take Cloud Nine as an example. Selling dreams is not a joke, it is a way of giving back humanity to humans.'

'Clear.' lied Paul, who didn't understand a thing.

'I mean, why else should we live if not to dream, create and share our ideas? We're not robots, we can't repress our emotions, they're part of our bloodstream, they... you know what?'

'No.'

'They're the only path capable of leading us towards happiness.'

'True.' the host commented, nodding like a pro.

'Why can't we have fun and experience an imaginary Glastonbury every day? Would it hurt?'

'Well... by the way, how are you? Can you tell us about the attack you endured?'

'Oh, it's nothing, really.' said Albert, his face still spectral white, dripping sweat from the bloody wound on his eyebrow. 'I'm a man.' he added, barely managing to keep his eyes open for the fatigue and the pain related to the vanishing morphine effect. Victoria was enjoying Albert's ordinary delusions, enjoying the second-hand hero costume he wore to protect himself from reality. But at the same time she was intrigued by a peculiar detail in his odder-than-usual behaviour. Albert looked stiff. Unnaturally stiff. She meant to ask why since they got inside the Mercedes, so what better moment than now, live on national television? She looked at him and fired:

'What's wrong with your left arm?'

'Uh?' both Paul and Albert replied together.

'It seems like you can't bend it, are you wearing a cast?' she insisted.

'I'd like to invoke the 5th amendment.' stated Albert, panicking.

The host burst out laughing.

'Mate, change subject.' Albert whispered to Paul although he was mic'd up and his words resounded loud and clear across the country. 'Shit.' he muffled, once more inside the mic. Victoria giggled like everyone else. And yet again she was determined to get to the bottom of that thing, resolute to find out what the heck Albert was hiding. But something else came up. A jingle jingled and

'Guys, it's time to meet one of your new fans.' announced Paul. 'Ladies and gentleman, please, give it up for the Mayor of London!'

'YEEEEEEEEEEEEEE!!!' cheered the whole studio.

'Good morning! It's such a pleasure to be with you, even though I couldn't be there in person.'

'We're honoured to have you, Mr Mayor. You said you wanted to congratulate our new heroes on their recent actions.'

'Indeed. First of all, I'd like to place an order of 150 blank books from Cloud Nine. Is it possible?'

Victoria's jaw dropped.

'You know,' he continued 'I'd like to humanise all the people working at City Hall, myself included.' he said, affably as only thieves and politicians can be, then he continued 'Jokes apart, I truly want those copies. I believe that even the slightest shard of magic can make the difference and I trust you will help us think differently, be more efficient and effective. We need all the help we can get to solve the many issues affecting this wonderful city called London.'

'Wow, that was quite a speech.' commented Paul. 'I'm afraid Miss Victoria just fainted from the shocking surprise. Our best guy is trying to reanimate her now.' he joked, jolly as ever.

'I'm fine, thank you so much, Mr Mayor.' mumbled Victoria, fidgeting, her cheeks crimson for embarrassment.

'You got it.' the big man replied 'Also, if I may, I'd like to offer a job to Mr Hoover. Are you busy at the moment?'

'Nope, free as a bird. Unemployed creep since 1986.'

Everyone laughed, amused, and millions of viewers couldn't detach their eyes from the screen. Hellen was on top of the world.

'Great. What about the position of consultant for all the social, racial, community matters of London?'

'It's better than nothing.'

'Oh, nothing's worse than better than nothing!' replied the Mayor, accepting the challenge.

'Aight, I'm in! Thank you, boss.'

'Brilliant. Victoria, are you still there?'

'Yep...'

'Can you please help me out with this bloke? I'm not sure why but I smell trouble.'

'Well...'

'Would you work along with him?'

'I'll see what I can do, sir. It's not an easy task.' she said, still holding Albert's hand, looking into his eyes as if searching for his emotions in there. Her heart was beating like a broken drum machine.

Meanwhile, Paul got distracted by a series of signs, gestures and notice boards directed at him. He waited for the cheering and the applause to cease and announced,

'Ladies and gents, as unbelievable as it may sound, we have another surprise for you. I've just been told that Lord Mortibar in person just called and is live with us. Good morning, Lord.'

'Good morning, my apologies for the intrusion.'

'It's our greater pleasure. Now, I'm sure everyone knows you, but let me remind the public about your career.'

'Please, don't...'

'Lord Mortibar co-founded the Morvar Company, the renowned factory of kites that sold dreams all around the world between the '70s to early '90s. Am I correct?'

Albert and Victoria looked at each other, stunned.

'You are correct, thank you. You know, I hate to brag, and as you may be aware, I stopped doing any kind of interviews after the death of my dear friend Anthony Morvar.'

'...' a poignant silence descended on the studio.

'Are you guys still there?' asked the Lord.

'We are indeed. Please, how can we help?' asked Paul, finding himself embarrassed as it never happened in his career.

'First of all, I'd like to tell Mr John Blake that one of the geezers enjoying Cloud Nine's opening the most, was actually me. I'd encourage the art critic to either experience the things he reviews or change his job since he clearly didn't understand a thing about that place.'

From the control room, Hellen Moore was fainting. She already became a star at the BBC for bringing the couple on air, then the Mayor and now... she would remember that morning for the rest of her life. Back in the studio, Victoria started placing a few puzzle pieces together and couldn't believe her mind.

'It can't be you...' she muffled.

'Guilty!' the Lord admitted like a brat kid caught stealing the jam. 'Sorry, I made a rule to travel incognito, you know, keep a low profile.'

'You're the old man who fell for our Wonderwall Waterfall!'

'I'm exactly that gaffer, darling.' he giggled.

'Oh Jesus, I'm so sorry, I didn't want to call you old, Mr Mortibar, I mean, shit, Lord.'

'Bollocks, no offence taken. And please call me Frank, enough with the formalities.'

'I will, Lord Mortibar, er... Frank. Now that I think about it... aren't you... ?'

'Precisely. The very first time we met was at Sherlintock train station. You were reading one of your blank books on the Morvar's bench. I'm glad you recognise me after all.'

'Are you a stalker?' she just said, without thinking.

Albert was delighted, as it was the audience including the Mayor who was still projected full-screen right behind Victoria.

'I must admit I've been following you ever since and I'm incredibly proud of what you achieved, Victoria. Yet, this isn't why I called.'

'????'

'Let me explain. I'm getting old and, even though I have done pretty much everything in my life, I still desperately miss that feeling...

you guys know what I mean, right?'

'Morvar! the Morvar Company!' shouted Albert, like a proper fool, like one of those quiz participants who can't wait to tell the answer.

'Precisely. I'd love to lose myself in the most beautiful dream ever dreamed. I know what I'm asking is probably too much, possibly impossible but, would you like to work on a project for me?'

At that moment the Mayor saw the opportunity of a lifetime right in his hands. He had to intervene:

'Lord Mortibar, can I speak?'

'Please.'

'If Albert and Victoria are ok with it, I'd like to offer the Serpentine Gallery and the surrounding areas, including the lake, for this project of yours. Would you guys be willing to create an art installation there? What do you think, Lord Mortibar?'

'Oh... I really don't know what to say, I'm flattered, Mr Mayor.'

There was a palpable tension in the air. Then, Albert stood up, literally dragging Victoria along, their hands still tied together. They exchanged an explicit look and:

'Frank, we would be honoured to work on whatever you are delusioning about. We're ready to start today.'

'Guys... I mean, is it Christmas already?' said Lord Mortibar with a trembling voice, this close to get moved and weep on air.

So, with a certain graceful pace, Paul also stood up. And he started clapping. In a split second, all the people roaming around the BBC studios followed him and the roaring applause became contagious. Rumour has it, a few million people cheered at that enchanting story that morning, as if they had been possessed by a supernatural, positive energy.

FIFTY-NINE

Lord Mortibar personally called Victoria right after the show.

He thanked her again and they agreed for him to visit Cloud Nine soon, so he could tell them a bit more about his story and they would start fantasising improbable solutions for that impossible project. Meanwhile, the most ludicrous Rolls Royce of the entire Lord's Rolls Royce collection, was waiting for Albert and Victoria to come down from the studios and get onboard. Frank dedicated that piece of design to bring them wherever they wanted, for all the time it would take to make the project real.

After signing a few hundred autographs and expressing their gratitude to everyone at the BBC, the odd couple exited the building and they were finally alone. The London sky was marvellous: a pale blue canvas stroked here and there with puffy liquid clouds which blurred on the edges like ink on water. Albert's mind was busier than peak-hour Oxford Street, with an insane traffic of thoughts fighting to get to the top of the list, one honk after another. 'Is it possible to spend a life together? Will we be strong enough not to surrender to routines, to keep seeing and appreciating each other? Most of all, is she still in love with me?' Albert asked himself, conscious that Victoria might have been overhearing his thoughts. Worried that she... but he simply said

'It went well, right?'

'How can you do it?'

'What?'

'Leaving me the way you did and then... I don't know, what's wrong with you? You're acting as if nothing happened.'

'You're right, and I'm so sorry. It's just...'

'I know what it is, you prefer imagination over reality.'

'...'

'I get it, I do it all the time too but, hey, who do you think you are? I mean, alright, nothing is truly special without a pinch of salt, a sprinkle of magic. Reality sucks, it's stale and crude. I can't think of anything sadder than a life lived without imagination and yet...'

'The truth is I was scared, Vic. Good things never last.'

'Right. Is that a statement, a bulletproof scientific fact, or is it just you, behaving like a fucking chicken?'

'The last one.'

'Great, 'cause nobody has an answer to your non question. But I thought you were brave enough to risk it with me, at least you fooled me into it.'

'Sometimes I wish I was like you...' softly sang Albert, lowering his eyes, ashamed.

Victoria observed him for a while. He seemed honest, genuinely sorry and, no matter how ardent the hate, she couldn't help but love him. 'Why?' she asked herself, surely knowing the incomprehensible answer a tad too well. With the slightest touch, her fingers caressed Albert's bearded chin like feathers and lifted it up, so that he could stare into her eyes as she whispered, '... easily amused.', finishing his sentence, completing the iconic Cobain lyrics from All Apologies.

'Fuck, you knew it...'

'Hello? You're not the one and only Nirvana listener in the universe.'

'No?'

'No. So, was it a test? A sort of *crack the code to win a trip to Hawaii* nonsense of yours?'

Sort of. Busted... I'm obsessed with Kurt.'

'You don't say.' she replied, smiling.

'Listen, I have something for you.'

'I know.'

'You know shit.'

'Did you really think you could fool me that easy? I know you're hiding something in your sleeve.'

'What? It's... I indeed have a plaster cast.'

'Bollocks.'

'Ok but close your eyes. I'm about to perform the ultimate magic trick.'

'Uh-huh.'

'Please?'

'I'm ready. Magic me up!'

'I will.'

'Do it.'

And, 'Tah Dah!' Albert *cha-chinged*, pulling a majestic so-called rose. Despite the surprise being totally spoiled, Victoria was genuinely stunned by that flower.

'Wow...' she kinda said, 'it's... wow!'

'Nah... yeah.' he blushed.

Victoria's heart was beating fast. 'Goddammit, Albert!' she thought out loud, and left a fleeting kiss on his flaming cheek.

'Where did you get it?' she asked as if to wake him up from a dream he was lost into.

'That? Well, I found a guy on my way to you.'

'The florist behind my shop?'

'Yep. I guess...'

'You know, a few days ago he told me that... nevermind.'

'So you've been there too! You should hire the guy, he's incredible.'

'Actually... I was thinking of offering the job to another fool.'

'Uh? And who's this lucky bastard male individual?'

'Oh my... it's you, you idiot!'

'Me? Ah. Clearly. I have all the required skills and a decent curriculum vitae for working at Cloud Nine.'

'Let's see about that.'

'...'

'Is that our car?'

'Bloody hell!'

Victoria walked incredulously towards the Rolls Royce. She had never seen such an elegant car in her life. The driver lowered the window and...

'Charlie?!' she shrieked.

'At your service, madam.'

'What the heck are you doing here? Sherlintock Police fired you for good?'

'Not exactly. Lord Mortibar hired me right after that scene at the train station.'

'No way.'

'I swear. He brought me back to the bench and told me the whole Morvar story, why it was so important to him and... since I gave a chance to your blank book, he considered me one of the team.'

'What team?'

'Er...'

Albert was puzzled too, he got closer.

'Don't tell me you've been on my tail all this time.' asked Vic.

'Yeah... me, and a bunch of other people hired by Lord Mortibar.'
'Jesus Christ...'
'He knew you were special from the very instant he saw you. He invested a large sum of money to have daily updates about you, your health and any new ideas coming on the way.'
'Woah, that's old-fashioned espionage. So, now what?'
'Now I'm your bodyguard, funny uh? Yours and Albert's.'
'Vic, you heard? We've become rockstars, like royal rockstars!'
'I'm not so sure it's a good thing...'
'Don't worry, I'll be a ghost.' swore Charlie, trying to reassure Vic.
'I don't wanna know nothing about you doing whatever you have to do. Deal?'
'I'll be invisible, trust me. Where do you want to go?'
Albert took Victoria's hand, he stared at her piercing eyes for a moment and, without saying a word, he gently asked. 'Would you come over to my place?' to which she never shyly replied, yes.
'Charlie, take us to Mile End! 45 Treby Street.' Albert announced, jovial.
Charlie felt a shiver coming up his spine. 'Are you sure? Isn't it a bit too dodgy for this kind of car?'
'Mate, trust me. I'm a respected local.'

SIXTY

The journey to Mile End was quick and pleasant. Victoria rested her head over Albert's shoulder as he caressed her hair, telling nonsense stories that made her laugh. The moment the Rolls Royce stopped at 45 Treby Street, a large crowd made of dealers, youngsters and all sorts of other shady/dodgy/younameit people gathered on the scene to check it out. When Albert and Vic stepped off the million quid vehicle, the mob rubbed their incredulous eyes.

'Charlie,' said Albert patting his hand on the glossy body of the luxury car 'what about getting rid of this?'

'Well, my orders are...'

'Don't worry about us, take a break, I've got everything under control. Das ma hood, innit?'

Victoria smiled at that. Charlie was dead worried. Knowing Albert, some major issue was just around the corner, ready to strike.

'See you later.' concluded Vic, shutting the door and waving goodbye. 'So... ?' she kinda asked Albert.

'Ready to live the East End dream?'

'It's quite a place...' she said, hesitantly. 'Is all this garbage included in the rent?'

'Obviously. JB Link is providing the best service in CrimeTown. Follow me into my humble castle, Miss.'

So, Albert searched his pockets for the keys. 'No shit. Again?'

'You lost them, didn't you?'

'Well...'

'Let me help.'

'Uh?'

'Flowerpot, oh, here they are!'

'No, no, Vic, put them back in there. Quick.' he whispered, like crazy scared. So scared that he made even Victoria anxious.

'What's wrong with you?'

'It's... my flatmate, Josh... he's very sensitive about this matter. They're his keys, he made me swear not to touch them ever again.'

'You can't be serious.'

'...'

'Seriously? So, how do we get inside?'

'Ah. I have a brilliant idea.'

'Oh, my... no... please, no.' said Victoria.

The plan was to climb the drainpipe to reach the first-floor window, the one leading into Albert's room. He always left it open, just in case. The whole thing was supposed to be a piece of cake. Two minutes top. If only...

'Are you sure you can do it?'

'Babe, I was born for this.'

'You came out of the hospital this morning, you're probably still dazed by the morphine...'

'I appreciate your concern about my premature death but, trust me. I'm a pro.'

'Yeah... What do you want me to do?'

'Put your hands together, right, like that. I need a leg up to get to the pipe.'

'You're lucky Rose is not here, otherwise...'

'I know, I know... now, push!'

'Argh!'

'Perfect, brilliant, you're amazing!' said Albert, now hanging to the drainpipe like a fucking idiot, like a terrified cat clinging on to a tree with its claws knifed into the bark. Stuck. Incapable of moving either up or down. Victoria was laughing.

'Should I call the fire brigade?'

'Give me a second, I'm not used to certain heights.'

'What? You're two feet from the ground, I can slap your back without even getting on my tips. Come on!'

'Umph... easier said than done.' he whined, then he thought 'Jesus, Albert, you can't make such a poor figure, not in front of her.', then he realised Victoria was listening and giggling. 'Fuck! Fuck! Fuck!' he cried.

'Please, don't mind me. You can get down if you like, we'll figure something else.'

But Albert was determined. Once he started a mission, he had to get to the bottom of it. He was still embracing the pipe like a silly monkey when he found the courage. He stuck one foot on the metal clip and pushed up. Great. Then he tried again and, wow, it was working. Two more of those moves and he reached the half-opened window. One foot on whatever the name of that bloody thing that almost snapped and, JACKPOT! He was inside. 'Woo-hoo!!'

At that very moment, Josh, concerned about all that noise, opened the door and found Victoria.

'Who the fuck are you?'

'I'm Vic, nice to meet you.'

'Yeah. Get lost and stop shouting, would you?'

'Actually...'

'What?!'

'I'm here with Albert.'

'You figure. Where's the motherfucker?'

'Ahem...'

Albert just came down the stairs, appearing from behind Josh.

'Don't even say it. You did it again.'

'Er...'

'Aight, I don't give a damn. Kill yourself if you fancy.'

'You're a real friend, Josh. So, you met Victoria. She's my...'

'Friend.' concluded Vic.

'Whatever. Just try not to be loud, uh?'

'Hey, wait a sec! Are you calling me a whore?' burst Victoria.

'I ain't calling you shit. I want no trouble, aight?'

'Cool.'

'Brilliant.'

'Can I come in, now?'

'Fucking hell...' commented Josh, sensing an infinite quantity of trouble nose-diving over his head like R.A.F. Spitfires. The door slammed shut and Victoria wondered inside. She only made two steps when she asked 'Who did that painting?', pointing to a huge canvas, that in fact was a blanket, painted with... colours that weren't actually colours and...

'NO FUCKEN SHITE, JOSH!!' shouted Albert. 'YOU DID IT!'

'Aye.'

'Seriously? Wow, it's impressive!' commented Vic.

'Well...'

Albert was trying to hug the big black man named Josh who was trying his best to get rid of the pale slim averagely tall Albert without committing a murder. Meanwhile, Victoria approached the artwork and studied the texture as if she had any experience whatsoever about techniques or styles.

'Unbelievable, is this... toothpaste?!' she asked.

'Innit?' replied Josh, lowering his eyes towards a pile of squeezed, exhausted tubes of all sorts, brand or colour.

'Oh, now I see...' she said, suddenly realising that Josh was only wearing a pair of Adidas slippers and boxer shorts, and that he used the latter like a bandolier, loading the elastic band with his "colours". 'Ingenious.' she commented.

'Well, it's cheap, and it does the job.'

'Fantastic. And...' she paused for a moment. Then she turned to Albert with a puzzled look.

Not only Josh was almost naked, he was also incredibly dirty. His face was smudged with any kind of substances: ground coffee, dried coffee, dried eggs, glittery toothpaste, striped toothpaste, neon blue, bright pink, chalk white toothpaste... he very much resembled one of those Native Americans or African tribe people who embellish themselves with circles and symbols, for their big celebrations. Victoria was undecided whether she was impressed or ew-ed by that. Either way, she seemed to have lost all words. So much so that she decided to shut up and act. She dip her fingers into the filthy bowl on the floor containing a disgusting turmeric-colour broth. Then, merry like a kid, she marked Albert's and her cheeks with it.

'What do you think, Josh? Are we a team now?'

'Aye. A fucken team of losers.'

'Sit down, please. I have an idea.'

They grabbed a couple of chairs and, but Albert was distracted. He was studying the painting when he noticed that the canvas had been fixed to the wall, over the tv set, with rusty, nasty iron carpenter nails. Now, he was perfectly aware that there was no hammer in the house so... and then he spotted his precious Italian moka lying on the floor, battered as if it had been used as a

'Fuck!'

He turned to Josh and, '*NOOOO!!! HOW COULD YOU DO THIS TO ME??*' he imagined shouting at him, crying like a baby, caressing his little metallic design jewel. He was incredulous, and furious, and sad at the same time, in his mind. In the real world, instead, he politely asked

'Shall I make coffee?'

'Please' replied Vic.

'Bourbon for me.' Josh.

'Fab.' Albert concluded, sticking a fag in his and his friend's lips and burning the tips with the free flame of his Zippo.

'Josh, are you crying?' asked Vic, observing the big man. Was he moving? I mean, no one ever appreciated or even cared about him and now...

'What? Nah, it must be the toothpaste fumes.'

'Clearly. You have it all over your face.' she agreed, avoiding the otherwise awkward conversation.

'...'

'Anyhow. How much do you want?'

'?'

'You know, I have a shop in Greenwich, I...'

At that point, Josh finally connected the dots and

'Fuck - me. You Victoria from Cloud Nine?' he basically shrilled.

'How do you know?'

'Everyone knows.'

'Josh, did you see us on the telly?' cut in Albert.

'Mate, we don't use that shit.'

'Makes sense, sorry.'

'How much do you want?' insisted Vic.

'What the fuck are you talking about?'

'I want to buy your painting. We can display it at the shop.'

'You serious?'

'Positive. What do you think, Albert?'

'I believe it's a great deal.'

'I ain't no painter...'

'Mate, you are. Look at what you did!' said Albert.

'...'

'I'll tell you what.' continued Vic, fully immersed in the businesswoman role 'Today we've been offered so much money we actually don't know how to spend it and, apparently, Cloud Nine is selling so quickly that we can barely keep up with the orders. We're gonna need more staff soon so, Josh, why don't you make a full series of paintings for us?'

'A series?'

'Yeah, on commission. We can pay you upfront and showcase your collection as soon as it's ready.'

'Collection?'

'Shit, Josh. I told you, you had to follow your dreams!!' cheered up

Albert.

'I... what can I say?'

'Perfect, we have a deal then!' concluded Victoria, sparkling of light for closing her very first contract.

So, Albert handed the stained mugs filled with steamy whatever to his mates and they all clinked the ceramics to celebrate that major event.

SIXTY-ONE

'You will dance, barefoot, on the warm waves of Blue in Green by Miles Davis, caressed by the gentle blow of a trumpet drawing celestial constellations onto your delicate skin. And I'll reach bliss as you twirl in the air without making a sound, your hair embracing the void like sinuous loops of red rose petals.'

That's what Albert didn't tell Victoria that night before falling asleep. And she silently listened to it all, safely nested in his arms, wrapped in modest sheets soaked with the scent of their naked bodies. 'Thanks' she hissed in his ears as her heartbeat sped up, and her lips quivered, longing his, touching them, falling apart into an intense kiss with no end. 'Peace.' Nobody said, right before they disappeared into the sweetest dream, protected under the cover of darkness.

The morning after, Charlie picked them up early and drove the Rolls Royce to Cloud Nine. Lord Mortibar was due to meet the couple there, to explain his vision. When Victoria and Albert entered the shop, they found Rose standing in the middle of the room, fuming, craving for a decent morning fight.

'Fuckin' hell, you're back. About bloody time.'

'How are you, Rose?' cheered Albert, foolishly happy as only a lover can be.

'Shut up and get lost, you punk. We've got some private business to discuss here.'

'Okay.' he immediately surrendered.

'Why are you so angry?' asked Vic, also glowing of silly joy.

'Why? Why?? You left us alone to deal with all the shit buzzing around this goddamn hole of reprobation of yours!'

'...'

'Do you have any idea of how many people came here yesterday after your fancy TV appearance?? We had to hire Steve, that dumbass, and Pete, and a couple of imbeciles from the cafe. Tommy was dealing with everything like a fucking dog, or a slave, considering his age.'

'I'm sorry, Rose.'

'WE NEED MORE PEEEOPLE!! AHHHH, I HATE YOU!!'
'Calm down, as a matter of fact, we did find new guys.'
'What? Proper weirdos?'
'Yeah... proper weirdos, am I right, Albert?'

Albert was distracted. Rose always scared him like hell so he sneaked out of the shop for a fag. He was staring at nothing when a car stopped and the driver helped an old elegant man out: Lord Mortibar marked his entry with an enthusiast smile. He brandished his brass and oak cane in the air and 'YO!, I'm here!' he shouted, feeling like a teenager. 'Are you ready, folks?'.

As he entered Cloud Nine he once again got overwhelmed by a sort of pinching-good electric shock. He was absolutely thrilled by that place.

'Vic, what a pleasure. And Rose, let's cheer up that grumpy face!'
'Cut down with the cocaine, grandpa.'
'Where's Tommy boy? Aw, there he is!' Lord Mortibar said, welcoming the kid who just popped out of the waterfall, still half asleep but smiling. 'Don't tell me... that your room?? You lucky bastard!'
'He's definitely high as a kite.' commented Rose, shaking her head.
'Shall we start, guys?' Frank was at full throttle. He couldn't stop touching, smelling, tasting everything (don't ask), and 'What's that?'
'It's a tape recorder, Lord Mortibar.'
'I know, Albert, but what do you do with it?'
'I see, sorry, Lord Mortibar.'
'Fucking hell, stop calling me that, I'm not a stuffed animal.'
'Absolutely.'
'So?'
'We use it to remind ourselves to never forget to remember, Frank.' said Victoria, who obviously knew every little detail of her shop. The Lord seemed to appreciate the nonsense and, with a smile, he asked
'Can I listen?'
'Of course.' she said, amazed by the energy sparkling from that old man, and at the same time touching the sky for having Albert on her side again. Rose, instead, was observing the scene from a distance, puffing like a chimney from a chunky Cuban cigar.
'Take the headphones.' Victoria added.

Frank put them on and closed his eyes. An impossible relax possessed him for the entire length of the track: *Aloneliness*. Two more seconds and, *click*, the recorder finished doing its job.

'What a beautiful sunset...'

'You know, I've searched it for a long time and... I only found it a few days ago, on Greenwich park's hilltop.'

'Marvellous. Marvellous. Please wrap me a couple of these cassettes, I'll pay later.'

'You don't have to...'

'Tut-tut. Let's get down to business.'

'Yeah, tell us whatcha want, grandpa.' said Rose, still crabby.

'Sorry, Frank, she's a bit mad at me for leaving her alone.'

'A bit? Mad? ME? You wish.' she grumbled.

'It's ok.'

'Please, have a seat. How can we help?' asked Albert, bringing their guest a refined vintage chair that smelled like France. Then he lay down on the floor next to Victoria and Tommy. They were focused, ready to be hit by Frank's words, so he raked his thoughts and started:

'You must know by now that I'm very rich, coming from an aristocratic family and blab blab blab. This is not important. I am not important. For this installation, I don't want anything fancy which talks about me or my story, so, in case, forget about mausoleums, statues or similar. She, instead... she was my everything and she died without taking me along.'

'...' they all replied together. Even Rose.

'I live in a huge house where I can't even die, damn good health! I own private jets, cars, yachts but... the world is meaningless without my Sally.'

'Do you have a picture of her?' delicately asked Victoria.

'Of course. I couldn't part from it for a single tick of the clock. I keep it here.' he said, patting on his heart.

'Can we have it? I mean, a copy would do great.' proposed Albert.

'I...'

'I promise we will treat it with maximum respect.'

'I don't know, Victoria... do you really think it could help?'

'It might. May I ask how the two of you met?'

'May you not?'

'Well...'

'I'm not sure I want to go back to that moment.'

'Holy cow. How the fuck do you think we can do the job if you refuse to open up a little?' burst Rose. 'It's clear you're stuck in there, you're probably reenacting those few minutes of your life ten times a day. On a freaking loop.'

Victoria and Tommy dropped their jaws simultaneously. Frank sighed, rolled his eyes and, finally, smiled.

'Christ, Rose, I guess you got me. Hit and sunk.'

'If you don't feel like sharing it's fine. We understand.' said Vic.

'No we don't.' replied Rose.

'She might have a point, after all.'

'Yes, Frank,' said Albert, 'that moment when you first met Sally seems to be hurting you like nothing else in the world... this particular story could be the key to open your gate.'

'Vic? Tommy?'

'Albert is right, Frank.'

'Okay then.' he accepted, his face not so jolly anymore. He sank into the chair, cleared his voice and... *'It was a long time ago.'* he almost whispered. 'I had just returned from the military service, R.A.F., I was a pilot. For all my life I did nothing but obey orders. First, they came from my father, dictating the path of my life and my future career, then they were given by my superiors, in the army. I never had a moment for myself so, right after finishing my service, I finally decided to escape. I went to the seaside, Margate. I used to spend plenty of time on the beach, walking, breathing in the sea breeze and thinking, a lot, about my life. *That day...* I woke up really early, I wanted to see the break of dawn. The sun was burning close to the horizon, setting all the clouds on fire and scorching my eyes with its indelible mark. I took off my shoes and started walking along the shore, keeping my eyes on the incandescent sphere that was coming into the world, bringing life.'

The story was flowing inside the room as spring breeze and even the clocks stopped counting their ticks, absorbed by Frank's soothing voice. Meanwhile, a large crowd of Cloud Nine fans gathered outside the shop and were listening through the huge glass windows. Frank was fully immersed in the ocean of his memories. Like a child without a watch, he seemed to have forgotten Time.

'... *the beach was desert and I felt free,* free as I never felt before. I kept following the light when a silhouette imposed her presence between the sun and my eyes. That dark shadow attracted me like a bee to its flower and, even though it was very distant, I was unconditionally intrigued by it. The more we got closer the more I was falling in love with that creature. Against the light, her long hair was shining like gold. Her feet danced the sand with grace, pirouetting the waves like a butterfly. I couldn't see her face, she was still obscured by the blinding sun. My eyes hurt but I kept watching, I couldn't stop staring at that elegant body. I was in love already and I felt like the most foolish idiot in the world. What was I thinking? I didn't even know her name, the sound of her voice. Was she married? Was she... and the sun kept going up, patiently losing the contrast, gradually revealing her colours. I was walking as slow as I could, so as not to waste a single instant of that fleeting moment. For some inexplicable reason, I perfectly knew in my heart that she was the one. We were two steps far from each other when I finally managed to see her face, and to my utmost surprise she was smiling. *Gosh, she was beautiful.* I was so embarrassed I wanted to run away but... she politely stopped and'

'Hi, stranger.' she joked. 'Finally, another early bird on this lonely shore.' she said to me.

'I was waiting for you. I waited all my life to meet you.' I didn't say, blushing, but she probably heard my thoughts, I know it sounds ridiculous, but I'm sure she did. I was ultra agitated, choking on my breath. Luckily, she took the lead.

'You look like a gentle soul. What's your name?'
'Me?'
'You.'
'Oh... Frank. I'm Frank.'
'Ok, Frank. Do you fancy a walk?'

'*I couldn't believe my ears.* My heart was beating so fast and loud I feared she would hear it too. And perhaps she did. All I know is that we never stopped walking that walk, hand in hand until fate decided to tear us apart.'

Inside Cloud Nine, a cosmic silence was roaring. It seemed like even mosquitos stopped flying. Not a movement, a sigh, nor from Vic's crew, nor from the outside public. It felt as if reality disappeared for a moment.

'So, what the fuck has this to do with your installation?' Rose said, shattering that magic spell, crashing it into a million shards.

Victoria couldn't believe she (aka her brain) came up with such a brutal straightforward question and literally lost it, so much so that Albert had to hold her tight in his arms. She wanted to execute her imaginary friend using Colombian-cartel methods, she would tie her with chains to a freaking nuke and send her into space, she... she was in complete denial when Frank simply admitted:

'I truly have no clue, Rose. There's probably no solution to my dilemma, no art or invention will ever bring my Sally back.'

'Well...'

'You know, the sole other person who heard this story was my dear friend Anthony.'

'Morvar??'

'Yes. He got so excited about it that he convinced me to create the Company. He believed only a dream could save us from reality. So, we tried many things, he had hundreds of ideas and we almost... anyway, I'm glad I found you guys, eventually.'

'You bloody fool. I mean, you really put your life in the hands of these two?' commented Rose, shameless, fearless.

'Don't worry Frank, we'll figure something out.' said Albert, unsure of his own words.

'Can you help me?' he almost begged.

'Absolutely.' lied Victoria, pretending confidence, gripping Albert's hand. What else could she say? What could anyone say in one of those occasions? 'Leave it with us. We won't let you down.' she added, giving some sort of foolish relief to the old gentleman.

'You people... we're fucked.' concluded Rose.

SIXTY-TWO

A couple of months later...
'Mission Impossible.' moaned Rose.
'...' no one was listening to her.
'Can you believe these idiots??' she told Pete, who couldn't care less, who was incredibly busy serving customers and helping out along with Steve. 'I mean, look at Albert:' Rose continued, 'he's been staring at that damn TV monitor for the whole day. Is he cretin or what? IT'S OFF, YOU STUPID CUNT!' she shouted at him.
'Uh?'
'Gosh, why do you even exist?' she commented right before switching her attention to Tommy. 'Here's another of God's mistakes.'
'How are you, Rose?'
'What the hell are you doing with all those circuits? You trying to invent the ultimate electric chair?'
'Oh no, that's bad. I'm working on a new system for connecting thousands of lights in the air, like, you know...'
'B-O-R-I-N-G.' she interrupted the kid. 'Try not to set this shack on fire, not that I care, but I'm not dreaming to become homeless again.'
'Deal.' he replied, and lowered the goggles back down, returning to his project.
'Rose?' called Victoria from upstairs.
'At your service, madam.' she replied, instantly appearing in front of her, like a ghost, I mean... yeah.
'Have you seen my canvas?'
'Which one? They're all the same.'
'No, they're not.'
'Let me explain it to you: the act of painting, *oh gosh, I'm getting old*, smudging a blank surface with water doesn't count as art. It's just stupid.'
'Says who?'
'Why do I even have to argue? You already wasted ten stretchers

and countless metres of canvas for this new idiotic idea. They're all blank. All the same. All, awfully, white!'

'Oh, there it is! Found it at last.' proudly stated Vic. 'Rose, would you pass me the colours?'

'Great, let's have some fun: tell me, which one? Transparent salty ocean, lukewarm lake, beck spring n.5 or, no, wait, don't tell me we're in the mood for fucking sparkling Scottish mist, aren't we?'

'No, I want to start this painting with a classic background. Give me tap water, please.'

'I give up.' concluded Rose. 'I'll be in the bathroom if you need me, hanging myself with a proper, man-made decking rope.'

'Ok, don't get too busy, I might need you.'

'SCREW YOU!!'

Victoria couldn't help but giggling at such insolence. She loved Rose, how could she not? Arrogant and stubborn like a Gallagher brother. However, Vic caressed the canvases with different kinds of fluids. In her bedroom study, she had glass jars of any shape and dimensions, each one containing a different *colour*: there was the chalky riverbed water, full of minerals, the salty ocean, perfect for a shot of vitality, muddy rain, for shadows and details, and many more, including original mixes of her creation. She let her brush dance over the stretched surface until she was satisfied with the result. When she was done, she usually left her creations dry for a day or two and finally hung them on the Cloud Nine's walls, using the space like she was a famous New York City gallery owner.

'That's it for today.' she told herself that day, giving a second look at her latest piece of art called: *Sunshine Thoughts*. 'Where's Albert?' she asked no one as she went downstairs. The shop was brimming with people roaming around the shelves, touching, smelling, experiencing all sorts of inventions and, of course, pestering Steve or Pete with thousands of impossible questions. Victoria dribbled the crowd and joined Albert on the couch facing the gigantic flat screen of their disconnected TV.

'How's tricks?'

'Vic, I'm lost. I've tried everything. And I mean every thing.'

'Should we remove it from the shop, then?'

'Nah... the TV works, most of the time. I've seen so many people successfully using it but this is a big one...'

'... *stare at your reflection inside the black mirroring glass and you will see through yourself.*' Victoria recited the instructions leaflet by heart.

'Well, I did it. No luck.'

'Have you tried the Music Bubble?'

'First of all, that gigantic plastic sphere is always busy with clients, they truly love it, dammit. Secondly...'

'Hey, you can always listen to the records outside the bubble, can't you?'

'Indeed. In fact, I cracked the whole *Sunsets Collection*, I spent two hours immersed in *Glances in the Dark...*'

'What about *Un-Given Kisses*? It's my favourite.'

'Absolutely, that one is a best seller, and I love it but... Tommy insisted that without the spherical ambient he created, the effect is diluted and, you know...'

'Yeah, you need it at maximum power, I get it.'

'...'

'Evening walk to the park?' proposed Victoria.

'Shit, you're amazing. I'll grab the jackets.'

And they were out.

Fresh air. Sometimes you need a rest, you need to wonder and get lost in order to find your way back. That's what Albert always told himself, a rule that Victoria also religiously followed.

They turned the corner and they were at Greenwich Park, one of the most beautiful places on Earth. The fact that it was free (*thanks Lilibet*) and royally huge, was a big plus too. They passed the gilded black gates and headed uphill, towards the Royal Observatory when Albert suddenly stopped. He hugged Vic intensely, as if some end of the world thing just happened although, no, it wasn't anything of sorts, it was just Albert acting like Albert. That's why she didn't worry, she knew her man, so she patiently waited for him to calm down and speak.

'I don't know, Vic, I think I lost it.' he almost cried, fully immersed in his drama queen mode.

'What? What did you lose?'

'I... I'm so ashamed to admit it but... I'm not able to do those magic tricks anymore. All the powers that you believed I had... well, they're faded, I'm not so special anymore. Sorry.'

Victoria was enjoying the drama. It occurred every day, at some point, usually followed/counterbalanced by an electric shock of energy, ideas and feel-good vibes.

'Don't worry, it will pass.'
'Yeah, maybe.'
'You know what? We should order pizza tonight!'
'Really?'
'You're so easy.' thought Victoria, secretly laughing. 'Sure!'
'Oh, my, I'm going for buffalo mozzarella and...'
'Yummy!'
'... double cheese, and...'
'What else?'
'... rocket, peppers and... hey, have you seen all these new people around the park?'
'Where?'
'Vic!, Vic!'
'Al!. Al!'
'Jesus Christ, are they really...'
'What?'
'Unbelievable, they're reading!!'
'Well, I'm glad, but that's not exactly special...'
'No, no, take a better look; their eyes are closed.'
'Shut up...'
'They're reading your books, goddammit, you did it, you did it!!'
'...' she blushed, incredulous.
'Vic, they're so many, holy shit...'
'Er... shall we go back home?' she stammered.
'Never. They love you, it's a mirac... look! They're even wearing Cloud Nine tees!'
'You sure?'
'This is insane. There: girl on the bench; guy under the weeping willow; mum sitting on the grass with her baby. All holding copies of your blank book.'
'Albert?'
'Wow, is there a single seat not occupied by one of your people?'
'Calm down, please.' she begged, increasingly embarrassed.
'Vic, Rose was right. Unleash *the weirdos and you'll see!* It's happening, it's not only in our shop or at the cafe anymore, it's spreading. It seems like everyone eventually decided to enjoy every single drop of their lives.'
'Shhh...'
'Bloody fucking hell, don't you dare to shush me, WE NEED TO

CELEBRATE!' he shouted, and he smacked an ardent kiss on Victoria's lips. So, Albert grabbed her by the waist and threw her slender body over his shoulders like a sack of potatoes. All the Cloud Nine fans turned at that and, recognising their idol, they clapped and cheered at Victoria. They even started a sort of ultra awkward standing ovation. She was so red-faced that she wished to disappear Potter-style, under the invisibility cloak and, but at the same time she couldn't stop laughing, and crying and slapping Albert's ass, imploring him to free her.

Like a proper fool.

SIXTY-THREE

'PIZZA!!' shrilled Tommy, super excited.

Louis Prima and his band were playing loud inside the Pioneer speakers, the turntable was spinning like a pinwheel and the excitement was at its top. At Cloud Nine, everyone was having fun: Vic and Albert were twisting and swirling around the room like old-fashion charleston performers; Steve and Pete pretended to be a professional tango couple; Rose was puffing cigars and guzzling exotic drinks sitting on the swing hung to the Victorian staircase. Ah, she was also barking football chants and all sorts of other obscenities at the top of her lungs.

'What a spree, what a spree, folks!' she shouted, among other things no decent writer would ever dare to put on paper.

'PIZZA!!' yelled Tommy again like a proper 19th century handbell ringer while chomping on his share of that mouth-watering meal. Beers were being cracked open like firecrackers, one after another as if it was new year's eve. The music got louder and the hours got smaller. It was pretty late when Albert decided it was time for a brainstorm. He turned down the volume and asked for a moment of attention.

'BOOOO!!' echoed everyone at once.

'Shall we recap the Lord Mortibar situation?'

'SHAAA UUUP!!' slurred Rose, drunk as a skunk.

'Ok, I get it, but...'

'BOOOO!!' insisted Vic, enjoying herself like a kid.

'We're all working on something different, right?' he tried again.

'YEEE!!' intervened Tommy, just to make extra noise.

'Alright, enough. Are you done?' burst out Albert.

'NO!'

'Pete, do you have an update on the music?'

'I have a few ideas. If only you'd give me a rough hint about the project...'

'Sorry, Pete. We don't have that. Steve?'

'What?'

'Do you have anything?'

'Nope.'

'Fab. Just fab. Tommy?'

'I am creating a system to connect like... mmm... hundreds of LED lights. I'm getting there.'

'Brilliant!'

'Do you think we can use it?' asked Tommy, excited.

'God knows, kid. Every little helps anyway.'

'Listen, you fucker, why don't you tell us your ideas instead, uh?' cut in Rose. 'Provided you have any.'

'Right. Nope. I have none.'

'Great, so LET's PARTY!!!' she shouted again.

'Wait, wait a second.' intervened Victoria. 'Let's be serious. Albert, I know you've been working on something. Tell us what it is.'

'Well, it's just a thought but I think we need to bring Lord Mortibar...'

'IT'S FRANK!! CALL THE BASTARD WITH HIS NAME, FOR CHRIST'S SAKE!!' exploded Rose, utterly drunk, aggressive, and this-close to be dangerous.

'As I was saying, I think we need to work on Frank's emotions.'

'Shit, you're a goddamn genius, Albert, who could have thought about it? Asshole.' burped Rose.

'What I meant was that we should find a way of bringing Frank back to that day on the beach. Can we recreate the glorious encounter with the love of his life?'

'No fucking chance.'

'ROSE!!' yelled Vic. 'Are you willing to help or not?!'

'Not.'

'Guys,' intervened Steve 'why don't we use the Serpentine lake as a film set? We could play with the reflections on the water, it won't be the ocean but...'

'That's clever.' commented Vic.

'Did anyone come up with ideas on Sally's picture?' asked Albert.

'Actually...' said Pete, 'What about using *Don't Look Back In Anger* as soundtrack for our installation? They're singing her name, it's epic, it's the definitive classic.'

'Innit?' Albert agreed. 'What else? Vic?'

'You all know I've spent a lot of time painting with water and...'

'Rubbish. I've had enough of that nonsense garbage.'

'Thanks for your support, Rose.' Victoria muttered.

'I love your paintings, I really do! What's your idea?'

'Honestly? I have no clue, Tommy, and forget about my art anyway. I was more into bringing up the concept of using something vanishing, like... ethereal.'

'A memory.'

'Yeah, Albert. If only we could bring Sally back to that beach once again...'

'Great, now we have to dig a corpse out of its grave too.'

'Rose, you're impossible.'

'As a matter of fact, I don't even exist.'

'I wish...' said Tommy.

'What the fuck did you say??'

'WOULD YOU SHUT UP, ROSE??' they all replied altogether.

'Can I speak?' insisted Victoria, trying to get to the bottom of her stream of thoughts. 'Obviously, no one wants a dead body on the scene. I think we might, I don't know, use a sort of hologram?'

'A what?' asked Steve.

'Vic, I have it!' cut in Tommy, out of his skin for the terrific idea that just popped in his mind. 'We could use an intricate net of LED lights to recreate his wife's face, up in the sky!'

'Wow.' they chanted at unison. 'Do you think you can make it?'

'I don't know...'

'Yeah you do, you're the worst pain-in-the-ass, stubborn kid I have ever met.' conceded Rose.

'I am?'

'Shit, don't be so fucking jolly and don't fool yourself thinking I made you a compliment. I still hate you, like I hate any other damn kid.'

'YEEEE!!!' screamed Tommy, hurrying to hug Rose, who looked totally disgusted.

'Marvellous. To recap:' said Albert, 'we want to emotionally bring Frank back to his most precious moment; we want him to see his wife once again; we have the right music but we must find a way for creating a fading version of Sally, copying the picture using hundreds of little LED lights thrown in the sky like a constellation the shape of her face. What do you think guys, do we have a plan?'

'YEEEEEE!!' shouted not only Tommy but the whole crowd.

'Sensational. Now, all of you: go fuck yourselves. Good night.' Albert concluded, and everyone smiled, thrilled about starting that hopeless project. Pete and Steve punched Albert's arm on their way out, like real mates; Tommy embraced Vic and did the thumb up to the others before sneaking into his private room, the magic waterfall; Rose stubbed her imaginary Cuban cigar straight in the middle of the TV screen and sayonara-ed away. Only Victoria was left in the room.

'Should I go fuck myself too?' she said, winking provocatively.

'Nah, you can stay.' Albert replied, bowing and kissing her hand like an 18th century gentleman. 'You're my hero, you've always been.'

'You're such a girl.'

'I know.' he replied as they stumbled their way up the Victorian staircase, to the bedroom, and: sock. Uh? Another sock. Sweaty t-shirt and, 'woah, you missed me!'

'Here comes the bomb!' Victoria announced, jolly, throwing her clothes in Albert's face and jumping around like a sugarhigh rabbit.

'Try me.' he dared her, and the ultimate clog of denim jeans was cast. It missed. Yet it centred the staircase hole.

'Slam dunk.'

'Ish.'

'What? It's 3 points for me.'

'Take this!'

But she didn't. Instead, she pushed him on the bed and pulled his trousers off.

'What are you up to?' he smiled, staring at her long bare legs as she stared at his briefs barely containing his erection.

'You sit there and watch.'

With her seductive doe eyes stuck into his eyes, she slowly took her white bra off, slipping one strap down her shoulders at a time till *voilà*, she threw it in his face.

'Victoria?'

'*Shhh...*'

Hands pressed against her breasts, she gave him one of those looks and started dancing like a professional stripper.

Shhh...

She got closer. And closer. Dressed in her lace g-string only, she danced on top of him, her back rubbing his lap, up and down, left to right as he licked her beaded skin, fingered her nipples, his hands playing with her secret spot. And she gasped. She could clearly feel his heat pressing on her sex when she turned and finally dipped her tongue into his mouth making him even bigger, making him shiver of lust. So he tried to grab her but she stared into his eyes and whispered:

'Give me your Mudhoney tee.'

'Uh?'

And she pulled it off Albert. She was ravishing. She was wet. She let her panties slip down to her feet and kicked them away with elegance. Then she entered the large grunge shirt, her head popped off and:

'Yo, touch me I'm sick!' she said, jumping on the bed too, dragging him along, grabbing his pulsing excitement and handling it fast, slow, strong. With her mouth. He was so hard it hurt so he spread her legs and disappeared between them, his tongue making her quiver, his ears blissed by her moaning as he tasted her taste till she pulled his head up. 'Take me' she never said, and she let him in. Out. In.

Shhh

They rolled from the bed to the wooden boards of the floor and back. Upright. Hands against the wall, bodies pressed, sweat oiling the motion, then down. Arms up in the air and knees riding the mattress. Front. Reverse. The mouth craves the lips and eats the spit. Again. Fire. Tongues sucking kisses. Fingers entering hot spots, they want more. Deeper. All the way. All night long. Hands gripping the hips. Face down on the pillow. Inside. Hard Stroke after stroke. Don't stop. Bashing on. For a while. For fun and for lust, tasting each other and thrusting their bodies into one another. Sweat. Heat. Sticky fingers.

Shhh

That night they fell asleep embraced like tiger cubs. Albert was exhausted. She was happy. In a sort of state of coma, he whispered 'Are you an Angel?' making her blush of joy and, as she caressed his head, they slowly dipped into a blissful sleep.

SIXTY-WHATEVER

It took a while to go from the first draft idea to actually put Frank's unique installation together. Hundreds of journeys to the Serpentine had been made, constant adjustments and countless hours of work were spent in order to fix the LED lights, the music and all the rest while everyone was ultrasonicly anxious (whatever that means). The air seemed to be brimming with a frenzyness the world never experienced before. Or maybe not, okay, I might be exaggerating a little. Anyway, the day had come and Lord Mortibar was on his way to pick up the magic team with his glossy-black Rolls Royce.

That majestic pearl of design arrived in front of Cloud Nine at 9 pm, as requested. Charlie lowered the window and, with the slightest nod, invited the guys into the car. Frank looked serious.

'How are you?' asked Vic, also disquieted by the unpredictable outcome of their installation.

'Dear, I couldn't sleep for the last four days... I have butterflies in my stomach and my head is numb. Muffled.'

'You need music, Frank.' said Albert.

'I know, and I listened to all of your tracks a thousand times but...'

'I get it, your mind is overloaded with thoughts, we have to free it. What else do you have?'

'Charlie? Do we have music in this car?'

'Indeed, sir. What do you fancy?'

'Did you buy that record... what was it called?'

'*All is Violent, All is Bright,* sir. It was delivered this morning.'

'Marvellous. Play it, please.'

God is an Astronaut's music gradually entered the spacious Rolls Royce with its soothing sound, filling the air. Frank laid back and closed the eyes, trying to find peace. Albert looked at Victoria, incredulous.

'Post-rock, seriously, Frank?' said Vic, quite amused.

'Post what?'

On the backseat, they exchanged smiley glances.

'One of your fans uses this album for his YouTube videos about you, that's how I found... wait a second. Are you implying an old man can't listen to youngsters tunes?'

'Chapeau, Frank.'

'Anyway, can I ask you something?'

'Shoot.' the couple replied in sync.

'What are your plans for the future?'

'Plans?'

'I mean... Yeah. Work with me. Please.'

'Jesus, straight to the point, innit, Frank?' said Albert.

'Is it a yes?'

'Don't you want to check what we did first?'

'Ah, screw tonight. This has nothing to do with it.'

'Er... no?'

'No. I know you guys tried your best and if it doesn't work... well, it wouldn't be the first time, I'm at peace with that. This is different.'

'Okay...'

'Look, the only exciting thing to do in life is play. And I must admit I truly love playing with you guys, so I was wondering... would you consider having me as a partner in your Company?'

'What Company?'

'Don't be silly, Victoria. Cloud Nine is an established brand already, it's clear you need to expand. I hear that you're barely keeping up with the orders, am I right?'

'Ahem... yep.' she admitted.

'I can finance any project, I can provide locations, people, but most of all, I'd like to stay close to you in the future. Would you allow an old man to enter your magic circle?'

'Are you trying to kill us with a heart attack?' asked Albert, serious, causing a pretty large, pretty pleased smile on Frank's face.

Meanwhile, the Rolls Royce was smoothly rolling around London on its way to The Serpentine. Inside the car, Frank was feeling a bit more relaxed now, enjoying the fact that the possibility of keep dreaming along his new friends seemed to be real.

'The world is divided into two categories of humans:' Frank said, after a moment of silence. 'People and the others. The first ones busy their existence with an array of material matters whereas the seconds are simply incapable of breathing reality in so they float a parallel universe, suspended amongst the clouds.'

'Ah.'

'Eh. You didn't know?'

'No. Not exactly.'

'So, listen up: you guys have the noble task of figuring out the unthinkable, editing the real and proposing alternatives to that in order to free people from an hopelessly static present.'

'Like adding zippers to straightjackets?' said Albert, fantasizing about the ultimate weird shit in his mind.

'Precisely. You're selling jailbreak plans to millions of humans who don't seem able to escape their days or nights.'

'Hold on, Frank, we ain't no Steve Jobs…' Victoria said like a rapper, feeling the pressure.'I mean, there's only one Walt Disney in this world.'

'I perfectly know it, dear. And there will never be another Anthony Morvar, no more Leonardo, Einstein or Galileo either, but the world keeps spinning, new visions keep appearing in the mix.'

Albert and Victoria were ecstatic. The flow of emotions was running too fast through their veins, overwhelming the hearts, flooding the eyes with pride and joy. The things to be said were so many that there wasn't much to say. Therefore, they just stared at each other. That simple gesture allowed them to break free from the fancy seats of the *Rolls* and enter their private bubble far from the world, a foreign place where their minds intertwined in the warmest embrace, shutting the reality door behind.

Outside the car windows, London was flowing like blurry memories of a lonely man when the majestic black panther finally approached Hyde Park. Tens of trucks were parked around the immense fields, rooted to the heart of the exhibition by kilometres of cables which brought life, energy and messages, from their metal boxes to the rest of the planet, in an endless back and forth. News Channels were present on that day to film something which was creating a buzz only comparable to the Moon Landing's.

Inside the car, Victoria and Albert were holding hands clearly lost in some celestial field and Frank felt a pleasant itch to his heart by observing them. They loved each other, no doubt about that, and, *yes, that's the only thing that truly matters*, he thought while trying to mask a warm smile.

'Sometimes the meaning of life reveals itself to us in the most simple ways. How come we can't appreciate the little things dotting our existences? How come I…'

Sally. Watching Victoria and Albert reminded Frank of all the great moments he shared with her and made him reflect on those charming fragments of life that happen to someone, somewhere, every single day. All those stories resembled each other. They were all differently alike like us, mortal souls, no matter our skin colour, background or gender. Everyone could see those fairytale stories and yet no one, nor the best Hollywood filmmaker, nor the greatest poet would ever be able to access their pages, written with water on the sheets of a blank, leather-bound book.

Frank and Sally.

Albert and Victoria.

Lone stars adrift in the buzz of the cosmos.

'Guys, we'll be there in a minute.' said Charlie, breaking that magic spell.

SIXTY-LAST

Throughout its royal life, the Serpentine witnessed all sorts of weird things but this last gig was one step ahead of imagination. At a first glance, you could have seen nothing. Zero. *Nada*. Yet, it was there, above your head, waiting for the right moment to appear, like a daydream or, yeah, love.

On the lake banks, only four slim shadows: Tommy, Albert, Victoria and Frank, dispersed around a strangely desert royal green. Animals gathered in quiet groups. No human was allowed. The water was calm too, and even the Princess Diana memorial fountain sounded mute as if she didn't want to interfere with the history that was about to be made.

The only signs of life were coming from the thousand red dots of the cameras, barely visible, masked with tape, screens, and whatever trick and gimmick to make their existence as faint as ghosts. Was that it? Not quite. From the hushed windows of the grand Lansbury's Lido Pavilion, a richful bunch of international guests observed the scene with immense curiosity, thrilled, amused, like kids. Not a word was spared. Not a whisper. Not a single nod when the burning sun set clouds and skies on fire as it forced his way out into the dark, performing his last act of the day. Gone.

Only a Moon scratch remained in the sky. The whole world couldn't wait no more.

'Ready?' gently asked Victoria.

'...' replied Lord Mortibar, panicking.

'Brilliant. Please, take off your shoes and follow the Serpentine.'

'What?'

'Trust us.' Albert added, giving the signal to Tommy, the director of that impossible show and, suddenly, the city lights went off too (thanks Mayor). It was pitch dark.

Silence.

Lord Mortibar started walking the frequencies of that buzzing stillness in a state of trance, curious but at the same time terrified by what was going to happen, if anything at all. His shadow was crawling the lake path, slowly, all eyes on him, when a music started colouring the air, fading in like a train from the past.

"*Don't Look Back In Anger*, Frank!"

Posted Victoria's fan club on every social media. But Frank didn't know, Frank just looked up and stared at that sublime dark mantle freckled with billions of tiny spots sparkling hope from afar. The whole thing was pretty moving as it was and when Noel Gallagher started singing, Frank found himself wondering about the power of nature, the overwhelming effect it always has on humans. Perhaps, the fact that we were made of the same matter explained why the simple sight of a waterfall or the cyclical blooming miracle of a million flowers with all their colours caused such a magical turmoil inside us.

'*Step outside, summertime's in bloom.*'

'Those words...' he hissed himself as he struggled to skim an old memory buried under the sand; as he zig-zagged around the constellation trails; as he... but something weird began appearing up there.

'What's going on?'

'Keep on watching, Frank.' whispered Victoria from a distance, gripping Albert's hand.

'*Take that look from off your face,
you ain't ever gonna burn my heart out...*'

That last phrase touched a soft spot, it felt as if his wife was speaking to him, 'Is it you?' Frank asked the stars, raising his gaze and, with the pace of a majestic elephants' parade, hundreds of tiny lights delicately started appearing, blending with the eternal patterns of the sky.

'I can't believe it...' Frank mumbled as the chorus invaded his heart, and

'*Soooo Sally can't wait...*' echoed all around Hyde Park, like a rumbling thunder.

He was increasingly confused. What was that shape appearing above his head? He ran towards it like a proper fool, an old emotional fool, while savouring each word of the song as if they were supposed to lead him somewhere.

'*Her soul slides away...*'

The music kept rolling as those faint, dim lights increasingly grew bright, gently conquering their space in the universe. That huge web of suspended LEDs was revealing itself. It was forming sort of a face, a figure that Frank couldn't mistake for anything else in the world so much he had it impressed on his heart, coded inside his DNA.

'Sally...' he barely hissed, close to tears, his breath getting shorter at every breath, as every splinter of the clock slipped away. He was trying to adjust to his newfound numb state when, no, that wasn't possible:

An orderly row of squirrels, foxes and ducks were following him in the most absurd yet glorious parade. Real? Unreal? What we know is that Frank raised his cane and led that ridiculous company towards Sally's face in the sky. He wanted to grab it, hold it in his arms for a moment. He wanted to jump and fly, the same way he used to do in his dreams when gravity seemed to vanish and he could flap his arms like a bird, to join her.

Meanwhile, the Oasis tune was shaking everyone, live or offline it didn't matter. The whole world was streaming, news channels broadcasting, radios transmitting.

Frank kept on marching.

And Albert was biting his tongue, hard, in the vain attempt to control his emotions. Embracing Victoria from behind, he buried his face inside her neck and tightened his grip on her waist. Despite they created all that, experiencing it for the first time was causing some unpredictable alchemy to burst inside everyone, even Rose.

It was when the solo started that Lord Mortibar completely lost it.

Noel's riff saturated the ears with its scratchy garage sound; Frank started running again, brandishing his cane, shouting her name, '*Sally, SALLY!*'; the animals broke the line and paddled, flew, whatevered side by side with him when a formation of swans spread their wings, hurtled right over his head, and *boom*! a drum fill charged on Frank's legs and, hell yeah, he was ready to take off as the last chorus stepped in, louder than bombs, it exploded like a nuke, sparkling notes in the sky as if a million fireworks had been shot at once. Madness. All set rules, the respectful silence and reverence towards Lord Mortibar suddenly shattered in a thousand shards and everyone sang along,

'*SOOOOO SALLY CAN'T WAIT*'

The intricate net of luminous spots was now clear enough for anyone to see it. It was her face. Sally's.

The ground fell out from under Frank's feet, he couldn't hold that load of tears no more so they ripped the plastic and flooded the eyes. He was crawling, and shouting, and 'THANK YOU, THANK YOU!' to

Victoria, and Albert, and Tommy, straight into the cameras like a damned rockstar at the end of the greatest concert of a thousand years long tour. And he kept looking up to his Sally who was probably watching him back from god knows where. Was she smiling? Weeping? Was she there at all? Whatever. Frank couldn't let her go so he kept stumbling his way towards her, and he dipped into, and ploughed through the dark lake waters as the music continued firing its notes like cannonballs.

That's when someone around London had the brilliant idea of clapping her hands, and the man next to her thought it was cool to follow the lead, and... within seconds, a grand roaring galloped miles and reached the Serpentine like a Pacific tsunami, drenching everyone with his cheering power poured from all over the city, from the people stuck on their screens, inside their homes, standing on the edge of Hyde Park. It appeared as if strangers from across the planet gathered together to sneak a peek of that mirage.

'Morvar did another miracle...' said Albert, trying not to break, still hiding behind Victoria's shoulders when she suddenly turned, in tears, and scorched his lips with a passionate salty kiss.

And the Oasis song was playing its final notes, singing *'You don't look back in anger... don't look back in anger...'* with a soothing tone, and by then Frank wasn't hearing Noel Gallagher anymore. It was her, lullabying those words to him with her hypnotic voice. The music was fading off, smoothly disappearing back to where it came in the first place. *'At least not today...'* Sally whispered to her beloved husband leaving space to a bottomless drop of silence.

Lord Mortibar, dripping water like a dog, managed to get off the lake and drag himself to the dusty walk path where he collapsed on his back, his eyes still pointing to the sky. Sally. Tripping through that absurd trip, he embraced the air convinced he had her tightly within his arms, forever, then he burst out crying without making a sound.

'A child dressed like a man.' wrote *The New York Times*, the day after.

Frank's emotive reaction spread instantly and infected millions of viewers from every corner of the Earth.

'Old-fashioned elegance. Refined dignity. On camera.' - *Vogue* -

Apparently, the aged tears of a man were more powerful than any atomic bomb, so electrically intense to lit up every single spot on the planet. Perhaps, that kind of energy was the genuine fuel for humanity.

'The only thing worth living for.' - *The Guardian* -

Finally, Frank stood up, turned to the cameras again and, wearing a blissful face he almost indelibly forgot about, he bowed to Victoria, and Albert and that little genius named Tommy. He even blinked at Rose who simply *prrrrr*ed an obscene raspberry in response. Done. The miracle was done. Time to go home.

Helped by his loyal brass cane and accompanied by a final, warm clapping embrace, Frank slowly made his exit with a tranquil smile kissed on his lips, holding a hand that wasn't there for our eyes to see. And

3

2

1

Cut!

It's a wrap. Although it wasn't. Although it's never. Not in the real world anyway, where the blue ball keeps spinning, tables turn and people say:

'What is love?' Victoria didn't whisper to her man, interrupting that incredible movie 'Is this it? A moment when your ego goes into hibernation for a second making room for something bigger and deeper?'

Albert, who obviously heard her thoughts, finally found the courage to do something he had in mind for too long. 'Vic...' he started, kneeling down as if he was about to propose, without losing sight of her dreamy eyes.

'What are you doing?' Victoria asked, trapped in between fear and... nope, it was just sheer terror, a disarming agitation she never felt before.

'Ahem...' he cleared his throat, looking for the right words.

'Albert?'

From the pocket of his military jacket, he pulled a crisp-white handkerchief. One with embroidered initials, pretty old but nevertheless graceful.

'Take it... it's, for you.' his trembling voice said.

'?'

'An old lady gave it to me as a present and she insisted that I... well, she wanted me to hand it to my lady.'

'...'

'The One.'

Victoria was staring at him, sweetly, amused by the incurable fool she had at her feet. 'It's beautiful...' she finally managed to murmur.

'...'

'Now, get up, please...' she tried, taking his hands but, clearly, he wasn't done yet.

'*Miss...*' he started '*I know I'm not a stranger to you... I observed you in secret for a long time, but I won't hide anymore, I know that the time has come.*'

'Holy cow, what the fuck is he doing?' said Rose, suddenly spotting the weird scene.

'Look... *before you, I'd never been in love. I hate the temporary. I know all about life. I know that everyone betrays everyone, but you and I will be different, we will be an example.*'

'Seriously? *Baisers Volés?*' Victoria said, but he continued

'*... we'll never leave each other, not for a single hour. I have no work, no obligations in life. You will be my sole preoccupation.*'

'Oh, my...' she thought.

'*I realise this is all too sudden for you to say yes at once. I know that you must first break your provisional constraints that bind you to temporary people, but I'm definitive. I am very happy.*'

'You're... you're the foolest weirdo I've ever met.' she said, trying to escape that, but he didn't lose the grip of his eyes on her eyes and recklessly thought out loud, 'I love you', his face shimmering like gold, making her blush.

'Alright, enough.' Victoria said in tears, grabbing his hands and pulling him up. 'Fuck, you made me cry!' she yelled, bursting in a laugh, overwhelmed by those staggering, still unnamed, emotions. Albert was high as a kite, high as only a lover can be and he melted when she took his face in her hands and their tongues licked the lips, and French kissed, speaking an ardent language which tasted like forever. Tommy, Pete and Steve were secretly watching from a distance.

'Disgusting. GET A ROOM!' shouted Rose, waking up the couple of birds that suddenly realised to be live, on-air, filmed by a smart BBC cameraman who managed to steal that fragment of time.

'Shi-p.' said Albert, totally unprepared. Then, as always, he tried to act like a rockstar. He blinked a not-so-secret blink at Victoria which, obviously, couldn't understand the meaning of it. And, although she immediately smelled trouble, she couldn't stop the fool as he was already making his move. Pretending to have a rose stuck in his mouth

he proposed,
'Tango?'
'No way!'

Too late. He grabbed her waist, pulled her close and, back fully arched, tilted head and an arm thrown in the air like a professional diva, he basically dragged them down to the ground. Stupid. Everybody laughed. A few memes were about to be made. Whatever. They looked embarrassingly happy into the lenses of the BBC camera which was still on.

Hand in hand, lying on the royal grass of Hyde Park, they were gazing at the future stashed inside each other's pupils when Albert opened his mouth and asked:

'What now?' with a funny voice, trying to imitate Alex Turner's moves, making her smile. Victoria's eyes were sparkling with love, excitement and fear. At once. She stared at her man and with no hesitation she replied:

'Let's change the world, babe.'

If you'll ever find a blank book
you'll know it comes from *Cloud Nine*.
Please read something out of it.
Or draw,
sketch,
paint your imagination
on it.

The world keeps spinning
and changes
thanks to these little,
silly
actions.

Enjoy the Ride.
Victoria and Albert

Victoria's BLANK BOOK
STRAIGHT OUTTA CLOUD NINE

THE ORIGINAL

Paperback and ebook available on Amazon

Printed in Great Britain
by Amazon